For Pauline Sweeney

The Deal

Michael Clifford is a Dublin-based journalist and media commentator who writes for the *Irish Examiner*. He is the author of the non-fiction books *Love You To Death*, *Scandal Nation* and *Bertie Ahern and the Drumcondra Mafia*. His first novel *Ghost Town* was published in 2012.

MICHAEL CLIFFORD

HACHETTE
BOOKS
IRELAND

First published in Ireland in 2013 by
HACHETTE BOOKS IRELAND

1

Cataloguing in Publication Data is available from the British Library

ISBN 978 1 444726 14 5

Typeset in Calson by redrattledesign.com

Printed and bound in Great Britain by Clays Ltd, St Ives plc

Hachette Books Ireland policy is to use papers that are natural, renewable and recyclable products and made from wood grown in sustainable forests. The logging and manufacturing processes are expected to conform to the environmental regulations of the country of origin.

Hachette Books Ireland
8 Castlecourt Centre
Castleknock
Dublin 15, Ireland
A division of Hachette UK Ltd
338 Euston Road, London NW1 3BH
www.hachette.ie

Prologue

When Kevin Wyman went outside, he drew in huge gulps of air, as if he had just emerged from the low depths of an ocean. The afternoon was grey, but there was warmth in the air.

He walked across the farmyard in jagged strides, moving like a man trying to pretend he wasn't drunk. He wasn't sure where exactly he was going. He had to get away from the house, as if distance could remove him from what had happened in there. He had to get the smells out of his system, the weed, the reek of death.

At the far end of the yard he passed the outhouse with its whitewashed walls and corrugated-iron roof. Maybe they could leave the body in there, take off and phone it in. That would blow everything sky high, but if the cards fell right, there was always some chance he could get back what was now slipping from his grasp.

Listen to him. The body. All that remained after a life had been taken, snuffed out, ended, just a few minutes ago. What had he become in these few short months?

Beyond the outhouse, the fields stretched across flat plains towards the brown bog lining the horizon.

Wyman stopped, turned and looked back up at the farmhouse. There were five windows on the first floor, set symmetrically against the stone wall, beneath a roof of grey slates. All the windows were blacked out with high-grade plastic, to keep the heat in, creating a climate, cocooned from the world outside.

The body was up there now, lying face down among the plants, dried blood congealing in dark stains on buds that had just reached full maturity.

He could run. He could take off across the fields, keep going until he arrived back in the life he had left behind. He could be at home in a few hours. But that wasn't going to happen. What had just gone down was part of him now. The clock was not for turning back.

He felt a great wave washing through his body, rearing up against his throat, and he was suddenly bent over, throwing up onto the grass, right next to a saucer of cow dung. Then, when there was nothing else to throw up, the empty retches coughed from his stomach.

He straightened himself, and it was all over. He wiped his face with the back of his sleeve, shivered, and took a few deep breaths.

A sound issued from the pocket of his jeans. He felt the phone vibrate against his leg. He reached for it, but when he looked at caller ID, it was not relief that met him. One word showed across the screen. HASSLE.

The phone kept ringing, demanding attention, until he heard something from behind. 'Aren't you going to get that?'

He turned to see the two of them standing at the back door, squeezing his options.

He let the call ring out.

I

SEEDING

Chapter One

Dara Burns found the lane he was looking for. He swung the Kawasaki Classic into it, downed gears and killed the engine. He could hear his own breathing as the bike groaned towards silence.

The lane connected one of the main arteries through the residential neighbourhood with a parallel minor road. It was five fifteen a.m. A full moon was wringing the last out of the night, with a hint of dawn bleeding across the horizon.

Burns would have preferred total darkness. An approaching engine droned closer from the main road. He tensed. A car crowned with the light of a taxi plate drove past towards the airport.

He dismounted, and swung the small green rucksack from his shoulders. He unzipped the bag, taking out a two-litre plastic bottle that had once held Ballygowan sparkling water. Now it was nearly full of petrol. He uncapped the bottle. Hypnotic fumes rose to his nostrils. He poured the petrol over the Kawasaki, then shook the last drops from the bottle. He took the navy balaclava from the pocket of his jacket and threw it on the bike's engine. There was no helmet to worry him. Charlie Small had taken both when Burns had dropped him off five minutes earlier.

He reversed a few steps from the bike and took a Zippo lighter from the pocket of his leather jacket. With one hand on the rucksack, he bent low towards the petrol and put fire to the edges of it. The ground lit up, like some biblical flame.

He was out on the street, walking at pace, when a muffled explosion sounded from the lane. He walked for another ninety seconds before a car came his way. It was heading south, towards him, a taxi with its light on. Burns flagged it down and sat into the front passenger seat.

The driver was white and fat and wore thick bifocal glasses. Burns didn't have a problem with black taxi drivers, but he felt somehow reassured that this guy was Caucasian. If there ever was a problem later, if this fella was put in front of an ID parade, the odds were good that he would develop memory problems. You just couldn't say the same for some guy who could scoot back to Africa.

The driver kept eyes front. 'Where to?' he said.

'Beaumont Hospital.'

The driver glanced in his wing mirror, and swung the car around.

'A and E is it?' he said, looking across at Burns, in search of the damage.

'Intensive care.'

His head turned again, as if he had missed something first time around.

'My gran's in there,' Burns said. 'She's on her last legs.'

'Sorry to hear that,' the driver said. Burns looked at his ID badge on the dashboard. His name was Sean Carson. He tried to memorise the number, just in case it was needed later.

'Comes to all of us, I suppose,' this Sean Carson said. 'She had a good innings?'

'She's eighty-seven. The innings? I don't know.'

He slumped into the seat. It hadn't been his gig. Pascal Nix had phoned him the previous evening, just as he was going out the door to the hospital.

There was a problem. Charlie Small was taking care of a body who had gone offside, and his chauffeur had pulled out at the last minute.

The guy had arrived from Limerick. He had agreed to the job over the phone. But after he'd walked into Nix's gaff, he'd taken one look at Charlie Small, another at the Kawasaki Classic, and asked Small what he weighed.

Small was straight up, shaving nothing off his twenty-two stone, not that he could have hidden it. The guy shook his head, said it wasn't worth the risk, starting out on a job with that kind of handicap.

He walked straight out, Nix shouting after him that there'd be consequences for his actions. Then Nix had rung Burns to step into the breach. Burns didn't like it but he knew it was one of those occasions when he couldn't say no. In any case, he hadn't done a lot of work lately. There wasn't much doing, the way things were.

He'd agreed and driven Small. It wasn't as bad as the other fella had made out. Even with Charlie Small on the pillion, the bike still moved like the hammers of Hell after Small did the target.

The taxi driver looked over at him. 'Rough night,' he said.

'I've had worse.'

* * *

Karen Riney didn't hear the sirens, if there were any, while she was walking on the beach. It was around six a.m., the dawn rising to meet the day. There was nobody else about at that hour and the tide was low.

She walked over and back on the sand, next to a line of spongy seaweed, from the ancient castle at one end to where the beach came to a stop at the other side, in the shadow of the huge house that had once been a summer home for nuns.

The only sound was of the seagulls nattering to each other as they wheeled above the shoreline, steering clear of a bank of clouds lurking with intent out in the bay. Beyond, a mist had settled on the mountain peaks. Ballinskelligs didn't wake up for another couple of hours at least. She owned the beach, the sky, the sea, even the little vessels anchored offshore, lapping against the dawn's gentle swell.

She made for a solitary figure traipsing across the sand, her brown bob of hair bouncing to her stride, blue eyes focused on the distance, a Jewish nose sharpening her profile.

She did three full laps, over and back, moving fast in her grey and orange lightweight Asics sports gear. By the end of the third, her back felt damp and she knew the colour in her cheeks had deepened to a bright red. She broke from her route and headed for the entrance to the beach, up through the dry silver sand, which kicked up to the touch.

The walk had served to reassure her about the course she was about to embark on.

She would sit down, have her grapefruit, a bowl of granola with strawberries and a nice cup of fruit tea. By then, Jake would be willing, if not ready, to meet the day. She would deliver the news, and await his response.

Any resistance would surprise her. This experiment hadn't worked out, and Jake knew that as well as she did. It wasn't going anywhere. The initial spark, for what it was worth, had flickered and died.

He'd known where she was coming from, bouncing around on the rebound, but he still wanted her down here and she had little better to be doing. But now that was it. She had to get out before she began to dislike him.

She was already halfway out the door, the bum-bag strapped to her waist holding her money, passport, phone and driver's licence. All of her that remained at the house was the packed rucksack, sitting in the kitchen.

There was the other issue, of course. She would assure Jake that her lip was buttoned. Her story, for anybody who enquired, would be that Jake had inherited some money and decided to get out of the city, move down to the wilds of south Kerry in order to . . . well, if it wasn't going to sound too corny, to find himself. She smiled. He'd be looking for a long time.

Once she hit the car park, at the entrance to the beach, she stopped, just to take in the sea air one last time. She opened the bum-bag, unzipped a little internal compartment, took out her silver wedding band and slipped it onto the designated finger. She held her hand up, just to give it the once-over. The gesture gave her a little lift. It was the first time she'd worn it in a few months.

Karen Riney walked through the empty car park and out onto the road. Once she got back to the city, she'd try again for a job. That was something she was taking away from these borrowed weeks down here. She was ready to work again.

It was a seven-minute trot to the house, which was set far enough away from the beach for privacy. The house in which she was staying was one half of a pair of identical bungalows done in grey brick and brown roof tiles, tilted towards each other inside a gate of timber slats. She and Jake were staying in one house, the plants in the other.

The road twisted and turned as it climbed. Just after she rounded the last bend, and the houses came into view, she saw the two vehicles parked outside the gates.

One was a white Mondeo garda squad car. The other looked like a Ford Focus, with a flashing light on its back windscreen, sending blue notes out into the silent morning.

Karen stopped and stared for a second. She moved closer, to where she could get a view. The front door to the house where she and Jake were staying was open. She couldn't see anybody, but she would have bet her bottom dollar that if she gave it thirty seconds or so bodies would spill from the house.

The door to the house next door was also open. While the blinds were down, she thought she detected movement behind one of the ground-floor windows. Each room of that house was more or less full of plants. Right now, the whole shebang had been blown through the roof. And with it poor Jake.

She took a deep breath. Not her fight. Not her life. She turned and walked back down the hill. Her clothes and toiletries in the packed rucksack would have to be sacrificed, but it was a no-brainer. She wasn't going back in there.

She didn't run. She concentrated on sounds. A procession of vehicles would be calling any minute now, and once they approached she had best adopt the role of early-morning jogger. It was a hell of a way to depart , but at least she was leaving.

* * *

Burns felt it as he was walking in through the lobby of the hospital, just after he nodded at the security guard. He knew then that Gran was gone. He walked down the long corridor, past a pair of nurses who looked spent after a night's work. He stepped into the lift to take him to ICU on the first floor.

He thought for a moment about that woman tonight, the wife. When he was on the front lawn, after Charlie Small had shot the target once, the woman had looked out from the front window. She'd had a baby in her arms, fear pulling at her face. Maybe the child couldn't sleep and she was up with it. There was no way she would ever be able to pick him out in an identity parade. He had on both the helmet and the balaclava. All she got was his eyes. You couldn't convict a man on his eyes.

He could see her now, sitting on a couch in that front room, a couple of shades holding her hand, telling her they'd get the scumbags.

When the lift door opened, Sharon was standing there, bathed in grief.

'Where were you?' she said. 'I've been ringing for the last hour.'

Burns had left his phone at home. Carrying it on a job would be like leaving a trail of fingerprints. 'My phone's down,' he said. 'She's gone.' It wasn't a question.

Sharon nodded, tear tracks on her cheeks. She looked completely worn out. She had been home from England for the last four days, since they'd known the end was near. All that time she'd rarely left the hospital. Gran and Granddad had raised the pair of them after their mother was taken. They had been the only real family Burns and his sister had had and now they were both gone.

Burns placed his hand on Sharon's arm, turned to go down the corridor towards the ICU. She shook her head and pulled herself free. 'We waited for an hour,' she said. 'I didn't think you were coming. They've taken her away. Where the fuck were you?'

For the last few days, Burns had been getting this sort of stuff from his sister. 'Where were you?' 'Why aren't you doing more?' 'She's your gran too. If she hadn't been around, you wouldn't have been so much reared as dragged up.' He hadn't reacted to any of it. Sharon had to let off a little steam, to compensate for having left her son and her asshole of a husband in Brixton to come over here and play undertaker for the family. And now, when it was all over, she couldn't just leave well enough alone. He was willing to go the extra mile, just this one last time.

'I didn't think for a second it would happen tonight. Something came up. I had to do a favour for a friend who was in a jam.'

The lift door swished open and a young guy wearing a medic's loose green rig-out stepped out. He nodded at the couple as if he was familiar with the disposition of the recently bereaved.

'You were doing somebody a favour,' Sharon said. She was straight into her I-don't-believe-it pose.

'Yeah. It doesn't matter now. I'm left with having missed this for the rest of my life.'

She gave him a look. 'I'd say you're really bothered.'

But he was. For the last few days, particularly when he'd come in and sat beside Gran, Burns had been thinking back over his life, and how this was a major juncture. She had raised them, and if she hadn't been there, they would have ended up in a home, and Burns knew the fuck-ups that came out of those homes.

He'd really wanted to be there at the end of something so major in his life. He'd really thought Gran would see through the night, as she had all the other nights for the last week since she'd taken the turn.

They went down in the lift, and walked the length of the corridor to the entrance. Outside, the day was opening up, cold and grey. In the distance, headlights fingered their way up the approach road through the dawn, the hospital coming alive for another round of fixing up and burying.

Sharon pulled a packet of John Player Blue from her handbag. Burns could see now that she was completely wrecked. She seemed unsteady on her feet, like somebody who was drunk or had just emerged from under the knife. She had on a new sky-blue blouse, bought just yesterday from Penneys in Artane because she had run out of the clothes she brought over. The jeans were the same ones she had worn since arriving, as were the high-heeled shoes.

'You better get some rest,' he said to her.

She peered at him through the smoke, nothing on her face. 'She wanted a wake. At the house.'

Burns shrugged. 'I'll go along with whatever.'

Sharon finished her cigarette and began walking towards the taxi rank, heels echoing in the early morning. She got into a car and it took off. Burns stood there for a minute, feeling alone. He had been on his own for a long time, but Gran was always there in the background, waiting, as he saw it, for him to fuck up. Now he could do it all by himself.

* * *

Karen had been walking for at least three miles. In that time, one squad car had sped past, en route, she was sure, to Jake's place. When she heard it approach, she turned and broke into a jog, ensuring that they wouldn't see her face. When it sped past, she saw the driver, a huge guy, behind the wheel. She expected to see the brake lights suddenly come to life, but the car kept going.

Now she was hot and her legs were protesting. She had been on the beach a good half-hour before all this had blown up. Cahirciveen, the nearest town, was still five or six miles away. When she heard the rumble of another engine behind her, she pulled in towards the ditch and, on an impulse, stuck out her thumb. Hitching was still safe in this part of the world – or at least it was until something happened.

The van slowed to a halt. She ran towards the pumping exhaust pipe and the winking orange light. The cab smelt of damp clothes and cigarettes. The driver was a large man with a crew-cut and a few days' growth on his face. He was wearing a blue V-neck jumper that had seen better days over an off-white shirt opened at the collar. It hadn't been that colour when it had started out in life, but it was now.

'Thanks,' she said, but he just pulled at the gearstick and took off. The sound of early-morning radio floated through the cab. Karen recognised the song, 'Start A War'. 'The National,' she said.

He looked startled, as if she wasn't supposed to talk.

'The National.' She pointed at the radio. 'Great band.'

His eyes fell to her outstretched finger. 'Yes,' he said.

Karen got the message. That was the extent of the conversation they would have. The National gave way to a haunting Elvis Costello song, something post-punk but before his middle-age phase. Karen concentrated on trying to recognise it while the Ballinskelligs Barbarian kept his eyes on the road, not a peek out of him.

She couldn't imagine how Jake was going to handle this. In the short time they had been together, she'd recognised he was good fun, but he'd never struck her as somebody who could withstand pressure. He'd taken on the job to sort out a debt for some small-time dealing he'd been involved in. He had never been arrested before, as far as Karen could make out. Prison would be a whole new experience for him. There was no way he was going to drag her into it. Was there?

They arrived in the outskirts of Cahirciveen as a light mist began to fall. She asked him to drop her at the Supervalu.

'Closed,' he said.

It speaks. She told him not to worry about it, and he didn't. She thanked him as she stepped from the cab.

She took shelter under the canopy for the petrol pumps outside the shop. Inside, men and women in what appeared to be uniforms were scurrying around, preparing the place for another day. A man emerged with a yellow docket in his hand. He stepped up into the cab of a truck. Karen took a chance, walked around to the driver's side. He was looking down at something on his lap and then he saw her. He lowered the window.

'Any chance of a lift?' she said.

He looked at her standing in the drizzle, a sheen of rain forming on her head. 'Where you going?'

'Where are *you* going?'

'I asked first,' he said. She laughed for the sake of a lift and shrugged.

'How does Killarney suit you?' he said.

She walked around to the passenger side and pulled herself up.

This lift was full of everything the last had been lacking. The guy said his name was George, and he worked right across Munster. Today's delivery was a one-off affair or he wouldn't have made it to Killarney. Usually he would have had to stop off at every branded store along the road. 'Selling, it's a mug's game,' he said.

'Maybe it's just become a mug's game,' Karen said. 'When the boom was here I was away in Australia, but whenever I came back I could see it. There was no selling. It was all buying. Nobody had to sell anything.'

'You left Australia to come back here?'

'It's a long story,' she said, her tone business-like to divert him down another avenue.

He took the hint, began going on about his job, how, bad and all as it was, there were cutbacks looming in the company and everybody was on edge.

She was looking at a sealed box of Snack bars at her feet. Right now, Jake was most likely being questioned by the police. None of this was going to be easy for him. A great hunger came over her. She must have walked a good ten miles this morning. She would have killed for a shower, but she'd make do with a tiny piece of nourishment. 'Mind if I have a bar?' she said.

He paused. 'Be my guest.'

* * *

Drizzle had turned to rain by the time she jumped down from the truck. He dropped her outside the railway station in Killarney. As she had guessed he would, he asked for her number.

She said she'd take his and give him a shout when she got back to Kerry. He scribbled it out with a pencil, resignation on his face.

There was an hour-long wait for the Dublin train. Under the platform's canopy she looked at the rain beating down. More than anything, this was what she missed about Sydney. Sure, it rained there, but the rain served notice and came down hard and fast, then stopped, and went about its business elsewhere. There was none of this hanging around like a threat of more to come. OK, she'd grown up here, but nearly a decade away had allowed her to forget. And here she was, over a year back in the place, and she was still having trouble returning.

There was no way Jake was going to haul her into it. He wasn't that kind of guy. He might get it into his head that she was using him. What if he came to the conclusion that she'd grassed on him? What if the police began planting that notion in his head?

Listen to her. You'd swear she knew this man, that she had deep feelings for him. They'd passed in the night, little more than that. If the opportunity arose, she'd try to help him out. But it was his gig. Nothing to do with her.

She dozed through the train journey, finally coming awake as the carriage pulled lazily out of Portlaoise. While she had been gone, a woman and a girl had sat into the seat opposite. The easy way they engaged with each other said they had to be mother and daughter.

Outside, the day was brightening. Beyond the town, as the ribbons of houses receded, she could see a film of rain on the grass.

She was bushed by the time the train pulled into Heuston.

As she moved up the aisle towards the door it occurred to her that the law might be on to her already. She ducked down for a sconce out the window, but all that occupied the platform was passengers moving to the exit.

Her bones felt stiff as she stepped off the train. Were they gaping at her, these passengers with their travel bags or handbags, wondering why she travelled so light in sweat gear, looking like she was in serious need of a shower? She kept the head down and thought about jets of water shooting onto her skin.

Stoneybatter was a short walk, over the low tide of the Liffey and up the hill until the steeple of the Greek Orthodox Church hove into view. And, beside it, the prison. Arbour Hill. She picked up pace as she walked past the grey walls. They cosseted the sex abusers in there for their own safety. Maybe that was where they'd bring Jake, to billet him with men who were a threat to children but not adults.

Five minutes later she pushed open the door to Heaven's Gate. The angel shop was tucked in among the convenience stores, hairdressers and off-licences on Manor Street, the main drag through Stoneybatter. The woman behind the counter looked up and saw her. She had a kind face, her hair tied back in a ponytail. She was shaped like an orange, round in the middle. A smile of surprise lit her up, but when she gave Karen a second take, it expanded into delight.

She walked around from the counter and approached Karen, who couldn't help but think that this angel was coming to rescue her. The angel wordlessly gathered her into a hug.

Chapter Two

Three chairs were commandeered from the kitchen for the chief mourners. Sharon sat in the first, near the head of the open coffin. She was a picture of mourning in black. Burns was next to her in a rented suit and tie. His white shirt was a few rubs of an iron short of presentable. When he stood next to Sharon, she towered over him, the heels giving her extra inches. Burns was below average height, but what he lacked in the vertical, he made up for in his muscled bulk, giving him the appearance of a handy rugby prop forward. His skin was sallow, eyes a steely blue, and he wore his black hair tightly cropped.

Next to him was Sharon's asshole of a husband, Steve, who found himself rising to shake hands with people he had never met before, nor ever would again. Steve had a round, bald head and wore a sleeper earring on his left lobe. He and Burns had never hit it off, and were unlikely ever to do so, now that Gran was gone.

They started at six thirty p.m., just as darkness began to smother the March evening. By then, a queue had formed down the road, and around the block. Eileen Burns's grand-nephew had been detailed to keep the queue manageable, and the traffic on the road outside flowing across the speed bumps.

She had lived in the neighbourhood all her life. She was well respected by some, feared by others, certainly until she entered the late phase of her life. Her tenure in this mortal coil had never been easy, but she had known it wasn't designed to be for women of her class and generation.

She had lost her husband to the pub even before her brood had begun to appear. And in the years that followed, a daughter had taken the boat, and eventually succumbed to cancer as a young woman. Her other daughter, who had been Sharon and Burns's mother, had turned to heroin to relieve whatever was ailing her.

In a life that had been weighed down with disappointment, one of the lowest points for Eileen Burns had been finding her daughter's body in the same bed where she had slept as a child. With their father already gone, she turned her hand to rearing all over again, doing what she could to mould Burns and his sister.

For the last few years she had moved through the neighbourhood in a stooped frame, as if already wishing she was in the grave, where there might be peace and even reunion with some of those who had gone before her. The mourners who gathered for the wake discussed these aspects of the deceased, but they did so in hushed tones, out of earshot of the woman's next of kin.

Passage into the house was tight, those entering squeezing past the departing. The kitchen was reserved for neighbours who were providing catering, pouring tea from an enormous pot, offering what looked suspiciously like surviving Christmas cake. There were also sandwiches of white bread, with ham, cheese, and ham and cheese.

Inside the front room, Burns was putting up with it all. He occupied himself by studying the wallpaper of sky blue with little sailboats, which he had hung less than a decade ago. He could spot a few swelled bumps now, where the years had been unkind to his work.

For the most part, the procession of mourners trooping past him resembled a column of ghosts. He stayed on his feet, offering a limp hand to all those who filed in. Some of the faces he recognised. Others required a rummage in his memory, particularly those who were shuffling into the departure lounge themselves. These were neighbours who had been in the prime of their lives when he was growing up. Some he had feared as a boy, but now they looked to be grizzled, worn, resigned to Fate's clammy grasp.

About an hour into it, Pascal Nix walked through the door. He was, as might be expected, the best-dressed mourner to appear. When he entered, a hush fell over the low voices of three elderly women who stood at the head of the coffin. His camel-hair coat was open, exposing a dark suit of impeccable cut, black shirt and red-and-black-striped silk tie. His shoes looked like a lot of energy had been spent on acquiring the perfect shine.

Burns got to his feet and Nix pulled him into a hug, both his hands slapping the bereaved man's back. Then he stepped back and ran his right hand over his own head where his rug had seen fuller days. He took Burns by the shoulders, looked into his eyes. 'She was some woman,' he said. Burns nodded.

'What would you know?' Both men turned to Sharon, who was still seated.

Her brother leaned down towards her. 'Sharon—'

'She was the pure finest, and you should know that,' Nix said.

'Did you ever as much as meet her on the street?' Sharon wasn't letting this go. Seated to her right, her asshole of a husband was focusing on the carpet. He didn't need to know Nix personally to realise that he was a man whom it was best to fear, unless otherwise instructed.

Nix said, 'She raised the two of you, didn't she? And look at the job she did of that.'

Burns nodded at his sister. He wasn't sure what Nix was saying.

Nix turned to the coffin, and bowed his head to affect an effort at prayer. After a suitable pause, he turned back to Burns. 'I'll be outside when you get a chance,' he said. With that, he moved along, down the far side of the coffin, and squeezed out the door against the incoming flow of mourners.

Burns resumed his seat. 'What's your problem?' he said.

Sharon didn't look at him. 'You can kiss that prick's arse, but don't expect me to do the same.'

'He's not the worst,' Burns said.

'He's a scumbag. I couldn't stop him coming in here, but you know Gran would never have let him darken the door of this place.'

Burns turned back to the column of mourners and found himself looking into the face of Jacinta. He never thought of her as his girlfriend, but that was how he described her to others, as if to demonstrate that he had a relatively standard private life. Jacinta was raising her three small children on her own, their father having scampered before the third was even born. For the last six months or so, she came over to Burns's place once a week. They rarely went out, and once Jacinta got used to it, it didn't seem to bother her any more.

Tonight she had made an effort, standing there with her brown hair piled high, her face light on the makeup and wearing a smile that reached out to him.

She hesitated before moving towards him with open arms. He knew she knew he would be touchy on public displays of affection, but he was willing to make an exception for a funeral. She whispered her condolences. He nodded, gently took her by the shoulders. 'Thanks for coming,' he said.

'Are you sure?'

'Sure I'm sure. Listen, I'll give you a shout later.'

'Maybe I can try to come over to you tomorrow, after the funeral,' she said, her voice full of hope.

'Sure,' he said, 'we'll see,' but he knew this week would be no different from every other.

* * *

Burns gave it twenty minutes before he said to his sister he was nipping out for a quick smoke. She responded with one of her special looks.

He got up and left. There would be the funeral tomorrow, and then she would be off back to England for a life of penance. He could keep things on an even keel until then.

Nix was out on the road, a mug of tea in his right hand, a cigarette burning between the fingers of his left. He was chatting to Burns's cousin, the crowd-control steward, a black armband fashioned from masking tape on his left arm. He was obviously star-struck to be shooting the breeze with a man of Nix's standing. When Burns walked up, the cousin greeted him, then copped that these two had things to discuss which weren't for his ears. He pointed towards the back of the queue and ambled off.

'Nice fella,' Nix said. He took a long draw on his cigarette.

'Yeah, sorry about Sharon in there. She's ... The whole thing is weighing in on her.'

Nix raised his mug. 'Don't worry about it, Dara. I've been around a lot of death. I know what it does to people.' He pulled again on the cigarette, and swivelled his head, scanning the queue and general area for any stray eyes. He switched the mug of tea to his left hand and reached with his right to an inside breast pocket, returning with a brown envelope that had been folded over on itself. He passed it across. Burns could feel the bulk of notes inside.

Nix said, 'Thanks for the other night. You took us out of a jam.'

The story had been all over the newspapers for the last few days. Usually, it would have been a twenty-four-hour wonder, but the detail of the dead man's wife at the window, holding their child, gave the story legs.

Burns knew the dead man, but not well. His name was Denis Stanners and he had been on the payroll with Nix. Burns tried to stuff the envelope into the inside breast pocket of his suit. It wouldn't fit. He prodded it, heard a tear of material as he tried to stuff it in. There was no shifting the pocket.

Nix looked around again. 'What about your flap pocket?' he said. 'On the outside.'

Burns looked at him. He tried the pocket on the left. The envelope made it in, but it was sticking out. There was no way he could go through the rest of the wake with ten grand sticking out like that. He pulled it out. He could leave it somewhere in the house, but the place would be crawling with all sorts until the early hours. It wouldn't take much for it to disappear.

Nix reached over and put his hand on the envelope. Burns let it slip through his fingers.

'You've enough to be going on with. I'll have it dropped off to you tomorrow after the funeral.'

'Thanks,' Burns said. He felt deflated, as if he had just lost something.

Nix said, 'Did you know him?'

Burns paused before answering. 'Met him a few times. Never really talked to him much.'

He could see the woman now at the window, the child in her arms. Nothing to do with him. The guy had gone offside.

'He was a lowlife, fucking rat,' Nix said. 'You know he was with me for the last five years. Not once would I have thought he was capable of that. Charlie the same. He and Charlie got along fine –

they worked together. When I told Charlie, you could have blown him over.'

Burns thought of Charlie Small and the size of him, and wondered how anything could blow him over.

Nix ran a hand across his head again. 'It was only right that Charlie did him. But I want to thank you for stepping into the breach. That other fucker who chickened out will get his in time.'

A man was walking past towards the back of the queue. He spotted Burns and leaned over, a hand extended. Burns knew the face but couldn't match a name. The man mumbled something, and Burns thanked him as he moved on.

Nix said, 'Look, I know you like working on your own, but I'm down a man as a result of that. Charlie needs somebody with him. How would you be fixed?'

Burns hated being put on the spot like that, but he needed the work. There was nothing doing at the moment, and from what he could gather, the dark clouds wouldn't be rolling on for a while yet.

Pascal Nix was involved in just about everything, but his main crust these days, as far as Burns could make out, was loan-sharking and debt collection. Word had it that he was sniffing around the grow-house business as well, but Burns had no interest in that.

Burns enjoyed his independence, the freedom. Take a job here and there. Shift some product when it suited him. It all added up to a nice lifestyle, where he could keep himself to himself and the wolf comfortably from the door. But those days had drawn to a close, for now anyway. He knew he should feel grateful. He tried his best.

Nix was reading his face. 'It's not Charlie, is it?'

'No problem with him.'

'Yeah, some people don't like him on account of his size and that he's eating all the time. But why should that bother anybody?

A man wants to eat, who gives a fuck? Once he does his job, and he don't step on any toes, he can do what he likes with his body.'

Burns nodded. The other night, before they'd gone out, Charlie Small had been chewing on a sandwich. It was a whopper in white bread, with layers of sliced ham and Swiss cheese, drowning in mayo. Small was having a serious problem getting it into his gob. Burns felt sorry for him. Just the sight of the man, who couldn't control himself, the mayo dripping down his chin, as if he was a baby getting to grips with the basics, instead of a grown man preparing to kill another.

'He's OK by me, Pascal. Is it collecting we're talking?'

'Yeah, I need somebody to ride shotgun for him with the Leopard work. The truth of it is, it's hard to get good people these days. I could do with somebody like you. Why don't you try it out and see if it suits? I'll make it worth your while one way or the other.'

Burns nodded. 'Maybe you're right,' he said. 'I like to operate alone, but comes a time when a man's got to move on to pastures new.'

'Jesus! That sounds like it's out of a song.'

Burns smiled.

* * *

Jake rang on the second evening. He had the landline number for Abigail's place, must have actually had it in his head, which surprised Karen. The two women had just finished a dinner of fish pie, which Abigail had whipped up in honour of her friend's return.

Since Karen had got back, Abigail had been all that could be asked for in a friend. She'd shut up Heaven's Gate early that evening, and they'd walked around the corner to her home, a cottage in a warren of similar abodes built a century earlier to house Guinness employees.

Abigail offered the ear of an angel, if not a counsellor, as Karen retraced her leave-taking of Kerry. The pair had been friends since first encountering each other at school. Their paths had diverged along the way, but when Karen had returned from Australia, they'd made contact, and rekindled their friendship. Prior to her sojourn in Kerry, Karen had been lodging with her friend.

The cottage was compact and well kept, with a living room, kitchen and two bedrooms from the original building. An extension, done over thirty years ago, housed the bathroom now, and a little alcove big enough to fit a washing machine. Abigail had bought it before the property boom had gone insane, and she'd even added her own little feature, a skylight in the flat roof over the kitchen, to let in a little light, which was at a premium. An ex-boyfriend who turned a buck as a handyman had done the job, but long after the relationship had ended, a leak had sprung on the window. She had tried to get a remedial job done, but had been told it would mean starting the whole thing from scratch, which she couldn't afford. Now, every time it rained, a drip fell to the kitchen table, and Abigail remembered her ex with fury.

A bottle of Sauvignon Blanc was still half full on the table between them when the house phone began its sing-song ring.

Abigail lifted the receiver, saw it was a blocked number. She moved her head over and back, debating whether to delve into the mystery or leave well enough alone.

She pressed the answer button.

'Karen?'

'Who's speaking, please?'

'Abigail? It's Jake.' She immediately handed it across the table, and mouthed Jake's name, her face full of drama.

Karen took the receiver. 'Hi,' she said.

'Hi, yourself. I tried your mobile phone number.'

'Where are you?

'Cork prison.'

'How are you?'

There was a pause on the line. Then: 'How do you think? The food is shit. I'm getting these looks from one fella in here – I don't know whether he wants to kill me or ride me. My solicitor says that the outlook isn't great, but I'd be better off pleading or I'm facing ten years. Otherwise, things are flying.'

Abigail was getting up from the table, a glass of wine in her hand. She reached over for a magazine on the worktop and walked through to the sitting room.

'What about bail?' Karen said.

'That's the scary bit. The solicitor told me it could be a problem 'cause I don't have what he calls independent means. He says the cops are coming down hard on these grow-house cases, that a lot of fellas caught are doing a runner.'

Another pause, and then, in a voice that threatened to break: 'I could be in here for a while.'

Karen thought of a little boy, afraid of what the world beyond his door might expose.

He went on: 'What happened you?'

'I came back from the beach and saw the law. I scampered. What would have been the point in sticking around? There was nothing I could do.'

He breathed hard down the line. In somebody not as harmless as him, Karen thought, it might sound intimidating. More likely he was just trying to maintain his composure.

'I didn't tell them anything,' he said, the voice still hanging in there.

'My name didn't come up?'

'Is that all you're worried about?'

'No, I'm just asking.'

'The solicitor told me that if I co-operate it'll help with the sentence. Ten fucking years.'

Karen felt her face going red. It wasn't her battle. What was the point in trying to drag her in? 'Jake, I'm sorry about what happened ...'

'Whoa. That sounds like the start of a PFO note.'

Now it was her turn to pause. On the train ride back to Dublin, she had gone through this conversation in her head. She would tell him that things hadn't worked out. It was unfortunate that the operation had been rumbled on the day she was going to leave, but she couldn't do anything about that. She would wish him well, tell him that if there was anything she could do to help, like contact a relative, she would gladly do it. But it was over between them. They had a thing going for a few months, and that was it. For God's sake, they both knew that the past was still clinging to her. And her fortnight in Kerry had told her that he couldn't get his shit together to save his life.

Hello, goodbye, good luck with everything, it was genuinely nice knowing you, but ... A PFO note? What else did he expect? But now he was locked up, his hand reaching out from behind bars.

'I'm not running out on anybody,' she said.

'Thanks. And I'm not going to drag anybody down with me.'

She had to stop herself screaming: It. Has. Nothing. To. Do. With. Me. *Comprende*? You . . . 'Do you want me to get in touch with anybody for you?'

'I was just coming to that,' he said, confidence creeping back into his voice.

Karen felt like she was going through an escape hatch. This was what she was looking for: the chance to pass it on to somebody who cared enough about him to invest some time and emotion.

'There's a guy who needs to know I'm staying schtum. Do you know what I'm saying?'

She felt herself stiffen. 'Keep going,' she said.

'This guy ... These people might get the wrong impression. They might begin to think I'm going to start singing, and if they get to that station, then this fella in here who I think wants to ride me will be the least of my worries. Do you see what I'm saying now?'

'Jake, I thought you might want me to put you in touch with, I don't know, family ...' She knew his parents were dead and a single sister was living in San Francisco. From what Karen had gathered, their relationship was non-existent. '... maybe a cousin, or an aunt?'

'Karen. This is serious. Do you know what I'm saying?'

She didn't want to know. Abigail sauntered back into the kitchen. Her face was full of mock drama and her glass was empty. She looked up at the skylight.

'OK, if you want me to pass on a message, I can do that.'

Abigail topped up Karen's glass.

'Thanks. And you know what to say?'

'Your lips are sealed.'

'OK. The guy you're looking for, I don't have access to his number, but I know somebody who does. You remember Creole?'

With a name like that, she couldn't forget him. He was a mate of Jake's, strange fella who lived alone and considered socialising an overrated activity. He dealt a little weed, but nothing you'd write home about. His one outstanding feature was his teeth, which, by and large, were as black as the ace of spades. Even if you didn't remember his name, his teeth would come back to haunt you at some stage.

'The guy with the chompers,' she said.

A snort came back down the line. 'That's him. He'll get you the number. Guy you're looking for, his name is Charlie. Charlie Small.'

* * *

It was shortly after three a.m. when Burns arrived back at his townhouse. A cousin, home from Manchester for the funeral, gave him a lift in a hired car. The pair of them had been about the only two sober bodies left in the house when the last of the mourners had left. As they drove through the silent and empty streets, the cousin told Burns how life was good in Manchester, even with the recession. He wasn't ever coming back to this kip, he said.

Burns let the cousin drive him down through Williamsgate all the way to his front door. Normally, he would get out at the top of the road. No harm in taking precautions, and the fewer people who knew his exact address the better. This was different. This was family, home to bury and advise the remaining natives to get the fuck out of Dodge before it blew through the sky.

Williamsgate was one of the mini cities that had sprung up on the edge of Dublin in the years of the boom, full to the brim with housing and little else in the way of infrastructure. It was made up of townhouses, and apartment blocks, all done in varying shades of brown and red, set back from the web of roads by grass margins, which boasted the odd skeletal tree, planted as an afterthought. Burns had bought a ground-floor two-bed unit near the top of the market, after a particularly busy year.

He thanked the cousin and stood on the pavement as the car's red lights receded up the road. At the wake, he had made a point of not drinking. He wanted to stay in control until all this was over. What his body needed right now was a workout, or a serious spin on his bike, where he could sweat out the tension. His mind could have done with a distraction like that as well, but it wasn't going to happen.

When he unlocked the door and reached for the light switch, he sensed something wasn't right. The living room was a shining example of minimalism. A brown leather two-seater and a couple of soft chairs in blue sat next to a long coffee table. The TV was compact, and fitted in a unit that also included a music centre. Next to the unit, on a stand, was his Lag acoustic guitar. The kitchen was all chrome and wood, including the worktop, which was a bastard to keep clean.

He checked the bathroom, his bedroom and the spare room, but nothing was out of place. Maybe it was his innate caution again, which could be a bitch but also ensured that he was still around. Everything was where he had left it, where it should be.

That was what irritated him about Jacinta when she came back here. She often seemed to forget that she wasn't at home with her gaggle of children. She left the doors of the kitchen presses open; when she used the bog, she took the roll from the rack and left it on the cistern; she sometimes brought magazines with her and left them lying around, as if the place was a dentist's waiting room.

He liked her; she fulfilled his needs; they had something, no question about it. She was good to be around, and she was around only as much as it suited him. But he was never going to change her, and that meant that the end was always hovering over her next visit.

He sat into one of the easy chairs and picked up the remote for his music centre. The album in his iPod was *Stripped*, a live acoustic effort from the Stones. He had downloaded it the previous week after reading that it included a mean version of Robert Johnson's 'Love In Vain'.

He located the song, listened to the sad opening guitar chords. He got out of the seat, picked up his guitar and sat down, pulling the grey plectrum out from between the strings on the first fret. He hit the remote to start again. And off he went, plucking along with Keith and Ronnie, following her to the station, a suitcase in her hand.

Chapter Three

They were leaving the city behind, moving out beyond the western suburbs where concrete, brick and glass gave way to virgin fields of green. Charlie Small was behind the wheel of the LiteAce, Burns riding shotgun. The funeral had gone well, but Burns was glad it had all finished yesterday.

'There's two types of creditors,' Small said. 'There's those who pay up when they're supposed to and then there's the ones who forget. We're the memory men.' He laughed, but it quickly turned into a wheeze, great rasps shuddering through his body. He took up a whole lot of space in the van's cab, like a great big cloud blocking out the sun.

He wore a goatee beard, which, Burns reckoned, was *in situ* mainly to deflect attention from his layers of chin. He was dressed in a black leather jacket that fell below his thighs, and a pair of brown slacks. His head was crowned with a grey pork-pie hat. He reminded Burns of a Traveller character in some TV drama.

'This guy we're visiting,' Small said, 'I like his type. Used to have his own construction company. He's one of these fellas who ripped the arse out of the economy, building houses to flog to workers coming here to build more houses, know what I mean?'

Burns was holding the overhead grip above the door on his side of the van. He had on his work gear: a canvas jacket, sweat pants and runners. He had shaved that morning, splashed a little Hugo Boss on his throat. He felt fresh, but when Small had collected him at the entrance to Williamsgate, he was immediately assaulted by the waft of sour milk in the van. He was also aware that he was sitting in the seat of a dead man. 'We're all paying for it now,' he said.

'Chalk it down. Anyway, this guy, Wyman, he takes care of himself, and he's got all sorts of tools at the house that he could use. But we'll be OK. Just stand there with the wheel brace and leave the talking to me. I'm not telling you what to do, understand, Dara. But just until you get the hang of things.'

Burns had no problem with that. He was happy to just go along. Small reached over and turned on the radio. Rihanna screamed out, 'We Found Love'.

Small was all over the road with the LiteAce, lurching from side to side as if he owned the highway, out here beyond the city limits. They were passing big properties, some hidden behind tall walls of stone or brick. Small kept looking left and right, trying to get a better view of how they lived out here.

'You're the boss, Charlie,' Burns said. 'The other night, doing Stanners, did you feel anything?'

Small looked across at him. 'What? You mean on account of having worked with him?'

'He used to sit in this seat, didn't he?'

Small said nothing for a minute, kept his eyes on the road.

'I didn't think about anything when I was doing it but making sure the fella wasn't going to get up. I had a few beers when I got home to bring me back down. After that, yeah, I thought about him. And you know what? It was him or me. If he'd landed me on a stretch in the Joy I'd have been thinking a lot more about him. What the fuck is this about anyway? It's not as if you've never done anybody yourself. From what I hear …'

Burns was shaking his head. 'It's nothing, I was just wondering about having worked with him, knowing him so well. Jesus, watch the road.'

A truck was coming at them full on, horn blaring. Small swerved back onto his side of the road. 'Did you see that?' he said.

Burns's eyes were closed. He wasn't a good passenger at the best of times. He preferred his own transport, usually sticking to his Trek bike, but he didn't mind using a motorcycle now and again. A recurring scene haunted his nightmares. He was lying at the side of the road, life seeping from his body, in the grip of total shock, because he had just been killed in a motor accident, rather than by a bullet.

Small said, 'There's one other thing, just to mark your card.'

Burns opened his eyes. The road ahead was clear. 'Yeah?'

'If Pascal brings up his hair, don't make jokes.'

'What?'

Small tried to shift his rump in the seat. He didn't get anywhere. 'Pascal has … issues about his hair. He's losing it, yeah? I'm not ratting on anything there. Anybody who looks at the fella can see that. But if he starts talking about it, don't make jokes. He'll hit the roof. You don't want to see that.'

Burns nodded, as if he knew what the other man was talking about. 'No comb-over cracks,' he said.

Small looked across at him, but he wasn't smiling.

* * *

Karen slept late. She had woken earlier to the sounds of Abigail preparing herself for the day. There was the pitter-patter of feet, a low hum that she knew to be Lyric FM, although she couldn't make out the music, the rising groan of the kettle en route to boiling, and then, here and there, snatches of Abigail humming to herself, happy to meet the day on its terms. Then she heard the door being pulled and the gentle thud of it shutting, a valiant attempt, Karen knew, not to interrupt her beauty sleep.

She dozed off again. This time she was visited by a dream in which she was answering the door of the house here. It had her in the kitchen, standing over the kettle, when an impatient knock echoed from the front door.

When she opened it, six or seven police officers, togged out in bulky vests, were all pointing guns at her. Beyond their orbit, Jake was standing buck naked but for a sandwich board suspended around his neck. It bore the legend 'Ballinskelligs'.

She turned to the sound of Abigail's voice from inside, and her friend appeared as an angel. Karen was fascinated by the wings, which were bordered with the most brilliant white feathers she had ever seen. Abigail was beckoning her back into the house, but when she moved to close the front door, somebody began shooting.

She woke with a start. It took a few seconds to bring her back.

She got up, showered and ate the other half of a grapefruit that Abigail had laid out for her. After that she plonked herself on the couch with a cup of brewed coffee.

A discussion was taking place on Lyric, so she fiddled the dial until she hit a pop channel that was playing a catchy number. She recognised it. 'Somebody That I Used To Know' by Gotye.

Her book, the latest Grisham, was on the coffee table. She curled up and began reading. Presently, the music died and the voice of a hyperactive DJ was squawking across the room. Then she heard the words 'retail' and 'position'. She lowered the book to her lap and tuned in.

The DJ repeated it.

'A sales person with five years' experience in mobile technology is required for a senior retail position with a major mobile-phone operator.' He read out a phone number.

Karen leaped from the couch, clutching the paperback, repeating the number to herself. There was a biro on the mantelpiece over the fire. She tried scribbling on the cover of the book, but nothing came. The phone number was now blaring out like a mantra.

In her bedroom, there was a pen she had picked up on the train on the way from Kerry. This one worked. She scribbled down the number and rang it immediately. She was put straight through to a voicemail. Already the legions of the unemployed had been prodded into action. She wouldn't hold out much hope there.

Ten minutes later, back on Lyric FM and deep into Grisham, her phone buzzed. It was the recruitment company. Interview set up. Come along tomorrow. A sense of giddiness came over her. Things were moving. She stretched, went back to her bedroom and slipped into a jogging suit. Nothing for it now but a walk in the Phoenix Park to form a strategy.

* * *

The place they were looking for was set back from the road, behind a long, timber split-rail fence and a black wrought-iron gate, topped with little golden arrows pointing towards the sky.

The drive was bordered by flowerbeds, beyond which lawns spread out. There were mini goal posts, and a trampoline penned in by its own nets. A large round garden feature, broken into quadrants, like an ancient compass, sat on the other side of the drive.

The house itself was two-storey, done in red brick. Burns spotted movement behind one of the large bay windows on either side of the front door.

Small brought the van to a stop. Burns reached into the back and picked up the brace. They got out and walked to the door. Small raised his hand to pull at the knocker, black and shaped like a horse's head. Just then the door opened. The man walking out stood a good three inches above his two visitors.

Immediately he saw Charlie Small, Kevin Wyman couldn't keep the fear from his face. He turned and shouted something, which must have been directed at kids, pulled the door behind him and went to step outside.

Burns moved in, put his foot in the door. Wyman turned towards him. He had arms like logs, handy for swinging hammers, even if it was just into nails. He had a square jaw and high cheekbones, the kind of looks that might have made a good cowboy in the movies.

He glanced at the brace in Burns's right hand. 'What's his problem?' he said to Charlie Small.

'Meet my associate, Mr Burns,' Small said, as if they had all just walked into a Tarantino flick.

'Mr Burns here likes to keep doors open. That way there's a better chance of proper communication. Anyway, the polite thing to do would be to ask us in.'

Wyman shook his head.

'Your missus inside?'

He shook his head again.

'Yeah, I forgot. She's the one bringing home the bacon these days.'

'Listen, things are really tight ...'

Small raised his right hand, as if he couldn't bear to hear what was about to be revealed. 'Please,' he said. 'You're late, you're late, for a very important date.'

'I had something lined up ...'

'Yes?' Small's eyes were closed, trying now to concentrate and understand.

'A job in the North. I was going back on the tools ...'

Now the eyes opened. Wyman was switching his gaze between the two men as he unfurled his story. 'It was all set up. I was going to move up there, big site on the M1 outside Belfast. The thing fell through at the last minute. I think they got some Polacks in to do it for half-price.'

A voice came from inside the house: 'Daddy.'

Wyman turned. There were two children, a girl and a boy, at the far end of the hall from the front door. Burns could see the girl holding something cuddly close to her face.

Wyman raised his voice. 'Go back to the telly. I'll be in in a minute.' The children scampered.

Small was nodding, all sympathy and understanding. 'Somebody was feeding you empty promises. Now, ain't that a shame?'

Wyman's face hardened. 'I'll get your money, don't worry about that.'

'The problem, Mr Wyman, is that I'm paid to worry about it. I mean, I come around here with Mr Burns and I see this beautiful house you got. I see your two beautiful children. Your beautiful wife is out cleaning up after your mess and I wonder how the fuck you can have such a beautiful life while you still owe my boss nearly thirty grand, and counting.'

Wyman moved quickly, his arms reaching out for the lapels of Small's jacket in a flash. Charlie Small's face was frozen in shock that somebody as powerless as this fool would actually make a move against him. Wyman caught the fat man and pushed him back against the wall of pointed brick.

Burns saw the situation for what it was. The guy was acting on impulse, letting off a bit of steam. He moved in behind and reached up to grab Wyman in a headlock. He could feel the guy's strength straining against him. He pulled him back, but the guy kicked out at Small. The fat man reacted with a flying kick of his own. He caught Wyman below the knee. Burns added pressure to the neck. His right hand was still free, still holding the brace, should it be needed.

Small moved in on Wyman, taking two fistfuls of the man's shirt in his hand. 'Who the fuck do you think you are? Give me one reason not to kick your head halfway into next week. Go on.'

Fear had replaced rage on Wyman's face. He knew he had been dealt a bum deal, out here in his home, where his kids cowered inside, where these two could do as they wanted, where he had still to tell his wife that he was drowning in a sea of debt. He held his tongue, but Burns guessed that he wanted more than anything to tell Small that, man to man, he'd kick his head in, but it didn't work like that.

Wyman kept staring at Small, his neck still locked by Burns's arm. Small moved closer, looking up into the other man's eyes.

'You ever try that again your missus will find you here with your head screwed up into your arse, you get that? Never, ever, disrespect me like that again, you fucking toerag.'

Burns tightened his grip in time with his partner's warning. He wondered how things might have gone if Charlie Small had been here on his own. He knew who his money would be on. Wyman grunted against the pressure on his neck.

Small went on, 'The next time we come by here it won't be in daylight hours and we won't be knocking on the door. If your next instalment isn't neatly tied and presented by Tuesday week, the debt-recovering strategy has to move on to a new plane, one that isn't as pleasant as this one. Do you understand me, fuckhead?'

Wyman stared at him. Small turned on his heels and walked towards the van. Burns released his grip and reversed, his eyes still on Wyman, who was bent over rubbing his neck.

As they drove back out onto the road, Small said, 'I really hope he fucks up, I really do. We'll be back for him. His future has just gone all black.'

Burns wondered what would have happened if he'd taken the wheel brace to the guy's head, what would have happened to the children if their daddy had been left unconscious on the threshold of their home. Fella should have thought about all that before he went and landed himself in hock to Pascal Nix.

* * *

When Kevin Wyman walked into the sitting room, Ciara was behind the couch. Daniel was standing at the door leading to the kitchen, poised as if ready to flee at a second's notice. The sense of playfulness that had permeated the room before the knock on the door had been sucked dry.

'What's going on here?' Wyman said. Ciara came around and walked towards him, the cuddly toy still in her arms. He got down on his honkers and gathered her into a hug.

'Who were those men?' she said.

'Just men.'

'What did they want?'

'Just to talk to me. There's no need to be afraid.' He gently extracted himself from her arms. Her mouth was turned down at the corners, showing she was afraid of the world as she was finding it. He looked over to Daniel. 'All right, Captain?' he said. Daniel nodded slowly. Wyman got to his feet. 'OK, let's go. Trampoline time – it's too fine a day to be stuck inside.'

The three of them walked through the kitchen, out the back door and around to the trampoline. Wyman had bought it on impulse four years ago, before the kids were ready for it, before the fall.

The children entered from a small ladder and began bouncing for the sky. Wyman stayed a minute until they were into their stride, then turned back towards the house.

He went inside, filled the stainless-steel kettle and switched it on, then sat down at the kitchen table to straighten out his thoughts. The morning's *Irish Independent* was still folded on the table, announcing more job losses and predicting that the country was facing a decade of austerity. A black Dell laptop lay closed beside the newspaper.

If he ever got that beached whale into a room, just the two of them, even give them both some class of a weapon – he would take a baseball bat – if he kept moving, dancing around, Fatso would get dizzy, turning like an ocean liner, trying to keep up with his dazzling feet. Then, when he began to sway, Wyman would move in for the kill, swinging the bat at Blubber's head, again and again, until the bastard fell to the floor and begged for mercy.

He contemplated whether he would keep pummelling him at that stage. He'd never thought before that he could be capable of such a thing. But never before had he been made to feel like he did now. His hands balled into fists, the knuckles turning white.

A ringing sound came from the marble worktop, next to where the kettle was bubbling towards a boil. The phone kept at it, notes rising and falling against the kettle's march, the sound of somebody else looking for him. He picked it from the cradle, all set to tell whoever it was to take a hike.

'Hi,' Brenda said.

Wyman held his breath long enough to ward the fight from his voice.

'How're you?' He tried not to sound like a man who was about to explode.

'What's wrong?'

'Nothing, nothing. Just … everything.'

She gave it a few seconds. They both knew there was little that could be said. 'Kids all right?'

He looked out through the window. Both of them were bouncing, but Daniel was reaching out to impede his sister's progress. They wouldn't get much longer out there before the sparks began to fly. 'They're grand. How's work?'

When she spoke again, the pitch of her voice had fallen. 'Everybody is bitching about last week's pay cut but, really, some of them would want to get a grip. At least we have a job.'

Suddenly Wyman had a shot of *déjà vu*. He was ringing home from the back garden of a house he was working on. It was a typical job, extension, knock a few walls, raise a few more, and fit a twenty-grand kitchen. On the day in question, they were pouring foundations for the external walls, and he'd had an impulse to share some good news with Brenda at home. He'd just got word that he'd won a contract for a total refurb of a block of eight apartments in the west of the city. Things were moving on up. The way business was going, he could make a few investments and be retired before his fiftieth birthday, maybe relocate for half the year to Spain. He had to share the feeling, the plans, with Brenda and the kids in the nest.

The refurb job never happened. From this distance, he could recall that the day in question had been about six months before things began to fall apart. Now the roles were reversed, their world turned upside-down, foundations of concrete exposed as little more than sand.

Brenda fished again for some uptake. 'Did you put that wash on this morning?'

Wyman leaned his head against the wall. 'Yes.'

'It's done by now so. There's good drying out there today from what I can see.'

'OK.'

'And I couldn't help noticing in the utility room. The ironing basket has grown into a mountain. You could make a start on it.'

'The ironing?'

'You know my sister is coming over tomorrow evening. We can't have the kids looking like ragamuffins, especially not now, the way things are.' Ragamuffins. That was one of her new words. He couldn't remember her using it before everything had turned sour.

He let the silence settle between them, but she wasn't finished. 'What have you got for the dinner?'

'The fucking dinner.'

'Kevin.'

The wall was cool against his cheek. He couldn't get it out of his head, the feeling that his balls had been sliced off. 'I'll think of something,' he said.

Brenda came back in a voice that was lower and had an edge. 'This isn't all about you,' she said. 'Where do you think I'd like to be right now? In here listening to all their crap? I should be at home with my kids, but there's nothing we can do about it. If I was at home right now, we'd just be waiting for the home to be taken from us. Somebody has to pay the mortgage.'

He didn't say anything now that she was into her stride. Her home had become his prison. Maybe he should put up some bars, keep him in and the Leopard Debt Recovery bastards out.

'The way things are looking in here, I'll be late today. So if you can have the kids' school stuff ready and their clothes. We can't have them going to school looking like ragamuffins, just because their father won't adjust to new realities.'

She hung up. Wyman walked to the worktop and put the phone back on its cradle. Outside, the kids were pulling and dragging out of each other, moving steadily towards an incident.

He stood by the table, keeping one eye on them, the other on the laptop. He opened the computer, watched it come alive and logged in. He scrolled down the favourites to Google, checked that the history bar was blank. He typed in the name of the site. Already, he could feel something change within. Things on the site had been advancing over the last fortnight. It was time to piss or get off the pot. His fingers moved slowly as he tapped in his online name, Steve. He felt like he was booking a day trip away from all the grief.

Chapter Four

'Any chance you could get some smoke?' Abigail was sitting cross-legged on the maroon mat in front of the TV. Her eyes were closed, and she could have been far away.

Karen was curled on the couch. She breathed in the sweet aroma of incense, spiralling from a candle on the mantelpiece above the fireplace. She raised her head from Grisham. They had agreed that spending an evening with the TV turned off would be good for both of them. It was an experiment, to see if they could engage in a little realignment, as Abigail had put it.

Abigail was dipping into meditation. The angel shop was beginning to rub off on her. She wasn't searching for an angel, but she said she could do with something more than bare reality as it now was. She had unfurled a yoga mat and plonked herself down in front of the dead screen. She wasn't getting very far in her flight from reality.

Karen was having more success. Her interview was on for tomorrow. She had figured out exactly what her approach would be. Now she wanted to lose herself in something, ensure that tomorrow wasn't going to weigh on her mind. She had disappeared into the novel until Abigail made her enquiry. Karen laid the book down on the couch. 'Pardon?'

Abigail opened her eyes. She would never be described as angelic, but she had a nice smile that could easily speak in mischief. To describe her as plump might be a bit harsh. Karen preferred 'cherubic'. Abigail mentioned her weight every now and again, but she didn't obsess about it.

'Come on, you have a suss. That guy with the funny name you met with Jake, lumps of coal for teeth.'

'Creole?'

'That's him, the kid. Could you give him a tinkle? I think the realignment needs to take off in a different direction.'

Karen ran a hand through her hair. She enjoyed a smoke, but Kerry had taken the pleasure from her. 'What would the angels have to say about it?'

'Karen, please. It's not angels plural. We all have our own angel. And mine is big into chilling.' Abigail closed her eyes again, her hands resting on her knees. 'I mean, just because I'm flushing out all the bad stuff in life doesn't mean I've turned into a dry shite. Don't you feel any itch for something?'

She raised herself up off the floor, as if her meditation couldn't survive the subject that had been brought up. 'I had a suss. A pure scumbag. Last time I caught him, he said he wasn't dealing in anything less than an ounce at a time. An ounce? I wouldn't be able to get out of bed for a week if that amount of stuff was lying about the place.'

She looked across at Karen, who was focused on the Moroccan rug hanging above the fireplace, following the hexagonal red pattern that ran around the perimeter. 'Karen, hello.'

She switched back on.

'Creole?'

Karen got up and stretched her arms. 'OK, I need to talk to him anyway.'

* * *

The evening was rinsed, the streets wet, as Karen made her way down to the quay and walked towards town. At Capel Street Bridge she stepped onto the boardwalk. The Liffey was dank, pools of streetlight bobbing around on the surface. She passed a man sitting on a bed of flattened cardboard. He extended a paper cup. Karen noticed he wasn't putting much energy into it. If he wasn't prepared to make any effort, then she certainly wouldn't.

She crossed the river at the Liffey Street Bridge, moved up through Temple Bar. A knot of women, looking like refugees from a hen night, were walking along the main drag. They seemed defeated, as if they had been told too late that things were not as they used to be in Dublin.

Grafton Street was pretty empty, even for that time of the evening. A man who had the streets written all over him was leaning against a lamp-post, one hand with a hat extended, the other bearing a piece of cardboard which said, 'I won't lie. It's for drink.' He had to be rewarded for initiative. She broke from her path, and dropped two two-euro coins into his hat.

Everything was shuttered for the night. Karen wondered how many were shuttered for good. She felt a pang of sadness. The thought of a shop, any shop, closing down was akin to a death. The bereaved owner must have opened the doors for the first time full of dreams. And then reality had kicked in. Doors had closed, lights died and the future melted into the ether.

She'd love a crack at selling again. Even now there were always opportunities for somebody of her talents.

She was feeling warm by the time she made it to Leeson Street. She'd been there once before, with Jake. They had arrived back after closing time in pursuit of keeping the night alive. She had been fairly out of it. The house was set back from the street, behind a lawn that looked more beaten down than mown. A hedge and rusting gate fronted the property.

There was no immediate reply when she pressed the buzzer. She wondered whether she had the right one. She looked again. Yes, Creole was on the top floor. She remembered that from the night she'd come back here. In her memory, the stairs went on for ever.

Caution prompted her to look out towards the street. She didn't know how much business Creole did, whether there was any chance it merited surveillance from the law.

'Yeah.' The buzzer cackled into life.

'Creole?'

'Who's that?'

'Karen, Karen Riney.'

'Who?'

Jesus, thanks a bunch. She'd obviously made a serious impression the night she'd been here. 'Karen. We met a few months ago. I came back here with Jake.'

There was another silence.

'How is Jake?'

We have lift-off. 'You heard about what happened?'

'Yeah.'

'Is there any chance we could continue this discussion upstairs?' she said.

'It's not a great time.'

'Look, I'm sorry, I've come across from the northside. I didn't have your number, and I thought I'd come on spec. I'd really appreciate if you'd let me in.'

'You're looking for something?'

'Yes.'

'I don't normally do business at this time.'

She could have guessed that was coming. From what she remembered Jake saying about him, Creole's solitary disposition meant he only did business within set hours, as if he was running a small shop or working to the strictures of trade-union rules. Apart from that, there was the power thing. Like all dealers, he had power over the mood and condition of his customers, and he liked to exercise it now and again.

'Could you make an exception?' she said.

There was no reply, until the buzzer for the door spluttered into life.

* * *

Kevin Wyman found himself drifting as he sat and waited. There were two couples in the bar of the budget hotel. Apart from that, Wyman was the only other customer. A barman in a striped waistcoat polished glasses, whiling away an evening when action was thin on the ground. The lights were dimmed low but there was no hiding the cheap décor.

Wyman surmised that the two couples were coming from the same side of the street as him. He'd been stealing looks at them, and it was obvious they lacked the easy familiarity of long-standing partners. He wondered whether they also had met on smooch.com. Maybe the website was a marketing ploy for the hotel. Maybe that woman was a plant, paid to lure illicit lovers into the establishment to give it a shot in the arm.

Brenda hadn't been impressed that he was heading out. He had the kids in bed when she arrived home from work. Sleep hadn't yet claimed them, so she went up to say goodnight. When she came back down, she kicked off her work heels and sat in front of the TV. He brought her the reheated lasagne, but she just picked at it around the fringes. She speared a few forks of lettuce from the side salad, but didn't eat much more. At any other time, he would have challenged her. There he was, making the fucking dinner for everybody, and she couldn't bring herself to eat it.

Instead he kept his cool, told her he'd got a call, had to meet a fella about the possibility of something on a couple of extensions in the city. There was maybe two weeks' work in it.

'Is it worth it?' Brenda said. 'I mean, what about the kids? Who's going to do childcare for a couple of weeks? We need to think about these things, Kevin. We need to think long-term.'

Right there, right then, all he was thinking about was shooting out the door. 'I need to start somewhere. I'm going out of my mind here at home all day. I have to ... get it back.'

'Get what back?'

'My mojo, my life, my ...'

'Go on, say it.'

'Forget it. I'm going out, OK?'

'Just don't be late. I'm on an early tomorrow so I'll be off before the kids are up.'

Wyman turned to leave. 'See you some time tomorrow evening so.' But his wife was already focused on the television.

Now he was waiting. He took a long draw from his pint. He'd give it to the dregs, but if she didn't show by then, he was off. He'd never done this before. At the height of the boom, he had strayed once in particular, but there had been what they call mitigating circumstances.

It was on one of those golfing breaks in Marbella. He had woken up one morning in a strange hotel room, next to a woman who was sleeping in gentle snores behind silky ropes of hair. He'd extracted himself from the bed as delicately as he could, found his clothes on a trail leading from the bathroom, and left. So what? It had been sex, nothing more. It wasn't as if he'd been off gallivanting while the rest of the contingent kept their dicks zipped up. Far from it.

But that had been abroad, on the lash, in a world that could be cordoned off from the everyday. It had been nothing more than part of the package, a chance to relieve the stress of living at the speed of light, making money as if it was going out of fashion.

OK, this was different. He was in Dublin, ten miles down the road from home. This wasn't party time. It was needs must. The flicker of passion from his marriage was dimming. What else could he do?

Online, insulated through cyberspace, anything was possible. Anything except the real thing. Wyman wasn't much up on technology, but the day would surely come when it was possible to have sex online. He wished to Christ it was here now and he didn't have to go through all this.

He took another draw, set the glass down on a napkin and looked up to see her coming through the door of the bar.

Their eyes met across the near-empty room by a process of elimination. She walked to his table in long, confident strides, her long black hair shining like that of the model in the ad who tells herself she's worth it. She had on a beige coat tied with a belt and her face was serious.

He got up and extended a hand. She looked all right, grey-green eyes, nice skin. If it wasn't her, he was making an ass of himself.

'Steve,' she said.

'Sabrina?' She smiled and it warmed up her face. She was all right, no question about that. As long as she wasn't a fruitcake, this might work out.

* * *

The apartment was up three flights of steps. When Karen got to the top, the door was ajar. She walked in and Creole was sitting in an armchair, eyes on the TV. He swung his head around and said, 'Hi.' There was a couch to one side of his throne and a small table that looked like it had been commandeered from a skip. The ceiling was high and could have done with a lick of paint. She walked to the couch. Over near the TV, in front of a tall window, a huge plant grew, branches reaching out into the room. On first glance, Karen thought it was cannabis, but she could see now that it was something more benign.

'Where did you get the beanstalk?' she said.

He showed his teeth, or the black stumps that had once been his teeth, and Karen told herself she wouldn't give him any more reason to smile.

His eyes were back on the TV, a football game of some sort. The couch looked like it could have something growing in it. Karen reckoned if she were to remain standing it might be interpreted as an insult. He made a gesture for her to sit. She perched on the edge, ready to leap up if anything emerged from its depths.

In front of her, on the table, there was an orange packet of Rizla papers and a tin advertising tobacco. There was also a mug, chipped at the handle. It didn't look clean. She hoped there wouldn't be any offer of coffee. There were some chances she wasn't willing to take.

Creole tore his head away from the football, turning towards her. She saw him up close for the first time. His mouth was closed, as if he knew the awful truth about his chompers. His hair was already in the departure lounge, a few blond wisps pulled back across his forehead, like the remains of a levee that had long since broken. He wasn't beyond redemption, but the drooping eyes suggested he had given up all hope of ever again being presentable.

'Coffee?' he said.

'Thanks, but I'm all coffeed out. How have you been?'

'Had a dose with a chest infection there last week but I got a good antibiotic. Before that, I'd a fall from a ladder. Couldn't work for about a month.'

'Oh, my God,' she said. She hadn't asked for his medical history. 'And how're you now?'

He considered the question for a few seconds. 'Right now I'm baked, so things are OK. But I worry a lot. About the future, the economy.'

'The economy?'

'Yeah, it's fucked. I mean really fucked.'

Karen took a look around the room. Never mind the economy, sunshine, I'd worry about you. 'Your own economy seems to be doing all right. I mean, you're still in business.'

He said, 'The way things are, people aren't going out any more. They buy the cheap booze, sit at home and skin up. Smoke is the new coke.' He looked at her again and raised himself up out of the seat with what appeared to be a serious effort. He steadied himself on his feet and said, 'What are you looking for?'

'What have you got?'

'Buds, a bit of Moroccan black, but there's some very good herbal going around. If you really want to leave the state of the country behind.'

She wondered how Abigail would be when really stoned. 'How about a quarter-ounce of the herbal?' she said.

He nodded slowly. 'Fifty spots OK?'

'Bit steep, isn't it?' she said.

'Going rate.'

'Any discount for friends?'

'I could do it for forty-five for you.'

'Tell you what,' she said, getting to her feet, as if she had just had an epiphany. 'If you can let it go for thirty-five, and it's as good as you reckon, I'll introduce you to my friend, who will grow into one of your most valued customers.'

Creole's face sparked into life. 'Thirty-five?' he said. 'Are you taking the piss?'

Karen reckoned he must be making at least a ton on an ounce. That made it twenty-five on a quarter, and throw in another five for chopping it down. Anything above thirty and he was still turning a profit. 'Think of the repeat business,' she said.

Creole just looked at her. 'You're something all right,' he said. He walked through the door into his bedroom. Karen noticed that she felt better about herself. The exchange had given her a little lift, like she used to get at work in Sydney whenever she made a sale. Affirmation.

He came back out through the door and handed her what looked like a severed green finger wrapped tightly in clingfilm. Somebody on the box suddenly got excited, capturing his attention. Creole pointed. 'Fuckin' goalie. Look at the replay here. Fella was rooted to the spot.'

Karen turned to the TV, pretending to give a shit. She handed him the notes, a twenty and three fives. She had come with plenty of change. 'Easy cash,' she said. He was looking at her now as if she had just brought up the splitting of the atom.

He shrugged. 'It has its own hassles. You want a smoke?'

'Naw. You ever think of trying to make serious money?'

'Doing what?'

'What do you think? Going into business for yourself.'

Creole sat back down into his chair, leaned forward and slipped three skins from the orange packet. He ran the papers across his tongue and, with one hand, stuck the three together, two long-ways, with the third joined at right angles at one end.

He opened the tin of tobacco and pulled some weed from it, kneading it as he dropped it into the skins. 'I don't know, lot of hassle,' he said.

'How much do you reckon your guy makes?'

He raised his head towards her. 'A shitload of money.'

'Exactly. And what about the guy above him? The higher up you go, the more money to be made. Amn't I right?'

'What are you getting at?'

'I'm just wondering. I first thought of it when I was down with Jake. There's serious money in the grow-house business if you could do it right.'

'Did you discuss it with Jake?'

'No, Creole, I didn't. I told you I was just thinking about it, that's all.'

'Yeah, well, you know, anybody can grow the shit if they have some cash up front, and a quiet place to do it. Where you going to get the cash? A bank?' At this, his mouth broke open into a black smile.

Karen said, 'Yeah, right.'

'Chalk it down. Hand you the umbrella when the sun's shining and take it away when it's pissing from the heavens. Anyway, apart from that, you have to sell it. That's when the hassle starts. Step on the wrong toes and you might end up on crutches, know what I mean?'

'Maybe,' Karen said. 'But tackling problems is part of business. Maybe that could just be another problem to take on.'

Creole raised the joint to his mouth and sealed it together with his tongue. 'You sure you don't want a smoke?'

Karen waved it away. She could see Abigail back at the house, beating the yoga mat off the wall, waiting for her rocket fuel. 'Listen, just one thing,' she said.

Creole turned to her.

'Do you know this guy Charlie Small?'

Creole's face darkened. 'What about him?'

'I need to talk to him.' Now she had his full attention. His fingers were moving up and down the joint, caressing it, smoothing out any lumps.

'Jake?'

'Yeah. What's he like, this guy? Funny name, Charlie Small.'

'He's not funny, not small either. He isn't big, but he's a fat fucker. I mean, he's huge. Jake needs to straighten things out with him?'

'I just have to pass on his best wishes.'

Creole fished in his pocket and came back with a Nokia mobile phone. He pressed a few buttons and reeled off a number. Karen got him to repeat it as she typed it into her phone.

'You know who Charlie Small works for?' Creole said.

'I haven't a clue. I don't know any of these people.'

Creole was looking at the TV when he spoke again. 'Pascal Nix.'

'Name doesn't mean anything to me,' she said.

He turned to her now. The joint was in his mouth, the top of it twisted into a little wing, primed for take-off. He flicked the lighter in his other hand, raised it towards the wing, and said, 'If I was you, I'd keep it that way.'

* * *

After the third drink, a silence swelled between them. She ran a finger around the rim of the wine glass, turned to him and said, 'Well.'

Wyman was floating nicely, half a gallon of stout to the good. 'Let's get out of here,' he said, and immediately wondered whether that line sounded too well worn.

'Let's not,' Sabrina said. 'I took the liberty of booking a room.'

Wyman allowed himself a smile. She was OK, this woman. He drained his pint and stood up with what he hoped was firm authority. 'Didn't realise I was that easy.'

'Just one thing,' she said, as she got to her feet. 'I'm not into anything rough.' For a second there, as she straightened herself, her face a stone, Wyman felt like he was engaging in a business transaction. But of course he wasn't. This was a coupling, no money changing hands, no favours, just two people getting it on, even if the circumstances were unconventional. Even if the circumstances were completely bonkers.

He nodded. The thought of rough stuff hadn't occurred to him, but the mention of it stirred something inside. It was on the tip of his tongue to protest that, no, all he wanted was to get his rocks off, but he edited that out, pronto.

She walked over to Reception and he took in the grace of her stride, even after the booze. By now the bar was empty, save for two men sitting in a conspiratorial huddle at a table near the window. Out beyond the lace curtains the traffic rose and fell against the night. A shadow ghosted across the window on the street.

He could hear sounds from hidden speakers, Michael Bublé, doing some damage to a Van Morrison song. Just this once. That was all he needed. Just this once to feel OK about himself again. If he could get away with it, he'd have his mojo back – maybe he and Brenda could rekindle things. Maybe all he needed was a little lift. He hadn't felt this good in a while.

'All set?' He turned and she was standing there, the key dangling in her hand like a crooked finger.

They walked through the room towards the lift. One of the two men was rising to his feet, an empty glass in his hand. The barman was smiling at them as they passed, wishing them a goodnight. Wyman exchanged glances with the man. Was that envy in the fella's eyes, or just an acknowledgement that he was in for a good night? A stab of panic gripped him. Did the barman know the woman? Was she a regular here to meet her cyberspace lovers?

He looked at her but she was focused on the lift, as if the

evening had moved into a different phase for which they were obliged to adopt new personas.

She kept her eyes on the floor light as they waited for the lift.

'You know this place,' he said, trying hard to keep the casual in his voice.

She laughed. 'It's a bit late to be asking do I come here often,' she said.

'I didn't mean it like that. I was just … How many times?'

'Not enough to matter,' she said. 'And, no, I haven't been in this place before. Like I told you, I'm married but nothing burns. You and I are kindred spirits, I think, and this suits me. Let's just enjoy the here and now and see where it takes us.'

The lift door swished open. A wicked impulse pushed him towards making a move now, but he beat it back. It would be too much like real passion.

They got out and walked down the corridor, she keeping an eye on the room numbers. At the appointed door, she took a swipe card from the pocket of her coat and a green light flashed on the handle.

Inside, she inserted the card and lit up the room. They looked at each other and he came at her. Her lips felt warm.

She pulled him in. He grappled with her coat, sliding it from her shoulders. Then he felt her hands at the buckle of his belt. This was what he had been waiting for. It was good, clean, no complications. He might even get away with it.

Chapter Five

Somebody was boring into Karen's brain. An angry, vibrating instrument was hammering away at her head, hauling her from the depths of sleep, dragging her towards the surface, until she began to hear it as a telephone. Her hand crept out from under the duvet and reached for the bedside locker. Her fingers felt the black plastic cover. She pulled it towards her, thumb and index finger searching for the button. The ringing stopped. She raised the phone to her ear.

'Karen?'

'Yes.'

'Did I wake you?'

'Who is this?' She could hear the hoarseness in her voice. Her mouth felt like it had been coated with sand and glue.

'Who do you think? It's me, Jake.'

This was all she needed right now. 'What time is it?'

'What … Karen, it's after ten o'clock. Will you listen to me, please? I don't have much time.'

She pulled herself up, refusing to believe that the day was already under way. She could see the light straining against the purple throw that served as a curtain. 'How're you?' she said, out of a sense of duty.

'How do you think? There's some guys in here, they're looking at me kinda strange. Guys who've been here a long time. You know what I mean?'

Last night was coming back to her now. She arrived with the smoke, stopping off on the way for a packet of large Rizlas and twenty Silk Cut Blue. Neither of them smoked cigarettes any more so the mildest brand would do the job.

Back at the cottage, Abigail had packed in the meditation. She was in front of the TV, engrossed in a documentary about the habitats of dolphins. Her eyes lit up when Karen pulled the weed from the pocket of her windbreaker. She killed the TV on the spot, reached for the music. Spiritualized drifted out from the speakers, filling up the room.

'How's the bail thing coming on?' Karen said.

'Not good. They're saying I'm a flight risk and I've nothing to put up. My guy, the solicitor, I get the impression he doesn't really give a shit. He told me that he's new to the free legal aid thing, and I believe it.'

'So, what's the future?' She swung her legs from the bed. The action sent the room through a wave. Her free hand reached for the pillow to steady the ship.

'The future? I don't want to think that far ahead. Listen, what about that contact you were going to make? The looks I'm getting in here, I don't know whether some of these guys have been tipped off to put the shits up me. I need to straighten things out with our friend.'

'The big guy?'

'Yes, yes, the big guy, Mr Small. Did you get his number?'

She stood up, her feet planted wide apart to withstand another lurch. More of last night was coming back to her now. The first joint went down well. Immediately after it they checked in with each other, but not a lot had changed in either of their worlds. The music had moved on. Abigail pulled out an old John Martyn CD, the one on which his wife Beverley had guested. She knew that Karen was a Martyn fan. They discussed how handsome he was on those old takes from the BBC and the album covers from the 1970s and how he had grown bloated from the booze and pot, had his leg amputated and then died a few years ago down in Kilkenny.

John Martyn's back catalogue took them all the way through the second joint. It was after that one that Karen moved to get up for a glass of water, but she couldn't raise herself out of the chair.

Now, she was standing in her bedroom. Her top from last night was on the floor, her black jeans at the foot of the chair where they had been thrown. She moved towards the bedroom door, her free hand out to ward off a fall. Water: it was all about water now.

'Yeah, I got his number. From Creole.'

'Was he asking for me?'

'Who?'

'Creole, who do you think?'

'He was. He said ... he's behind you all the way.' She was making this stuff up as she went along. All she wanted was to get Jake off the phone. There was something on today, something that should have her full attention. Shit. The interview.

'Listen, Jake, I have to go. I've got an interview.'

'An interview? For a job? Jesus. If you get it, you could go bail for me, maybe.'

'Jake, I'll ring that guy this afternoon, OK? I'll get it sorted with him, but that's it. After that—'

'Whoa, what are you saying? You can't abandon me. Not now.'

She reached over and ran the cold tap, rinsed out a glass and drank long from it. Relief washed down her throat.

'Karen.' His voice rose, as if she had already scampered and he had to holler after her. 'Karen.'

She put down the glass. 'I'm not going anywhere. Look, I'll get back to you later. I have to prepare for this thing.'

She rang off and walked out into the living room. A foggy pall hung in the air. The door to Abigail's room was open. The angel had fled.

* * *

Dara Burns was obsessing about Robert Johnson again, how he'd lived his life, and how he'd messed up. Burns couldn't buy it. The king of the Delta blues had had a unique gift. Apart from possessing fingers made for dancing on frets, he could write songs. Man, if Burns had that ability, he'd mind how he'd go. But that Johnson dude, he was something else. Pissing it up wherever he went, sticking it into any woman who came into his space, flushing his future down the drain.

If Burns had been given those breaks, he'd have nurtured his gifts, treated them with respect and kept them close. Fuckin' Robert Johnson. Who said he was the king anyway? What about Charley Patton? What about Son House? When you came to think about it, Johnson had lived more after he died than he ever did when he was alive. Fella gave the blues a bad name.

Burns was sitting in the LiteAce, the window rolled down to take in an unseasonally warm March day. There wasn't a cloud in the sky, and none in Burns's sight either. His head was bobbing, his right foot tapping on the heavy-duty rubber mat on the floor of the passenger side. He could hear Johnson wailing about a kind-hearted woman, doing the twelve-bar thing, that bass descending as if it was en route all the way to Hell.

The van was parked in a housing estate on the west side of the city, just beyond the M50. Charlie Small was in conversation at the front door of a house across the road, his head tilted to the heavens, a priest hearing the confession of a woman who had sinned against her moneylender. The woman's face bore the concern of one who wants to repent. A cigarette burned between the fingers of her left hand, and a child clung to the red polka-dot pyjama bottoms.

Dara Burns was taking to his new role. They had made three calls that morning and he had been required only once to make his presence known. That case had involved a wiry guy, in for ten big ones on foot of a coke habit, and still not getting the predicament he was in. Burns had been required just to stand there, cracking knuckles, as Charlie did all the talking. Charlie enjoyed doing all the talking, and that was fine with Burns.

Most of the time, it left him with the space to wander, and right now he was down in the Delta, trying to get past Mr Johnson.

When his grandfather had been near the end, his body breaking down in a raft of complications associated with decades of excess, Burns used to keep him interested by bringing up Johnson and his wasted talent. Granddad was a Johnson man, but Burns used to chide him that Johnson owed everything to Charley Patton and Son House, the proper heirs to the Delta blues who had plucked their talent for all it was worth. In those final days, Burns had got a kick by watching Granddad come alive again, his passion fired by the music that had brightened his dull existence.

The blues was the one thing that Burns carried from a childhood he'd rather forget. Granddad had had all the records going back to the twenties, thirties and forties, most of them sent from the States. He lived for the old country blues, all that acoustic guitar and stories rolled out in song.

They were all there, Johnson, Patton, House, Big Bill Broonzy, Sonny Terry and Brownie McGhee, Willie Moore, and then all those guys who couldn't see too good. Blind Blake, Blind Willie McTell, Blind Lemon Jefferson, Blind Willie Johnson, Blind Boy

Fuller: Burns's imagination used to see all of them, their heads tilted to the heavens, eyes far away, pulling strings, keeping time with the bass, the sounds giving them sight on the world. That stayed with him always, how those who are blind could see so much. And there was Johnson, the world at his feet, and he went and got himself poisoned to death at twenty-seven for riding another man's wife. Dumb fucker.

His grandfather had been a purist, though, and Johnson was the man. That kid represented the high-water mark of the acoustic blues, a time before electrics were put on a guitar, and the blues moved north from the Delta and drifted into what Granddad used to call 'that Chicago shite'.

The car door opened and Charlie Small manoeuvred himself into the driver's seat. After a pause he sighed, like a deflating balloon. 'These people,' he said.

'Yeah?'

Small pointed across the road at the house where he had come from. 'She's in for over two grand. Six months ago she came to Pascal for money for the kid's first communion. Five hundred spots. You know, the kid isn't getting married, she's making her communion. And now she's giving me this round-the-houses spiel about her labour getting cut and the kids having no shoes and, man, I don't need to hear about this. I mean, I have to tell her, "Listen, honey, I'm not the guy from the Vincent de Paul. I'm here to collect."'

'So, what are we going to do?' he said.

Small reached for the ignition. 'She said I can come along with her when she's getting the labour next week. She'll fix me up straight after. Hey, I might even get fixed up with something more. The dole office, where love stories begin.'

The engine kicked into life, as Small began laughing. Burns didn't want to think about Small and the woman. Jacinta was coming over tonight. He thought about her and the remainder of the day ahead took on a soft glow.

* * *

The floor was open plan, with little beige dividers corralling the work stations. Karen had a quick gander as she sat waiting. Right around the room the walls were made of glass, looking out across the city-centre skyline.

Maybe it was her imagination, but as far as she could make out there wasn't much happening in this place. A knot of them stood around one desk, a woman on the fringes using the toes of her stockinged right foot to scratch the calf of her left.

A few of the faces were stretched in what had to be anxiety. One man, overweight under a receding tuft of jet black hair, was staring into space, his countenance more appropriate for a funeral. OK, everybody knew the job scene was tight, but this recruitment outfit was supposed to be among the best. Did they have no work to go to?

'Miss Riney?'

She got up without turning around. He was leaning in towards her, tall, slim, in his white shirtsleeves and black-and-grey-striped tie that added a few years to him. He wore silver cufflinks, and a hint of sideburns crept down in front of his ears. He looked the business, she'd give him that.

'I'm Richie Reynolds.' He took her hand in a firm grasp and wheeled around to his side of the desk. His right hand bore a brown A4 envelope holding her CV. He pulled the contents from the envelope. 'You found us no problem, I assume.'

'Your directions were on the button.'

He looked at her, as if he was seeing something for the first time. 'So, I've had a look at your details, and there's a few things

I'd like to explore with you.'

Karen nodded, straightened herself. She felt something, a tingle, like a nervous bell going off. She hadn't felt like this since she was in school. This was the first time she had subjected herself to a formal interview since her first job in Sydney. She wore a white blouse that Abigail had rooted out for her, and the black trouser suit that was getting its first outing since the funeral.

'OK, well, working backwards, as we like to do, I see that your last job ended in Sydney over a year ago. Where have the missing months gone?'

She coughed away something in her throat. 'I'm back here since a few weeks after I left that job in Pitt Street. I've been readjusting to being home, I suppose. I was in Australia for ten years since finishing up a training course in sales here. Things went well for me over there. They're not sticklers for qualifications, especially in telecom retail where I worked, and I got on fine. But now I'm back and I suppose I was just taking some time out.'

'Did you go travelling?'

'No.'

He looked down at the sheet of paper again, as if he'd missed something. 'You haven't worked for over a year.'

'That's right.'

'So what brought you back at a time when the place feels as if it's about to fall apart?'

Her laugh was dry. 'Things changed for me over there.' She didn't want to go into it, not now, not with this man.

'Are you going to share with me your reasons?'

'My husband died in an accident. I didn't want to stay on.'

His face softened. 'Sorry to hear that.' He opened his mouth to say something, but a bell sounded from the far end of the floor. Karen looked over and saw a woman of around her own age pulling a rope attached to the bell's tongue. It was hanging from a faded yellow wrought-iron frame. All eyes were now on the woman and the bell. It sounded like a summons.

Richie Reynolds said, 'Oh, for fuck's sakes.'

'What's wrong?'

'Sorry?'

'What's the story with the bell?'

'Oh. It's just a thing we have. If somebody makes a sale, they have to ring the bell to let everybody know. It worked well when times were good but now . . .'

'Now it's used to piss everybody else off,' Karen said.

He looked at her like she was full of surprises. 'Officially, that's a terrible thing to say. Off the record, you're bang on.' With that, Richie Reynolds got up and joined others who were moving towards the bell, like condemned prisoners.

They gathered around and offered the woman handshakes. She bent her head to receive pecks on the cheek, her face a picture of pleasure. Karen looked on. She wondered about the condition of the soul in these people. Richie Reynolds did his duty and hurried back to his desk.

'OK,' he said. 'Now, where were we? Right, Karen. Look, the deal is I have a client who's looking for somebody special. Let's just see if we can match your wants with their needs.' She told herself to chill.

'Just to let you know the kind of candidate I have in mind. The client is a big organisation. I'm sure you've heard of 4Fone, the latest entry to the mobile-phone market?'

She nodded.

'Good, always good to know the client. Well, they're embarking on a huge retail-sales drive and they're looking for the right person to fit into their culture. You know where I'm coming from?'

Karen nodded again. She was trying hard to stay with the programme. An image kept flitting through her head. She was standing in a house somewhere, a bedroom, looking out across rows of plants, calculating the weight involved and how much could be made from this room.

'So, what gets Karen' – at this Richie Reynolds looked down at the CV – 'Riney out of bed in the morning?'

'Sorry?'

'What drives you? What ignites your passion?'

'Mobile phones.'

'Mobile phones?'

'Yes. I wake up in the morning and my head is full of mobile phones, and mobile tones.'

'What?'

'What do you want me to say? Listen, I can sell, OK? I know how to deal with people. I worked in retail for ten years in Sydney. I could wipe the floor with most of the salespeople there. I'm just good at it, and I know I'm good at it.' She leaned back in her chair, finally arriving at a relaxed state. 'The jargon? The – excuse me – the bullshit? That might do something to mask your shortcomings if you can't sell, but I don't have that problem. You can put me forward for the job. I'll probably get it and when I do I'll make a good go at it. Mark my words.'

'Jesus,' he said, his mouth open. He looked down at her CV, searching for some clue that he might have missed earlier. Karen kept her eyes on him, but her mind was on money. If she went into that business, where would she get the dosh?

'Are you attached now?' He was looking at her differently, like she'd just been swiftly promoted from a long shot at a commission to the only show in town.

'What's that got to do with anything?'

'Just … you know, can I be frank? I couldn't help noticing the wedding band you're wearing. We live in the real world. It's a patriarchal society. If you were, let's just say, in a committed relationship, intending to' – here his fingers jabbed in fresh-air inverted commas – 'start a family? Well, nobody's going to say it outright for obvious reasons, but it might influence a decision to take you on.'

The fresh-air commas did it for her. Curiosity had kept her tuned in, but she couldn't handle that. 'I see,' she said. 'You want to know whether I'm about to get knocked up.'

He shrugged his shoulders. 'Not to put too fine a point on it, these things matter.'

'I thought I explained that my husband died. I'm still wearing my band. So what?'

'Just as long as you make it clear in an interview that you're … not, you know, all set to start a family, that the ring belongs … You know where I'm coming from.'

'What if I told you that I wasn't attached, but on the look-out?'

She thought she could see Richie Reynolds's chest swell. A smile opened across his face, celebrating his obvious attraction to any woman with a pulse.

'What say we continue this interview at a little pub just down the road from here?' he said.

Karen Riney got to her feet, took her shoulder bag from the floor. She looked Richie Reynolds in the eye and said, 'Mr Reynolds, does the term "asshole" ring a bell with you?' He reared back, as if she had just slapped him across the face.

She turned and walked towards the door, and found herself passing right by the bell. She leaned over and began ringing it with all the swing she could muster. She walked right on through the door without looking back.

* * *

Jacinta arrived early and let herself in with the key Burns had given her. Even now, six months down the line, she couldn't get over the order of the place. It was as if he didn't live there at all, or he was about to sell it, and had got it dolled up for inspection.

When things were quiet at the salon, she told her friend Irene about it in hushed tones, after Irene had asked her how it was all going, the thing, as she called it. They looked at each other in the mirror, over the high chairs, and she told Irene she couldn't get over the cleanliness.

'Ah, come on now,' Irene said. 'Tell the truth. I'd say he can be dirty when he wants to.'

Tonight's meal came from Jamie Oliver. The book had been a present from her mother. It wasn't easy with three kids, and her mother could do only so much. But look at her, and how she was managing. She wasn't on the labour. She could sit at home on her arse and get what she was entitled to. But she didn't believe in that. She wanted independence. She wanted to provide a proper example to her kids. They would grow up knowing the value of work, and that, if nothing else, might help keep them on the straight and narrow. Their father was long gone, and not a word from him. She had heard through different channels that he was in London, shacked up with a floozy from Blanch. Well, good riddance. She felt nothing but sorrow for any woman who ended up with him.

Not that she was heading for happy ever after here. Dara Burns was a strange fish, with his guitar and not really ever wanting to go out to the pub. She should be grateful for that, in light of her experience with men, but damn it all, there was no harm in a few sociable drinks every now and again.

And then there was his thing with the music. It just seemed so old, like something out of – who knows? – *The Black and White*

Minstrel Show or something. The only song she could relate to at all was that one 'They're Rd Hot', by that Johnson man he was always giving out about. At least you could jive to that, but the rest of the stuff . . . She put up with it because it seemed to mean so much to him, but she'd never get to a place where she would enjoy it.

Even as they paddled through the shallows, she could see that they wouldn't be heading off into the deep blue yonder. Dara wasn't the marrying type. She wasn't sure exactly what type he was. He had a good heart, and the sex was a few notches above fair to middling, and what more could she, at this station in life, want?

She was looking forward to the evening.

Within half an hour, everything was ready to go. She set the table with two little mats she had bought for him in Arnott's on a rare visit to the city. A scented candle burned in the middle. She had her wine glass. He had a half-pint glass for the German beer he liked.

When he came through the door, his eyes darted around in concern. She knew what that was about. The scan stopped dead on his guitar, mounted on a stand next to the music centre. If, by some quirk of Fate, she had even touched the instrument, the evening would have gone south. She knew better.

After they'd kissed, she said, 'See? I'm learning. It's as if I haven't been here at all.'

He just nodded, said he'd have a quick shower and disappeared into the bathroom. Jacinta checked the oven. She debated with herself whether to have a cigarette now or to wait until after the meal. She knew the wait would be worth it, that she'd get more pleasure after a feed. She went into the bedroom, unzipped the overnight bag she had brought and took out a copy of *Image* magazine.

As she left the bedroom, the shower jets fell silent in the adjoining bathroom. She walked out into the living room, heard Dara call her from the doorway of the bedroom and she turned around. He was standing there in the nip, giving her plenty of his perfect body. She let the magazine fall to the floor.

That was when she heard the bang and felt something slam into her back. The room began to spin and then smacked her hard. She knew it had to be the wall. A blinding pain was boring into her. The floor had come up to meet her. She could smell her own blood. Something was all wrong.

Dara was going to go through the roof with the state the place was now in. Where was he and him with no clothes on? He couldn't have done this to her. What about her darlings? She had to see them again, touch them, say goodbye.

She didn't want to leave here, away from them, but the darkness was moving in. She didn't have the energy to fight, everything was draining from her. Confusion had her in a grip, but it began to dawn on her that she was dying. And then there was nothing.

Chapter Six

When the shot rang out, Burns ducked back into the bedroom. He dived for the floor, pain shooting up through his scrotum as he slid across the polished boards. His right hand reached under the bed and gripped the hurley at the top of its taped shaft. He pulled it out into the open, and, on his fours, hopped across to behind the door, like a Neanderthal grasping for survival.

He lengthened his grip on the hurley, waiting for them to come through the door. He knew that he might as well be using a feather to attack a bulldog, but he wasn't going to make it easy for them. He wouldn't plead for mercy or logic. It had never meant anything to him when he was the one out there, at the right end of the gun. And he sure as hell wasn't going to look for it now.

The sound of moaning came from the living room. Everything was amplified as his senses went into overdrive. He heard feet running, fading into the night. Then nothing but Jacinta out there, life draining from her body. Only a fool or a suicide would stick a head out now.

He didn't want to be remembered as the man who died in the nip. They could say what they liked about him, but he didn't want any songs written about how he'd left the world as naked as he'd entered it.

Across the room, on the bed, his laundered navy jocks lay on the duvet, where he had thrown them from a drawer seconds ago before he'd gone out to give Jacinta a little surprise.

Now he wondered how much blood she was losing. If the wound was in one of her limbs, there was a chance she might make it.

He shouted her name. The moaning had stopped. He called again. He rested his head back on the wall. Nobody was coming. He could go out now, walk into a trap.

He moved back a few feet from behind the door, lifted the hurley and offered it as a target in the doorframe. It hung there in the air. Nothing happened. His hand was steady, and for this he was grateful. He waved it up and down. No response. They had to be gone. He thought he felt a chill on his skin, air blowing in through the broken window.

'Jacinta,' he called again. The silence answered. He threw himself across the doorway and onto the bed, sliding over and falling down on the far side. Nothing. Now voices were coming from somewhere out there, voices full of fear and dread. He grabbed the jocks, poked his legs into them and walked out, the hurley hanging loosely from his right hand.

Most of the room was as he had left it when the shot had rung out. A tall candle still burned on the table, between the mats and the cutlery and the wine and beer glasses. His guitar was still on the stand next to the music centre.

The front window was in shite. A hole had been blown through it and the blinds were now hanging on. He turned to where Jacinta had got up from the couch. She hadn't gone far. The wall was red with her blood.

Her face was already turning blue. He knelt beside her, took her head in his hands. He was sure that he was holding her when the last drop of life drained from her body, by a twitch at the corners of her mouth. He had never been this close to death before. Sure, he'd got in close a couple of times, dished it out from inches, but it wasn't as if he had ever hung around to see it set in and take over.

The blood was all around him now. He could feel it on his knees. From behind, he heard noise, somebody shouting to open the door.

He lowered Jacinta's head to the floor and stood up. There was a face at the window, wide-eyed and afraid. 'Are you all right?' the face asked. He stared for a few seconds, then turned and walked back into his bedroom to get dressed.

The paramedics were on the scene in seven minutes. By then, Jacinta had grown cold.

* * *

'How do you feel?'

Burns looked across at his questioner. 'We're doing feelings, now, are we?'

Detective Sergeant Paul Gohery stared at him through cold, blue eyes. He was a big man, a few years on the wrong side of forty, a lot of muscle from his time playing senior county football now turning to flab. He wore his hair tight, a number-two short-back-and-sides. The days when he'd elicited instant recognition from passers-by on the streets of most towns in his county were behind him, but he wasn't living on faded glory. Despite all the cutbacks, the force still held out a bright future for those who pursued it with any vigour.

'Nothing hangs on it,' he said, to the detained man. 'I'm just curious. Whoever fired into your home, I don't think they were looking to kill Jacinta Maguire.'

The other person in the room, Detective Garda Nora Cummins, looked up from where she was writing. 'Jacinta's mother said she had no enemies,' Detective Cummins said.

Burns noted her casual use of his girlfriend's first name, as if the cunt had actually known her.

'Of course she didn't,' Gohery said. 'A girl like that spent most of her time either working or trying to raise her children – and, God knows, that can't have been easy where she lived. No, it would seem, Dara, that she was in the wrong place at the wrong time. So I'm just wondering how that makes you feel, your girlfriend having taken a bullet with your name on it.'

Burns shifted his gaze to the camera trained down on the chair where he sat. Paint of a dull yellow was peeling from the walls up near it. The chair, with steel armrests, was bolted to the floor.

Burns thought of Old Sparky, where they used to fry people in all those songs. Lots of folk who were just trying to make their way in the world ended up being fried in Old Sparky. Or else the gallows. Mississippi John Hurt, he'd sung a lot about fellas meeting bad ends on the gallows.

A voice brought him back. 'Burns?'

He looked across at the shade again.

'You're not bothered by that, are you?'

'What?'

'Your girlfriend taking the bullet for you. Her kids left orphans because somebody was shooting into your home. None of it bothers you.'

Burns leaned forward in his chair. 'What bothers me is that you're saying somebody shot into my home and killed Jacinta Maguire, and you know that couldn't have been me. Why are you not out there chasing down this killer rather than hassling me?'

'You know the rap. You're under arrest on suspicion of

involvement in the murder of Denis Stanners. You remember him? His wife was standing at the window, watching somebody shoot him to death?'

'I don't know anything about that.'

'Sure you don't. Let's start at the beginning. You're working for Pascal Nix now, right?'

'Who?'

The detective straightened in his chair. 'Pascal Nix. The man who's paying your wages. The guy with the rug issues.'

'The what?'

The female garda looked up again. 'Mr Nix is going bald. It's breaking his heart. You must know all about that. Everybody on the street seems to be aware of it.'

Burns gave her the once-over, but there wasn't a hint of sarcasm on her face. They knew about Nix's stubbly head. Who could have told them that but Stanners, the rat Stanners? He felt reassured about that hit again. If he'd had any doubts about Stanners deserving it, they were gone now. 'Fuck this,' he said.

The bastards hadn't even allowed him to go with the body to the hospital. They'd showed up and arrested him. He was the victim of a shooting, some lunatic firing a shotgun through his front window, and the law comes along and arrests him for another shooting that had nothing to do with him. At least they'd no evidence against him. How could they do that? All he wanted was to go with the body in the ambulance.

As they were leaving his place, standing outside, his hands cuffed, the neighbours looking on, Jacinta's mother had stepped out of a car.

They had never hit it off, Burns and Iris Maguire. In the early days, when he'd called by Jacinta's place, the mother had eyed him as if he was something the cat had dragged in. That was one of the reasons he'd stopped going over there or at least it was a good excuse.

On the phone, when she picked up, Burns usually just identified himself, and the mother responded by saying she'd get Jacinta. Neither of them made much effort to bridge the divide for the sake of their common interest. Now her worst-case scenario had come to pass. He had led her daughter all the way to a violent death.

She'd been wearing a white dressing-gown, which he'd thought he recognised as Jacinta's. Her head was crowned with what looked like a shower cap. But Burns couldn't avoid the look on her face. He had seen terror before, close up. But this was different. This wasn't a job. This wasn't somebody who had deserved what was coming to her.

She saw Burns, the cuffs, the two shades flanking him, and he could see that her imagination had already passed judgement on him. What was the point? They would put her right on that. He hadn't killed her daughter. But they would also make sure she understood that the bullet had been meant for him. In the end, that was all she wanted to know. He mightn't have pulled the trigger, but he had killed her daughter.

She'd stood before him, a silent blue light from one of the cars flashing on her face.

'Where is she?' the mother had asked. What was the point? He was in no mood to talk to this woman who was here only to condemn him.

'Mrs Maguire ...' One of the shades had reached out to her elbow.

She waved him away, her eyes burning into Burns with hate. 'What did you do to her?'

'Mrs Maguire, this man wasn't responsible for—'

'So why is he tied up? Why are you taking him away? Where is my daughter?' She turned from him, facing the knot of neighbours who had assembled behind a police tape. 'Where is my daughter?' she asked the night, her voice now rising to a scream. 'Where is she?'

* * *

The early-morning flight to Málaga was delayed. A groan rippled through the seats adjoining Gate 32 in Dublin airport's Terminal One. The man from Nerja didn't need this. He got up from his seat and stretched out his legs until he could feel his hamstrings strain. The whole place was heaving with bodies. Everybody seemed to be getting on with it. No eyes were looking his way. No plain-clothes cop was whispering into a sleeve or reaching behind his back for a weapon.

The recurring image that had haunted him for the last twenty minutes played on his mind again. A commotion on the escalator followed by the sight of a band of plain-clothes and tooled-up uniforms thundering down with weapons drawn. He makes a run for it, out the door onto the concrete platforms full of the sound of screeching engines and snake lines of passengers queuing to board planes. Can he make it?

Never before had he envisaged himself to be in a situation where he could transmogrify into a lunatic, but of one thing he had his mind made up. He wasn't going to prison. There was no way he would see the inside of an Irish jail, because all that awaited him in there was a painful death.

As far as he could tell, Dara Burns was well connected. He, on the other hand, was an outsider, long gone in Spain. It wouldn't take much to get some serious hard chaw to do him in once he was on the inside.

What was bugging him more than anything was that he would

have to come back. The job didn't get done. The dish best served cold had been returned to the kitchen.

Finding Burns's place had been the easy bit. He'd got word about the funeral, and on the night of the wake, he'd followed the car that dropped Burns to his door. If only he had been sorted for a weapon that night. It would have been sweet, a perfect turn on the wheel of justice. But it wasn't to be.

After he had reeled off the shot – Christ, nobody told him the recoil would pack such a wallop – he had been consumed with a high, as if he was running a few feet above the ground. Everything was cool with the motor. He stopped on his way back into town at the spot he had identified earlier, and dispatched the sawn-off shotgun to the bottom of the Tolka.

He parked the motor in the Ilac Centre car park and went straight to his hotel room. Inside, after he had splashed water on his face, he looked at the bathroom mirror. He couldn't remember ever appearing so pale. He lifted a hand and his fingers trembled in the reflection.

Yet he was also flying high. The job had been done. Seamus could now rest in peace.

The next morning, as dawn pushed at the curtains of his room, the man from Nerja reached for the remote control. Sleep had eluded him through most of the night. He felt heavy around the eyes, but the TV might while away the time until he had to leave. He'd catch the news on teletext.

Nothing. The only killing recorded was that of a woman. Doubt began to crawl to the centre of his thoughts. Even in the worst-case scenario, even if he hadn't killed the bastard, surely the shooting would have been recorded.

He scanned the list of items again. NAMA, a motor accident, job losses, and then just the woman. It said she'd been shot. He had presumed it was one of those wife-killing numbers. He punched the three-digit code into the remote and the screen filled with a story: 'A mother of three was shot dead last night in Dublin in what is believed to have been a gangland killing. The woman, who was 34, did not live at the address in the Williamsgate area of north Dublin. It is understood that she was not the target of the shooting.'

He was wide awake now, in the grip of something awful.

'Gardaí believe the intended target was the owner of the house who was present at the time. A single shot was fired through the front window of the ground-floor unit, killing the woman instantly. One man was arrested at the scene last night but a spokesman for the gardaí said they are still looking for the man who fired the shot.'

He turned and buried his head in the pillow. The phone began ringing, like a round of machine-gun fire. He picked it up with a shaking hand.

'Sir, your wake-up call.'

Now, here at the airport, there was more delay. The intervening hours had served him well. He went over what had happened. He tried not to think of the woman. Three kids, just like himself. Well, she was another victim of Dara Burns. Seamus first, now this woman. Another innocent victim of a depraved animal.

By the time he reached the departure lounge he had his mind made up. He would have to return, whatever the dangers. The way things had unfolded, he now had a duty to take Burns out of circulation. Society had to be protected from the likes of him.

* * *

They put Burns back in the cell a few minutes after eleven a.m. The place reeked of must and socks and booze and even, his nose hinted, a class of hair oil. Burns examined the bed. Some filthy fucker had left a few bloodstains on the sheet, and these pigs hadn't even cleaned it up. He felt heavy, weighed down with lack of sleep and last night's madness. He swept his hand across the sheet, erupting a cloud of dust. Jacinta's smiling face presented itself before him. *Don't worry, honey, the sheets don't bite.*

Jacinta knew who he was when they hooked up. She knew he didn't work eight to four to bring home a slave's wage. He didn't have to spell it out for her, but she must have known that danger stalked him. Still, she didn't deserve it. Her kids didn't. Even her pain-in-the-hole of a mother didn't deserve it. Something would have to be done.

He had occupied himself in the interview room running through a list of candidates. The man in charge, Sergeant 'I have the body odour of an ox' Gohery, kept getting in his face, driving him further into his own thoughts, where he tried to figure out who might have been responsible.

No point in denying it: there were plenty of lads who might want to do him. Running back through the last decade or so, he had been involved in seven terminal jobs. All of them, he told himself, had it coming to them. Well, all except one, the one he always pushed to a dark recess of his memory whenever it popped up.

The others, they could have no complaints about an early exit. They were in the life. All of them knew that the odds were stacked against arriving at middle age, and if they didn't they needed their heads examined.

Like him, they'd made their own choices a way back. He was only a conduit, detailed to keep the machine churning, to eliminate those who were either too stupid or too greedy to remain in the game.

He had been the trigger man for five of them. None presented any problems.

Like much in life, chance had thrown him into the game. He was working as muscle for an operator out in the west of the city, a guy who vanished a few years later and was now believed to be under a bed of concrete in an industrial estate on the Costa Brava. He got a call one day, telling him there was a job that required a little more than just muscle. He hesitated at first, letting it sink in. He had always known this time would arrive. Ever since he first went to work, people had referenced him as Sean Burns's son, as if lineage alone meant his fate was predestined.

He had no recollection of his old man, no memories to feed on. His grandparents never spoke of Sean Burns. Growing up, he'd asked now and again, but he was usually met with an air of irritation, as if his father was parked away in some institution for the insane, an embarrassment to be swept out of memory.

His grandfather let the mask slip once, when Burns was about twelve. The pair of them were in the good room, listening to Granddad's records. Every Sunday evening, the old man would return from the pub, his head softer than usual as the Sabbath was reserved for a session that began in mid-afternoon. Invariably, his words would fall into each other, as he fumbled with the key to the good room, where he went to listen to his records.

The room was like an icebox in the winter, apart from when a fire blazed through the days of Christmas. Yet Burns used to await his grandfather's arrival home each Sunday with a sense of expectation. He loved just loitering in the room, where everything was in place, free of clutter, free of smells.

On the evening in question, he remembered that Granddad was feasting on a Lightnin' Hopkins record that had been sent from Boston by a nephew. For at least four Sundays in a row, it was all Hopkins this and Hopkins that, and Burns could see that this guy had wrapped up the blues in his own guitar and taken it home.

At some stage, Granddad began to retreat from the music, his head lost inside a cloud of cigarette smoke, eyes falling as he slipped further away from the here and now. Then, in the crackling break between songs, he said, 'You know he was going out to the chemist's for you when they shot him.'

Hopkins launched into 'Coffee House Blues', a twelve-bar number with a high tempo. Burns sensed he wasn't expected to respond. He might not even have been in the room for all his grandfather knew now. Then, in a voice raised to compete with Hopkins: 'They killed your mother that night too. A piece of her died and after that it was only a matter of time before she gave up.'

When he was fifteen, Burns went in search of something more. He found it in the newspaper library in the Ilac Centre. His father had been shot dead on the street on a winter's night. The report said he had just left home on an errand. 'Sean Burns was associated with one of the factions in a Republican feud that has already claimed four lives,' the report said. 'He is suspected of having been involved in two murders associated with the feud over the last twelve months.' Burns never discussed it with his sister. They carried their baggage separately.

When he got involved in the life, he noticed that older fellas often gave him a second take when introduced. Some he knew had been around since his father's day, and were curious whether he was his father's son. With others, he often sensed a wariness. Maybe some had been involved in the feud, and wondered whether he harboured a grievance. Their worry was misplaced. It was all from another world, one he wasn't interested in dragging out of a vault of history.

His attitude stood to him. He soon realised he was regarded with respect rarely afforded those of tender years. When the first offer came, it was nothing unexpected.

The job, as these things go, was very straightforward. He was driven to the location, the Westwood estate, out west, a large affair with a green in the middle. It was soon after midnight when the target showed up. He left a friend outside a row of shops and began walking across the green.

Burns got out of the car and followed at a light jog in the man's wake. The moon was high on a clear night sky. Here and there, lights still burned behind drawn curtains. He picked up pace, his grip tight on the Smith & Wesson in his right hand. He was less than ten yards away when the target sensed something and turned. There wasn't time to run. There was confusion on his face. Burns could see his acne, something this fella would now never grow out of. He raised the weapon, and the target's hands went up, a plea issued from his mouth, and then the shot rang out, and the fella was on the ground. He looked up at Burns, eyes pleading. Burns stood over him and emptied two shots into the kid's head, to be sure to be sure.

He was back inside the car in fifteen seconds. Within two minutes the motor was burning half a mile away. Burns and the driver were collected and driven off.

Afterwards, at first, he was on cloud nine. The power of holding the weapon, the move he had made onto a higher plane, fed his buzz.

When he came down, he dealt quickly with a few doubts. The newspaper reports had said the dead man had had a large drug debt. Burns was satisfied that he'd had it coming to him. He also resolved that the next time he would enquire beforehand as to the reasons why a target was getting it. One thing he was sure of was that there would be a next time. That wasn't long in coming either.

The second job he was offered was to do the man who had driven him on the first job. Guy had gone offside, was making moves to do his own thing, set up in competition. Burns was satisfied that the hit was justified. He picked up twenty grand for that number.

Now, a decade down the line, here he was, in a smelly cell, being hassled by the law at a time when he should have been free to grieve. He heard a sound from beyond the cell's thick walls, a drunk lashing out, then a door closing, and nothing but muffled protests. Somebody would have to pay for this.

Chapter Seven

Kevin Wyman's eyes followed the mothers as they stepped from their vehicles outside the school. He noted that, despite everything that had befallen the country, many of them were still driving around in well-preserved SUVs. He scanned the reg plates. Most were pre-08, but there was one with a 2010 plate and another that looked like it had been driven there direct from the showroom.

He was also acutely aware that he was the only man present. The only man, behind the wheel of a VW Golf, a car fit for a hairdresser, and all these women on school runs in those high-octane babe magnets.

The school was a long, low building of white-painted brick, located on a minor trunk road between rolling fields of green, pockmarked with bungalows. Out here, within commuting distance of the city, sites were valued and quickly gobbled up by dwellings of varying taste and design.

The March sky was low, clouds drifting in light shades of grey. He willed the rain to hold off. On dry days, the kids could amuse themselves outside for the afternoon, freeing him to perform his duties as a house-husband. He also had plans to build a tree house, do something useful, tell himself that he was actually engaged in real work.

He got a load of the mothers as they made their way through the school gates. They moved to the sound of Arcade Fire coming from his radio. One in particular had exercised a pull in his attention over the last few weeks. She was taller than the rest, nice face, auburn hair cut tight, like a model from a black-and-white reel of 1960s London. She nearly always wore dresses of bright colours, as if she had just stepped out from the display window of Marks & Spencer.

There she was now, closing the door on her blue Kia Sportage brightening up the day in reds and purples, her head tossing around in his direction. Her face widened into a smile when she saw him. He raised the fingers of his right hand above the steering wheel and reached for the door handle, but the muffled ring from the phone in his pocket hauled him back. It had to be Brenda, getting ahead of herself again, enquiring how the kids had got on at school and them not even out of the place.

But it was a blocked number. It had to be about work. Please let it be about work. He pressed the call-answer button.

'Steve?'

'Sorry, wrong number.'

'No, it's not.'

The voice, he knew it from somewhere. 'There's no Steve here.'

'There was plenty of him there last Tuesday evening.'

He straightened in the car seat. Steve. 'How did you get my number?'

'Now, that's no way to talk to a lady,' she said. 'Even one who you've whammed, bammed and said thank you, Ma'am.'

Wyman reached for the radio dial, cut it off. He'd known this was going to happen. Some class of karma had told him there would be no clean getaway.

He had left the hotel that night in a jumble of feelings. The sex had been good, better than he'd had in a long time, better than nothing. Once they were done, though, the pair of them lying in a tangle of sheets, their bodies sweaty and separate, his first concern was how to get the hell out of there on the right side of polite.

She'd probed, but he'd resisted any intimate talk. Then she'd asked the question he'd dreaded: 'What now?'

Now he wanted out, back to the ship of his marriage, which was taking water, but still afloat. The few hours of shore leave had been great, but it was time to man the rigging once more.

She didn't say much, made a few noises about the harsh life of living in a loveless marriage. Then she asked him straight out: 'Are we meeting again?'

He danced around the whole thing. It was all coated with embarrassment, but what could you do? Having posted his relief, the priority now was to get the fuck out of there.

They parted in the lobby. She offered her hand. They actually shook hands, as if they'd just conducted a business deal.

All the way home, he'd listened to soothing late-night radio music, trying to tamp down a feeling of dread. It couldn't be as easy as that.

After a pause, he said again: 'How did you get my number?'

'You sound surprised. Good. That's the beauty of an affair. The thrill of the unexpected.'

'An affair?'

'Ah, Steve – or should I say Kevin? – lighten up. A little joke.' She knew his name. 'Aren't you going to ask me how I've been? Don't you want to know how I've coped for the last two days without you?'

Wyman's hand was gripping the phone tightly, as if he was trying to squeeze the life out of what he was hearing. 'Where did you get my name?'

'Your real name? It's not that difficult, Kevin. I like Kevin. Steve is just … a little cold.'

He exhaled deep and long. 'And what's your real name?'

'I'll stick with Sabrina. It's … out there. What do you think?'

He held the phone away from his ear. She isn't Glenn Close. This isn't *Fatal Attraction*. Not yet, anyway. Jesus, he knew women dug him, but he couldn't have made that big an impression in just a few hours. Or maybe he could.

'Sabrina, it was fine. I mean it was great, but let's just back up the truck for a moment. I told you where I stood. I'm not … ready for … an affair. I just needed …'

'You just needed to get laid for the night.'

'You weren't looking for love on smooth.com,' he said.

'I don't know, Kevin. Love comes in many forms.'

He wished to Christ she'd stop using his name. Across the road, beyond where a flock of mothers had gathered in a huddle, he could see the first kids exploding through the front door of the school. 'Look, don't ring this number again. Give things a week or two and I'll mail you on the site. OK? But you're freaking me out, phoning out of the blue like this. How did you get the number?'

'I'll tell you all about it when we meet up.'

'We're not meeting up. Not now, not—'

'Kevin, Kevin. Listen to me. You will be at the Liffey Valley Shopping Centre, upstairs in the eating area. Tomorrow at three o'clock. We'll discuss where things go from here.'

Daniel came through the school's front door. He ran to a standstill and looked around. A question mark fell across his face. Ciara would be out within the minute. Wyman reached for the car-door handle and stepped out of the vehicle. He lowered his voice: 'What is this? We had a pleasant evening together and now you're turning it into something crazy. I'm not meeting you tomorrow. I told you I'd be in touch. I'm going to hang up now.'

He shut the door with more force than he had intended. Daniel's eyes lit up as he spotted his father.

'Oh, you'll be there. Because if you're not, Mrs Wyman is going to receive a little gift in the post, showing how active her hubby can be in the sack when he puts his mind to it. She can have a peek at the film before it makes its way onto YouTube. Three o'clock.'

Wyman turned back to the car, as if to protect his son from this stuff. 'What are you saying?'

'Our liaison the other night? It was all captured on what I have to admit was relatively high-quality film. I arranged to have it all recorded, Kevin. Just in case you didn't turn out to be a proper gentleman. And I don't think you'd really claim to be behaving like one now.'

He remembered that she had booked the room. Where could she have put the camera? The room was standard cheap hotel fare. She had to be bluffing.

'I'll meet you and we can discuss this like adults,' he said.

'We'll be waiting,' she said. The line went dead.

He broke into a jog, moving across the road. Daniel was standing by the gates. Wyman took his son's school bag, ruffled his hair. 'How was your day?' he asked.

Daniel launched into a spiel, but his father wasn't hearing much of it. What did she mean, 'we'?

* * *

Karen breathed the air long and deep when she emerged from the Internet café. Inside, the place had been a soup of smells, from the failure of some customers to address basic hygiene to hints of food that had travelled from the East. She had been in there for the guts of two hours, researching, downloading, printing out her future. She carried the plans in a cardboard A4 folder as she stepped back out into the day.

Abigail was still operating off the dial-up Internet back at the house. After twenty minutes' dealing with the hiss and cackle of a phone line crawling at the speed of a snail, she'd given up and sought out the café.

Now, the task complete, her head was lightened by the plan that was coming together. Facts and figures shot through her imagination like flying rocks. She needed some air and space to think things through. She walked to the Luas platform in Abbey Street. Once home, she was going to change and head for the Phoenix Park, where all her good thinking was done these days.

Fifteen minutes later she was turning the key in the front door when her phone buzzed. The lock responded, and she got inside, reaching for the answer button.

'Hello.'

'Hi, it's me.'

It was him too. Jake. 'How are you?'

'Do you want to know or are you just being polite?'

Already, Karen felt resentful. Here she was, trying to be nice to him, and he was pushing her away. No problem, if that was the way he wanted it. 'I was just asking.'

'OK. Well, things are worse than they ever were. I've got this prick of a judge who remanded me without reducing the bail. Just before I went before him, he was sentencing this other guy in another grow-house case. He said something about the guy being a dealer in death. A dealer in fucking death. Growing a bit of weed. Man, I'm in serious shit if he hears my case. It's no picnic in here, Karen. I can't sleep. Anytime I doze off, the nightmares come down on me, like a shower of hailstones. I have to get out.'

Karen was clasping the phone to her chin as she slipped out of her jeans. 'But you're holding up?'

'Just about. Any word on that job you went for? I seriously need to get my hands on some money.'

She threw the phone onto the bed, pulled her top up over her head, and picked it up again. 'Dead end,' she said. 'I'm looking into other stuff. Look, Jake, I'll do what I can but I don't have the kind of money you need.'

A silence settled on the line. What did he expect?

'There's one thing you might be able to help me with,' she said.

'That's what I'm here for.'

'The male plant, yeah? Is there any point in growing it at all?'

'What?'

'The male plant. The female is the one that flowers, right? She produces the goods. But as far as I can make out the male is only there for mating purposes, in order to get her going, you know, up the pole. So if you've got something less than an industrial-scale operation, is it worth your while to be growing the male?'

This time the silence was full of incredulity. When he spoke, his voice was lowered. 'What the fuck are you at?'

'What do you think?'

'I don't believe it,' he said. 'You're working for Charlie Small, aren't you? You went to him and he's taken you on as a gardener. Karen, do you have any idea what you're getting into? Do you want to end up like me?'

She reeled in an impulse to tell him that in her worst nightmare she couldn't imagine herself ending up like him. 'Jake, I haven't met this Charlie Small yet. I'm just—'

'Wait. You haven't met him yet. Karen, the one thing I asked you to do, the one thing to save my bacon, and you haven't done it yet. If you can't find him on the phone try Philly John's, it's a pub out west that he hangs out in with his boss. Do you realise that every minute you fail to make that connection is a minute closer to me getting my head kicked in? And, no, you don't need the male plant. The male plant is good for nothing these days. You need to weed him out, get him away from the female, so she can flower and bloom. The fucking male is redundant, out in the cold. Just like me.'

* * *

Within minutes, she was on the North Circular Road, striding past the four-storey red-brick houses and full maples that lined the street. The sun sat low in the March sky, a sharp chill in the air. Perfect weather for a brisk walk.

She hit the park and followed the road around. There were few other pedestrians in the lull of the afternoon. The way she saw things, the business plan could be divided into subsections. First thing was the premises. More than one house would be required. Economies of scale demanded it. Apart from that, natural wastage might occur. There was always the possibility of a house getting rumbled. Having all your weed in one basket was not the way to go.

Location was the next issue. Like everything else, a mix-and-match approach would be best. In cities, from what she could gather, the best locations were in middle-class areas, where neighbours knew less about each other and were less likely to get nosy. Otherwise out the country would be ideal. She made a mental note to check out large houses in the middle of nowhere, preferably within reach of Dublin.

She crossed at the roundabout at Chesterfield Avenue, and moved on down past the Wellington monument reaching for the sky. A young couple were sitting at its base in the green area on her left, looking like they had not a care in the world.

False ID would be needed for renting. These days, estate agents were probably so eager to get things moving that close attention wouldn't be paid to documents. That shouldn't present any real problems.

The seeds could be bought on the net. No issues there. She'd have to weed out the males once it became obvious who was who. This was going to be a fully female operation. She smiled to herself. Less chance of a cock-up with women on top. Peter would have liked that one, even if he wouldn't have agreed with it.

The equipment wouldn't be a big deal. Industrial lighting, sheeting, hoses for watering and nutrients – you used that kind of stuff even for growing tomatoes. All of that was Easy Street, but then you began heading down into the badlands, where problems hung out.

She would need some serious help with the electricity. The only way to go would be to tap into the national grid in order to supply power for the lighting. Otherwise, the electricity bill would read like that run up for a U2 stadium gig.

Funding was the other big issue. Everything depended on that. Then there was distribution. That was something else, but she had up to three months to worry about it before she had a product to harvest.

She was eating road now, the city away and down to her left, the old magazine fort rising on a ridge to her right. The sound of traffic came at her like the sea, a sound that still brought back Coogee.

This was going to be a temporary thing, of that she had no doubt. She wasn't going to get stuck in the business. All she wanted was seed capital. Then she would follow the dream of going legit. How she wished Peter was here now. This was his road. He was the one who had awoken the impulse in her back in Sydney. He was the ideas man, she the nuts-and-bolts operator who made flesh of the dreams.

Every so often he would have an idea, something he'd said would carry them down the road to success. Her favourite had been the salmon skins.

* * *

Peter had brought the product home one evening when he arrived back from work. It was a typical summer's day, warm and clear, a fuzzy blanket of heat hanging in the air, tamped down by a gentle breeze fanning in from the ocean. Karen usually made it back an hour before he did, bussing it from the city. They lived in a fourth-floor two-bed, with a little balcony that looked out on Coogee beach and the ocean.

They had fashioned a home from the rented property, adding wicker furniture and a few large, framed prints. The clincher was the balcony. Once you pulled back the sliding door and stepped out, the sea came at your senses, waves crashing and salt spicing the air.

The day's mood was all there in the sound of the waves. If it was full on, the breakers turning and crashing onto the sand, it meant the elements were agitated about something. A fair to middling day was felt in a steady flow, the sand squealing under the advance and retreat of broken waves. And then there were gentler times, when they crept in, as if trying not to disturb anyone.

On nights that she couldn't sleep, or now and then when Peter nodded off quickly in the aftermath of love, Karen would pad across a shaft of moonlight in the living room, slide open the door and step out into the night.

She never took it for granted. Every day, when she walked back from her swim, togs still clinging to her body, flip-flops dragging on the pavement, she knew she had landed a good one. The same line always lodged in her head on days like these. *You're never going back now.*

What was there to go back to? When they had left, nearly a decade earlier, Peter had done all the running. He had a sister out there, sending back dispatches about how she'd found Paradise. Why not see the world, or at least that corner of it Down Under?

At the time, both had set out for the foothills of a working life in Dublin. After completing what she regarded as a half-assed business course, Karen had picked up a job in a mobile-phone shop. She was open to learning and the commission was good.

Peter had pulled a number as a draughtsman in an engineering firm that had work coming out its seams. But he wasn't happy. He couldn't leave the wander itch alone.

'It's a simple choice,' he'd told her one day after work, when they'd met in a darkened city-centre bar. 'We can stay here, continue in our good jobs, climb' – he grappled the air in a climbing motion – 'that thing called the career ladder, settle down, make babies, grow old and die.'

'Don't think I like the last bit,' she said.

'That one's not negotiable. Anyway, the alternative is that we get up off our asses, go see Australia, hang there for a few years, take in a little of the world on the way back and then get into the babies, old, die bits. What do you think?'

She was happy to stay, apprehensive about going, but in the overall scheme of things, she regarded those as minor decisions. The main one was they were together.

She hadn't planned it this way. She had been looking for nothing more than a good time when they had met. But whatever had taken off between them was dear to her now. Go, stay, who cared? In the end she'd been a pushover, and these days, whenever she sought refuge in the editing room of her memory, she often wondered how different things might have been if they had stayed put in Dublin.

They got married three years after moving out there. The ceremony was on a boat in the harbour, just the pair of them, with Peter's sister and her fella. Karen loved it, making vows as the sea lapped around the vessel, the sun sparkling on the water like shards of glass. They repaired to a pub in the Rocks, the Hero of Waterloo, and she told him at the end of the night it had been all she could have wished for.

On the day in question, the day he brought home the fish skins, Peter walked in just as she was emerging from the shower, wrapped in a towel, holding her togs between thumb and index finger, en route to the balcony.

He was carrying maybe half a dozen suits wrapped in cellophane and folded on his arm. He knew how she felt about the suit racket. An Irish guy he worked with, fella from Cork by the name of Kelliher, had a little number going. Once every six or seven weeks, he sourced up to two dozen top-quality suits that had fallen off the back of a lorry. Kelliher had cut Peter in on the deal. He knew a few heads around Coogee and Randwick who were always in need of sprucing up for work. The nixer netted five or six hundred each time, or so he told Karen. Her only worry was the chances of getting nabbed. Why risk all they had for a few hundred bucks? If things went wrong – and she neither liked nor trusted Kelliher – they were on a plane back to Dublin in a jiffy. In the end, she ignored it because he had set his mind on it.

On that day, she knew straight away from the twinkle in his eye that he couldn't wait to share something.

'The salmon of knowledge,' he said, moving in and taking her shoulders as he kissed her on the lips.

She held the togs at arm's length, so as not to get his work shirt wet. 'That rings a bell from school.'

'Fionn MacCool, the salmon of knowledge. He was … a dude back when dudes used to go around with hatchets and make legends.'

'Right. He's a legend,' she said, pulling the sliding door open and throwing her togs onto the back of a white plastic chair. 'Let me guess. You've decided you want to be a teacher. Those who can't do, teach, and you're not going to do my head in with more ideas.'

Peter affected a wounded look. 'The salmon of knowledge is the line, skins are the game.'

'Skins?'

He pulled something from the back pocket of his tan chinos, handed it over to her. It was a wallet. 'Feel it,' he said.

She ran her fingers across the patterned texture. It might have been crocodile skin, but she knew it wasn't. She held it up. 'Salmon skin?'

'All the way from Howth,' he said, then added in a mock-yaye Australian accent, 'Cown-ty Dab-leen. Kelliher is just back from Ireland. He gave it to me. He picked it up from a fella in a bar. He was tanked when he got it, but the wallet was still there when he woke up the next morning.' Peter grabbed her by the shoulders again, large hands pulling her in. He had that look in his eyes that saw into a future shining with success. 'Nobody's doing that out here. We could be in on it. This could be the big thing. Salmon-skin products for the fashion industry. Salmon could be the new crocodile. Throw in a few Irish legends and Bob's your uncle. We have a brand.'

Karen immediately moved into the role she adopted anytime he brought up the big thing. 'Off you go,' she said. 'I'm right behind you, giving you a kick in that nice little ass of yours.'

'No, listen, this is the chance. We're both wage slaves. Here's an opportunity to get into something. Come on, you're the business head in this house. Think about it. This could be the way to go. Let's at least do the research. It's sure as hell not going to happen if we don't try it.'

She looked at him and told herself again how lucky she was. 'OK,' she said. 'Let's do it.'

* * *

The sea was still on her body the day the cops called to give her the news. It was about a month after Peter had brought home the salmon skins. In the interim, she had begun looking into possibilities and, she had to admit, Peter's instincts were on the button. There was huge potential in this salmon-skin thing.

Down at the beach the waves had been particularly big, as if the elements were cranky about something. Earlier in the day, while she had been having lunch in town, a thunderstorm had fallen on the city like a rinsing agent, great big drops thudding down and bouncing off the street as if to wash away, for a little while, the stifling humidity.

By the time she got home from work, it was ideal for a swim. She was just back, all set to peel off her togs and pop into the shower, when a knock sounded on the door. She reached for a towel and wrapped herself in it.

When she saw them, the first thing that entered her head was that he had been nabbed over the suits. She went into lock-down mode, determined not to tell them anything. She saw Kelliher fingering Peter for the whole racket. She saw him banged up in a cell somewhere on the North Shore. Now all that was left was deportation, a fate worse than death.

These thoughts flitted through her head, like, she would later recall, the last vital signs of a life that was about to end.

'G'day, Ms Riney,' the older one said. He was a large man, in both height and width. She looked at him and saw for the first time that he had removed his hat. 'Could we come in for a minute?'

Reality began to dawn on her. They stepped in and she stood there, growing cold inside her towel, until he explained that there had been a road traffic accident up in Neutral Bay during the thunderstorm. Peter had been travelling in a vehicle with a work colleague. The car was a write-off. There was no way anybody could have got out of it alive.

She lost the hours that followed. All she could remember

afterwards was Peter's sister showing up at the door, her face already blotched with red stains. The cops left at that point.

The following days passed in a blur. There were trips to the morgue, to the Irish consulate, as they made the arrangements to officially bring a close to Peter's life.

She never swam at Coogee Beach again. Various impediments meant it would be ten days before the body could be flown home. Whenever she left the apartment and noted that life was going on as before, she wanted to grab people passing, shake them awake to the new reality. Everything had changed.

The details of the accident didn't do anything for her pain. Peter and Kelliher had been in the car during lunch break, en route somewhere, when, at the height of the rain, as she'd sat in a city-centre café munching on a sandwich, their vehicle had ploughed straight into an eight-axle truck. The two men had told work that they were going to check out a new apartment for Kelliher. Karen knew what they were doing, but never let on to anybody. Peter had told her that the suits were sourced from a lad in Neutral Bay. In those early days, as she rummaged around in the depths of bereavement, she wondered whether karma was at work. But then she dismissed it. They were flogging suits, not murdering somebody, or abusing children.

She flew her husband's body and their dreams home in a plane that felt like it was going between worlds.

Back in Dublin, the funeral was awful. The body was brought to Glasnevin Cemetery for cremation. The little chapel was half full. They had both lost contact with most of their previous circles, and many others hadn't got word of what had unfolded.

She had assured her mother there was no need to come back from Canada.

Tupelo Honey played in the chapel. She felt like a stranger in a strange land, rather than a widow returning to be comforted in the place from which she had sprung. Friends approached and tried to repair ties sundered by a decade in exile, but beyond Abigail, she failed to reconnect.

At least she was spared her family. Her brother had long since moved to Vancouver, where her mother had also been based since the early days of her own widowhood, soon after Karen had emigrated.

The months that followed were filled with little beyond efforts to keep going. Her appetite for work disappeared. Not that opportunities were knocking down her door, but she knew that whatever state the country was in, she could pull a number if her mind was in the right place.

It was during that time that the Phoenix Park became her refuge from the world. She got to know every track and path as she tried to walk her way into a new life. She watched the seasons turn, the thickened branches on trees stripped bare, frost settling across the plains abandoned by deer that didn't have the stomach for the cold.

Christmas was hard, but brought with it a sense of renewal. As January dawned, she felt ready to emerge from under the duvet of bereavement, to find out whether the world still had anything to offer.

That was when she ran into Jake. Of all the men in all the towns at all the times of her life, why did she have to meet him just at that point? Maybe it was the vulnerability she saw in him that ignited attraction.

His sense of humour resonated with Peter's, and that seemed to have been enough to draw her in. What had she been thinking? She could see now she had been on the rebound, but at the time she didn't care.

When Jake asked her down to Kerry, she didn't hesitate. The

country air would do her good, and he was teaching her to laugh again.

The grow-house in Ballinskelligs had been a surprise, but also a thrill. It blended with the concoction that was injecting energy back into her life. And it also planted seeds in her mind. She spun through the figures, never sharing the idea with Jake because it was becoming more obvious by the day that he was flakier than her wildest nightmares could ever have conjured.

Everything would have worked out fine if he hadn't been rumbled that morning. He wouldn't be hanging around now, like a niggling cold, if only she had been able to make the clean break.

Then again, if she hadn't met Jake, the world of grow-houses would never have crossed her imagination. If he hadn't been rumbled, she would never have had the opportunity to seek out people with money. And that, right now, was where all her energies were focused.

The colour in her face had deepened by the time she was walking past the entrance to the American ambassador's residence and out towards Chesterfield Avenue again. She would walk back down the avenue and home, having had her fill of thinking for today.

Everything was in place now. She had her business plan prepared, albeit in her head rather than on paper. And she felt Peter at her side, as she often did up here. He was leaning towards her ear, whispering long thoughts. The salmon skins. *It's a runner, babe, it's a runner.*

Chapter Eight

The Leopard Debt Recovery van pulled in fifty metres up the road from the halting site. Charlie Small killed the engine. The day was clear and bright. His laboured breathing filled the cab. He turned to Dara Burns. 'Can I make a suggestion?'

Burns nodded.

'I can understand where you're at. If I was in your shoes I don't know if I'd be able to handle it the way you are. But maybe it would be best if I took the lead here, did what's needed in the persuasion department. We don't need to fit this fella out for a coffin.'

Burns nodded again. He was a lot cooler about the whole thing than Charlie Small gave him credit for.

The two men stepped out of the van. Charlie Small swung his pork-pie hat onto his head. He reached back in under the driver's seat and came out with the wheel brace.

Currents of burning drifted up from the site. Burns could see a few columns of smoke. Little else was happening on the road, ditches both sides, until just up ahead, opposite the camp, two squat concrete buildings sat behind cast-iron gates in a yard of sorts. Inside the gates, tufts of grass pushed up through the cracks between concrete slabs. If the place had ever been a hive of industry, that day was long gone.

As they walked, Small said, 'I know it's none of my business, but I got to tell you, Dara, her family were right out of order.'

Burns said nothing. Arriving at the site, the acrid smell of burning grew sharper.

Small said, 'The way they were, you'd swear you'd killed the woman. I mean, you did everything you could to save her life. Ask me, I think you were a hero. And then the filth comes along and locks up you for the day. You! Man, they don't even have the decency to let you grieve. It shows you, doesn't it? They treat the likes of us as sub-human.'

Jacinta Maguire's family had sent word to Burns through a solicitor. They went and got a fucking solicitor to write to him, telling him they didn't want him to attend the funeral.

He'd phoned, kept his cool and spoken to Jacinta's uncle. After a bit of back and forth, they'd agreed that Burns could come to the house and view the body ahead of the wake.

When he arrived at the appointed time, nobody was in the house but the uncle and a young girl busying herself in the kitchen. The mother wasn't there. Neither were Jacinta's kids. It was as if the family didn't want to be contaminated by his presence.

He looked down at the lifeless body and resolved to make somebody pay. It just wouldn't be right for her kids to let it go unanswered.

Charlie Small's voice had dropped a notch. 'You have to wonder, how do these people live like this?'

Burns counted six caravans lined up in a row set back from the road. Behind them, a mound of earth and stone rose up to form a little hill. An orange domestic gas cylinder could be seen sticking out of the earth, along with what looked like long plastic handles that might once have been used for cleaning or beating. At the far end, Burns made out a garage of sorts, or at least a lean-to, with concrete walls but a roof of corrugated iron. It could have housed four or five motors, not to mention the odd Hiace.

As they passed the first caravan, Charlie Small raised himself onto his tiptoes at a curtained window. No sign of life made itself known.

They passed another two caravans, encountering nobody but a long black cat, which eyed them warily from its vantage on the tow bar.

At the last but one unit, Small rapped on the door. Burns thought he heard something moving inside. The door pushed open. The man wore only a string vest, against which a beer belly strained. White stubble grew across his face, and his eyes were watery. This, Burns assumed, was Mickey Rickshaw. He looked at his visitors, and took a few seconds to register who they were. 'Fuck off,' he said, and reached to pull in the door. Burns caught his wrist and jerked him out onto the road, Mickey Rickshaw losing his footing as he came down. He rolled over and went to raise himself with his arms, but Small moved in, landing a kick to the man's kidney. A howl rent the air. The two men looked about, but nobody emerged from the other caravans. The sound of a motor came from the distance.

'Inside,' Small said. Burns reached down to the man, and caught a waft of booze. He grabbed a clump of Rickshaw's hair with one hand, hooked his other under the man's left armpit and hauled him to his feet. He closed his two hands around the man's throat. Mickey Rickshaw struggled, but Burns was too strong for him. They fell through the door of the caravan, Burns managing to keep his balance.

Charlie Small squeezed through the door and pulled it in after him, just as the black cat shot past outside.

* * *

Wyman's fists were balled under the table, which was nailed to the floor. If it had been free-standing, he might well have lifted it and thrown it at the woman opposite him.

She insisted on retaining the name Sabrina. It was a minor thing, but he was aware that it set out the stall, provided her with a little edge from the off. On the phone, she'd made mention of 'we', as if she would be accompanied. Right now she was all on her ownio. At least, that was the way it appeared.

'OK, so what do you want?'

She kept her hands below the table. What bugged him was that she was dressed much the same as she had been the other night. Business-like suit, white blouse, albeit with a higher neckline, and big earrings that threatened to shine. All she was missing was the coat. He saw her again as he had that night, striding across the lounge.

'The eternal question, isn't it, Kevin? What do women want?'

'Where did you get my name?'

She lifted the cardboard cup, brought it to her lips and blew on the steam rising from the coffee. 'That's something I wanted to ask you about. Names. You had my name—'

'Bullshit.'

She tilted her head back, in mock surprise at the swearing. 'That is my name.'

'You use your actual name on that site?'

'Why not? I've nothing to hide. But even after we met, after we fucked our way through an hour, you still held back. I thought at the very least you could have opened up and told me your real name, the same name your wife uses.'

Wyman cast an eye around the food hall. They were upstairs in the Liffey Valley Shopping Centre. Only stragglers were hanging on into the mid-afternoon. Most of the chairs were empty. The background din of cutlery and plates was low. Some God-awful pop music drifted up from the main concourse downstairs. Ciara and Daniel were down there in a shopping crèche.

As he swept the place, Wyman made out two or three candidates who might be accompanying her. There were also at least two couples who could be in the frame. Was paranoia tugging at him? He looked across at her again.

He had made a mistake. He had messed up big-time. But he didn't deserve this, not now, not when he was already drowning in stress. He wasn't going to play her games any more. Wherever she'd got his name, she had it now. That was all that mattered.

'What's this about?' he said. No matter what she said, threats, promises, ultimatums, he wasn't going to shag her again. Whatever it was that had prompted her to address things this way, he wasn't going to shag her again. No.

'Money.'

'What?'

'Don't get me wrong. The other night was good. Not spectacular, but not awful either. But once the whole business became clear, that this was to be a brief and clean break from your drab existence in the suburbs, I thought, Why should I be left high and dry? So, let's just say I feel entitled to compensation.'

Wyman leaned across the table. 'You want me to pay you. For the other night.'

She laughed, the sound dry and cynical. 'Don't kid yourself. I said I feel entitled to compensation. You brought me to that hotel under false pretences. That wasn't nice and now you must pay the price.'

His eyes swept the hall again. Why wouldn't she talk English? She was blackmailing him. 'And what if things were different, say we were to … meet again?'

'Some sunny day, as the song says.' She smiled, but the sight made him want to hit her. He had never thought he could feel like hitting a woman.

'Too late for that. To tell you the truth, Kevin, and sorry to break this, but you're not my type.'

He was back there again, the lights low. She had just sat down. He couldn't take his eyes off her legs. He remembered the cool look she wore, as if she was sussing him out, as if to check that he wasn't a psychopath or rapist. She was checking him out all right, but for something else. 'This is really crazy,' he said.

She placed her arms on the table and moved her coffee aside, getting to the meat and drink of the meeting. 'Kevin, I don't care. What you make of the whole thing, I really don't care. The bottom line is you get your hands on five grand in cash in the next three days. We'll arrange to meet and you'll give me the money. If you don't come up with it, Mrs Wyman will be receiving a parcel in the post. To her work address. *OK?* After that, who knows? Maybe the bright lights of YouTube.'

'You were there too.'

She laughed again, this time with the wry bitterness of a stabbing motion. 'Of course I was, Kevin. I'm the one who had the camera planted, remember? I've actually reviewed the footage and, if I may say so, I'm quite proud of the fact that my face is more or less obscured for the whole thing. You, on the other hand, you're there in all your glory. If you could only see the look on your face as you—'

He reached across the table, a hand extended towards her to do some serious damage. Her eyes widened. She went to stand up. 'Don't ever do something like that again. If you ever as much as raise a hand in my presence your wife and the whole world will be introduced to you. I'll be in touch, but three days is all you have.'

She turned and walked across the hall. She didn't appear to

make any eye contact with any of the other diners. Wyman gripped the underside of the table and pushed against it.

* * *

The interior of the caravan smelt of piss and baked beans. A bottle of Paddy whiskey, empty but for a few drops, rolled on the floor. Two tins of Strongbow cider sat on a Formica table at one end of the room. There was a pair of boots, caked in dried muck, under the table. Burns noted a slash-hook hanging from a nail.

He dragged Rickshaw towards the table and sat him down. Small came to them, kicking a pair of trousers that had been on the floor.

Without uttering a word, he pulled back his right fist and slammed it into Rickshaw's face. The man's head jerked back, hitting the window behind him. Burns looked out through the soiled curtains, saw a car droning by.

The guy, this Mickey Rickshaw, his hands were up around his face, a low primal sound, like that coming from an injured dog, escaped his lips.

'You finished?' Small said. 'Or will I keep going?'

Mickey Rickshaw kept his head bent low. Burns looked at him, a pathetic figure. On the way there, Charlie Small had told him where the knacker'd got his name. Used to run a few of those rickshaw-type things that the tourists went in for in the city centre. Small didn't even know the fella's proper name.

'It's not the time of month,' Mickey Rickshaw said.

Small stood over him. 'The time of month is for women. You owe the money. You haven't paid it as you said you would. That gives us the right to come round here when we want. We own a piece of you. Are you clear on that, fuckhead?'

Rickshaw's face twisted into hate. Burns was looking at him now. If he'd been a betting man, Rickshaw was on the point of spitting a glob of blood at Charlie Small, but he hoped he was wrong. Right now, Dara Burns wanted to hear what they'd come for and get the hell out. How did these people live like this? He was in the place all of two minutes and scared shitless he might pick something up.

'I don't have it,' Rickshaw said.

'Ain't that a pity?' Small said. He turned and looked around the caravan, as if seeking out collateral. Rickshaw was into Pascal Nix for close to ten grand. 'Maybe we can give you a little break on this occasion, but onlys if you give us a steer.'

Rickshaw straightened his bulk. A little light had appeared to guide him out of the enveloping darkness.

'You heard about that shooting out in Williamsgate, woman killed by a bullet through the window?'

Rickshaw's face said he knew all about it. 'I seen it on the news.'

'And what about the motor?' That was where Rickshaw made his money these days, buying and selling cheap cars, clocking miles, sometimes doing them up, more often giving the impression of having done them up.

'Nothing to do with me.'

Small pulled the wheel brace from his pocket. Rickshaw moved to rear back, but there was nothing behind him except a window, looking out on the world as if from a prison right now.

'I got a day job, you understand,' Small said. 'But I'm a person. I'm a human being and I got feelings. Right now, I have feelings for my man here, Dara. You understand? Dara's woman was the one who bought it. And we really need to know who the shooter was.'

Rickshaw looked across at Burns, searching for a sign of bereavement, or even humanity. Burns didn't give him anything.

'You know who we're looking for,' Small said.

'I sort people out for wheels. That don't mean I know what they want them for.'

Small straightened himself, moved back from the table to give the man room to talk. His voice softened when he said, 'If we thought you'd anything to do with it, we'd have left by now and an undertaker would be on the way out here, arranging one of those big funerals you people go in for. All's we want is information.'

Rickshaw's head moved from one to the other. He nodded. 'There was a fella, over a week ago, maybe ten days. Never saw him before, but he said he needed wheels for a job. Didn't say what and I never ask.'

'What he look like?'

'Normal.'

'What the fuck is normal?'

'He was same height as you . . . well, maybe an inch or two taller. Wasn't carrying your kind of weight, but he wasn't thin either. Tanned. Looked like he got a lot of sun.'

'A name?'

'No. Called himself Rogers, but that wasn't his name.'

'How do you know that?'

''Cause afterwards I axed around and, from what I can gather, turns out his name is Coulter. Small-time operator who moved to Spain after making a score a few years back. Had a brother who was …'

Burns wasn't listening any more. He just stared at the knacker's lips moving. He knew who Coulter's brother was. At least, he knew how Coulter's brother had ended his days.

It was supposed to be a straightforward job. About three years before, when business was still ticking over, twenty grand, ten of it up front. The target would be presented to him in a parcel. He just had to attend and dispatch. When he asked, he was told that the man in question had done the dog with some coke, made out he hadn't received it and was trying to set up in business himself. That was enough for Burns.

On the night it went down, he was having a guitar lesson in the city but had agreed to leave his phone on. When word came through, he told his teacher he had to scamper, urgent family matter. He went to the john, took the 9mm Sig Sauer from his guitar case, and slid the Lag into the case. When he came out he asked the teacher if he could leave the guitar on the premises till the morning.

Then he got on his Trek bike and made off for the South Circular Road, his destination less than a mile away. The text had told him the target would be arriving in the passenger seat of a Vauxhall Astra.

He was waiting around the corner when the car pulled in. He lay down the bicycle, walked up, with the sleeve of his right arm covering the Sig Sauer in his hand. He knew something was wrong the minute the target looked out at him. It was as if the fella was expecting it, not in the way that he wasn't surprised, but that he was actually expecting it there and then.

Burns put three bullets through the windscreen. The fella in the driver's seat fell out of his door and took off. As far as Burns guessed, he was in on the job himself, although he gave a good impression of being scared shitless.

Later that evening, after he returned home from a movie in town, he got the call. The wrong man had been done. He was supposed to be the one behind the wheel but the target had insisted on doing the driving. The dead man's name was Coulter, small-time operator, who had agreed to set up the target.

'Shit happens,' the voice on the phone said, but Burns didn't like it one bit. The whole affair upset the order of things, and threw him out of kilter. Now here it was, rising up out of the grave, coming for him.

Charlie Small managed to hold his tongue all the way back to the LiteAce. The look on Burns's face when the name was mentioned had spoken loads.

Just as Small turned the key in the ignition, his phone began ringing.

'Mr Small?'

'Who wants to know?'

'My name is Karen Riney.'

'And?'

'Jake sent me. Jake O'Sullivan?'

'How is Jake getting on in his new surroundings?'

'That's what I want to talk about.'

'OK, where are you?'

I'm in the city centre, but I can meet you anywhere.'

'You familiar with Eddie Rocket's?'

'Yes.'

'That's a good start.'

* * *

Karen arrived early and stood by the sign that instructed patrons to wait to be seated. There were half a dozen other diners that she could spot. None of them fitted her image of Charlie Small.

A man was hunched over his meal on a stool at the counter. Two girls, teenagers, Karen reckoned, were practically joined at the head in a booth, talking and listening, drinking in all the world had to offer. Roy Orbison was singing in heavenly tones about how he drove all night.

A waitress approached and Karen told her she was expecting somebody else. She was led to a booth in the centre of the restaurant. The waitress wore a white army-style hat with a red Eddie Rocket's logo.

She spotted Charlie Small the minute he came through the door. It had to be him, enormous guy waddling around under a pork-pie hat. There was another man with him, which was not as she had envisaged things unfolding. This guy was medium build, not bad-looking either. He saw her first, looking their way, tapped Small on the shoulder and pointed over.

When they arrived at the booth, Small nodded at her and they exchanged names. Small didn't look like he would make it into the booth. He took a glance at it and decided he wasn't going to risk it. He looked around, and nodded towards a more open-plan booth at the window, which could seat up to six. Karen followed the two of them towards it. Charlie Small slid in as delicately as he could, as delicately as a truck reversing around a corner.

The waitress hovered. After a cursory look at the menu, Karen said she'd just have coffee.

'You're not eating,' Small said, as if she had delivered him a personal insult.

'Not hungry,' she said. Small looked at the other guy. No introductions had been made yet. 'I'll have the triple-deck cheeseburger, fries and a strawberry milkshake,' he told the waitress. The other guy said he'd just have a cheeseburger.

'Do fries come with that?' Small asked.

'With what?' The waitress spoke in a foreign accent.

'With his cheeseburger. Is there a meal deal?' 'I don't want fries,' the other guy said.

Small turned to him. 'Could you let me take care of this? Can he get the cheeseburger on a meal deal?'

The waitress picked up the menu and pointed to a meal deal.

'OK, we'll go for that,' Small said.

The other guy was about to say something, but Charlie Small laid a hand on his arm, reassuring him that the situation was under control. The other guy stayed silent.

'Do you want me to get fries?' Karen said.

'What?'

'Sorry, I just … Will I get fries as well?'

'Do you want fries?'

'No, but neither did he, and he's getting them.'

'Are you trying to be funny?'

'Oh, no, I'm just trying to help.' She was too. The guy obviously liked fries. He was already on a promise of two bowls, and from the size of him she imagined he could easily put away a third.

'Sorry, forget the fries,' she said. The waitress stood there, saying nothing in her foreign accent, waiting to be told she was done. Charlie Small put her out of her misery and she walked off.

Karen was staring at the other guy, so Charlie Small said, 'This is Dara.'

They exchanged nods.

'How's Jake doing?' Small said.

'I don't think he's cut out for prison.'

Small nodded. 'I'd worry about that all right.'

'He wanted me to reassure you that you don't have to worry about him.'

'What's there to worry about?' Small said.

'He wants you to know that he won't talk.' There was caution on his face now. 'About what?'

'Just … everything.'

Small looked across at Dara. 'Karen, I don't know you. I know your boyfriend …'

'He's not my boyfriend.'

'Whatever he is to you, he got himself in a spot of bother.

That's a pity, but it has nothing to do with me. If it did, I might be involved in something illegal. You get my drift?'

The waitress appeared with cutlery, Karen's coffee and Small's milkshake.

When she left, Karen leaned across the table. 'I understand perfectly where you're coming from. All I'm saying is that whatever Jake may know about anybody, he doesn't know.'

Small lowered his face to the milkshake, took the straw in his lips. The level in the glass began to drop, like a swamp being drained. For a second, his eyes closed, as if he was experiencing the height of pleasure. He lifted his smacker from the straw. 'Run that by me again.'

'Anybody who might worry that Jake will start talking about anything he knows, they don't need to. He's going to take what's coming to him and make no big fuss. But if there was anybody out there who believes he might get notions and begin talking, they can put their minds at rest.'

Small nodded. 'Good for those people. You know that your boyfriend, or whatever he is to you, is facing a mandatory ten. That's a lot of years to be thinking about. When a man does a lot of thinking, his mind can begin to play tricks.'

Karen said, 'From what I can see, he won't get ten years. The judges don't go in for that unless they're dealing with big fish. Anybody can see that Jake's about as small a fry as you can get, with, God love him, a brain to match.'

The two men looked at each other.

'So I just wanted to straighten that out before moving on.'

The waitress appeared with the triple-deck burger, the cheeseburger and two bowls of fries. She put a bowl of fries in front of each man, keeping an eye on Charlie Small to check that this was the way it was meant to be.

Small popped a chip into his mouth. Dara wrapped his hands around the cheeseburger.

'You want to move on to something else?' Small said.

'Yes. I'd like to meet Pascal Nix.'

Small stopped chewing. He swallowed the fry.

'You'd like to meet . . . What was his name again?'

'Pascal Nix, the man you work for.'

'The man … I see.' Whatever about Small, the request hadn't knocked a feather off Dara. He was mowing into the cheeseburger. She thought she caught his eye straying towards the bowl of fries in front of him.

Small said, 'What. The. Fuck. Is. This. About?'

'I have a business proposal for Mr Nix.'

'Tell me more.'

'First off, Jake, as I understand it, took on the job in Kerry to pay off a debt, or at least a part of it. He told me he owed Mr Nix around three grand for some merchandise. Now he's messed up down there so the money isn't going to get repaid and a business venture has gone to the wall. Are you with me?'

'I'll let you know. Keep going.'

'I have a proposal for Mr Nix. I'll cover Jake's debt if he invests in my operation.'

Karen noticed that Charlie Small had stopped eating. He was looking at her now, his mouth open. The other guy, Dara, had eased up on his assault of the cheeseburger. Maybe he was getting the most out of it, or maybe she had lassoed his full attention as well. The scene gave her confidence a shot in the arm.

Small said, 'What operation?'

Karen looked around, as if the walls had ears, and lowered her voice. 'I'm going into the grow-house business. Not in the half-arsed way that Mr Nix was involved and not with people like Jake running the show. I'm going to do it properly and I'm going to make some money, and seeing as Mr Nix is already on my radar through his association with my ex-boyfriend, I'd like to give him the opportunity to invest.'

She sat back, took it all in.

Charlie Small looked down on his bowls of fries. He turned to the other man, their eyes meeting to share a conspiratorial secret. And then he began to laugh, a great rasping sound coming from him, as if he had just heard the funniest thing ever to pass his ears.

Chapter Nine

Philly John's was dead, as would be expected for a few minutes after midday, when Burns and Small pushed through the front doors. Even before the pub business had begun to eat itself at the tail end of the bubble, you'd have been hard pressed to find Philly John's hopping at this hour of the morning. These days, you'd be hard pressed to keep the doors open, if it wasn't being used to wash Pascal Nix's money.

The building was a low squat concrete structure, fronted by a car park that could, when full, accommodate forty plus vehicles. The signage over the mahogany front door was done in tall lights, with the J missing from 'John'. It had been quite a while since the name was lit up after dark.

The two men walked down through the lounge. Behind the bar, Tall Phil, in his white shirt with the sleeves rolled up, straightened when they came through the door. But then he recognised them and he just waved a long arm before returning to his glasses.

The room was dark, the floor dotted with small round tables and stools, a wine-coloured couch running around the walls.

Pascal Nix was in his usual spot, down at the back, like, Burns reckoned, a caveman retreating as far from the mouth of his dwelling as he could. He was togged out in the customary bespoke suit, this one with wide pinstripes. Before him on the table was a plate that looked like it had once hosted a full Irish breakfast. All that remained was a strip of bacon fat.

He looked up from his newspaper, saw the men, and ran a hand through his hair. The gesture reminded Burns of what Charlie Small had said. No rug jokes. Touchy subject.

Nix waved the newspaper. 'Man City. They're going to win the league. It's the only way for football clubs to go these days. Get yourself and oil sheik.' The two men sat into lounge stools opposite him.

Charlie Small said, 'We met Jake Sully's bird.'

'What's she like?'

'She's not your type, Pascal.'

'What had she to say for herself?'

'She said Jake's cool about everything.'

'I'm sure he is. I've somebody keeping an eye on him in Cork. If we start getting worried, his face can be rearranged.'

'It sounds like he knows where his bread is buttered.'

Nix turned to Burns. 'What do you think?'

'She's fit.' All three men laughed.

'There's something else,' Small said, bringing the focus back to himself, where it belonged. 'She wants to meet you.'

'She what?'

'Yeah. She . . . she says she has a business proposal. She's setting up in the grow-house game.'

Nix ran a hand across his head. He threw the newspaper onto the table. Burns noted that it had landed on the greasy plate. Why couldn't the fella have left the paper in a condition that others could read it?

'Are you taking the piss?'

'Dara, am I?'

Burns shook his head.

Nix said, 'Now I'm worried.'

'I thought the same. She's not what you'd think, Pascal. She's got the cut of somebody who knows what they're doing. All confident, but trying to suss out at the same time. What do you think, Dara?'

Burns said, 'I was expecting something different.'

'She obviously made an impression on the pair of you. How the fuck did she end up with that nitwit O'Sullivan? Is she looking for money?'

'I'd say so,' Small said.

'Chalk it down,' Burns said.

'OK, run the whole thing by me.'

Small adopted what he considered a dramatic pose, and got started. He told Nix that he wasn't to laugh until the end. Then he went through the whole meeting, how she was cocky, even to the extent of making a joke about the fries.

Jake O'Sullivan had obviously told her about his debts, which wasn't necessarily a good thing, but there you go. And then she'd set out what she called her business proposal.

Nix didn't find any of that funny. He said, 'But you didn't say anything?'

'Fuck, no, we were, I mean, Dara hardly opened his mouth and I made out to be completely at sea as to what she was on about. When she finished I just told her she was a gas ticket.'

'And that was it?'

'Well, no. I finished my dinner.'

'Did she stay to observe that sight?'

'Hey.'

'I'm joking, Charlie, take it easy.' He pulled a piece of paper from his pocket. 'Fella out in Citywest. He said you were out to him last week. Guess what? He can't wait to cough up. Could you take a quick run out there? Dara, you can stay here. I need to talk to you about your bird.'

* * *

Wyman looked at the clock next to the fridge. Twelve twenty p.m. His day was drawing to a close. In twenty minutes, he'd be doing the school run, handing the rest of the day over to his kids. Make no mistake, he loved his kids as much as the next man. More, maybe. But it wasn't natural that he would spend this excessive amount of time in their company. Wasn't healthy for the kids either. They needed to be with their mother or, failing that, in some institution for the afternoon, where professionals knew how to make them happy, keep them quiet.

He closed the laptop, planted his elbows on the oak table and massaged his temples. At times like these, stress seeping into every pore of his life, he fantasised about the road. He could pack a few things, drive into Dublin airport and take the next flight out of here.

During his youth, before he met Brenda, he knocked a few years out of travelling. A stint laying pipes in London provided the funding for a trip down to South East Asia, where he took in Thailand and Vietnam, before moving on to Sydney, where he stayed for the guts of three months, working on a site shuttering concrete for the 2000 Olympics. Then it was on to New Zealand – what a country, Ireland without the grief. America was Disneyland on wheels after New Zealand. In LA, he hooked up with a guy he'd worked with in London, and they drove right across the continent, setting down in New York.

That was the beauty of having a trade. There was always work for a chippy, and, because he was handy with electrics, he sometimes passed himself off as a sparky on small jobs. By the time he got back, he was ready to roll into Life Phase II. For four years, he worked for a contractor, always with one eye on setting up himself and, if he could manage it, bringing some of the work with him.

He'd been on the razz one night when Brenda walked into the place, like a messenger from his future. From soon after that, he knew he wouldn't ever let her go. The couple of years on both sides of their wedding were the best. They were young, together, in love, and rolling in dosh. Brenda knew the insurance game and had worked her way steadily up through the ranks. By then he'd set up on his own and his operation was taking off at a rate of knots.

Initially, he just did attic conversions. Easy work, compact, had a few guys on full-time. But he was snowed under and soon saw that the big bucks were to be made in extensions.

After Ciara was born, Brenda went part-time and took over his books. Her presence drove things onto another plane. She had the business head, he had the working hands. Back then, between them, they'd had enough ambition to heat their home.

The ultimate plan was retirement at fifty, when the kids would be coming out the far side of their secondary education. Gradually they could begin a move out of the country, maybe to Spain. Live there for six months of the year. Take things easy.

He could see now where his big mistake had been. It wasn't the expansion of the business, driven, even she would admit, mainly by Brenda. She had been right then. That was the way to go when the roof was being blown off the market. No, it had been the comedown, the clean-up operation at the fag end of the party. Instead of winding things up, accepting that a mighty change had come over, he simply didn't believe it and ploughed on. He kept going, like a man trying to drink his way through a hangover.

He cut a few corners. VAT invoices were falsified here and there. These were temporary measures, designed to see him through to the other side. But the far side kept receding, disappearing into the mists of infinity.

When the banks cut off his credit, he still didn't get the message. He thought they had reverted to type, wrapping themselves in a comfy caution blanket.

That was when he went to Pascal Nix. He'd heard about him through a friend in the business who had done likewise.

Straight off, it was obvious where Nix was coming from. They met in that pub, Philly John's, which he seemed to use as an office. The guy didn't look like any banker Wyman had ever come across, and maybe that meant he was honest. But he wore hard years on his face, and Wyman could see that he wasn't to be messed with.

A casual conversation on the economy served as an introduction, and then he laid it on. Twenty grand. That was all he needed to see him through. Once things were back on track, he'd be in a position to repay that, along with the 25 per cent compound in the space of a month.

Nix didn't push it on him, not like they used to when he'd visited the bank, refusing to let him leave until he'd taken out more loans. The moneylender gave his opinion that maybe the economy wasn't going to turn in a hurry. Had he considered that?

Wyman assured him he had an exit strategy, and soon after, Nix had agreed to front the cash.

That was by far the biggest mistake. If he had walked away when the banks turned him down, all he would be hassled by now was ordinary, decent debts, which were most likely to run into the sand. Pascal Nix's debt wouldn't be disappearing so handy. Twenty had quickly risen to thirty. And now there was another call on his credit, another debt mounted on the back of a dumb decision.

He'd had enough to be going on with before this bitch and her five grand walked in and sat on his face.

The whole thing was making him ill, had him feeling as if there was a balloon in his stomach, slowly expanding, pushing out, literally squeezing the breath from his body as he sat there, waiting to explode.

Right now what he could really do with was a taste of freedom, the road stretching out ahead and nothing to keep him awake at night but curiosity or company. If he wasn't going to run, his options were limited. He had spent the morning beating back a scenario that stalked his imagination, like a smack deal outside a methadone clinic.

He would agree to meet her. They would go back to her place, she all ready for some rock and roll, him moving to seal the conclusion of their brief, crazy mix-up. Could he do it? Was he capable of actually killing her?

Look what she was threatening to take away from him. There was no way Brenda would allow him to stay in the family home if this came out. She would hunt him all the way to the edge of reason. And the kids? How could he manage as a weekend dad? He couldn't bear to think of the resentment they would carry through their adolescence. And all this at a time when he was in hock up to his eyeballs.

He saw the pair of them walking into an apartment, maybe one of those newish jobs that were thrown up like dolls' houses. He saw her slipping her arms out of her coat, turning to him with an air of expectation. And then he would hit her, full force in the face with his fist. Floor her. Bend down over her injured body and take her neck in his hands and squeeze the life out of her, just as she was trying to squeeze the life out of what he had built, what he was still clinging to by his fingertips.

He felt his fists ball in anger. He saw her face turn blue in surprise and pain, the realisation that she wasn't going to get her way, that he wasn't the fool she'd made him out to be. And then what?

He would rise and exit the place pronto, after a quick sconce to ensure he'd left no clues. What about DNA? He wouldn't leave any traces, no trail back to his door.

He opened his eyes to the here and now. He wasn't a killer. Besides, knowing his luck, he'd be nabbed within hours and dispatched to a prison cell for the rest of his days, as his kids grew up with a dad behind bars.

He could let his imagination lead him down that path but he knew he would never take it. Christ, things were bad, but he wasn't a killer.

Ultimately that left him with just one other option. The clock was pushing for twelve thirty-five. He'd have to go by quarter to. He got up and climbed the stairs, walked into the marital bedroom.. He and Brenda shared a king-size bed, which now served to widen the gap between them.

He fished in a drawer until he found what he was looking for. He returned to the kitchen, picked up the phone from the worktop and dialled.

'Mr Nix. Pascal Nix?'

* * *

'Yeah. Who wants to know?'

'Kevin Wyman.'

'Who?'

'Wyman. I owe you some money. You sent your goons around last week.'

'Mr Wyman, I have you now. Builder, living in a pad out there in the arse end of Meath. You have some class of a memory problem when it comes to your debts. By the way, I don't have any goons, and accusations like that might ensure that this is a very short conversation.'

'I just want to meet up with you.'

'Any negotiations on your debt, Mr Wyman, are to be conducted with the staff of the Leopard Debt Recovery Agency. I can't help you. There, things have to be kept above board.'

'Look, it's not about the money. I have a very different problem and I'm looking for some help.'

'What the fuck am I? Fix-it Friday?'

'I need some help. If I can't sort this problem, I won't be in a position to pay you what I owe.'

Pascal Nix ran a hand back across his head. Sitting opposite him, Burns tried to avert his eyes. Every time the guy did that checking-his-head thing, he thought of Bruce Willis dying hard, as bald as a coot. Anyway, he had more pressing issues. The way things were looking, he reckoned he'd have to go back to guitar lessons. He'd have to finally put his hands up and admit it. He just wasn't advancing like he thought he ought to. If he was ever going to get a proper handle on the blues, he'd have to bite the bullet and just do it.

Nix said, into the phone, 'Now you got me thinking all kinds of wild and crazy thoughts. You've got my attention, Mr Wyman. Why don't you make your way into my office some time tomorrow? I'll have somebody ring and arrange with you when I know what I'm doing, OK?'

He rang off. He looked at Burns. 'Everybody wants to meet me all of a sudden. Ain't it great to be so popular?'

Burns smiled out of a sense of duty. The fella was paying him enough that he could make an effort to appreciate the wit.

Nix called Tall Phil behind the bar to bring more tea. He gestured to Burns, who said he'd have an Americano.

'What is this Americano shit?' Nix said. 'When did black coffee become Americano? Makes it sound as if it was brewed by Mexicans.'

Burns laughed this time because it was funny. 'Don't know, Pascal. I think it's that you ask for it, and if they say they don't have Americano, you know the black coffee will be piss poor.'

'So what do you do then?'

'Ask for tea.'

Nix sat back on his chair. When he spoke, his voice had fallen a pitch. 'How's it going?'

'Grand. No complaints.'

'You and Charlie?'

'He's cool.'

'Once you get used to his size. Just one thing. Don't go to Eddie Rocket's with him.'

'Too late.'

'Well, you'll know the next time. Anyway, the main thing is you're happy. That stuff with your bird, is there anything more we can do?'

'I need to know who the shooter is. From what we heard he's over in Spain and just scooted here to do me. He's back there already, I'd say.'

'You want to go over?'

'I don't know.' He didn't share with Nix his doubts. How could he go over there, chase this guy, Coulter, who was only looking to even up the register? He couldn't explain to Nix that this whole affair had thrown his order upside-down. He could go over and kill the guy, but he didn't have the right to do so. Nix wouldn't understand any of that. Nix didn't see the world in those terms.

Burns said, 'If I get word that he's coming back to finish the business, I'll go over. Otherwise, might be best to leave it.'

Nix sat forward. 'Jesus, you're cool all right. If that was me, if my missus had got done, I'd be over there now, shooting the shit out of the place until I found the bastard. And then he'd die slowly.'

Tall Phil arrived at the table with the drinks. Burns sipped from his cup of Americano. It tasted more like black coffee. He looked at Nix's pot of tea with a sense of regret. 'I'm a big boy, Pascal. I know the game. If it gets that I feel I need to do something, I will. But I'm not rushing into anything.'

Nix raised his hands, palms flat, in a defensive motion. 'It's your life, bud. All I'm saying is, if you need any help in sorting out your problem, that's what I'm here for.'

'Appreciate that, Pascal. I'm grateful.'

'Yeah, well, I can tell you one thing. You aren't the only one with serious problems. There's plenty of that to go around.'

'Yeah?'

Nix raised his hand to his crown again, this time tugging a wisp of thin hair at the front of his thatch. 'I badly need some cash,' he said. He tamped his hand down on his head. 'I'm losing it,' he said. 'It's no fucking joke, but I'm going bald. My old man was bald. When I was a kid, I promised myself there was no way I was going to turn into him. Couldn't stand the bastard, the way he treated my ma. And now look at me. How're you fixed?'

Burns raised his right hand and smoothed his hair to reassure himself that it was there. His gran had always been a big fan of his rug. She used to say that strong hair ran in her family. She'd had two older brothers. Both of them had popped their clogs on the right side of eighty, and both had had hair as black as coal until the very end. Anytime she'd run her fingers through his hair, even when he had grown to adulthood, she'd referenced this genetic triumph. Say what you like about her family, but they had hair to die for.

'I'm doing all right,' he said.

Nix looked at him, envy twisting his face. 'Ever been to a hair-restoration clinic?'

'No, Pascal, can't say I have.'

'You don't want to either. They have separate waiting rooms. That way the clients aren't sitting there comparing their heads. It makes sense, but you're there on your own in this little cubicle with piped fucking music and men's magazines, as if you had the clap. Which I don't, by the way.'

Burns nodded. He had known Nix from a distance before recent days. Always the guy seemed to be on top of things. Right now, talking about nothing more than the hair on his head, it was like he was shedding a skin and a human being was emerging. Just shows you, Burns reckoned, you never really know what's going on with people.

'Anyway, you don't have to wait long and they bring you in. The doctor – he's a fucking doctor – old guy, must be heading for the exit, he's got a big thatch of silver on his head. I mean he's more hair than I've ever had, and you know just by looking at it that it's strong. Guess what his name is?'

'I don't know – Samson?'

'What?'

'Samson. The guy in the Bible with the—'

Nix was nearly out of his chair. 'Are you taking the piss? I know who the fuck Samson is.'

Burns put his hands out flat in front of him to ward off any offence. 'Pascal, I thought it could have been. You ask a question like that, man, I don't know any other name to do with hair.'

Pascal sat back into the seat. 'Thatcher.'

'Thatcher?'

'Yeah, like Margaret Thatcher – or Ben Thatcher. Used to play left full with Spurs?'

'Thatcher?'

'Yeah, he thatches … Forget it. Anyway, the thing is, you have to fill in this form, asks why you're there. I'm telling you, this thing begins to sound like a place for bozos.' Nix looked beyond Burns's shoulder, as if he was checking that nobody was in earshot. 'On the form, they ask you how often do you think about your hair. You have to tick a box. Sometimes, most of the time, all of the time.'

'And what did you put down?'

Nix leaned across the table. Burns could smell the man's cologne. He was surprised: it reeked of cheap, no class. He would have expected more from a man of Pascal Nix's standing.

'What did I put down? You know they say men think about sex once every seven seconds? These days I think about my hair more than that.' He retreated, straightened his back, as if he had just divulged a primal secret.

'Then get this one. Why would you consider treatment? I didn't want treatment, I wanted some fucking hair. Do you have low self-esteem? Do you have a negative self-image?'

'That's heavy shit, Pascal.'

'Tell me about it. Anyway …' he looked out into the bar again, lowered his voice '… and I don't want this going anywhere else. The guy, the silver fox, he put me on this drug. It's called finasteride.'

'He put you on a drug for your hair?'

'They … It's used for prostate cancer. If you get the big C down there, they give you this shit. But they found out that a side effect is that it can make your hair grow.'

'On your head?'

'On your head. So he has me on that and, if it works, there might be no need for the big leap.'

'OK,' Burns said. He'd never been in this position before, somebody unloading all their shit onto him as if he was a priest or a counsellor. What could he say to the fella? He had no problem in the rug department. He couldn't share Pascal's pain.

'If it does come to that, it's twenty grand. Can you believe that? Twenty fucking big ones at a time when this austerity is crippling everybody trying to make a buck. Some of these guys, they don't know what it's like to be hungry. If it does come to that, you know what they do?'

Burns offered a face full of curiosity, hoping that it was convincing.

'They take two thousand hairs from the back of your head. The back of your head, it's the safest place for hair. Yeah, best place to plant a bullet in a fucker too, but that's neither here nor there. They take the hair and transplant it onto the crown. And off you go, new man.'

'Wayne Rooney.'

'Exactly. Look what it's done for him. But hopefully it doesn't come to that. I've three months on this drug but if things don't get fertile up there I have to go for the big one. Twenty grand. Twenty fucking grand. And you think you got problems?'

Chapter Ten

The day didn't require shades, but she wore them anyway. Over there, in the life she'd left behind, her pair of Dolce & Gabbana glasses were never far from her eyes or her fringe. These days, she usually left them at home, but something prompted her to bring them for this task.

Back at the house, she mulled over what to wear. On the day she'd gone to the interview with that recruitment creep, she'd worn the black trouser suit, her funeral and interview outfit. While this was going to be an interview, it wasn't standard fare. And, she told herself, she hoped to Christ it wasn't going to be a funeral.

In the end she settled on a pair of indigo trousers, a matching blouse and a cream jacket with a light purple scarf.

She walked down to Manor Street, keeping her eyes peeled for a taxi. When she spotted one, the driver pulled in, and she sank into the back seat. At the mention of Philly John's, he gave her a second take in the rear-view mirror and just nodded.

The journey took little more than fifteen minutes. En route, the image of *Dragons' Den* kept flitting through her head. She'd first seen the programme over in Australia, but hadn't thought much of it. The presenter had been the one doing the pitching to the Dragons, not the entrepreneur.

Since she came home, though, the RTÉ version began to draw her in for her weekly dose. She had often wondered how she would fare with one of her ideas in front of the Dragons. One thing that bothered her was her patience. The Dragons at times were so smug and condescending. Would she have been able to take their crap without telling them where to go?

The car park in Philly John's was empty but for a Lexus, a Ford Mondeo and a van with something written on the side. She paid the driver, and he said, 'Good luck,' as if he sensed she must have a serious purpose in going to a place like that.

Once she stepped out of the vehicle, she felt drizzle on her head. She removed the shades, put them back in her shoulder bag.

The plan was simple. She would enter and enquire if this Pascal Nix was about. If he wasn't, she was prepared to wait. She would wait all day if she had to. And if that didn't do, she would come back tomorrow and again the day after. Right now, her body was buzzing, as if she had just downed a few cans of Red Bull. There was nothing to be afraid of. She wasn't a threat to anybody. She just wanted an audience with this guy. Nobody was going to do her harm. She wasn't going to disappear.

As she walked through the door, she told herself that Peter was at her shoulder, walking with her, as he had since the day he left this life. Well, apart from that time when she lost all reason and hooked up with Jake.

The interior was dark, all dull carpeting and frosted glass. A row of lights was lit above the mahogany bar, where a tall man was now looking out at her. She gave the place a quick once-over. Nooks and crannies all around, the faintest waft of beer, a radio playing in the distance. She didn't recognise the song.

Within seconds, her eyes had adjusted to the low light. She

caught two men sitting down at the rear of the lounge. One was on a stool with his back to her. The other was facing her. He wore a suit that didn't seem to sit easily on his shoulders. Middle-aged, light on top. He swept his hand back across his head in a gesture that suggested deep thought at work. That had to be him. Now, did she just walk straight over, risk encountering wrath, or sit and wait until he was good and ready? She was still mulling over the option when a voice came at her from behind. 'Well, looky here,' it said.

She turned and the fat man was there, eyes narrowed, carrying an air of menace. 'Hi,' she said, a high note of innocence in her voice, as if they were bumping into each other on a crowded Henry Street.

'Well, well, well.' He wagged a stubby finger at her. 'Who's a naughty girl, then?'

Beyond him, hovering in the shadow of his shoulder, she saw the other guy, Dara. He looked as if he was standing there ready to intervene if Charlie Small lost the run of himself.

'Didn't we have an agreement?' Small said.

'Did we?'

'Yeah. I told you that it wasn't possible to set up the meet you wanted. I said I'd see what could be done, just as a favour, like, and get back to you. And what have you gone and done?'

She tilted her head, putting on a little-girl face, trying to be cool, shitting bricks. 'A little birdy told me that this was the happening place,' she said. She turned and looked over towards the corner. Pascal Nix – it had to be Pascal Nix – was tossing his head back in a laugh.

Charlie Small wasn't buying it. His face turned dark. 'The best thing you could do now is fuck right off out of here. You've been a naughty little girl but I'm still going to try and see what I can do for you. I'll be in touch.'

'Could you just check with him now?'

'No.' He put a hand out towards her elbow, but she was too quick for him. She turned on her heels and began walking towards the back of the lounge. She felt him at her shoulder. She broke into a jog. Pascal Nix looked up at her, panic momentarily flying across his face as if she was coming to do him harm. Then she was standing there, nearly out of breath, delivering her bullets.

* * *

'Mr Nix?'

She felt a stab of pain in her arm as Small grabbed flesh and began to squeeze. She tried to break free from him.

'What the fuck is this?' Nix said. The other man, the one whose head was now a few inches from Karen's left knee, looked up.

'Sorry, Pascal,' Small said. 'This is the woman I was telling you about. She appears to have lost all reason. I'll get rid of her.'

'Mr Nix, I just want a few minutes. I'm not going to waste your time. I have a proposal you may be interested in.'

Pascal Nix swept a hand back across his head and looked over at the other guy, who seemed confused.

Nix turned to Small, waved his hand, signalling that he lay off her. 'We're off to a bad start, Miss …'

'Riney. Karen Riney is my name.'

'… Miss Riney, but seeing as you're so full of persuasion, go get yourself a cup of coffee and I'll be finished here in a few minutes.'

Wyman turned to see who this woman was. She looked all right from his vantage on the stool. Mostly, though, he wanted her to disappear. His business was of far more importance. The woman, this Karen Riney, looked like she didn't know what to do, as if she hadn't expected to be brushed off, as if she should be allowed to muscle in on his business.

'OK. I'll be at the bar.'

'You do that,' Nix said. 'Charlie will keep you company.'

She turned to go. Charlie Small gave his boss the eye, looking for the word to turf her out, but Nix remained impassive.

He turned back to Wyman. 'Some day, man. I'm in serious demand.'

Wyman nodded. So far, this was going all right. He was waiting for a catch. There had to be a catch.

When he arrived a half-hour earlier, the first person he saw was Charlie Small, a smirk on the fat fucker's face as he stood at the entrance to the lounge, a doorman in a pork-pie hat. Guy even opened the door for him to let him know he'd been expected and that Small was going to make the most of it.

The other fella was there too, the one who didn't say much, but had arms like logs. Wyman could still feel the pain across his neck where the guy had put him in a headlock.

Nix had given him a welcome that was a few notches below warm, but what had he expected? Then they got down to the matter at hand. He unreeled the story slowly, stretching out the background as if to delay revealing the meat of the thing. As he did so, it began to remind him of those visits to confession when he was a child, mumbling in the darkness into a steel grille, the priest's breath rising and falling against his story, sensing that the fella was waiting for the juicy bits.

Nix said, 'Sorry about that. Anyway, run the thing about the website by me again.' His face was serious as stone. If he started to take the piss, Wyman didn't trust himself as to how he might react.

'It's for people who want an affair.'

'Sex,' Nix said. 'We're talking about sex, aren't we? I mean, nobody's looking for happy-ever-after here.'

'That's right.'

'We're just talking about the ride.'

'We are.'

'A free ride. No terms or conditions apply.'

Wyman held it tight. Was the guy trying to get a rise out of him? For the first time since he'd entered, regret surfaced on the horizon of his thoughts. 'That's what I thought, anyway.'

'I hear you,' Nix said.

His right hand went to the inside left breast pocket of his suit and came out with a sheet of notepaper. A tabloid newspaper was open at the racing page on the table in front of them, a pen lying beside it. Nix lifted the pen and handed it with the paper to Wyman. 'Write down the address, will you? Sounds like the kind of place I might head myself one of these days.'

Wyman scribbled it down and raised his eyes again to Nix. 'Anyway, we met up, me and this woman. It went OK, and then I took off for home.'

'Only OK?'

'Yeah. It was fine.'

Nix nodded. 'OK. Fine is better than OK. But that was it, end of story. Ships in the night.'

'You could put it like that. Then, two days later, I get the phone call.'

Nix raised a cup to his lips, looking over the rim at Wyman. He replaced the cup, nodded. 'She had a few terms and conditions.'

'She did.'

'That she didn't bother to mention when you were doing the deed.'

'That's it.'

'How much?'

'Five grand. She had the whole thing on camera.'

'Resourceful. You didn't see that coming.'

'Mr Nix, the way things had been going for me, my business, my personal life, I couldn't see anything coming. My head was lodged so far up my rear end the sun stopped shining a long time ago.'

Nix leaned forward. 'You saw something and you thought it was for free.' He began tapping on the table with his index finger. 'You thought that you could get away with this without there being any cost. How long have you been alive, fella? Nothing in this world is for free. Everything has a price. Even a little night like the one you're talking about. But, to be fair to you, there are some circumstances here that most people wouldn't have seen coming. I mean, and you mightn't like to hear this, but I admire her balls. She's after pulling a scam that you would expect a man to maybe do – but the likes of you, Mr Wyman? You never saw that coming from a woman. You thought you were getting a free ride.'

Wyman had to admit that it was true. He was still not sure that this was happening. 'I don't know if she was acting alone.'

'Muscle?'

'The day I met her, out in Liffey Valley, there were people around, but it wasn't obvious that any of them were with her.'

'Maybe she figured she didn't need muscle. I mean, what were you going to do to her in a public place? Give her a few digs? I don't think so.'

Wyman thought it best not to give this guy the benefit of his darkest thoughts. For one thing, he didn't want to be putting any ideas in Nix's head.

Nix said, 'Not to put too fine a point on it, this woman has you by the short and curlies. What I don't know is what you want me to do about it.'

An image came to Wyman as he considered the question. He was on a diving board at a swimming-pool. The water looked dank. 'You can see how this really fucks me up from a financial point of view?'

'I can see that all right but, Mr Wyman, I ain't your solicitor, and my shoulders ain't tender enough for your tears. What exactly do you want?'

Wyman exhaled deeply, ready for the plunge, unsure of what would meet him below the water's skin. 'Could you … engage with this woman?'

'Could I what?'

'Get her to see the error of her ways, get her to back off, to leave me alone, to get out of my life so I can begin to try to put things back together again.'

Nix sat back, began rubbing the flats of his palms on his suit trouser legs. Wyman wondered where those hands had been, what they were capable of.

'What we have here is a sex tape, yeah? You want me to get it and return it to you?'

'I just want it destroyed, removed from my life. But, apart from that, there's the woman herself. Could you … have a word with her, explain that she should leave me alone because – well, for one thing, I need to concentrate on paying what I owe you before dealing with anything else.'

Nix closed his eyes, conveying the impression that he was deep in thought. 'I might know somebody who could see if she would be willing to look at this matter in a more reasonable way.'

'Thank you.'

'Obviously, I can't guarantee anything. I don't know how unreasonable she might be.'

Wyman held up his hands. 'Once she gets a message, that's all I'm asking. No more than a message.'

'Right. And what about you? What are you going to do for me? I'm getting worried that your obligations are shooting through the roof.' Nix pointed his index finger at Wyman's head, the thumb up straight, as if he was holding a gun. 'If you can't get work, then I'm going to have to organise some for you. OK?'

Wyman hadn't bargained for anything like that. He had seen a straight deal: you get the woman to back off, and I've a better chance of meeting the debt. Now the water was turning black. 'What kind of work?'

'Don't worry. I'm just talking about using your skills. Nothing specific, but if an opportunity comes up, you got to take it. My patience isn't endless. But as far as the other matter's concerned, let me see if I can arrange something.'

He rose to his feet and extended a hand. Wyman took it, aware that his own was now damp with sweat.

Nix said he'd walk Wyman to the door; he needed a smoke. As the pair of them exited, Wyman saw the woman at the bar, her eyes following their progress. Maybe she was afraid Nix was doing a runner, Wyman thought. He wanted to go over, explain to her that if she had any other option, she'd be better off giving this man a wide berth.

* * *

Karen thought he was making a getaway. 'Where's he going?' she said.

Small swivelled his head towards the door. 'Maybe you've scared him off.'

Karen stepped down from the stool. Small laid a hand on her arm. She looked down at the stubby fingers, as if they were contaminated. The idea that this article would physically impose himself on her was too much to bear. The other fella, Dara, he was standing back at a distance, like some insurance policy to be called in if anything went wrong. She pulled her arm free, checked the sleeve for any paw marks he might have left.

'Are you that hard up for trouble?' Small said. 'You can't go out and interrupt him again. Take my word for it. Have some more coffee. He'll be with you in a minute.'

It was actually three minutes before Nix walked back in. He was alone, and made a beeline for his corner booth, as if Karen wasn't there.

Small got up and walked over to his boss. They exchanged words before he turned and motioned Karen over.

Nix's breath was stony with tobacco. His handshake was surprisingly soft. When Small had left, they both sat down. There was a small silver teapot on the table, from which Nix began pouring into his cup. Small appeared at her shoulder again, like an irritating shadow, but he was just dropping over her cup of coffee. Nix put down the pot, poured a little milk, and sat back.

'First off,' he said. 'You're out of line. You walk in here as if you have a right to badger me. I don't know you but Charlie does and he says he told you that a meeting wouldn't be possible.'

'I know,' she said. She had rehearsed this moment maybe a dozen times in her bedroom in Stoneybatter. Already the script was being torn up. She felt a dose of stage fright coming on.

'But you didn't listen to him, and now you're here. Lucky for you I'm in good form. Because otherwise you'd be out that door like a blue-arsed fly. You're what the Yanks call a pushy broad, no doubt about that. Now, what can I do for you?'

This was where she should have pulled out paperwork, facts and figures, given him a little presentation, but all her stuff was in her head, where it was bursting to get out before she forgot it. She took a sip of coffee and tasted tar. She leaned forward on her stool. 'I'm going into business.'

'A recession is a great time to be getting stuck into something.'

'I know you don't want to talk about Jake and his grow-house.'

'His what?'

'I'm probably telling you what you already know, but I spent some time with Jake down in Kerry.'

'Lovely part of the country.'

'I saw what he was at. On one level it was an impressive set-up.'

'Are you sure you should be telling me this and not the poo-lice?'

'On another level, Jake was all over the shop. He didn't realise what he had, the potential. He didn't have a business head.'

She had him now. She could see he was all ears, but trying to play it cool, holding back in case he wanted to make a quick exit.

'As you're aware, I didn't know your boyfriend all that well. But from what I gather he didn't have a huge amount between his ears.'

'No argument there. Jake is a stoner. What you needed down there—'

'Hold it, Miss Riney.'

'Karen.'

'Karen can hold it too. I didn't need anybody down there. It had nothing to do with me.'

She held her hands up. 'OK, let's forget Jake and his disaster. I just want to tell you about me and what I'm going to do.' She went through the whole shebang with him. She had her figures, showing that at the very least eighty grand could be made with one crop in the space of twelve weeks. She explained the renting scheme, the equipment needed, showed him how she would get around the electricity problem. She knew that little of this was new to him, but he had to be impressed that she was on top of it.

She reckoned that a little over six grand could send her on her way. Nix's face remained impassive when she came up with that figure. But he was staying with her, glancing over her shoulder just once when somebody entered the premises. She had him all right. Then she decided to throw this in:

'The only thing I haven't made room for is the males.'

'No males.'

'It's a woman's operation.'

'In a man's world. What in the name of the sweet blessed divine are you talking about?'

'The male plants are only good for their reproductive functions. The crop, the stuff, all of that comes from the females. You know the business jargon they go on with these days? Well, the female is the wealth creator. So we get rid of the males as early as possible.'

Nix was shaking a head full of disbelief. 'Life imitating pot,' he said. 'Men good for nothing except – what did you call it? – reproducing.'

She laughed, and it suddenly occurred to her that she was now relaxed about all this. Why wouldn't she be? She was a natural.

'All very interesting, Karen. But what has any of it to do with me?'

'I'm looking for an investor.'

He peered about him, as if the walls had ears, swept his hand across his crown, drama lighting up his face. 'What you're talking about is illegal.'

'No shit, Mr Nix. Can we talk as adults?'

The phone on the table began vibrating, a light flashing on its display window. Karen felt the tension ease from her body. Just when she was moving in for the kill. Nix held up a hand, and brought the phone to his ear.

He sat there, nodding, throwing in a word here and there. This wasn't good. She shouldn't be left hanging, like a gangster's throwaway moll. She needed him in the palm of her hand, and right now he was slipping away in distraction. Removed from the pitch, left hanging there, she could feel her bladder serving notice on her.

She caught his eye, pointed towards the door to a toilet halfway between their booth and the bar. He nodded, although he was already far away.

She got up and walked to the bathroom and pushed the door through into it.

The ladies bathroom, she concluded, was alien territory for the tall guy behind the bar. It could have done with a good scrub, and something to sweeten the air. She entered the cubicle with a sense of trepidation, as if she were venturing into an untamed world. Pipes hissed somewhere nearby. Afterwards, the sink tap outside responded with a trickle when she turned it on. She gave herself the once-over in the mirror. All OK, she was looking good, alert, on top of the job. The towel in the machine looked suspicious. She was standing there, shaking the water from her hands, when the door opened and Pascal Nix walked in.

Immediately Karen felt something deep in her bowels, an instinct that this was all wrong. One look at him and she knew he hadn't stumbled into the wrong toilet.

'Take off your clothes,' he said.

'Wait a second—'

'I said take off your clothes. Now.'

She could scream but the sound would only travel out to the bar, where those thugs were probably smirking right now. She had to hold it together. The bathroom was moving out of focus. Her head was full of the sensation of falling, of having been pushed from a perch on a cliff and heading into a black hole. The man before her had changed instantly from a shady business type to a thug capable of extreme violence.

'You wanted us to be adults. Here I am,' he said.

She extended her hand to the countertop housing the sink. Suddenly the room was sucking air from her body. 'You're out of line,' she said.

'Or else you are, Miss Riney.' He raised his hand, showing her a mini tape recorder. 'This is my little friend. He's taken note of everything that was said out there, just in case it's needed. Whatever happens now, I'm covered. You approached me with a proposal to cultivate drugs. What I need to know is whether you have a little friend too. Like a wire hooked up for some of our finest constabulary. I need to know, Miss Riney, that you aren't trying to entrap me. Take your clothes off.'

'You've got the wrong end of the stick here—'

'I won't ask again. Down to your underwear. I need to see you in the flesh.' He turned and put his hand on the door handle behind him. 'You do it now, or I call Charlie Small in here and he'll do what he has to to protect me.'

'You've been watching too much American TV.'

'And you, Miss Riney, have no choice, unless somebody is listening in to us and is about to burst through the door there. Criminal justice has moved on here in the last few years. The law now means that hidden recordings can be used to entrap people. Shocking development, but fuck-all to do with me. Strip. Last chance.'

The image of Charlie Small thundering into the bathroom flitted across her mind. She tilted her head to a defiant angle, loosened the scarf from around her neck, held it tight in her right hand, as if it might provide some protection if needed. He held out a hand and she passed it to him. His fingers ran through the material. She slipped the jacket down her arms. She caught it with her right hand and placed it on the countertop. His hand was out again. She passed it to him, then began on her blouse. She bent her head to follow her fingers, which were trembling as they undid buttons. And then it was done. For some reason, she was glad she had worn a white bra. She looked up at him.

'Off,' he said.

'No.'

'I don't need to see your titties, but I need to see no wire. Take the blouse off, and then your trousers.'

The cotton left her shoulders and fell from her arms. She kicked off the ankle boots, and opened the button on the trousers, kicked them down too, and stood there in bra and knickers and stockinged feet, the man looking at her as if he was about to slip something into her bra for a lap dance. He picked up the garments and ran his fingers through them.

How would she explain any of this if something happened? What if that disgusting article outside was going to come in anyway?

Nix stood there, like a leech, she felt, for seconds that stretched in her imagination to minutes.

He handed her back her clothes. 'OK, you're clean,' he said. 'Sorry I had to do that, but that's the way things are these days.'

She reached for her blouse first, fingers still fumbling as she buttoned up.

'If it ever turns out that you're setting me up, I'll kill you. We're clear on that? If you're really bad, Charlie Small will take you somewhere and do with you as he pleases before killing you.'

'I'm not setting anybody up,' she said, her voice trembling like a leaf. 'There's no need for threats.' She tied the scarf around her neck again, confidence creeping back to her with the clothes, telling herself she should have expected all this. And yet there was no escaping a feeling that she had walked through a new door, opening up on a world that was alien from everything that had gone before. Pascal Nix had just arrived from the pages of tabloid newspapers into her life.

'No threats. I'm just letting you know the rules. I'll have five grand for your start-up costs by the end of the week. Your boyfriend owes me just short of four at this stage. You cover that. In twelve weeks I want twenty-five grand or else the collateral is mine. All that clear?'

Karen was bent over, trying to get her foot into a boot. She looked up at him. 'Twenty-five,' she said. The sum beggared belief.

'Take it or leave it. I'm not a bank shoving this money down your throat. You came to me. If this goes ahead, you can tell your boyfriend to relax. I'll try to make sure he sleeps soundly in his cell at night.'

She gave it a second, just to show she wasn't a pushover, but one way or the other, there was no going back now. 'OK. I'm in,' she said. She extended a hand and met his eyes. He took it and held her stare.

'Just one other thing,' she said. 'He's not my boyfriend.'

Chapter Eleven

It was two days before Wyman got the call. Immediately after it, he rang the number he'd been given.

'Hello.'

'Yeah. Who is this?'

'Is that Charlie Small?'

'You first, who the fuck is this?'

'You know me. I don't want to use names.'

'Ah, yes, yes, yes. I know that voice now. The tough guy, Kevin, isn't it? How's life as a house-husband these days? You looking for me to make some inroads into your financial management?'

'I was told to ring you if anything happened.'

'So I heard. You've got yourself some woman problems. Your little pecker ran away with you and look where it led. Sex, lies and a videotape gone missing.'

'Look, I don't have to listen to this shit. Our friend, P—'

'Who?'

'P, your boss.'

'P, P, P. Aha, I have you now. OK, Kev, keep going.'

'He gave me your number, said to ring when the time came. Well, the time's here now. The woman, the blackmailer, she wants to meet in town, at the Central Hotel on Exchequer Street. I told her I would only have some of the money right now.'

'And when exactly are you due to go for your second helping?'

'Three o'clock today.'

'That's not much notice, Kevin, but thanks. I'll see if we can get somebody who might be willing to clean up your mess after you. Take care and we'll be in touch.'

* * *

At three twenty-one p.m., the woman who went by the name Sabrina walked out the door of the Central Hotel. She stood on the threshold, looked to the sky. It was fair to middling up there, plenty of cloud cover but nothing bearing an imminent threat. She dipped a hand into her shoulder bag and pulled out a pair of shades. Her eyes suitably shielded, she began walking.

Burns liked her walk. She was wearing a belted trench coat and her legs looked promising. Her hair bounced in brown waves off her shoulders as she turned onto George's Street. Burns was reminded of the thing Jacinta had made him sit through a few times, *Sex and the City*. Except this piece of work wasn't no movie star, or pretending to be one, and she wasn't going to be involved in any laughs anytime soon.

She kept going, head high, confident that any oncoming pedestrian traffic would veer to the side, because she sure as hell wouldn't.

All according to plan so far. Charlie was parked around the corner, the motor facing this way. Burns pulled out his phone and hit the button.

'She's on George's Street, heading out of town.'

'OK. I'll stay put until you give me the word. If she gets in a taxi we're going to have to move fast.'

She didn't make any moves to suggest a taxi was on her mind. There was no effort to step out onto the street, or even to keep an eye on what might be coming.

He kept back about twenty yards, far enough away that she wouldn't cop anything. She didn't once turn her head.

They crossed another junction. Then the woman's pace slackened. She turned at this point, as if checking out the approaching traffic. Burns instinctively lowered his head. She had to be on the look-out for a taxi. And then she came to a halt. At a fucking bus stop.

Burns turned and looked in a shop window. And what do you know? It was a music shop. Two acoustic guitars, an Ibanez and a Yamaha. Apart from a couple of tin whistles, the rest of the display consisted of sheet music books. He recognised one, *Play Acoustic Guitar with Eric Clapton*, but the rest was all rock 'n' roll, folk and generally useless stuff. He had a quick scour for a teacher's ad. There was one, but it was for classical guitar. The way things were looking, unless he got somebody who specialised in the blues, he'd have to go back to his old teacher, tail between his legs.

When he looked up, there were three others waiting under the bus-stop canopy. He punched his phone again. 'She's getting a bus.'

'Tight bitch. You stick with her and let me know. She can't be going too far.'

As he rang off, a double-decker lumbered up the road, bearing the route number 65. The woman extended her hand and the bus came to a halt. Burns held back, watched the others board, and then his prey. Once she stepped in, he ran to the door and jumped on as she was walking down the aisle. The driver looked at him, eyes enquiring about his destination. Burns couldn't remember the last time he'd caught a bus.

He patted his jeans pocket, but knew there were no coins there.

Then he pulled out his wallet, slipped out a five-euro note and dropped it into the fare box. The driver was still looking at him like a question mark. Down the aisle, half a dozen pairs of eyes were staring up in search of an explanation for the delay. She was sitting one seat from the back, looking down at something in her lap.

'Where to?' the driver asked, exasperated that he had to concede speech.

'End of the line,' Burns said. He knew it sounded ridiculous.

The driver was nodding, as if he'd heard it all before. 'End of the line,' he said.

He tapped in something and the machine spat out a ticket with a credit note. He looked at it and shook his head, then glanced into his wing mirror and pulled out.

Burns sat into the second seat back from the stairs to the upper deck, three ahead of her and across the aisle.

He punched in a text: 'On 65. Sorted.'

He stayed alert, ready at every stop to follow in her wake if she got up. The bus lurched and swayed through the traffic. Burns noted the people boarding and departing, wondered about the kind of lives they had that they found themselves on a bus in the middle of the afternoon. If things had been different, if he had ever really tried to make it as a musician, maybe he'd be an afternoon bus person, struggling to put food on the table, living in some shithole as if he had walked out of a Charley Patton song.

The passenger traffic thinned as they moved out of town, heading for Tallaght. Burns began to wonder whether she was actually taking the bus to wipe clean her trail. If so, this thing wouldn't go as smoothly. But then, at the next stop, she moved up through the aisle and stepped off. Two schoolkids arrived down from upstairs and Burns let them go ahead of him.

He didn't know the area, but it was dominated by apartment blocks. He rang Small, who was caught in traffic on the canal. Burns kept back a good thirty yards. She left the road, moving under a canopy. By the time he arrived there, she was inside the entrance to a brownstone complex. He saw her through the glass frontage, waiting for the lift.

* * *

'Where were you?'

'Who is this?'

'Don't play games with me. You know who this is. Where were you today? Three o'clock. The Central Hotel.'

She kicked off her heels, sat into the couch. Her left hand reached for the remote to the TV.

'I couldn't make it,' he said.

'Sorry. Not good enough.'

'Something came up. My kids—'

'Oh-oh. No kids routine. You were supposed to be there. Two thousand euro. That's a cock-up on your part. First payment is now delayed. The clock is ticking.'

Her fingers moved through the channels. Daytime telly was such a drag. She was annoyed that she found herself back home at this hour. But after he hadn't shown, she just hadn't been in the form to stay in town. She felt riled, abused. She had trusted him when he'd said he'd be there.

'So how are you going to make this up to me?' she said.

A silence responded. She raised her voice. 'Are you trying to play games with me? Because if you are, you're making a big mistake. I've been entirely reasonable with you – I even allowed for you to pay in instalments – and now you stand me up. I think perhaps, Kevin, you need a little reminder of what exactly you've got yourself into ...'

Her front door was buzzing. It had to be one of the neighbours at this hour of the afternoon. How would any of them guess that she would be here? She got up and walked across to the door. 'I'm going to have to give you a shout back,' she said. 'Don't go anywhere, and I'm warning you, you'd better pick up when I call.'

She bent to peer through the spyhole. A stocky man wearing a peaked cap had a large box in his arms.

'Who is it?' she asked.

'Delivery. Number three one three,' he said. Usually a delivery had a name attached rather than an apartment number, but curiosity got the better of her. Nothing like a surprise in the afternoon to give you a lift. She turned the latch to pull open the door and suddenly felt it fly from her grasp.

***

Charlie Small was first inside. He pushed her back and she stumbled, but didn't fall. A high-pitched sound escaped her mouth, but Small hit her with his open hand and sent her flying. Burns stepped in and closed the door behind him.

Small bent down over her, pulled a little square piece of sticky tape from the pocket of his jacket, peeled off the back and applied it to her mouth. Burns stood over him, looking down at eyes that had gone wide with terror.

Small pulled a plastic tie from his trouser pocket. He grabbed her arms roughly, pulled them behind her back, and applied the tie. Then he turned her back around. Her eyes were closed, as if she could shut out the unfolding nightmare.

'OK, honey,' Small said. 'Where is it?'

Her eyes widened into a question.

'The sex tape. You and Lover Boy. I'm going to pick you up and you're going to lead us to it. And if you do it fast, and you behave yourself, there's a great chance that you might walk away from this in one piece. If you give us the runaround, well, hey, I might get to have some fun with you. We're clear?'

She nodded, letting him know she'd never been as clear about anything in her life.

* * *

'Hello?'

'Wyman?'

'Yeah, who's this?'

'Your friendly banker.'

'Mr Nix. What's going on? I was talking to—'

'Whoa, whoa. Just listen to me. Our little arrangement. I've managed to get you some work.'

'That's great, but I got a call from the woman earlier—'

'Stop. Listen. Learn. I have a little construction project. You're handy with electrics, aren't you?'

'I know my way around.'

'Take down this name. Karen Riney. She has some work lined up for somebody like you. She's going to contact you, make you an offer. And before you ask, no, you can't refuse it.'

'What about the other thing?'

'Don't worry about it.'

'Have you got something for me?'

'Like what?'

'The thing, the … tape.'

'I said don't worry about it. It's in safe hands.'

'What do you mean, safe hands? I thought it was going to be destroyed.'

'All in good time. What you need to know is that your problems in relation to that other issue have been dealt with. Now, what I'm interested in is that you get your arse into gear to get me my money. I'm organising a start for you. Your new life is just about to get under way. What more could you want?'

Pascal Nix listened but there was no response.

'Wyman?'

He heard the line click and go dead. Nix took the phone from his ear, looked at it as if it was about to explode.

'How do you like that?' he said to Charlie Small. The two men were sitting at the bar in Philly John's, Tall Phil the only other person in the hostelry. 'The fucker hung up on me.'

Charlie Small shook his head. 'Told you, boss. One of these days that guy is going to bring out the worst in me.'

Nix turned to the barman, handed a DVD to him. 'OK, Phil, put it in and let's see whether this is likely to make the porn charts.'

The tall guy turned to look up at the TV mounted on a bracket at the far end of the bar. 'Want me to close up?'

'Naw. Why bother? Who's going to come in here this hour of the day? And if anybody does happen to, well, they're in for a bit of a treat. Let's go.'

II

HARVEST

Chapter Twelve

The first time Kevin Wyman saw the Chink was round about midnight, two weeks shy of harvest. Wyman was doing his round of calls. The Golden Eagle Valley house – Pure Mule he had dubbed it after a TV series – was last on his list. He was stepping out of his car into a clear June night under a half-moon, when a guy ambled down the road, coming from the heart of the estate, like he was heading out for a midnight walk to the village.

As he shuffled past Wyman, the guy kept his head down. There were none of the greetings you might expect this far into the country, or this late at night. Wyman wouldn't have taken him for a Chink except he caught a quick glimpse of the guy's face. Otherwise he was slight, wiry, wearing a jet-black fitting of hair that fell over his ears, a leftover from a 1980s pop group. He wasn't wearing a jacket against the evening chill. Wyman knew from Vietnam War movies that some of these guys were hardy out.

Wyman thought little more of it until he happened across the guy a second time. That was ten days later, soon after five a.m., the day not yet awake. Pure Mule was first on Wyman's list that morning. He liked to call to this house when most of the neighbours were tucked safely in their beds. Of the three operations, this one was potentially the trickiest, but so far everything was motoring along nicely.

This time, the guy was walking into the estate on the far side of the road and Wyman was coming out of the front door of the house. He had to fetch a monkey wrench from the car to deal with a minor issue that had arisen in the sprinkler system. Their eyes met across the dawn, and straight away Wyman saw caution, maybe fear, on the guy's face.

'Early doors,' Wyman said, the guy passing ten yards away. He didn't respond, put his head down and kept going. The morning was cold for summer, but the guy still wasn't wearing any jacket.

For the rest of that day, the Chink was on his mind. Wyman was operating out of number five, and he reckoned that fewer than ten of the other forty-odd houses in Golden Eagle Valley were occupied. He had, over the last few months, spotted a young mother pushing a buggy. There had been sightings of sour teenagers belting a ball along the road to the estate's entrance. A woman driving a VW Golf similar to his own – most likely a hairdresser – scooted in and out at various times when Wyman was there. But he'd never seen any Asians. And this guy, this sullen midnight prowler, was preying on his mind.

This was not the time for the unexpected. The plants were about to mature. He would be down here a hell of a lot over the coming week or so, cutting, packing, taking the stuff away, reconfiguring the eco-system for replanting. Most likely, he would need help. There would be a fair bit of activity, and the last thing he needed now was any uncertainty bouncing around in his head.

What if? What if somebody else had had the same bright idea that Karen had come up with? What if there was another operation going on in there? What if the chances of getting rumbled were about to go through the roof? He had to find out. DAY ONE

* * *

Karen spotted the parking space up ahead on the left, a break in the line of cars that were parked along Leeson Street. A red Citroën had just pulled out to join the flow of traffic. She applied the brake hard and hit the indicator. An angry blast sounded from behind her. She didn't have to look to know that it was the latest He-man to be under the impression that he owned the roads. Dickhead.

He pulled across onto the next lane and overtook her, his face all rage as he stared at her. She gave him the benefit of her sweetest smile. It never ceased to amaze her how some of these men treated the roads like a shrink's couch.

She leaned across to the glove compartment on the passenger side and took out the purse where she kept the parking coins. Three euro would suffice for what she had to do. As she stepped out of the car, she was taken with a fleeting, warm glow of affection for the vehicle. It was serving her well, this 1998 Honda Civic, the colour of iron filings. A good buy, which she attributed entirely to luck.

Five minutes later she was walking up the path to Creole's place. This was the third time she had come here since she'd arrived home and it didn't get any better. Still, in mapping out the secret of her success, there was little doubt that the evening she had been there to buy weed had lit the fuse that was now burning.

She was dressed for business: jeans, runners and sweatshirt. No makeup, no jewellery. She badly needed a visit to the hairdresser, but she had made a point of deferring it until this meeting was sorted.

Creole answered on the first ring, buzzed her in. He was expecting her. At this time of day, evening light fading, the stairwell was dark with a heavy smell of decay.

At the top, the door was ajar, nobody in attendance. She pushed it open and entered the room. Creole was at the far end, pouring water from a jug into his beanstalk on the windowsill. Two other men were seated on the couch. She wondered whether they had lowered themselves onto it with the same trepidation she had felt on that first visit here.

One had a shaved head and a stud in his left lobe. He was bursting out of a denim jacket. He could have looked threatening, but his eyes were full of grey humanity. The other guy was stock thin, salt-and-pepper hair, and deep crevices on his forehead. She liked his lime green V-neck jumper, a collarless shirt underneath. It was the sort of thing she might have seen on Peter.

Creole put down the jug and waved a hand at the men. 'Shamie and Jamie,' he said, his mouth collapsing into a crooked grin of black stumps. The one in the denim jacket, Shamie, she would have guessed, showed his teeth. The other threw his head in the direction of Creole.

'This fella thinks he's Tommy Tiernan. I'm James, and this is Seamus. Creole the donkey likes to play around with our names.'

Karen relaxed. She hadn't known what to expect, but these guys were making all the right noises. She walked over to the couch with purpose and stuck out her hand. They both looked surprised, as if she was introducing some obscure ancient ritual.

'OK,' Creole said, reaching down to the coffee table, picking up his pouch of tobacco. 'Let's do the thing.'

Karen unhooked her shoulder bag and took out a transparent Ziploc bag full of weed. She placed it on the table and stood back. Shamie reached down and picked it up, opened it, ran his fingers through it and brought it to his nose. He closed his eyes and his face broke into a dreamy smile. Jamie snatched the bag from his fingers and went through the same routine. Creole began putting together a couple of skins, his eyes on the two boys, as if wanting affirmation of something he had told them before her arrival. He began licking the skins.

Karen said, 'First things first, lads. I'm not here for a smoke.'

Jamie gave her that look again, as if she was from a far-off place. 'We need to sample the stuff,' he said.

'No problem,' she said. 'Once I've left. I've too much to do and you need at least two hours' floating time for that weed. Let's just discuss a little business.'

Shamie spoke for the first time. 'Shoot,' he said, like a man who had suddenly found he was in a hurry.

'I need to know how much you can handle. I can front you twenty ounces. After that we'll see how we go. You can take that bag as a little introductory gift and use it as you see fit.'

Creole looked up from massaging the assembled skins between his fingers. 'An introductory gift,' he said, rolling the words around on his tongue. 'How much?'

'One fifty an ounce.'

'Jesus.' Shamie's head was thrust forward, as if he hadn't heard right.

'The market won't like that,' Creole said.

Karen said, 'The way I see it, the market will be out of its tree. It's blue cheese. Top notch. This stuff is so good you can double your money. Trust me, you'll be back for more before the waft of it sails out to sea.'

Jamie looked down at the bag in his hand. He extended it to Creole, who was now balancing the skins on his left wrist.

Shamie, said, 'There's people who mightn't be too happy about this. People who'll be wondering why the likes of us are no longer doing business with them.'

Karen was enjoying this. She could feel the buzz welling up inside her. She had rehearsed the whole thing before walking in here, and so far it couldn't have gone better than the best she'd hoped for. She needed this deal, a base from which to launch even bigger things. If Creole and his mates didn't go for it, then a new strategy would be called for. The worst-case scenario – going cap in hand to Pascal Nix – kept bugging her. Now, though, it looked as if she was blasting off.

'All I can tell you is that I have help who is willing to protect my operation. I don't want any hassle with anybody. I'm just running a business.'

The room fell silent. Shamie's mouth was hanging open.

Creole said, 'You just want to make everybody happy.'

'Yeah,' Shamie said. 'If you can get enough people smoking that shit you won't have much trouble there.'

Karen smiled, her body now flushed of any tension. She had a mind to sit down with these men and partake in a smoke right now, a little celebration. But that just wasn't on. There was a lot of road to put down yet.

* * *

Wyman exited the house through the utility room and the back door. He walked around the concrete path and out the front gate. Number five was near the entrance to Golden Eagle Valley, set back in a small cul-de-sac with four houses. After you entered the estate, through the large gateway between the huge stone eagles, it was in on the left. The houses were standard detached fare, thrown up at the height of the building bubble, an inch on the right side of habitable.

When Karen had taken it on, she'd done her Greta Garbo thing. 'I vant to be alone,' she'd said, mailing the estate agent that she was going through a divorce and, as a writer, needed somewhere isolated to get working. She had visited the village and it looked just the job. She did her homework, knew the layout and requested number five. There would be no real traffic directly in front of the house, but it wasn't set back far enough that it might awaken suspicion.

The estate was touching the outer reaches of Coomray, a one-horse town that was en route to the knacker's yard. It nestled in the shadow of the Slieve Bloom mountains, rising like a frozen eruption from the soft midland bogs.

Back in the days when the property furnace was raging, some bright spark had hit on Coomray as ideal for a commuter estate. You could be in Dublin in just over an hour on the new motorway yet come home in the evening to the country.

Coomray's commercial district ran to a single convenience store, two pubs, a sub-post office and a service station in need of a canopy. Golden Eagle Valley was hailed as a new model for young commuters. It was here that dreams of domestic bliss would foment and materialise. For those who had bought before the market began to descend towards Hell, it was here that their nightmare had begun.

Wyman moved out onto the main drag and turned towards the innards of the estate. He could feel the falling June sun on his back. Three teenagers were seated on a wall fronting one of the houses, heads lost inside their hoods, like a pew of monks awaiting divine intervention on their boredom. Wyman nodded at them but got no reaction. He knew he didn't have a face that melted easily into a crowd. Over the months since he started work, he had managed to wear caution like an extra skin.

This thing they were doing, it was no big deal on any moral plane. But the law didn't see it that way. Around every corner it could come tumbling down, and with it much else in his life. What they had here was a nice little operation that would see him out of his difficulties. After that, he would be happy to go back to the real world. Well, maybe not just yet. Depending on how things went, they might wring a year out of it, and if his sums were correct, he would then be well placed to restart a business with some to spare.

As he moved further into the estate, there were few vital signs of life. A roll-on lawn that remained unrolled here, a bare tarmac driveway there. A Fiat Punto sat outside one house. Another property was corralled inside a series of tall, steel-fabricated fences. Plastic guttering hung from the eaves at one end of the frontage, and a couple of roof tiles looked to be a gust short of taking flight.

He scanned each house for clues. Upstairs curtains shut tight, to give no hint of the black-out blinds. Nothing coming from a chimney that might betray a ventilation system. Nothing so far. Nothing except lots of nothing, most of the houses resigned to never being homes.

The main drag came to a halt at a T-junction on the inner reach of the estate, where the Slieve Bloom grew bigger. The mountain's dark mystery was melting as the shapes on the slopes came into focus. He could see a couple of goats and a lean-to halfway up the ridged slopes.

He looked left. The driveway was empty. On the right, there was nothing either. He turned down that way. He took it handy now, no rush, his gaze switching between the houses, left and right. There was nothing there. Until, at the last but one, number thirty-nine, the curtains on the first-floor bedrooms were drawn. He felt something move inside his body, prodding vague suspicions.

Apart from the curtains, the place gave away few hints. Wyman turned and looked back up the road. Nothing. He was alone, unless somebody was inside the house.

If he had been the man he was three months ago, he would have turned and left right now. There could be only trouble behind those walls. But he had a stake now. His future was tied up with the business. To leave now would be a dereliction of duty.

He stepped from the road through the open gateway into

number thirty-nine. The ground beneath his feet turned soft. Up close, he could see that the front bay window was covered with a blind. Nothing growing in there so, but still, it obscured the view. He walked up to the window, looking for a crack at either end of the blind. No crack, but a faint hint of light was coming from somewhere beyond the front room. He turned and went around the side of the house, moving carefully on the spongy earth.

At the rear, light poured from a large window out into the dusk. He stood with his back to the pebble-dashed walls, sharp stones tickling his spine. He inched his way closer to the light. The Slieve Bloom looked down on him. He spotted another goat up there. He knew he should leave now, while the going was good, but he couldn't.

There was no blind on the window. He leaned over and saw a kitchen, a man sitting at the table, his head bent into a book. Most of the table was taken up with cans of food – noodles, peas, coconut milk. The guy sitting there was the Chink Wyman had seen before. At the far end of the room another man was kneeling, his head bent all the way to the floor.

In front of him there was a small table, waist high, fronted by three stubby purple candles, faintly alight. On either end of the table there was a vase of roses, one bunch pink, the other red. Between the vases stood a little statue of Buddha, sitting cross-legged, looking totally chilled out.

Wyman ducked back against the wall. This was trouble. Hurried sounds came through the glass, voices. He turned again and looked in. A face, Asian, eyes narrow and suspicious, was looking out at him. The man's mouth opened in a cry. Wyman turned and took off.

* * *

'You gotta brush, man, you gotta brush.'

Burns looked up from the Lag guitar. His teacher, George Ribbon, was pushing down hard on the strings of his Fender, offering patient example. His voice was raised against the sound of Big Bill Broonzy singing 'Hey, Hey' from the laptop, at a pace that had been electronically slowed down.

Burns tried it again, fingers flowing down across the strings, but the notes just weren't the same. He couldn't make it sound like his teacher's playing and he sure as fuck couldn't come near to sounding like Broonzy.

George Ribbon reached across and killed the music on the laptop. The screen was purple with a white jagged line running across it, which always reminded Burns of the bedside of a dying man.

The pair of them were sitting in a basement room in a lane off North Great George's Street, under a pet shop that had been shuttered for the last six months. A single bulb hung from the ceiling, brilliant without a shade. Outside, the night had not yet arrived.

The room was too bright for Burns's liking. He preferred shadows where he could find refuge, if need be. He sat in a folding chair next to George Ribbon. There were half a dozen more chairs with easels in front of them scattered around the room. Usually, George Ribbon taught groups of adults but when Burns had first approached him, he said he was only interested in a one-on-one session. This was a private element of his life. He didn't want word going back to whoever about his dirty secret. And now that he was coming again, it would be on the same basis.

'Don't get me wrong, I'm not saying it's easy,' Ribbon said. He was looking intently at Burns from behind thick-rimmed glasses. He had two days' stubble on his face, and the guitar was pushed out on his lap by a commercial girth. Now and again, Burns wanted to warn him that he'd better watch himself or he'd end up like Charlie Small, even if this guy didn't know Charlie Small from Adam.

'But it's all about practice. When you strip it down, the blues is not rocket science. It's a few chords, a lot of repetition and a shitload of practice, you know what I'm sayin'?'

Burns nodded. 'Broonzy didn't know much about rocket science,' he said. The other man grinned as if he was making a concession. Since he had recommenced the lessons, must be six weeks now, Burns had noticed that George Ribbon rarely laughed. Now and then he conceded a smile, in deference to the blues.

If he knew jack shit, Burns said to himself, he'd know that the bluesmen were by and large funny guys, who knew how to party, not morose bores broken on lost women, dead pets or burned-out homes.

'Thing about Broonzy,' Burns said, 'was that they tried to make him into something he wasn't. See, they got him to do tours, right across the States and over to England. That was back in the fifties. But Big Bill, he knew what was what. From the Delta, but he made a name for himself in Chicago. He was a right snazzy dresser too. But on those tours they wanted to sell the idea of the blues, not just the music. So they got Broonzy to dress up in these mothballed shirts and trousers that you'd see on people picking cotton. They wanted to sell an image.'

Burns noted that Ribbon had lifted his guitar down, placing it on a steel stand. The clock said it was two minutes past eight. His time was up. He enjoyed this, talking to somebody about those guys, because there weren't too many people out there who would appreciate what you had to say. 'So they had Broonzy going around the place like some kind of a dumb greenhorn, and him with a whole closet of top-notch suits back in his place in Chicago. I tell you, they were really selling thirty shades of shite.'

'Yeah,' George Ribbon said, with the air of somebody who felt maybe he should have known this shit, what with him teaching the blues and all.

'That guy has some special fingers.'

Burns got up and slid his Lag into the canvas case. He pulled a twenty-euro note from his pocket and left it on the table beside the laptop.

'So you're happy with the way things are going?' Ribbon said. 'You're OK with this set-up?'

'Sure,' Burns said. 'I was hoping maybe we could do something from Lightnin' Hopkins pretty soon.'

'No problem, man. Let me go through it and see if there's something we can pull out that suits where you're at.'

Burns got to his feet, picked up the case.

Ribbon looked up at him, a request on his face. 'Mind if I ask you, man, but you wouldn't know where I could get some smoke?'

Burns turned and looked him in the eye. 'Why would I know that?' he said.

The teacher put his hands up. 'Hey, I'm just askin'. Lots of people smoke. I'm just throwin' it out there.'

Burns shook his head. 'Don't have much to do with that stuff. I wouldn't even know where to look,' he said. 'Anyway, see you next Wednesday.'

* * *

Wyman suddenly felt hungry. He hadn't eaten since morning, and now a great weakness was coming over him. He was behind the wheel, approaching headlights flashing across his face as he slowed down outside Kilcormac, little place on the main Birr–Tullamore road towards home. The radio was playing music for somebody on the road, looking for solace, Liam Ó Maonlaí belting out a sweet rendition of 'The Lakes of Pontchartrain'.

He could hang till he got home for a bit of grub. He'd be there within an hour, but he couldn't imagine there would be anything waiting for him.

Since he'd got stuck into the business, they had been relying on this kid down the road for child-minding. She came in for the afternoons once Wyman dropped the children home, and she stayed until either he or Brenda made it back. Her idea of a wholesome meal was to rustle up a few slices of iceberg lettuce, served as an excuse for a side salad beside an ordered-in pizza. And Brenda, who must be home by now, certainly wouldn't have been performing in front of the cooker.

Traffic through the town was light. At the far end, a square opened up on the right. He looked over and saw a chipper, nestled in the corner like a mirage. Red and white lights lit up the Café Royale, as if it had just landed there from Monaco or somewhere.

Within ten minutes, he was back in the car, the window on his side rolled down two inches to set free the deep-fried waft that would linger. Two girls, must have been teenagers, were huddled together in conversation near the car, oblivious to his presence.

The chips made short work of his hunger. He drank deeply from a can of 7-Up. Afterwards, he felt better, but no less agitated. The day had been good up until a couple of hours ago, harvest nearly here. Now this.

Once he had rounded the house, he had kept running, out into the road, the soles of his shoes slipping on grit and pebbles. Only when he'd reached the T-junction did he turn around. One of them was back at the entrance to the house, stopped, looking like he was mulling over whether to give chase or go back inside.

He slowed down as he walked. He arrested his pace further when the pew of monks hove into view again. As he approached them, he threw his head over his shoulder once more, but there was nobody behind him.

The youths fell silent as he walked past, and when he'd moved on, he heard a rippling snigger.

Back at the house, he'd been too agitated to do anything else. He gave it ten minutes, peeking out through the blinds at the front-room window every now and again. Nothing. They weren't coming after him, not now at any rate.

Once he finished the chips, he got out of the car, startling the pair of girls as the door opened. A bin on the lip of the square was overflowing, but he managed to stuff the wrapping paper in.

Back in the car, he pulled out his phone and scrolled down through the contacts.

She answered on the second ring.

'Hi.'

'How're you?'

'Grand. Where are you?'

'Kilcormac. A stop on the road home.'

'You're coming from Pure Mule?'

'Yeah, a little problem has reared its head.'

'Go on.'

'The fella I mentioned to you, foreigner, walking around at strange hours.'

'You're not going to tell me he's a gardener.'

'He's a gardener and he's got a friend.'

There was a silence on the line.

Karen was the one who had researched the Vietnamese. She'd found that they were pioneers of sorts in the business. They'd set up first in places like Canada, where they'd perfected the art. Then they'd popped up in Britain and north of the border here. Over the last couple of years, some Vietnamese gangs had crept down here from the North, looking for drug markets. Already, the law had fingered a few of them.

Wyman was sceptical at first. These fuckers arriving in a strange country and doing a reverse takeover of the market in drugs. Still, when he'd first seen the Chink, he couldn't rid himself of the nagging suspicion. Now he'd gone past scepticism. They were here, and they were going to be a headache.

'You're sure?'

'I did the neighbourly thing, paid them a visit to welcome them to the estate.'

'What do they know about us?'

'I didn't wait to find out. One of them saw me outside his back window, and I took off. Jesus, my heart was thumping. I don't know what they know. But I do know that they know that I know what they're up to.'

'The guy, the one you met, you saw him a second time?'

'Yep. Bright and early Tuesday. They can't be stupid, Karen.'

There was another silence, before Wyman said, 'Can I make a suggestion?'

'Go on.'

'We leave it for a few days. The drying room is full, humming away. That stuff will be ready for cutting and packing within a day, two tops. We go back in two days and get to work. Take this crop, and let things lie after that for a few weeks, maybe a month or two. Who knows? Maybe everything will be hunky-dory.'

'I was thinking along the same lines.'

'See? You'd be lost without me.'

'Just go home to your family. We've a busy few days ahead of us.'

'Karen?'

'Yeah.'

'You should see what they've set up in the kitchen down there.'

Chapter Thirteen

Sleep didn't come easy to Karen that night, but when it did eventually fall, like soft snow, she found herself walking into a dream. She was being shown around a property out in Killiney, where millionaires gathered and celebrated themselves.

The estate agent was a creature of chic. She had a great figure and a mane of chestnut hair stolen from Cheryl Cole.

Karen was trying to double-guess her, gauging her selling capacity, picking holes in her technique, noting where she was coming up short.

And then the viewing was interrupted by a commotion at the door. Karen turned to see two Asian men, little guys, wiry, not a pick on them, tearing into the house, squealing in a language she couldn't make out. As they barrelled their way into the room, she could see that the two of them were each cradling potted plants under their arms.

She woke and lay motionless in the grey dawn.DAY TWO One of her first moves once she'd got her hands on some serious cash would be to find her own place. Their friendship had sustained Abigail and herself over the last few months, but the walls on the cottage were squeezing in on them. Abigail's decision to come on board the operation meant they saw even more of each other. Both enjoyed their space, and now there was the added complication of Abigail's romance, if that was what you'd call it. Whatever happened, Karen didn't want things to get to the point where their friendship was damaged.

She rose, showered and sat down to a bowl of strawberries and granola and a cup of fruity tea. She was just making a few quick notes on her iPhone when Abigail emerged from the bedroom, her head still drooping in sleep. 'Early bird,' she said. She looked up at the ceiling window, as much out of instinct as any fear that rain might be on the way.

Karen said, 'Lots to do. I'm hoping to get to all the houses today. Things are beginning to move.'

'Busy, busy.'

'You're OK for road tomorrow?'

'The great flat midlands, here I come.'

'There's just a small change of plan. Have you been talking to Kevin?'

Abigail's face woke up in surprise. Kevin's name rarely passed between them. 'No,' was all she said.

'There's a small issue with Pure Mule. But if all goes to plan, Kevin will still be down there late tomorrow.'

Abigail walked over to the worktop by the sink, dipped her hand into a drawer, pulled out a pair of pruning shears and wielded it as if she was ready to do some damage. 'I'm all set,' she said.

'Careful who you might use that on,' Karen said.

'Don't be giving me ideas.'

They laughed away the tension that the subject of Kevin might have raised between them.

'There's a lot of work to be done,' Karen said.

'And?'

'Abigail, come on, I'm just saying. Once the work gets done, I don't care what ye get up to. But we need to get things moving, that's all.' She clicked out of the notes window in her phone, stood up and drained her cup of tea. 'Listen,' she said. 'This is going to be a seriously big week for all of us.'

Abigail held up her hands in mock defence. 'I'm all on board, honey, you know that.'

Karen extended a hand, placed it on her friend's shoulder. 'I do, and I appreciate it. I know this is eating into your hours in Heaven's Gate.'

'It's not an issue. Angels go through their ups and downs too, especially in a recession.'

Karen lifted the tan shoulder bag from the back of the chair. 'What I'm trying to say is that I'll be out of your hair in the next fortnight or so. Once the cash begins flowing, I'll be OK to get my own place.'

'Karen, hold on ...'

Karen reached out a hand again. 'Hey, listen, we're mates. That will never change, OK? Everything is cool. But this place is getting a little too small for both of us. And, besides, you need your own space.'

Abigail looked into her eyes. 'You're not doing this because ...'

'No.'

'Because don't get the wrong impression.'

'I'm doing it because I want us to stay friends. OK?'

* * *

Rush-hour traffic had thinned out as she made her way west. The interior of the Honda Civic had no air-conditioning so she lowered the window on her side. A warm gush hit her cheek. The day was muggy, unforgiving, building up to something serious under a low, dark sky. It was the kind of day she would have described as cranky back in Sydney, but over there the sea rolled in like a balm.

The only sound was from the engine. The radio was acting up, and the CD player was banjaxed. She didn't mind the silence. It gave her room to think.

Kevin's news had to be digested in the cold light of day. So, there was another operation in Golden Eagle Valley. So what? Once he had told her of his suspicions last week, she had taken account of the dangers.

When she was starting off, Karen had mulled over the possibility of getting a couple of Viet gardeners on board. Their reputation was second to none. They worked for half nothing. They stayed on the premises, chained to the job, hardly ever going out, surviving on dried food and dreams of living off the money. Because they were there 24/7, the quality of care for the product was top class, and the market duly rewarded.

But there could have been complications. Getting a gardener who wasn't tied into one of the gangs would have been next to impossible. And you didn't want to mess with any of those people. From what she had read, they made the likes of Pascal Nix look like Ronald McDonald.

No, she had been better off hooking up with Kevin Wyman. So far, their partnership had worked out a dream. On first meeting him, she was cautious. They circled each other, both trying to suss out whether the other was in cahoots with Nix.

It didn't take long for trust to come dropping slowly into the conversation. He told her about the business, and how he had chased his losses all the way into Nix's cave. She was interested in the business angle, threw him a few questions as he charted the demise.

'Bless me, Father, for I have sinned too,' she said. She told him of her sojourn in Kerry, how she hadn't bargained for it initially, but then realised it was no big deal. He was full of questions about the grow-house and she filled him in.

He was cute, Kevin Costner with a Meath accent, but he wasn't her type. Once she sent out the smoke signals that their relationship would be hermetically sealed in work, he seemed to relax.

Where he really came into his own was turning her half-baked notions of fitting out the houses into a plan of sophistication. Had she made any provision for smells? Ventilation? How would she operate a sprinkler system? How was she going to get the maximum return from the lighting? What about the electricity? If she diverted the mains, she would have to do it in a way that still registered some use. An occupied house using none might as well have a red flag draped across its roof.

Soon she realised that he was an asset. By the time they arrived at discussing money, she was ready to cut him in for 25 per cent of the business. He thought about it for a few seconds, made a further pitch as to his usefulness, and said he felt he was worth 40 per cent. Now she knew she really had an operator on board.

They settled on two-thirds to one-third split, with a review scheduled once the first crop was harvested and sold. So far, he was worth every penny. She shuddered to think of the shortcomings in the operation if she'd been left to her own devices.

The only bum note was his thing with Abigail. He was married, and Abigail was at an anxious age. Karen didn't want to see anybody get hurt, including the business. But now there was a much bigger issue. Everything would have to be speeded up. She had long been expecting the unexpected: all the business manuals she'd read had told her it was inevitable. Now that it was here, she was ready to meet it head on.

She had no fear, not yet, anyway. And as for loneliness, it only reared its head on rare, vacant moments. She had managed to compartmentalise her life. The work kept her up. She would never get over Peter, but she was learning to live without him. Time did heal, even if it took its time.

It wasn't that she was leaving him behind. He was still there with her, just in a different form. He would have enjoyed this. She allowed herself a dry laugh. 'Yeah, you and your hot suits, flogging them for a few dollars more. Welcome to the big time, honey. Up here, the air is fresh and clean and smells of serious money.'

* * *

Wyman's childminder was on the razz. Rosanna was missing, presumed drunk. Her mother said she didn't know when to expect her back. She had left home the previous evening, en route to the cinema with her boyfriend. The first her mother knew that she hadn't shown up was this morning: a quick glance into her bedroom revealed an unslept-in bed. A text was recorded on the mother's phone, sent at six forty-three a.m., informing her that she couldn't get back, 'slept in Mark's'.

'If you ask me,' the mother said, 'she won't be back this side of tomorrow. Two of her friends are heading off for Germany this week, so, you know the way they are today, they'll probably go drinking all day. What I want to know, Kevin, is how they can afford it. I wasn't shy of a skite myself when I was their age, but it was a once-in-a-blue-moon affair. We just didn't have the money.'

Kevin Wyman couldn't have cared less where his twenty-year-old childminder had got the money. His only concern was that his kids were off school for the day, and he had booked her to show up at eleven. Now that she was on the missing list, his plans were shooting south.

'Drink is cheaper today than it ever was, Mrs Fox,' he said. She had asked him repeatedly to call her by her first name, but he preferred it this way, addressing the mother of his childminder with a matronly regard. There couldn't have been more than a decade between them, but her daughter was acting as substitute parent – that was how Brenda put it – for their children.

'I know, I know,' she said. 'They don't go to pubs any more. They drink at home, they get – and there's only one way to describe it, Kevin – rat-arsed, and then go out on the town and drink water. I don't know, I worry about it all the time. With that kind of an attitude, what is to become of them?'

Wyman placed his cheek against the cool kitchen tiles. Who gives a shit?

Mrs Fox went on: 'It's all ahead of you. How old are they now?'

'Six and four.'

'Oh, sure, you won't feel it now before they're off out gallivanting, breaking your heart, and sometimes you wonder about the whole thing.'

'What thing?'

'Bringing children into the world. Why do we bother? Nobody ever told me it would be like this …'

He didn't hear much after that. He let her on her way, down the dark avenues of woe where she went to comfort herself. When she stopped for a pause, he threw a final call out into the wild: 'Mrs Fox, you don't see any way that she'll turn up for work this afternoon?'

Silence settled on the line. It took Mrs Fox five seconds to formulate her reply: 'Kevin, you gave that girl a chance to do something useful with herself rather than lolling around the house doing nothing but drawing the dole. I can't tell you how sorry I am that she's let you down now. I really can't …'

Don't, please don't, for Christ's sakes, don't tell me any more. 'That's OK, Mrs Fox. Just let me know if she turns up.' He replaced the receiver. TV sounds were coming from the sitting room. He didn't need this, not now of all times. He'd have to phone Karen again. Gardeners and now childminders were messing with his head big-time. Nobody'd told him there would be days like this.

* * *

Karen turned into the Westwood estate, half a mile beyond the M50. The recession was fraying at the edges here. A few of the houses were boarded up. Front gardens had gone untended; shards of glass littered the shadow of a redundant streetlight. A man stood at the window of Life Cycles, looking out over the bank of bicycles he had placed hopefully outside his premises. The Westwood Inn was shuttered, its doors closed during the day, opening only to the toll of the Angelus from the nearby parish church. That place was shut most of the time too. Even the retailers of religion were doing poorly in this time of lost souls.

Karen took it all in, and thought about Sydney, a world away.

She pulled up outside the house and sat in silence for a minute, her eyes switching between rear-view and wing mirrors. The house was terraced, three bedrooms, the front wall of navy, wanting for a fresh lick of paint. An elderly woman shuffled along the footpath from behind, coming towards the car. Karen leaned across to the glove compartment, busying herself with nothing at all. The woman passed. A few spits of rain fell on the windscreen. She looked up at a sky that was turning a deeper shade of purple. Driving down to the Middle Kingdom would be no joke if the rain really turned it on.

This had been the easiest house to rent. The estate agent did everything on the phone, not even looking for references. She sent him her IDs by snail mail, never having to meet him face to face. The guy was over the moon that he was actually getting somebody to take the property off his hands.

The rent was paid at least four days before it was due, presenting a model tenant.

She stepped out of the car and locked it. Nobody else was about at this time. She made what she hoped was a casual sweep of the front windows in the neighbouring homes. Nothing.

A rusty iron gate led to a narrow concrete path that flowed, like a river, to the front door. She pushed past the gate and raised her eyes to the roof, where a faint wisp of something misty was rising from the rust-coloured chimney cap. You'd want to look closely for a while to wonder why a chimney would be in use at the height of summer. Then again, summer was a relative concept in this country. Beneath the eaves, curtains were drawn tight on the two first-floor windows. Nobody would give that two seconds' thought.

* * *

Once she opened the front door, the smell came at her. By now she was getting accustomed to it, the overpowering stink that the plants gave off. Back in the day, when she'd been a casual smoker, she'd enjoyed the smell of weed, either dried or when it enveloped a room as a joint was being passed. She'd always taken the aroma to be part of the hit, easing her into that place from which she could look out on the world through a soft, easy lens. Even when she had caught a current of the stuff, in a pub, on the street, it always greeted her with a sense of warmth.

These days, whenever she checked on things, there were times when the smell might make her puke. Once, about six weeks after planting, she arrived at the house with a dicky tummy. She wasn't in the place ten minutes when a wave of nausea washed towards her. She ran to the toilet bowl to throw up, her head thumping, the sound of gurgling coming from the bath beside her.

Still, it could have been a hell of a lot worse. If Kevin hadn't been around to knock together the ventilation system, she doubted that things would still be on track here. The neighbours would most likely have taken in the smell, and ended up high as kites before they'd copped what was going on.

After she closed the front door, another feeling came over her, this one all good. Here she was, in her little factory, manufacturing, getting down to business, striking out on the road to freedom. A low hum came down the stairs from the makeshift fuse board on the first-floor landing. The only other sound was of the sprinkler system, as if a stream was flowing across smooth stones between the bathroom and bedrooms upstairs.

She took a quick glance at the ESB meter in the hallway. Everything OK. A series of cables led from the meter up the stairs, bunched together on the steps by a couple of plastic ties. At the top of the stairs, she looked at the wooden panel nailed to the landing wall. This was covered with sockets from which dozens of wires ran across the landing in blues, browns, reds, leading to the three bedrooms and the bathroom. Diverting the electricity before it could register on the house meant that it was both free and beyond suspicion. Kevin had arranged it that a small volume was still being used legit. That was one of the little things she would never have thought of.

The landing was also littered with a maze of small tubes, running from the bathroom to the bedrooms. A quick peek into the bathroom confirmed that everything was flowing fine. One of the taps on the sink was broken and attached to a hose leading to a pressure pump and timer, feeding water to the plants. The bath was filled about two feet, looking like an algae pond, thick with nutrients, and industrial chemicals, which fattened up the THC levels.

The heat hit her like a wall when she opened the door to the master bedroom. Inside, her little babies, about eighty of them, each in its own pot, were almost fully mature. You had to give it to weed, she thought. It takes humans the guts of twenty years to arrive at the outskirts of maturity, yet these little girls were up and ready for the world after three months.

It had taken about a fortnight to recognise the male plants. When they began to bloom, little prickly bits formed on the stalks. The females bloomed in tiny little balls. Once identified, the males were dumped. You couldn't have them fertilising the females, stunting their potential. Those little boys wouldn't have been able to keep their dicks in check.

The little babies were now more than a metre high, all set to be moved into the drying room, where they would be hung upside down on lines to dry out. Then the cutting would begin, and they would be sent out into the world to make a lot of people happy.

Plastic sheeting covered the floor under the pots in the master bedroom. A series of tubes, punctured with small holes, ran through the maze of plants, a top-class, home-grown sprinkling system. A matrix of high-wattage bulbs hung from the ceiling on metal chains, attached to hooks. Two eleven-inch pipes were also cut into the ceiling, leading up to the attic, where they snaked between the beds and other furniture piled high up there. The pipes led to the chimney flue, through bored holes, providing for a ventilation system out of the top drawer.

The room's walls were covered with industrial tinfoil, which, along with the light, codded the plants that they were growing in a fine climate, many miles from the west side of Dublin. Kevin's other little detail was the timers. The lights were on for only sixteen hours of the day, giving the little darlings eight hours' rest in the dark, just like the real world.

The second bedroom presented a different scene. In here, the cutting had already been started, with three-quarters of the plants

shorn of leaf. This room had been the pilot project, up and running a few days before the others. Now it was the first to be harvested, the plants removed to the third bedroom for drying. She and Kevin had spent the last weekend cutting down and drying. Now one batch had been dried and was packed into a brown suitcase on wheels, parked in the drying room.

At the current rate, the whole house should be harvested by the end of the week, the buds dried in three days, tops. Then it would be time to reconfigure the system, and begin replanting. If everything went as smoothly as this little factory had done, they would be on the pig's back.

The broad plan was to go to work here, down in Pure Mule and over in the other midlands depot, the old farmhouse they had taken to calling the Middle Kingdom.

The fourth operation, in salubrious Rathfarnham, had been abandoned after a few days. One of the neighbours had had a couple of brats who kept coming in over the fence in search of their stray football. It was never going to work out so she terminated the lease, and left the place more or less as they'd found it.

In the drying room, she felt the handle on the suitcase, tried to lift it, but found it too much. She dragged it out, lifted it over the lines of cables, and trailed it after herself down the stairs. At the bottom, she paused for breath, just as a tremble came from the pocket of her jeans.

'Karen?'

'Yes.'

'More bad news.'

She didn't respond.

'My childminder is on the razz. Won't make it over to you today.'

Small issue, she reckoned, but no less irritating. 'And tomorrow?

Will she still be partying, or will she be fit to go back to work?'

'I know. Couldn't believe it. I was all set today.'

'OK. We can put it back. How about you get down to Pure Mule tomorrow evening? Nothing's happened on that front. We might as well get the product down and out of there.'

'Will do.'

'I'll manage the suitcase here, bring it over to the guy I was telling you about.'

'Perfect. I've a feeling about this, Karen. I think the week ahead is going to be very good to us.'

* * *

The pinkie on Burns's left hand just wouldn't play ball. Every time he tried to slide it, it slipped off the fret, giving a good effect, but making a balls of the song.

Burns was sitting at his living-room table, the Lag on his lap, over a music sheet. The sheet had the tabs for 'Got The Blues, Can't Be Satisfied' by Mississippi John Hurt. George Ribbon reckoned this would be one of the better ones to try on, considering where Burns was at and all with his progress.

It got on Burns's wick sometimes, the way the guy set it out during a lesson, making it seem that this shouldn't be any problem. When he ran through it, there in the room, that was the way it always seemed. But something happened by the time Burns got home. He could never replicate what the stoner did during the lesson. Even when he recorded Ribbon's efforts on his phone and played it back, his fingers still seemed to be encased in concrete compared to the poetry flowing from the recording.

He kept it up for a few minutes, but it was just no good. He wasn't up to speed, and the way things were looking, he might never be.

He sat back and listened to Mississippi's silken voice, full of warm empathy, yet telling tales of killing and dying, and not in an easy way.

A thought that had been hanging around for the last few months occurred to him again. Why didn't he try to write a song about Jacinta, and how the end had come here in this very home where he was perfecting the blues? When you got down to it, his own life was straight out of a Mississippi song.

Some bad motherfucker had come to his home and shot in, killing his girlfriend, scaring the life out of him. That was worthy of a song. Except there were a few verses to go yet. He still hadn't got the shooter. Maybe when that was done, he'd sit down and try to put something together. Maybe even get somebody to record it.

Burns laid down the guitar and got to his feet. He had been sitting there for more than two hours, since soon after he'd got up that morning.

He went into the kitchen, opened the fridge, just as he had done an hour ago, and looked again, as if somebody might have sneaked in and restocked the thing. No surprises. Two bottles of beer, half a pound of butter, the dregs of a litre of milk, and a jar of marmalade, with a best-before date that had passed last week.

He was still looking, trying to magic something into existence, when intrusion sounded from his bedroom. The phone was recharging on his bedside locker and still ringing when he got in there. Blocked caller ID, but it could only be one man.

'How goes it?' Charlie Small said.

'OK.'

'Let me guess, you're playing the blues, banging away at that shit.' Small's voice broke into a rasp. It was one of Burns's most recent regrets that he had ever opened up to Small about his life.

A month or so back they'd spent a stuffy afternoon in the LiteAce, waiting for a debtor to come home, when they would introduce him to the concept of facing the music.

Whiling away the hours, suffering through one of those over-forties pop stations, Burns asked about Small's taste in music, which turned out to be bad, like really fucking awful. He was into eighties stuff, the New Romantics, Duran Duran, Spandau Ballet, that kind of gunk. He even gave a tortured impression of Tony Hadley doing one of those hits. Burns was glad he didn't know the song, but it was scary.

Burns had tried to explain to him about the blues, its history, where it had come from, what you could get out of it, but none of it seemed to register with Small.

'Let me get this right,' he'd said, his face all twisted for a rummage around in his brain. 'It's nigger music, but not like rap and that stuff. I mean it's old-time nigger music, right?'

Then, his tongue loosened, Burns's passion awoke. He made the cardinal error of telling the guy about his guitar. He might as well have said he had taken up ballet dancing.

Now, any time Small rang, he had to crack some joke. Burns couldn't make out whether the guy was more stupid than he'd first thought, or whether he just didn't give a shit. One way or the other, he was fast moving from taking the piss to reaching the point of serious disrespect, and he should know that that kind of situation couldn't be maintained for too long before something happened.

'The big chief,' Small said. 'He wants to meet up in Blanch this afternoon.'

'No problem,' Burns said.

'Looks like somebody has been a naughty boy,' Small said. And then that laugh again, coming all the way from Hell.

Chapter Fourteen

Burns spotted Pascal Nix from across the car park at the shopping centre. The early-afternoon sky was closing in low and black. The car park swept down to the entrance where Burns could see Nix walking towards the sliding doors. Burns and Charlie Small had just got out of the van, and were about to plough through the matrix of cars.

He could see that the boss was bareheaded. From where Burns stood, looking down on the back of the guy's head, the hair drug didn't seem to be working. Maybe it was just the darkened day, or maybe he had never seen the guy from this vantage before, but it looked like he was going to be as bald as a coot before long if he didn't get that transplant.

When the pair of them entered the emporium, Nix was standing there, just on the right side of impatient. They turned to walk through the centre, Burns and Small on either side of their boss.

The broad aisles were light of traffic, a few women here and there pushing buggies, the odd besuited man wearing the demented look known best to males who consider a shopping centre to be one step away from a gas chamber. Piped music wafted through the air. Ben E. King was asking somebody to 'Save The Last Dance For Me'.

'Rickshaw was lifted last week,' Nix said.

It took Burns a few seconds to remember who Rickshaw was. Now he had it. The knacker who supplied the car for that guy who did Jacinta. His interest went up a notch.

Charlie Small's wild eyebrows raced up his forehead, but otherwise he kept any surprise under wraps.

Nix said, 'He got careless. They nabbed him for clocking a rake of motors, and handling two others that he knew were nicked. On top of all that, stupid cunt was drunk when they brought him in. He was climbing the walls with the DTs while they were turning him over.'

Small said, 'He did his James Blunt impression?'

Nix looked at him? 'Who?'

'The singer.'

'Fuck the singer. Rickshaw told them he had an in with me. Said he owed me big-time, which was about the only thing that wasn't lies. Said he'd set me up with something for them, if they'd cut him loose. They went with it.'

Small stopped in his tracks. 'Somebody in there telling you all this shit, Pascal?'

'Naw. Those fucks really have it in for me. It was the same with your old buddy Stanners. They're pegging away at anybody who's close to me, or even a clown like Rickshaw, who barely knows me. Rickshaw ... You couldn't make this up. Once they let him go he's off on the tear, out in the Westwood Inn. Then he starts blabbering about all this stuff and he thinks it won't get back to me.'

'How soon?'

'Today. I don't want him having any more cosy firesides with the law. Looks like it's going to be down for the afternoon. My guess is he'll be inside his dump of a caravan pissing it up.'

Small said, 'He always smelt like a rat.'

'He'll probably be hammered on cider, but let him know it's

coming. See if he shits his pants.'

A woman walked towards them pushing a buggy, a little boy trailing her in a grumpy wake. She leaned down towards the buggy, hair falling on her face. For a second, Burns was grabbed by a notion that it was Jacinta. But then the woman raised her head to reveal a face of harassed freckles. Burns shook his head. It wasn't right that Jacinta's kids were growing up without a mother, just like him.

'You're OK with this, Dara?' Nix said.

'Sure, no problem.' He thought of the gypsy in his filthy caravan, surrounded by bottles, living like an animal. Doing him maintained a sense of order. He had it coming to him. He had played his role in disrupting order in Burns's life, chaos blasting its way into his home. Nobody was going to miss that toerag.

They arrived at a pool in the middle of the centre, the sound of water falling all around. A few small boys were sitting on the marble plinth at the pool, throwing copper coins into it. Nix sat down on the plinth. Charlie Small stayed on his feet.

'Charlie, you wouldn't get us a coffee? I like to sit here sometimes, watch the world go by,' Nix said.

* * *

By the time Karen made it back into the city, the rain was driving down in sheets. She found a parking bay, no bother, on Leeson Street. She turned off the ignition and sat there for a moment. Once the wipers were stilled, the view through the windscreen melted with falling rain.

Outside, a few brave souls scurried from one place of shelter to another under the cover of umbrellas. She could see across the street to where little rivers were running tight against the pavement, flowing madly to a drain. One young guy, togged out in navy sports gear , under a black beanie, walked along the pavement as if he was bathed in sunshine. Karen wondered whether he was out of it or just in a defiant mood.

She was torn on what exactly to do. A quick scope of the street failed to locate a pay-and-display machine. Did she get out and go in search of one, like a stray animal seeking out the Ark? Or could she take a chance that no parking attendant in their right mind would venture out in this storm?

Why take the chance? To get soaked would be a minor inconvenience. To attract the attention of a narky attendant could lead to all sorts of problems. She took a small pink umbrella from the passenger seat and opened the door. It took her a long, soaking twenty seconds to locate a machine and shell out. Back at the car, she threw the ticket at the dashboard, locked it again and opened the boot. She had to heave the suitcase out. There was no question of it getting damaged in the rain, she told herself. She dropped it down onto the road. On just touching the handle, she could feel something coursing through her body, adrenalin, definitely, fear, maybe, but whatever it was it would keep her on her toes.

This was the real deal. The product was out in the open, out where it could be stumbled upon, where she could be nabbed. Over the last three months she had grown accustomed to visiting the houses armed with caution. Now she was no longer behind closed doors but out where disaster might lurk.

She slammed the boot and heard the voice from behind, raised against the driving rain. 'Do you want a hand with that?'

He was dressed in a beige trench coat, the collar pulled up as far as his ears. The umbrella was blue, with an insignia that included a rugby ball. He had a hand out, to help or to take.

'No,' she said.

He recoiled in the rain. 'Suit yourself,' he said, and walked on, his feet dancing around puddles. She looked in his wake, drops of rain falling from her fringe to her nose. The suitcase had wheels, which was just as well. Here she was, dancing through the rain, suitcase in one hand, umbrella in the other. Mary Poppins never had to put up with this kind of weather.

Within thirty seconds she was standing at the door. Creole answered on the first ring. 'Could you give me a hand?' she said to the intercom. She turned and looked out at the street. The cars were swishing through surface water. There was nobody out there, nobody in sight. She was sure she'd get used to this, but right now her nerves were at her something awful.

* * *

Charlie nodded and waddled off. Burns wondered whether he would come back with a big, dirty bun for himself.

Nix looked up at him. 'What's the odds that he won't be able to resist ...?'

'Fella's unreal,' Burns said.

'Fuckin' cholesterol. How is he still alive? Sit down, Dara.'

Burns sat, and Nix leaned over towards him. Burns got a whiff of bad aftershave.

'Charlie's a good man, and he's loyal.'

'I can see that,' Burns said.

'But he's not the sharpest tool in the shed.'

'I can see that too.'

Nix looked at him, checking whether he was taking the piss. 'What I'm trying to say, Dara, is that we got something coming up that I want you to take a lead in, but you gotta do it in such a way that Charlie doesn't take offence. You get me?'

Burns wasn't sure where this was going, but so far he didn't like it. Easing himself out of Nix's operation, rather than getting further into it, was on his mind. He had a few euro put away. This whole deal wasn't working out the way he had envisaged it. He missed his own company. The only way he would have any interest in staying onside was if a big payday was in the offing. So far, nothing was showing up.

Nix sighed, ran his hand across his head. Burns tried to avert his eyes, in case Nix thought he was focusing too much on the thatch.

'You remember that woman who came to see me a few months back, the grow-house bird?'

Burns saw the woman now. Not bad-looking, she'd had a bit of attitude, which he liked, but meant she could wade beyond her depth without knowing it. 'Sure, couldn't easily forget her.'

'Well, it's harvest time. I'm meeting her to begin calling in the money I laid out. Are you with me?'

Burns nodded.

'Except she doesn't know it yet, but we're taking over the operation.'

Burns wasn't surprised. He hadn't thought about it much in the months since the day the woman – what was her name? Karen – had walked into Philly John's. But when he heard afterwards what she was at, he was blown away. Who did she think she was dealing with? There was no way Nix was going to let her earn big money on the back of his. 'You want me to take care of it?'

'Yeah, but, like I say, bring Charlie along with you. Don't make him feel as if he's getting frozen out 'cause he's not. It's just that he doesn't have the brain needed to do this thing properly.'

'What about the woman?'

'We'll have to see how she takes it. I can't guarantee anything. If she gets all crazy on us, I don't know. Thing is, there's some serious bucks at stake here. Last time I was talking to her, all she'd say was that she had three houses on the go. So for starters, that should be the guts of a hundred grand. Then, with everything set up and ready to go, we get a second crop under way and another ton comes in for us by the end of the summer. There'll be lots of euro to go around for everybody.'

Burns found himself switched on. If he went through with this, he could be out in six months, well padded into the future. Besides, the job had all the appearance of taking sweets from a child. He said, 'What was she at anyway? How was she going to sell the stuff?'

'Exactly what I asked her, Dara. Told her I could help her out, but she said no, she had her own channels. Channels. That's what she said.'

'She have anybody working with her?'

'Yeah, another old friend of yours. Remember our porn star?'

'Who?'

Nix swung his head in an arc, turned back to Burns and spoke in a lowered voice. 'The guy on the sex tape. Looks like he arrived in Meath straight from the Hollywood hills?'

'Oh, yeah.' Burns saw him again, fella he and Charlie had visited out in the country. Couldn't pay his debts or keep his dick buttoned up. 'The sex tape.'

'I don't know if you'd call it that. There wasn't much sex there beyond the sight of him grunting beneath the woman. You remember her?'

He had no problem recalling that woman, Charlie Small standing over her, unbuckling his belt, her face full of terror. Burns remembered being as afraid of what might fall out of Small's trousers as what he might do to the woman.

'Yeah. She didn't take kindly to Charlie getting up close and personal with her.'

Nix laughed. 'Anyway, that Wyman, he's working with Karen.

I fixed him up and put his debt on the slate until harvest. If he becomes any kind of a problem, he'll have to be introduced to a dose of reality. I'm meeting with her tomorrow, get what you might call a progress report. I'm going to tell her that I need to see my investment in the operation, and that's where you come in. She's going to bring you to all the houses, show you around.'

'Like an estate agent?'

Nix leaned back, as if he'd just seen something in Burns for the first time. 'I like that. She's your estate agent, showing you around the place you want to buy. Or rent. Or just fuckin' take off her.' Nix bent forward and slapped his thigh with his right hand. His eyes widened, and Burns saw in them an unsettling hint of what the man was capable of.

Burns said, 'How was she going to distribute?'

'Hold your horses there. She's not as stupid as all that. I got word last night about this guy, Creole – he's done a bit of business for me before. Depressive fella, sits in his pad getting high all day. He's apparently begun shifting something new.'

'Where did she come across him?'

'He was buddies with my old friend Jake who got nabbed down in Kerry. Cooling his heels in Cork prison at the moment. And guess who he was shagging down there among the plants?'

'Small world.'

'It's about to get smaller. You hook up with the woman, I'll get Charlie to pay Creole a visit. Way I see it, this whole thing could be wrapped up in a few days. It's nice when a plan comes through, Dara. We could all do with a few extra euro.'

Burns stood up, stretched his legs. 'Can't see a problem, Pascal.'

'Me neither. When Charlie comes back, the pair of you can go and take care of that other matter. I just want it out of the way.'

* * *

Creole came down from his turret. He opened the door, looking dry and cautious. He barely took in Karen in her bedraggled state, his eyes wandering over her shoulder in search of trouble. There was nothing out there but cars going by in the rain.

Karen gave him a look. He reached out and took the strap of the suitcase, and pulled it inside, throwing one last glance out at the rain.

Once the door was closed, he seemed to take in her state. 'Jesus,' he said. 'Have you a change of clothes?'

Before she could answer, a door pulled closed somewhere up the stairs. Feet sounded on the steps. A woman, young, twenties, wearing a see-through mac, hair piled up under a knitted purple hat, appeared before them. 'Hi, Creole.'

'Maggie.'

Karen felt as if she was shrinking into herself. She didn't want to meet anybody in this state. And how did it look anyway? Here she was, suitcase in her hand, moving in with Creole. Maggie gave her a half-and-half look, sympathy and curiosity. And then she was gone.

Creole heaved the suitcase to his turret. He laid it down flat on the floorboards, the timber darkening from the dripping rain. He ran the zip open, looked down and then up at Karen.

'How much?' he said.

'Twenty kilos.'

'Jesus. Maybe I could …'

'No. Do whatever you want after I'm gone, but right now I want to get this done and get out of these clothes.'

Creole got to his feet, went to the sink and filled a stainless-steel kettle. 'We have a problem,' he said.

Karen reeled in the impulse to sigh. It could only be one thing. 'Shamie and Jamie?' she said.

'Shamie. Jamie's kosher with the whole thing. Actually, he's mad for road. I think he sees all sorts of possibilities. Shamie doesn't have the same vision.'

'What's the issue?'

'He doesn't want to tangle with the big boys. After you left the last day, we had a smoke. Fuck me, we couldn't even go out after it. You sure there isn't acid or something in that stuff?'

Karen smiled, shook her head.

Creole said, 'Anyway, we just sat here in front of the TV. We hardly spoke. Before I knew it, there was a late-night psychic on the box, giving it loads. She said she knew she was a psychic since she was born.'

Karen could feel the wet seeping into her bones. 'And?'

'Yeah, well, that's when Shamie sort of freaked out. He said he could see the future and it was full of his blood. There hadn't been a peep out of him all night and suddenly he started into how we'd all get blown away, that you were totally out of your depth and if we hitched our wagons to you we'd end up a statistic on the side of some lonely road.'

'And Jamie?'

'He was just laughing at the whole thing, egging Shamie on, but it all ruined the night. It was funny for a while, but then Shamie stormed out. I got a call from him yesterday, didn't apologise or anything but said he was out. He didn't want to step on any toes and said there was a lot of competition out there at the moment and it was too dangerous.'

Karen began peeling off her jacket. A dizzy notion came alive behind her eyes. She could feel it pulling her in. The sneeze issued down onto Creole's floor. She raised her head, and he came to her with a hankie. The last thing she needed right now was a dose, not when there was so much to do.

'You and Jamie?' she said.

'Chalk it down. He came over this morning and we talked about it before sparking up. He's on board. I reckon we can unload the lot between us.'

'You're not going to step on any toes, Creole?'

He looked at her as if she had two heads. His eyes were drooping, she could see now, heading down his cheeks, ready to fall off his face altogether. Karen realised for the first time since she had arrived that the guy was fully baked.

'Me? I'm out to make everybody happy, just like you,' he said. 'If I see any toes, I hop around them, pronto.' He got down on his honkers, picked up one of the vacuum-packed bags, bounced it in the palm of his hand, as if he was weighing it.

He looked up at Karen. 'By the way, you hear anything from Jake lately?'

'Jake?' she said.

'Yeah, Jake. You remember him?' He got to his feet, showed her a row of black stumps. 'Guy who introduced you to this business, you went—'

'OK, Creole, let's leave out the funny-man routine. No, I haven't heard from him for a while. Still no bail. Last time he phoned, things had settled down for him in there. He was playing a lot of table tennis, said the lads who were in a long time were very good at it.'

'I'd say they are. No, I was just thinking. When all this money begins flowing in, maybe you could, you know, put something up for him. Give him a chance to see the outside before his case comes up.'

The thought hadn't occurred to Karen, and she was annoyed now that somebody else was trying to set her off on a guilt trip. She hadn't spoken to Jake for more than four weeks. The last time he had been pushing her for info about what she was up to. He suspected something, but he just didn't know, and she had no intention of broadcasting her business to the likes of Jake. Maybe she could go bail for him when the money rolled in, but he sure as hell wasn't at the top of her list of priorities.

'Yeah,' she said. 'We'll have to see how it goes. No money in the kitty yet, not until you get cracking with that stuff.'

She walked to the door, feeling the need to leave behind any complications about Jake. She'd enough to be going on with.

'I'll give you a shout in a few days, see how things are going,' she said.

'No problem,' Creole said. 'Take care of yourself, get out of those clothes. And, listen, thanks for the credit.'

* * *

The rain was coming down cats and dogs, Charlie Small behind the wheel, leaning forward, trying to see out through the wipers beating against the deluge. He turned to Burns.

'She advertised herself as the best cocksucker in Munster,' he said. He rolled out a laugh, which descended from a cackle to a fit of coughing.

Burns looked across at him. 'Munster?'

'Yeah. Munster. I thought all they did in Munster was play rugby. And there I am, sitting in this hotel in Cork, and the ad on the website says this one, Marigold, like the biscuit, was the best cocksucker in Munster.'

Burns looked out on the rain. That was the other thing that was getting on his wick: Small's appetites.

The wipers beat against the downpour, sounding like an ominous march. Normally, on the way to a job, Burns would have been pumped up, alive, alert, going through all the angles. Not today, and he didn't know why. He turned to Charlie Small. 'It was your first time down there?'

'Yeah. Pascal had half a ton of weed coming in on the coast down in the arse end of nowhere. I holed up in the city for the night. And, looking for a little action, I saw the ad so I rang up and she came over.'

'And was she?'

'Was she what?'

'The best cocksucker in Munster.'

'Fuck knows. I'd never been to Cork before. Where's Munster? Is Tullamore in Munster? I got blown down there one time and it was as good a job as I've ever had. So I just don't know.'

Burns didn't say anything. He didn't use whores, never had. He couldn't understand how anybody would take risks like that, the type of things you could pick up from them. He listened to the beat of the wipers, marching them to where they were going to end the life of a toerag, who had fucked up one too many times, who didn't deserve to live any longer. He couldn't be bothered showing any more interest in Small getting his todger sorted.

Charlie Small said, 'I tell you one thing. She was the best cocksucker I had that night.' And off he went again, rocking in a laugh, the cab gently shaking. Burns tried to prepare. If there was anybody else in the caravan, they would have to go as well. Hopefully, it wouldn't be a woman. He had never clipped a woman, and now, after all he'd been through himself, it would be hard. But what could he do if one was there? Any woman in the caravan with that guy couldn't be right in the head.

The van came to a stop. Once Small switched off the engine, the wipers were stilled. Rain beat down relentlessly, like a warning not to get out. Charlie Small turned and reached his arm around behind the seat. He groaned at the effort of turning. When he came back he had a blanket in his hand, wrapping a Beretta 9mm.

He handed it to Burns. 'Thing is,' Small said, 'there's no standards, no quality control, you know what I mean? Did she ever enter a competition or anything that would allow her to claim to be the best? Did somebody ever give her an award based on performance? Now that I think if it, maybe I should make a complaint to that outfit that puts the hammer on false advertising. What do you think?'

Burns listened to the rain. This knacker had a direct involvement in Jacinta's death. Maybe doing him would help with that dream, the one where he was driving into a cul-de-sac, a brick wall up ahead, his foot stuck on the accelerator.

Small said, 'Are you sure Tullamore isn't in Munster?'

* * *

At least one of the caravans was occupied. As they moved past, Burns could see the yellow glow of a light. They kept going, moving towards Rickshaw's. Burns's focus switched between the caravans and the road in front, as he danced around deep potholes full of bouncing water. Drops were falling onto his nose. Charlie Small had already landed his foot in a hole that reached up to his ankle. He cursed out loud, giving Burns a fright. Concentration was the game now.

Burns was taking up the rear. Just ahead, under a caravan, he could see the black cat peering out from shelter, its fur glistening with rain. Charlie Small turned, looked out at him from under his Yankees baseball cap. His eyes said it was all systems go.

Small nodded at the door, his eyes on Burns. Well, this was it again. Another day, another dollar, the world cleansed of another dumb fool.

Through a window beside the door, Burns could see a shadow moving behind the dirty lace curtain. Rickshaw, eking out the last moments of life. Burns knew one thing. If it was him, confined to a filthy caravan on the side of the road, debts mounting around him like rubbish, he wouldn't have much interest in carrying on.

Small rapped on the door. Burns stepped back a few inches, feet planted apart. The curtain on the window was pulled back, Rickshaw's face pressed against the pane. His mouth was open, eyes somewhere far away. Burns nodded at Small, who turned the handle and pulled the door open.

They stepped in out of the rain.

'Oh, Christ,' Rickshaw said, like a man who was annoyed at the persistent calling of a pair of Jehovah's. 'I don't have it.' He was wearing a shirt that had a dark stain running down its middle. Burns saw that the fly on his brown slacks was open. On the fella's head a salt-and-pepper untamed thatch. Pascal Nix would kill for hair like that, Burns thought, his finger now caressing the trigger in the pocket of his jacket.

'That's OK, Mickey,' Small said. Rickshaw's eyes were alternating between his two visitors, as it slowly dawned on him that this wasn't a routine visit. The rain was now making a racket, drumming on the roof of the caravan.

Burns pulled the gun from his pocket, pointed it between the target's eyes.

Rickshaw's mouth opened, releasing what sounded like a yelp. He bent down, hands around his head, curling up like a man trying to locate the foetal position, as if adopting the pose of his entry into the world might delay his exit from it. A low animal-like whine came from him. 'No, no, please, no.'

Burns pulled the trigger, but it wouldn't slam home. Nothing happened. The fucking thing jammed. He couldn't believe it. This was the kind of thing that happened to amateurs. He looked at Small, who was now full of confusion.

'What the fuck?' Small said.

Rickshaw peeped through his cradled hands. He saw a gap through which his life might leap. He drove at Burns's midriff, pushing the gunman back across the caravan. Burns slammed the butt of the weapon into Rickshaw's head, trying to regain a sense of composure. He knew now why he hadn't been pumped up on the way here. He'd known that this was never destined to go according to plan. He slammed down on the back of Rickshaw's head again, matted blood now forming through the man's hair.

Rickshaw seemed to retreat. Burns looked up to see Charlie Small hauling the knacker by the collar, dragging him away.

'Wait,' Rickshaw said, the momentum now surrendered. 'Wait. The guards have somebody. They have a rat on the inside.'

The two killers looked at each other.

Rickshaw straightened up, his hands stretching out now, looking for help. 'They told me they have somebody feeding them shit on Pascal. They just wanted me as back-up.'

Burns was fiddling with the gun, careful where it was pointing, but determined not to be beaten by this inanimate object. He looked at Rickshaw now, a man inching back in from the edge.

'Who?' Burns said. 'Who is it?'

The shot sounded like an explosion in the confined space. Rickshaw fell to the floor, his head crashing onto a stray can of Strongbow cider. Small was holding the weapon, a snub-nosed pistol that had materialised from somewhere on his person.

On the floor, life was ebbing from Mickey Rickshaw. The second shot rang out, and the air was now thick with smoke.

The two men said nothing, and moved to the door. Burns was first out, stepping back into the rain. There was nobody else in sight as he broke into a jog towards the van. Behind him, Charlie Small moved as fast as his bulk would allow.

Chapter Fifteen

The Ryanair flight from Málaga was five minutes early, the pilot advised his passengers on touchdown. Coulter looked out the cabin window and saw a day that was dull but dry. There were large pools of water in the grasslands off the runway, hinting at a recent downpour. He'd heard that yesterday had been pure cat here with the rain. Some things never changed.

He hadn't been to Cork before. It was like travelling to a new country rather than going home.

He half expected to be rumbled as he walked through the doors into the arrivals hall, but there was no reception awaiting him. The airport felt small but airy, almost homely, compared to what he was accustomed to in Málaga and Dublin.

He picked up his wheels at the Avis desk, from a coiffured attendant who wore a twenty-four-hour smile. All his identification papers were in order, acquired at a knockdown price of two hundred euro in Nerja three weeks ago. He was Henry Reynolds, ex-pat businessman, returning for a short working holiday. There was no need for a disguise.

Now that he had landed, he was in the form to get on with things. The adrenalin was pumping, awoken by the rising sense of righteousness he recognised from his first attempt three months ago.

Earlier in the day, as he was leaving Nerja, he had been lumbered with a great weight. Jan held him tight on the threshold of their home. She had picked up on something, sensed that he was flying into danger. The boys lapped around his legs, begging for hugs, and demanding that he return with Power Rangers and Bob the Builder. As he stood there, an impulse pushed him to walk back in, close the door and put this whole business in the past. But he knew he couldn't.

He was doing right by his family, performing an ancient ritual so that his brother could rest in peace. More than that, though, he knew that if he didn't address it, this thing would haunt him for the rest of his life. The weight had lifted now that he had arrived back.

Once he had the car keys, he needed phone credit. On entering the convenience store, the headline on a newspaper caught his eye. He felt a chill. The front page had a headshot of a face he knew, and a larger photograph beside it of a scene cordoned off with blue and white police tape.

The headline screamed: MAN GUNNED DOWN IN HIS CARAVAN.

The Traveller who had supplied him with the car the last time he was here. He picked up the paper, paid for it at the counter and bought twenty euros' credit for the throwaway phone.

Outside, he laid down his bag, and read the story. The guy, Mickey Rickshaw, had been at home the previous afternoon when two men were reported to have approached his caravan, entered and shot him. The victim had had a number of criminal convictions and was known to the gardaí for supplying vehicles to members of crime gangs.

Coulter felt dizzy. This was the world he was heading into. He was just a day-tripper. All he could hope for was a clean in and out. He wondered whether anybody had ever visited this Rickshaw guy after his last attempt to put an end to Dara Burns. There was no way that this killing had anything to do with him getting a car from the man three months ago.

Outside, the day had a rinsed feel to it. He made his way up through the car park, following the directions he had received at the desk.

This wasn't the time to get nervous. Whatever had happened to the Traveller had nothing to do with him. He wasn't stupid enough to have gone to the same fella again this time around. That was why he was coming through Cork. Not for the first time, he congratulated himself on the precautions he was taking. There would be no trail to Dublin airport, no connection with anybody in the city.

Coulter stepped into the car, an Avensis, his senses drawing in the artificial feeling of newness that rental vehicles always seemed to have. He fished his wallet from an arse pocket and dialled the number. It answered on the third ring.

'Yeah.'

'This is Henry Reynolds,' he said.

'Who's Henry Reynolds when he's at home?'

'I've just got in from Málaga.'

Seconds passed in silence.

'OK, I have you now. Where are you?'

'Cork. Looks like the place is just drying out.'

'Welcome home. You missed the downpour from Hell yesterday. Are we going to meet up to talk about your plans for the garlic business?'

'That's the idea.'

'Right, well, my man is travelling from Limerick, heading for the capital. There's a little place that might suit both of you, town called Kilcormac, on the Tullamore to Birr road. You with me?'

'The midlands might as well be Timbuktu to me, but I'll find it.'

'There's a square in the town. He'll be there at five o'clock.'

Coulter rang off, switched on the engine and eased the car out of the bay. With any luck, this thing would be down and dusted within two days, three tops. There would be no fuck-ups this time around.

* * *

A dozy ambience had settled over Philly John's, now that the few lunchtime stragglers had drifted off. Down in the darkest recess of the lounge, Pascal Nix was spearing the last of his carvery. Sitting opposite him, Karen Riney had her hands wrapped around a cup of sour coffee. She wasn't eating. She had a rule about pub carveries. Only eat them in establishments with which you're completely familiar. And Philly John's was not a place she would ever be familiar with.

The trepidation that normally stalked her ahead of these meetings was absent today. She was feeling good about herself, having made the long-postponed visit to the hairdresser, who had fixed up her confidence in the shape of a concave bob. Now that ching-ching was around the corner, she'd expected more nerves, but all was fine at the moment.

She gave Nix a minute to chew. He was spearing the last piece of his beef, his fork twisting like a mop into the gravy. He didn't suffer from the Irish culinary inclination to horse it down like a chore. She wondered if he had the same patience when it came to business. Well, to give him his due, he hadn't hassled her since they'd made the deal. This was only their fourth meeting, but she sensed it mightn't be as routine as the others.

Nix laid down his knife and fork, pulled a napkin from his lap and touched the corners of his mouth. His right hand moved to his crown and tapped the invisible hat down on the thinning hair.

'You look like you enjoyed that,' she said.

Nix raised an index finger towards the bar, like a man putting in a bid at an auction. 'Fair,' he said. 'Fair to middling. That's the thing about these carveries, they're all about pot luck.' He pointed at her cup. 'You're OK?'

She nodded.

He did a drinking motion to the tall lad behind the bar. His shoulders eased, as if now that he had dealt with that outstanding issue he could give Karen his full attention. 'So how's things going?' he said.

'Things are fine,' she said. 'Getting to the point where we're going to have some cash coming in. I'd expect that I'll be able to begin sorting you in the next fortnight.'

Nix's eyebrows crept up his head in an expression of pleasant surprise. 'And the quality?'

'It's good. I reckon it's going to be a hit wherever we unload it.'

'What is it exactly?'

'Blue cheese,' she said. She noticed how easily the term rolled off her tongue. She had, in such a short space of time, become something of an authority on weed.

The tall man came with Nix's tea. He put the silver pot on the table and departed. Nix righted a cup that had been face down on a saucer. He sat back and let the tea draw. 'There's one other thing,' he said. 'Now, I've been very trusting of you, you appreciate that.'

Karen felt something in her stomach. She nodded.

'But trust is a weird thing. Sometimes, if you're not careful, it can fall into stupidity. You get my drift?'

Karen's face hardened into offence. 'You're not suggesting …'

Nix raised a hand in protest. 'I'm not suggesting anything. I'm just explaining to you why I need to have a look right now at my investment.'

On one level, Karen couldn't say that this was unexpected. Over the months, it had occurred to her that he might want greater input or, at the very least, to get a sconce at the operation. As time had worn on and he hadn't made a move, she had relaxed a little about it. She'd got to the point where she'd told herself that this was the way some of these people conducted their business. It suited him to be hands-off. If anything went wrong, his fingerprints wouldn't be anywhere near the thing. He'd made his investment and let her get on with it. Now those delicately constructed notions were beginning to shake in the wind.

'We had a deal,' she said. 'I'd take care of the business, and you'd get paid your dividend. Mr Nix, this is my operation. That's why it's got to the point that it has. There's nobody else involved to make a hames of it.'

Nix's hand swept back over his crown. He lifted the pot of tea and poured. When he was done, he replaced the pot and looked over at her again. 'Calm down. I'm not saying I think you're doing me. If I thought that, we wouldn't be sitting here. All I'm saying is that it would be foolish of me not to check up on my investment. I like you, Karen, that's why I went for your proposal. I think you're smart. But that doesn't mean I hand over my money to you and disappear.' He leaned back on his seat, hands coming together in his lap. 'I can't do that.'

She didn't like any of this, but what choices did she have? She could tell him where to go, but where would that lead her? She could argue with him, maybe get his back up and introduce tension where up until now there had been benign trust. At the back of her mind, she saw that day when they had been in the ladies' room, her down to her underwear, him looking at her, letting her know that she had now entered his world, and in there he could do as he pleased, and there wasn't a thing she could do about it.

What would be the consequences of allowing him to see the operation? There was nothing there that would be a surprise to him. She had told him there were three houses. It wasn't as if she was making more on the back of his money than she had let on. He could come along, have a look, satisfy himself that the whole thing was kosher, and with a bit of luck he might clear off back to his cave.

But even as she figured it out she felt something slipping from her grasp. Control. And without control, things could begin to shoot off in all directions.

'This wasn't part of the deal,' she said.

'It is now. Look, I need to know what's going on.'

'So what are you proposing?'

'I'd like one of my people to have a look at the operation. That's all.'

'With a view to what?' she said.

'With a view to nothing. I just want to make sure that it's all there, and that everything is coming along nicely. You're new to this business. How do I know that you haven't made a complete balls of things and are just covering up now?'

He had that look now, pained innocence, as if all he was trying to do was get an even break for himself. She wanted to believe that it was genuine, but no way.

She knew there was no arguing with that. It was just . . . why hadn't he done this months ago when things were just getting off the ground? There was something off about him moving in, squeezing her space, right now when the product was about to go to market.

'OK,' she said, 'but not Charlie Small.'

Nix's face fell into mock offence. 'What did poor Charlie ever do to you?' he said.

'He's not great in the people skills department.'

'Charlie'd be very upset to hear you say that.'

'I'm sure he's good at other things.'

'Like what?'

She shrugged. 'Eating.'

Nix wagged a finger at her. 'You're very cruel. I was going to get Dara to go with you. You've met Dara?'

'He's the guy whose girlfriend was shot,' she said.

'Yeah. Bereavement can do awful things to people. But he's getting on with it. It would take more than that to knock him back.'

Karen thought about him, the few occasions they met. He hadn't said much, but his pose was all menace.

Nix said, 'Sure you know yourself.'

She felt that pain again in her stomach. 'Sorry?'

'Bereavement. Your husband. Sydney.'

His face was full of compassion, but it gave her the creeps. Letting her know that he knew all about her. He raised the cup to his lips again, his eyes looking out over the rim at her.

'When?' she said.

He replaced the cup. 'Today,' he said.

'No.' Her voice was firm, reaching out to wrest back some control

'Why not?'

'I can't arrange it at that kind of notice. Tomorrow would be the earliest.'

'OK,' he said. 'Tomorrow it is.' He stood up and extended a hand. 'Our relationship is about to move onto a new plane.'

* * *

She saw the LiteAce approaching, its left indicator blinking orange, as she was pulling out of the car park. The van turned in. She exchanged glances with the slob behind the wheel, made fleeting eye contact with the other guy, Dara. She had his number now, but she was damned if she was going to deal with him on anything but her own terms.

Traffic was light on the way back to Stoneybatter, but her head was full. Now was the time for a calm hand. Within fifteen minutes, she was pulling up outside Heaven's Gate. A part of her wanted to get out of the car, enter the shop and seek out a guardian angel who might look out for her in the near future. But she didn't really believe in that shit. To go looking for inspiration among robed figurines would be an admission of defeat.

Abigail had on her angel face when she emerged from the shop, all sweetness and light. No question about it, she got to drink deeply from a cup of serenity while flogging angels and their wares.

'Hi,' she said, sitting in. Karen reckoned that her friend had lost more than a few pounds over the last month or so. She was looking good. Love was taking her to places that were beyond even angels.

Karen told her they had to get out to Westwood to cut and dry what remained of the crop. First they had to stock up on some nutrients and plastic sheeting to get the next lot under way.

'And what about down the country?' Abigail said. 'Shouldn't I be getting to work down there?'

'I'd like you to head down tonight, if that's OK with you,' Karen said.

'Are you coming?'

'No. It'll just be you and Lover Boy.'

Abigail looked across, her face lit up with a crooked smile. 'He's Lover Boy now, is he?'

'Not saying it again. Be careful. I like Kevin, but. Be. Careful.'

'My guardian angel is—'

'No, no, please. Leave the angels out of this. They can't get their hands dirty. Do whatever but just get the work done. That's all I'm worried about.'

'That's all?'

'You know what I mean.' They were stationary now on the quays, traffic backing up from O'Connell Bridge. Karen had her window lowered. The Liffey was giving up its smells from a low tide bed. She was looking ahead, focused on more than what was in front of her eyes.

'There's something else,' she said. 'I don't know how this is going to work out.'

'Karen, I'm not expecting happy ever after. He's married, for Christ's sakes.'

'I'm not talking about your love life. The business, things might take a turn, I just don't know.'

Now Abigail was looking out at the traffic too, her face changed from serene to dramatic. She was waving an index finger before her. 'Excuse me, Karen Riney. Excuse me, but is that doubt I just heard somewhere in your voice? Doubt?' She glanced across, looking her friend up and down as if to take in how she was dressed. 'Did you get up this morning and put on my clothes? Hello. Doubt is my department, girl. You're the rock, the compass. You're the one driving this thing all the way to success.'

Now Karen looked over, like a startled bird. 'You weren't smoking back there in angel heaven, were you?'

Abigail laughed. 'I'm just saying, you've never had any doubt about this or about your ability to see it through. Don't start letting it in now that we're well on the road.'

Things were freeing up now, traffic shaking itself into acceleration as they exited from the far side of the city centre.

Karen pulled the window up a touch. 'I'm just marking your card. If things get tricky, all of this is on me. I don't know if it would be worth my while sticking around.'

'Tricky-dicky-bicky. Everything will go fine.'

'Sure. But should anything happen suddenly I just want you to be on notice. I brought you into this.'

'I'm a big girl, Karen. And, no, don't answer that one.'

Now it was Karen's turn to laugh. 'I don't know,' she said. 'I just don't know. Back in Sydney, before I got into the technology, I worked in this car-sales place, big outfit in Randwick. There was this guy there, Billy, he'd been in the game a long time, must have been around the fifty mark. Anyway, he told me about one of his best techniques. He reckoned he got the smell of somebody who wasn't yet set on buying, but just had that half-notion. He'd go out to them, suss out what they wanted, and guide them towards the best one on the lot. He'd always have a clipboard in his hand. It was just a prop. But he'd have the purchase form clipped to it. And the killer, he always waved a Montblanc pen, a real pricey one. So when he sensed that the sale was within reach, he'd put the pen on the roof of the car, exactly where he reckoned it would fall. Then when it slipped from the roof, he'd let on not to see it and the customer would grab the pen, save it from falling to the ground. Billy reckoned once they had the pen in their hand they were more than halfway to signing.'

'Wow,' Abigail said.

'I know – amazing when you think about it.'

'And what if the customer didn't reach the pen before it fell, or if he was a real bastard and made no effort to catch it?'

'Billy said you just put it back up there and waited for it to roll. If they didn't bite the second time, do your damnedest to flog them the biggest crock on the lot. Anyway, the thing is, I was feeling like I'd got Pascal Nix, the banker for this thing, with the pen in his hand. He was ready to sign off, to let us get on with the job and just sit back and enjoy a great return from his investment. At least, that was what I thought before I met him today.'

The car was sitting three back from a red light. Karen lifted her hands from the steering wheel. 'Now I don't know. I just don't know.'

Abigail said, 'I'll tell you what you need.'

'No.'

'Yes. She'll be at your shoulder every minute of the day. You can't go wrong.'

* * *

'Did he shit his pants?'

The three of them were standing outside Philly John's, Nix pulling a cigarette from his packet of Major. Charlie Small had his hands buried in the pockets of his fleece jacket.

Burns said, 'I didn't see, Pascal. I wasn't hanging around.'

Nix turned to Small. 'If he had a chance, he must have.'

Charlie Small said, 'But I got him good, right behind the ear. Made an awful fucking mess.'

Nix said, 'But he saw it coming. He knew he was about to die.'

'Sure, Pascal. Jesus, we walked in there and Dara pointed a gun at his head. He knew we weren't fucking around.'

Nix lit his cigarette, pulled hard and exhaled. Burns could smell currents of nicotine sailing by his face. He hadn't smoked in over a decade, but he still felt a moment of pleasure from the waft of burning tobacco.

Nix laughed, but not at anything funny. 'I like them to know that they have it coming. The fear. Let the cunt smell the fear.

What do you think, Dara?'

'I never hang about to find out, Pascal. Just do the job and get out of there.'

Nix transferred the burning cigarette to his left hand, made a gun shape with his right. 'Bang-bang,' he said.

Burns nodded. 'Bang-bang.'

He didn't know whether he should say anything. On the journey back, and over here today, nothing had passed between him and Charlie Small about the knacker's final words. The way things were, the way Pascal was capable of getting, who knows what kind of notion might enter his head if he heard anybody else was going offside.

'He didn't 'fess up, did he, admit the whole thing?'

'Naw,' Charlie Small said. 'I didn't give the fucker a chance to even plead for his life.'

Dara Burns nodded.

* * *

Locating the M8 was a cinch. Coulter was amazed at how the roads had changed in the years since he'd left the country. From his memory of travelling outside Dublin, you were lucky to encounter a run of a dual carriageway here and there for a few miles. Now it was complete motorways between cities, as if the country was a modern European state.

He kept the needle on a steady seventy as he made his way north through the wide, curving roads. He tried to take a note of features that he would remember on his return journey. He slowed passing the sculpture on a hill at the Cashel bypass, a column of thin men – they looked like high kings of old – overseeing the ebb and flow of modern life on a modern highway.

Thing was, back in those days, when there was no faffing around, those kings decided who should answer for their crimes. Justice was handed down in a proper manner. Not like today. If he hadn't decided to do this himself, his brother's execution would have gone unanswered. Back when those dudes on the hill ran the show, Burns would have been dragged out into a public square, hanged till he was half dead, then his limbs stretched until every bone in his body was on the point of breaking, before being cut to pieces with a well-oiled blade, his balls falling out before his eyes.

That would have been the proper end for the likes of him.

He consulted the map on the passenger seat beside him. The Horse and Jockey up ahead was the place to turn off and hit cross-country. Once he left the motorway, the ease of passage decreased. He found himself behind a cattle truck, the waft of manure sailing through the lowered window. After Thurles, he hit across for Birr, moving through flat plains and undulating hills, the kind of terrain that would have been ideal back in the day for chasing down a murderer on horseback.

He was a modern-day avenger, exiled but returning to set the record straight. He thought of Seamus, what remained of his body rotted under the soil up in Balgriffin Cemetery, just a few miles from where they had grown up.

Fifteen minutes after leaving Birr, his destination hove into view.

He drove through the town. There was a large stone building in its centre. Coulter would have bet his bottom dollar that some wing of the Church owned it. It had that look about it.

He was upon the square before he knew it, if you'd call it a square at all. He pressed hard on the brake, and turned sharply, pulling into the space.

There was a chipper, the Café Royale, right here in downtown

Kilcormac. Beside it there was a butcher's, a man swinging a cleaver behind the counter. The time was four fifty p.m.

He turned off the radio, concentrated on the rising and falling sounds of vehicles moving along the main drag. At six minutes past five, a car pulled in. Coulter knew immediately it was his guy.

A man got out, tall, carrying a satchel, which reminded Coulter of what he used to carry his schoolbooks in a lifetime ago.

The man nodded at him, walked around to the passenger side and folded himself into the seat. He was thin and wiry, and wore his hair like a tight-fitting cap. Coulter detected a strong waft of BO. The man placed the satchel at his feet.

'You have something for me,' he said. The accent was flat, full of Limerick City's feuds. Coulter turned his head, looking for stray eyes or ears, but there was only a couple of teenagers within range, bent into a flirtatious huddle. He reached across to the man's feet, but the man placed a hand on his wrist. 'The money,' he said.

'Can I see it?' Coulter said. The man did his own scoping of the square, bent down, and undid the straps on the satchel. He opened it wide enough for Coulter to see the weapon inside, dark, oily, grooves running along the grip.

He leaned across again, his hand flicking open the glove compartment to reveal a brown envelope.

'Do I have to count it?' the man said, taking the money.

'Go ahead.'

'Do I have to?'

Coulter looked out through the windscreen. 'No.'

'Good. There's a balaclava thrown in there for good measure. Just to show that we offer a friendly service.' The man reached for the door handle. 'You're living abroad, aren't you?'

Coulter hesitated. The less this guy knew about him the better. 'Yes,' he said.

'Anywhere nice?'

'Spain.'

'Cuntish weather here at the moment,' the man said. 'Fuckin' summer was over in a day and now we're just waiting for Noah's Ark to hit town.' He opened the door, lifted a foot out onto the ground. 'Anybody I know?' he said.

'No.'

'Business or personal?'

'It's a debt. Overdue.'

The man nodded. 'Good luck with it so,' he said. He stepped out and leaned back into the car. 'And if I was you I'd stay put where you are. This place is going nowhere fast.'

* * *

The minute Brenda came through the door, Wyman saw trouble on her face. She dropped the car keys onto the mini oak table that stood in the hall. Her look was a foretaste of a rant to come, but before she could get started, Ciara and Daniel came bounding out from the kitchen and smothered her skirt in hugs. The fight went out of her face. Temporarily, Wyman feared. Well, fear wasn't exactly the right word. He wasn't in the form for a strop from his wife, but in light of all that was going down, it would be relatively harmless stuff.

The kids wove images of their day for their mother. Wyman retreated to the kitchen. He removed the plate covering her dinner and placed it in the microwave. It was nothing special, Thai green curry, one of the few dishes he had mastered beyond the basic staples since taking up his current domestic role.

It was still bothering him that he'd had to text Karen and tell her he couldn't make it to Pure Mule for a second day. The house was less than an hour away, but with his babysitter lost on the piss, he had been left high and dry.

Momentarily, he had considered bringing the kids with him, but a paternal instinct reeled in that impulse. Despite his hands-on role in recent months, he wouldn't claim to be Dad of the Year but he balked at the notion of bringing his kids to a grow-house, as if it was a trip to the zoo.

Karen texted him back an hour later, said another day wouldn't make that much of a difference, but it did mean he'd have to head down tonight once Brenda got home.

From the sitting room, he could hear the two children unloading their day. Once that was done, they'd be dispatched to bed and a war-council meeting would commence.

Fuck that. It was the last thing he needed right now. Later, when the week was over and the tide gone out on his stress, he'd sit down and explain why he had to do what he did.

A screech of sibling rivalry came from the sitting room. Wyman walked to the back door, turned the key, opened it and slipped out into the mild night. He walked around the long way to the front, to avoid his shadow passing the living room.

He opened the driver's door of the Golf with great care. He winced as the engine came to life, but there was no going back now. The car reversed, and turned towards the gate. As he went out onto the main road, he thought he saw the front door opening in his wake. He gunned the engine to freedom. Driving down the road, he couldn't get out of his head the image of Brenda opening the front door, seeing the departing red rear lights.

* * *

'Hello, is that Dara Burns?'

'Who wants to know?'

'My name is Karen.'

'Yeah.'

'We're to go on a trip tomorrow, I think.'

'That's right.'

'I understand you don't drive.'

'I drive all right, just don't own wheels.'

'Will I pick you up?'

'Sure.'

Karen removed the phone from her ear and looked at it, as if it was malfunctioning, swallowing up the fuller responses she'd expected from the man. OK, two could play at that game.

'Where?'

'Where are you coming from?'

'Town.'

'You know Williamsgate?'

'No.'

He began to relate instructions, the words flowing as if from a tap that had been locked tight but was now loosened. She scribbled down his words on a notepad.

'See you then,' she said.

'OK,' he said.

* * *

The room was retreating into a soft cushion, sleep creeping over her, just about drawing her into its warm embrace, when the phone rang.

The first thing she thought was that it had to be Kevin: some other problem had arisen, the babysitter had been found alive but not well enough to take on his kids.

She pressed the answer button without looking at the call display.

'Karen?'

That wasn't Kevin.

'Who is this?'

'Who … who do you think?'

Her head fell back onto the pillow like a stone. 'How's your table-tennis game coming on?'

'My what?'

'Nothing. How are you?' Even as she asked, she knew that the answer would not be all sweetness and light.

'Still no sign of bail.' His voice lowered. 'The solicitor wants me to tell them everything. He says it will take a huge chunk off the mandatory ten years that's looking down a barrel at me. I don't know what to do. I couldn't survive ten years in here. There's one guy got done for shifting a few kilos of heroin. Only one of the ten suspended. You should see him playing table tennis. Fuckin' unreal. He's in his sixth year now, and after a while you realise the fella doesn't know his arse from his elbow any more. That's what this place does to you, Karen. I don't know if I could handle that.'

She lay there, seeing him in a cell, lying on a bunk, a mobile phone clamped to his ear. They both knew that their relationship consisted entirely of her taking up the role of Good Samaritan. She was tiring of it, but whenever he flew across her radar these days, he always left a trail of guilt in his wake. His stupidity and bad luck were nothing to do with her. If only he would just learn to stand on his own two feet and leave her to get on with her life. She didn't want to ask him how much bail was.

'So what are you going to do?' she said.

'I don't know. You see much of the big guy these days?'

'Who?'

'Mr Small.'

'Jake, I met the guy to sort out your problem. I could live very happily and never see his face again.'

'Are you up to something, Karen?'

'What are you talking about?'

'You just seem … distant.'

'I'm trying to get by, Jake. It's not easy for any of us these days.'

Chapter Sixteen

Abigail was sitting astride Wyman when they heard the commotion.day three There was a screech of tyres, and then the sound of engines barrelling through the dawn into the estate. Wyman could feel the polished floorboards through the sleeping bag, bouncing off the cheeks of his ass. Everything in the world had been fine and pure and cleansed of worry for those few minutes before the commotion bored into his brain, like the first belt of a kango hammer on a shaky Monday morning. He looked up at Abigail. Her face had stiffened from pleasure to panic, and he just knew that her concerns were not his. He wanted to find out what was going on. She still wanted the earth to move.

He had arrived the previous evening just before midnight, and got to work cutting down the plants and hanging them in the drying room. He was a demon with the garden shears when he put his mind to it. He had got through about two-thirds of the master bedroom when she arrived down a few hours later. She produced a bottle of Sauvignon Blanc, which they drank from kitchen glasses until the passion would wait no more.

They started out on the peach-coloured couch, but that Abigail, she could eat a man alive and the two-seater was never going to accommodate her needs. When they were spent, both fell into a fitful sleep, full of the smells of cannabis, and the odd cough from the pump in the bathroom, sounding like the slow death throes of some wild animal.

Come the dawn, he reached out to her through the shallows of sleep, and she responded full of hunger. And here they were, en route once more to distant peaks when the screech of tyres told him that something was wrong, very wrong.

He grabbed Abigail around the waist, feeling through her flesh to something he could get a grip on. She misinterpreted and thrust down with greater force, thinking that he wanted to hurry up the hill. In one movement, he lifted her up and over. Her ass slid down the outside of his left thigh onto the boards.

The couch was the only furniture in the room not flush with one of the walls. There was a unit of hardwood veneer against the wall on one side of the fireplace. The lower part held a sliding-door cabinet, inside which sat the two empty canvas hold-alls. Apart from that, the only other item of note was a stand for the TV, a pre-flat-screen box that only broadcast TG4.

Wyman got up, walked to the bay window, and pulled back an inch of curtain. Outside, the sky was deep purple, brightening from the east. Another car drove past at speed down through the estate, headlight pushing against the dawn. A silent blue light flashed out from inside the rear window.

'What is it?' Abigail said, behind him. She was off the floor now, the sleeping bag draped over her shoulders like a cloak, hoping for an interruption rather than conceding termination.

'The Chinks,' he said. 'They've got the fucking Chinks.'

'Who?'

Wyman walked past her as far as the door leading to the hall. He turned and walked all the way back to the curtained window, willing pace to sharpen his thoughts. 'I knew it.' He turned to her sharply, as if she was to blame. 'I knew it.'

Abigail was standing on one foot, the other poking into her knickers. 'Calm down, will you?'

'Calm down?' He pointed at the curtained window. 'They've got the Chinks. A pair of gardeners.'

She answered with a face full of confusion.

'There's another grow-house in the estate,' he said, words slow and deliberate as if he was talking to a child. 'And the cops have just rumbled them.'

'Oh,' she said. 'Shit.'

'Shit is right. It's shit all the way from here on in.'

Wyman dressed quickly, his eyes never leaving the window, as if somebody or something was liable to come crashing through it at any minute.

'Should we leave?' Abigail said, doing up her bra.

He looked at her. Should we leave? He liked her. This thing they had, he had got to enjoy it, especially after the disaster of his only other foray from the marital home since things had gone sour. She was funny. She made the most of the fact that, apart from one hurried occasion, the only place they ever got it together was in one of the grow-houses. Sure, she was ditzy, but there was no harm in that, not until now. Now that a crisis had arrived, the last thing he needed was ditzy.

'I don't know about you but I'm getting the hell out of here,' he said, sitting down and pulling on a sock.

'Well, thanks very much for that.'

'Let's just go,' he said.

He walked through to the kitchen at the rear of the house. Like the sitting room, it was a paragon of minimalist fashion. Two chairs and a small table sat on linoleum with purple and red patterns. The back window above the sink looked out on a half-built fence. Beyond that lay a field where cows grazed in hides of black and white.

The two cars were parked out front, a careless detail that had crossed his mind last night after a few glasses of vino, but he couldn't be arsed doing anything about it at the time. Now he wished he had been more alert.

Abigail was at his shoulder. She was wearing a long white blouse, her legs bursting out of tight paisley trousers. He noticed that she was shod in sandals. That might be a problem if they had to run. 'What about the curtains?' she said.

'The curtains?'

'In the front room. Once the estate comes alive somebody might notice that the curtains are drawn here in the middle of the day. I mean, hello?'

He gave her a look that said she wasn't as stupid as he had thought. He told her to stay put. He walked back into the sitting room, scooped his canvas jacket from the couch. He pulled back the curtains. The dawn was unfolding before his eyes.

He wondered whether the Chinks had scampered the evening he'd rumbled them, whether they had come back since, and if they had, whether they had any English, whether they could fill in the cops on the competition.

He took the stairs two at a time, checked the bedrooms and bathroom. The master bedroom looked forlorn with most of the stalks bare, as if a blight was making its way across the floor.

He shut the doors, and tried Karen's phone. It rang out again. Something told him he shouldn't be abandoning ship without word from the absent captain.

Fuck that for a game of soldiers. If this place was going down, he had no intention of going with it.

Abigail had moved back into the hall downstairs. 'Is it really bright of us to be sneaking off through the back door and around, like we were burglars of something?' she said.

Wyman watched as she rose once more in his estimation. 'It's early yet,' he said.

'Why take the chance? Why not make it look like we're heading off to work? We could just walk out of here like any normal couple. OK, obviously we're not a normal couple, I don't know what exactly we are, but you see where I'm coming from?'

He nodded. 'You're on the ball this morning,' he said. 'Better still, maybe we should leave separately, especially when we've two cars.'

'Yes,' Abigail said. 'If we leave separately we won't have to put on any act. At least, you won't.'

Wyman's eyes raised to the ceiling. 'Jesus Christ,' he said. 'This is the wrong time, Abigail. This is really the wrong time.'

Abigail smiled at last, a little victory at the corners of her mouth. 'I know,' she said.

* * *

Coulter rose early, did a few press-ups and sits-ups in the hotel bedroom, showered, then rang home. They were an hour ahead over there, but his wife and kids were still in the sack. The boys were doing her head in, acting up, making the most of his absence. 'How long will you be?' she asked, as if his schedule might have tightened since last they spoke.

'Still early next week at the latest,' he said.

'And the earliest?'

If things went well today there was no reason why he couldn't be on a plane tonight. After he replaced the receiver he had that feeling again, the one bursting with dread that told him he was making a big mistake.

He showered and dressed and went down to the dining room

where he put away a full Irish, because he didn't know what the rest of the day would bring.

Traffic was just about heading towards the rush-hour when he hit the streets. He wanted to get out to Williamsgate before things got clogged up. For the most part, he was going against the traffic. He turned on the radio, where there was a heated discussion about vacant hospital beds. They never let up over here. At least in Spain they knew they were in trouble and tried to ignore it. Back here they gorged on misery.

Within half an hour he was touring through the warren of roads that made up the Williamsgate estate. He wanted to get his bearings, ensure that he had all angles covered, both for the hit and the afters. He drove slowly past Burns's townhouse; no sign of life inside. The window was repaired, looking good as new. There was not the slightest hint of what had been visited on the house just a few months ago. Two doors down, a woman was sitting on her doorstep, keeping an eye on two boys who were fighting over a tricycle. He smiled to himself. He thought of his own lads back home, safe and secure.

For a fleeting second, the dead woman came into his head. If things turned out all right, he would, somewhere down the line, try to find out where her kids were. He wasn't a wealthy man, but if fortune favoured him in the future, he would attempt to make some reparation. It was the least he could do.

The reccie took just ten minutes. There was only one entrance on Burns's side of Williamsgate. He checked the time. Just shy of eight o'clock. Most likely, the fella wouldn't be up and about for another hour or two. He took a chance that there would be no action in the next ten minutes, retracing his tracks to a convenience store he had passed a few minutes previously. Inside, he stocked up on coffee, water, three sausage rolls and a couple of red tops. He was back outside the entrance at eight twenty. Now he just had to wait. His hand reached under the seat, felt the cold steel of the gun. The sense of doom that had permeated his thoughts earlier in the morning began to lift. It wouldn't take huge luck for this thing to be wrapped up by lunchtime, certainly before the end of the day.

* * *

Wyman gave Abigail all of three minutes. She had walked out the front door, local resident, en route to work, got into her Seat Ibiza, done the three-point turn and was gone in a puff of exhaust fumes. Once he got the text from her to say the coast was clear, he went to work. He pulled the two hold-alls out from the unit by the wall. Upstairs, he packed the dried buds into the bags, pretty much filling them out. By his calculation, the stuff in them must be worth something north of thirty grand.

Not for the first time, he wondered if a couple of bags of that size would be missed. If he'd had the wherewithal to take it and find a dealer himself, he'd make serious inroads into his debt with Nix. Whenever he thought of that bastard, a sense of entrapment fell over him. The man still had the tape. Once he'd paid him off, he could expect to get it back. But most of all he just wanted to be shot of the guy.

There was a stepladder on the landing, next to the makeshift fuse board. He stepped up and stuck his head into the attic. Cool air blew across his face. The place was packed with much of the smaller furniture from downstairs, laid out on sheets of plywood spanning the joists. For a while now, his main worry about the house was that the ceilings over the bedrooms might collapse under the weight of holes for the lighting. So far, the work was a tribute to whatever cowboy builder had put together this estate.

Downstairs he checked everything, glanced at his watch. She'd been gone a good ten minutes. He walked to the front window and threw what he hoped might look like a casual glance out onto the estate. On the far side of the road, two uniformed teens were ambling towards the entrance, one of them twisting a head of curls back in the direction they had come from.

He stepped into the Golf. For once, he was proud of his wheels. Who in their right mind was likely to suspect a Golf driver of running a grow-house? As he pulled out of the estate, another squad car approached and turned in, this one cruising at a lazy speed.

Wyman switched on the radio, fiddled the dial until it registered a midlands station. That would be the first media outlet to get word of this morning's raid. He really needed to find out what was going on.

* * *

Karen wasn't familiar with this part of the city, so far north, just inside the M50. She would have preferred to meet Burns in town, and right now she was cursing herself for the moment of weakness in which she had offered to pick him up.

Out of curiosity, she would have preferred to collect him at his doorstep. She wanted to know how these people lived. Did they deck out their homes like gangstas from the TV? On their brief encounters Burns had struck her as understated, quiet, shy almost. Maybe he was just an inarticulate psychopath.

She was passing an industrial estate on the left, prefabricated units in greys and greens inside a fence of black steel. The other side of the road was necklaced with a row of tan-brick townhouses, which looked neater than she would have guessed out this way.

Up ahead, the lights were red. She craned her neck for one of the landmarks Burns had mentioned. There it was, Charlestown Shopping Centre, sitting beneath a tower of apartments. The lights turned just as her bag on the passenger seat moaned for attention. She reached across, fished around inside for the phone, pulled it out and glanced at the dial. Kevin.

She tapped down the indicator and pulled in. Please let there not be another cock-up. He had assured her the babysitter was sorted for today.

'Kevin?'

'We've a problem.'

'The babysitter's still on the missing list.'

'I wish. The law arrived in Golden Eagle Valley this morning. Our friends from South East Asia? They've been nabbed.'

'Are you sure?'

'Well, it's that or somebody in there has murdered their family. The place was crawling with squad cars.'

'Were they in the house?'

'I don't know. It's a break for us if they weren't.'

Karen massaged her temple with her free hand. She had been prepared for this, but she wasn't ready. Not right now, not with the other complications. There was always the prospect of breakages, a house going up in flames, but she had assumed that might be a couple of harvests down the line.

'Where's Abigail?'

'She's sitting here beside me. We took both cars and met up here. We're in this one-horse town, Kilcormac, about eight miles from Tullamore.'

'How is she?'

Karen heard Wyman repeating the question, and Abigail's response: 'Surviving,' she said, her voice sounding far away. 'Takes a while for the morning to get under way out here in the country.'

Karen closed her eyes. At least her friend wasn't put out. 'What do you think?' she said.

A silence swelled on the line, as Wyman strung together his thoughts. 'Nothing's set in stone,' he said. 'If they've got the gardeners, then who knows? Those lads are a long way from home. They might be clued in to what we were at, especially after our introduction a few days ago. Maybe they'd talk. If I scared them off the other day, then anything's possible. Maybe the law will be in and out by lunchtime and we can go back again. But I'd stay away for a day or two. If nothing happens by then, check it out and see what's what. It's not dead yet, but it's in intensive care.'

Karen was grateful that Wyman's take on the situation chimed with hers.

'OK. I have to pick up Nix's guy, Burns, and bring him down today.'

'You've got a ready-made excuse to put him off now.'

'I want it over with. Look, why don't the pair of you go to the Middle Kingdom and I'll meet you there with him? I want to let Nix and his people know that there's a few of us involved, makes things look a bit professional.'

'Maybe we can put on a show for him, a little pantomime or something.'

'Don't go there.'

'Karen?'

'Yes.'

'This can't go completely wrong, can it?'

Karen tried to envisage him sitting there, parked up in a lazy midlands town, Abigail beside him, wondering where the hell her guardian angel was.

She softened her voice. 'Kevin. This is the business. We knew we weren't making woolly jumpers. There were always going to be problems cropping up and we've just hit a few. We can manage this. I told you, I have all bases covered. Trust me.'

'OK,' he said. 'We've done well to get this far. No reason why we can't bring it all home.'

'You should go into motivational speaking, Kevin.'

'Fuck off.'

'See you in a few hours.'

The instructions on the passenger seat said she was now on the right track. A mile or so up the road, a sign done in stone and slate, rising to the size of an adult, said that she was now entering Williamsgate. She pulled in, checked for his number and dialled.

* * *

Coulter's first instinct was to duck down behind the steering wheel. Then he copped himself on, just in the nick of time. What a wally he'd look if anybody clocked him.

He couldn't believe it. Dara Burns was presenting himself for death. He was standing there, just down the road at the entrance to Williamsgate, as if inviting his executioner to give it his best shot.

He dipped his hand beneath the seat, felt the cold steel. The gun was at his feet now, trembling in his hand. He'd get out of the car and walk over. Burns would have to see him coming. Then what?

Burns didn't know what he looked like. The chances were he wasn't carrying. He could turn and run, back down into the estate, but he'd never escape a bullet that way. Coulter considered himself to be pretty fit. He'd keep up with the guy. He'd make sure of it.

But all of this wasn't right. He had envisaged a run-in during which he could get accustomed to Burns's routine, pick a time and place, preferably after dark, certainly not mid-morning out in the bright open.

No matter, it had to be done. This was it. He reached for the door handle, heard the click.

Then he saw a car pull out beyond Burns, heard a horn sound. Burns turned and the vehicle pulled in beside him. Coulter cursed, a long sigh deflating his lungs. Burns sat in and the car took off. Coulter tried not to look as they passed him, but he reckoned it was a woman behind the wheel. He looked in the rear-view mirror, shut the door again, and turned the ignition key.

He couldn't make out whether he was angry or relieved.

* * *

Right across town, over on the southside, in the heart of Dublin 4, Charlie Small pressed a buzzer. While he waited for a reply, he turned and looked out on Leeson Street. Nice address, this. He wondered how Creole had found the place. One thing for sure, the spacer had made a good move. As long as he didn't have a procession running down the garden, it was unlikely to attract any attention.

The buzzer crackled into life.

'Yeah.'

'Mr Creole, it's your friendly sales director here.'

There was a silence, the sound of Creole's mind trying to figure out a way to avoid a visit that was already on the threshold of his home.

'Hi, Charlie. Jesus, it's a rotten time. I'm really fucked with this flu I've picked up.'

Not half as fucked as you're going to be, sunshine.

'Buzz me in,' Small said, congratulating himself on his patience.

'I'm in bed, man. I should be all right tomorrow if that will do.'

'This is the second time. Buzz me in. There won't be a third.'

The line went dead and the front door began buzzing. Charlie Small walked through. Any time he visited this toerag, the stairs killed him. They went on for ever. Fella hardly ever went out. Small wondered whether he got whores in to keep him company. He laughed to himself. Yeah, probably fills 'em full of smoke and jumps 'em when they're paralysed from the stuff.

Charlie Small would be the first to admit that he was not in a good mood. A feeling had enveloped him that he was getting the short end of the stick. When Nix had told him about this operation, he had assumed that he would be dispatched for the inspection job. He'd liked the idea of going around the houses, casting a cold eye over them, letting the bird and that other clown know he was running the show. It would have provided him with an opportunity to revel in his power without actually having to exercise any violence. That was the kind of gig he loved best. Letting people know that he was in charge. No threats, at least none that weren't buried deep below the surface, just the force of his personality making it plain that he was the man, the brains, the organiser, and, if really necessary, he could provide the muscle as well.

Instead Burns had got that gig. He'd nothing against Burns, even if the fella was as odd as two left feet. But Charlie Small didn't think Burns had much between his ears that you could rely on. The fella was a shooter, cold, focused and alert, but he didn't seem really clued in to life. And when he had spilled out about playing the guitar, well, only that Charlie had professional respect for him, it would have provided endless material for taking the piss. The guitar. The blues. The greatest load of bollocks Charlie Small had ever come across and, God knows, he'd seen a lot.

On the second floor, a door opened and a petite young woman emerged. Her face turned serious when she saw Small blocking out the light. He tried to put on his best smile, and spoke between heaving breaths. 'How do you manage those stairs? They could kill a man.'

She offered a nervous smile, but had to wait until he made room before she could escape. Small watched her descending the stairs. She moved well in her nice little ass.

By the time he got to the turret, the door was ajar. Creole was wrapped in a brown towelling dressing-gown, sitting on his throne. Maybe the fella really had been in bed, not that it mattered. Small thought he heard a sniffle from Creole's general direction, as if for his benefit.

He shut the door. He gave it a few seconds for his breath to return. Creole didn't even turn to greet him.

'That bird on the floor below?'

Now Creole's head wheeled around. 'Maggie?'

'Have you poked her?'

'Naw.'

'Is there a jockey in there?'

'Don't know.'

Small walked around, stood in front of the scarred coffee table. He noted that there was no sign of smoke, which was a first. He clasped his hands together in front of his crotch. 'You don't know?'

'I don't see much of her.'

'Creole, when's the last time you went chasing skirt?'

'Jesus, what's this? The Spanish Inquisition?' Creole showed a line of black stumps, which did nothing for Charlie Small's mood.

'I axed a question. When's the last time you've got laid?'

'What's that got to do with anything?' Creole's lips were buttoned again. He pulled the dressing-gown tighter around himself, against the cold, or maybe thinking it might offer some protection.

'That's twice I've asked.'

'No, it's not. You've asked me two different questions.'

Charlie Small said nothing. His breath was still laboured. He looked down on Creole, conveying his displeasure at this insolence, but offering one last, unspoken, chance.

Creole said, 'Last week.'

'Last week?'

'Maybe it was the week before. I don't keep count.'

'A whore?'

'Charlie, what is this?'

'I'm getting tired of asking a second time.'

'No, it wasn't a whore.'

Small walked over and back across the floorboards, his eyes wandering as he moved, taking in everything in this shithole. 'I'm just curious. What woman in her right mind would ever allow you to fuck her?'

'Christ, you're hardly Casanova yourself.' Creole had barely got the words out when a dark cloud of regret came down over him. He sat up, aware that he had just handed this man a platter with his head on it, if the guy so wished to take it. Charlie Small just nodded without offence. 'Sorry, Charlie, I didn't mean that. It's just you come in here and …'

Small held up a hand. 'Forget about it,' he said. 'Your insult has no impact on what I'm about to do.' He pulled from his pocket a snub-nosed pistol and pointed it at Creole's head.

'Stand up,' he said.

Creole got to his feet, his hands shooting towards the ceiling, fully awake and alert now.

'Charlie, I didn't ...'

Small straightened his shooting arm.

'This is the last time I'm going to convey something to you for the second time. Get my drift? Speak again and you might as well be shoving your head between the cheeks of your arse to kiss the world goodbye. Now, take off that robe.'

Creole's mouth opened, but shut again sharpish. He pulled open the corded belt, let the gown fall to the floor. Small looked him up and down, a scrawny specimen in a pair of green boxers, a guy who couldn't even handle a good dinner if it was put before him. For a second Charlie Small wondered what it would be like to be that thin, to live day to day without having to wonder where your next feed would come from. But he knew that a body like that required Olympian effort, and a form of denial that was nothing short of religious. It wasn't the life for him.

'On the floor,' he said. Creole's mouth opened again, the hint of a 'Ch' sounding. But he stopped on the precipice of Charlie Small's patience, and let his eyes do the pleading instead. He was shaking now, like a leaf at the height of winter, hanging on for dear life to a tree's limb.

'What the fuck did I tell you about having to say something twice?'

Creole got on his knees. His eyes closed as Small walked towards him.

Charlie Small's boot connected right between the eyes, in exactly the location where he would have shot the toerag. Creole sprang back, falling to his side onto the floor, a pool of red forming by his face, eyes all over the shop.

'OK,' Small said. 'You're allowed to talk now. And you're going to tell me all about your dealings with Karen, the woman who thinks she's running a nice little business for herself. You're going to tell me everything, and I'll make sure that when I leave you'll be able to get yourself to a hospital. Hold back, and it's a coffin they'll need for you, although how the fuck they'd get it up those stairs is beyond me.'

Chapter Seventeen

They weren't in the Middle Kingdom ten minutes before she started into him. They had arrived in convoy, Wyman leading the way in his Golf. Once they left the main trunk road, he kept the speed constant at around fifty m.p.h. He surprised himself at how disciplined he could be behind the wheel since he got involved in this business. Once the stakes had been upped, he had no problem observing the rules of the road.

The morning was chilly for the time of year, but he kept the side window lowered. Paul Weller's 'Wildwood' drifted out from the speakers.

Wyman switched his gaze to the rear-view mirror now and again. Abigail's face in the following car was a picture of concentration, eyes on the road, her head off someplace else. He had begun to notice that look in recent days, as if she suspected she was getting done and was trying to figure out how exactly it was happening to her.

Not his issue. She knew the score. Keeping balance was what it was all about at the moment. A mirthless smile passed his lips as he thought of the performing seal again. There he was, leaping from the water in cool, smooth arcs, a ball balanced on his beak, turning full circles to give everybody a piece of the action. He was the focus of their attention. He was the one carrying the show. It was all about balance, all about keeping everybody happy, Brenda, Abigail, Karen, and the other thing as well. Not to mention that scumbag Nix. Pressure was bearing down on him from all angles. This was where the men got separated from the boys.

He took a sharp bend, where branches of hawthorn hung over the road. He looked once more at the mirror. She wasn't happy, no question about that.

The road straightened, and he recognised the stretch. A bank of poplars on the right gave way to the entrance to the house, their pride and joy, the Middle Kingdom.

The gate to the property was centred on a semi-circular stone wall, set back from the road. A faded brass nameplate could still be seen to the right of the gate. Mountain View. He always got a kick out of that. There was nothing more than a drumlin within sight whichever way you looked from here. Whoever had the place back then obviously possessed a sense of humour. He pulled up outside, and stepped from the car, engine still running. Abigail pulled in behind him.

He unlocked the padlock and pulled the chain off. Just then, a drone sounded from the direction they had come, and a tractor came into view, bouncing along at a fair clip. He stopped and waited. The vehicle slowed as it approached the stalled cars. Wyman raised his hand and smiled at the driver, a young guy wearing a woolly hat despite the time of year. The guy waved back, his eyes taking in all that was before him. Wyman could see him already filing away the scene, to be reproduced somewhere locally later, among friends, in a pub, whenever they mused on the presence of strangers in their midst.

The tractor disappeared up the road. Wyman walked over to the Seat Ibiza, where Abigail had lowered the window. 'Everything cool?' he said.

'Sure, why not?' she said, letting him know that it was anything but. He nodded and returned to his vehicle, then eased it through the gates. The entrance road to the house had been laid long ago, but time had moved in, punching potholes, and tearing at the surface. A strip of corn-coloured grass was breaking through at the centre, and on both sides rows of beech provided a guard of honour behind a split-rail fence all the way to a large gravelled space in front of the house, where there was enough room for half a dozen vehicles. Wyman came to a stop and sat there for a moment.

This had been one of Karen's best moves. The house was ideal, tucked away here on the border of Westmeath and Offaly. It would take a lot to raise suspicions in anybody local. The nearest neighbour was the guts of half a mile away and, Wyman had discovered, he was a recluse, who farmed a living from a few acres around his abode.

This place, though, had once been home to farmers of a far more prosperous bent. The main residence dated from at least a hundred years ago and was fronted by nine tall windows, fixed on two floors symmetrically around the entrance door. The front wall was done in stone the colour of slate, the roof tiled in black.

Inside, there was a large kitchen at the back, and three other rooms, which estate agents referred to as 'reception rooms', as if they were reserved for soirées with visitors where everybody would drink out of tall-stemmed glasses. Upstairs, there were four bedrooms, walls papered in a fashion that had been all the rage when Moses was a boy. Three of the rooms were in use for growing, the fourth set up for drying. The only concession to the late twentieth century was an en-suite renovation in the master bedroom. This had proved particularly pleasing to Wyman because it provided the irrigation system for that room, leaving the main bathroom to cater for the other two. Sorting out the electricity had been no problem, and he hadn't bothered with much beyond a primitive ventilation system as nobody was around to take in the smells.

The big plus about this place, though, was the future. At the back, three outhouses hugged the perimeter of the large yard. Two were large enough to cater for serious growing operations. Once the second crop got under way, this place could turn out to be a real gold mine.

All of that was in the future, but right now Wyman was more concerned with the present. That thug was going to arrive with Karen in the next few hours. A couple of Vietnamese gardeners were at large somewhere in the midlands, if they weren't in custody. And Abigail was wearing a look that was as dark as yesterday's skies.

* * *

Traffic thinned as they made their way out of the city on the M4. Once they left Lucan behind, Karen put a little pressure on the pedal. Burns had been out this way as recently as a fortnight ago. He and Charlie had travelled to Maynooth to negotiate with a student who had completely forgotten that he had to cough up for a debt on foot of what, these days, was an unfashionable coke habit.

They had approached the student and explained that he appeared to be acting unreasonably. After two minutes of negotiation, when that tactic hadn't worked, they'd bundled him into the van and driven him out of the university town to a quiet spot where a humpback bridge crossed high above a shallow river. The student had been held by his ankles over the bridge until he'd come to his senses. Half the debt had been duly delivered to Philly John's just short of a forty-eight-hour deadline. As they now drove steadily past the turn-off for Maynooth, Burns wondered whether he would be called on to retrieve the other half.

Burns was growing bored now, the woman, Karen, doing little to lighten the mood. After explaining briefly that they were heading down to the two houses she was using in the midlands, she lapsed back into silence. She was acting as if she didn't want to risk conversation, afraid of where it might lead, what she might let tumble out about the operation.

'No music,' he said.

She looked over at him, satisfied that this line of conversation was safe enough.

'Radio's broken,' she said. 'Can't afford a proper iPod, or to hook something up. Usually I'm in the car on my own. Do all my thinking here.'

'Is that a hint?'

Her laugh was short and perfunctory. 'No. That's just the way it is. You big into music?'

Now it was his turn to hesitate. Sharing the blues with Charlie Small had been bad enough. Who knows what this woman would make of it. Still, he didn't get much opportunity to talk about it.

Karen pressed down on the indicator and overtook a truck. She could drive, he'd give her that.

'Older stuff really,' he said.

'Yeah? How old?'

'Ancient.'

'OK,' she said, all slow and deliberate and full of questions. 'Is this a quiz? Do you want me to guess what you're talking about?'

'I like the old acoustic country blues, the authentic stuff that … It's just … It's not like what you hear on the radio.'

'I know the blues,' she said. 'My husband, Peter, he was big into Eric Clapton. I got him an album once, *Me and Mr Johnson*. It always reminded me of that song that was out at the time. 'Me And Mrs Jones'. Robert Johnson, that was his name. You ever heard of him?'

'Don't talk to me about that fucker.'

Karen shifted her eyes from the road, gave him a look of surprise. 'I remember now,' she said. 'Peter, after I got him the album, he went and looked up this stuff about Robert Johnson 'cause the guy was Clapton's hero, and Clapton was Peter's. Anyway, he gave me the rundown. Was there something about him selling his soul to the devil so he could be a great musician?'

'He did in his bollocks,' Burns said. That was what happened when people got stuck into this. They had no cop on. They just didn't know what they were talking about.

'Look, the fella could play guitar, he could write a song too, but then he went and got himself killed and years later, in the sixties, when all these guitarists like Clapton and Keith Richards copped on to the blues, they raised Johnson up as if he was Jesus Christ himself.'

'So he didn't get down with the devil?'

'Did he fuck. He went away for a couple of years and got to grips with his craft. When he came back he was so good, nobody could understand it. But then he couldn't keep his hands off other men's women. Some guy whose missus he was fooling around with poisoned him. But after he died, all this shit grew up about him having made a deal with the devil, that he'd sold his soul for his talent.'

'Wow,' she said. She was behind an eight-axle truck now, looking impatient about overtaking, but she'd got him going. He could never have had this conversation with Charlie Small.

'Thing was, Johnson pissed away his talent, drinking and

whoring. I heard of that Clapton album. Didn't get it because it was imitation stuff, like those bands that call themselves tribute bands.'

'Jesus,' Karen said. 'I don't think anybody would call Eric Clapton a tribute band.'

See? She didn't understand. Even when he tried to have a civilised conversation with her about the blues, she couldn't see the wood for the trees. 'I've nothing against Clapton. He can play the guitar. But he's not the real deal. Those guys way back, they were the blues. All those musicians like Clapton, they go on about Robert Johnson. But what about Son House? Who remembers him? He could wipe the floor with Johnson.'

'Son who?'

'Son House.'

'That's his real name?'

'Yeah, far as I know.'

'Mr and Mrs House called their son Son?'

'How the fuck do I know?'

She laughed. 'So he grew up in the House of the Rising Son?'

Burns gave her a look that was full of menace, and she stopped laughing pronto.

He said, 'How many grow-houses you got going anyway?'

* * *

Coulter could feel the buzz. There were four vehicles, three cars and a small van, between him and his prey. They were heading out west, hitting the midlands. He felt reassured. Most likely, they would be meeting on neutral ground. The car radio was on, some fella waffling about shopping for men. You'd have to wonder about the calibre of person they got on the radio here.

The Beretta was under the seat. His night-bag was in the

boot. Once the thing went down, he would make straight for the airport. He had an open return ticket from Cork, but he'd have to see where they ended up.

He tried to imagine where they were headed, who the woman was. Obviously, it hadn't taken Burns long to get back on the horse after the death of his girlfriend. Of course, a bastard like him was beyond any basic feelings of regret or bereavement.

He wondered about the woman. She'd looked OK from the fleeting glimpse he'd caught of her. You'd have to presume she had half a brain, and possessed feelings that weren't frozen. How could she have anything to do with that animal? Still, no matter what, she was a civilian, and he would make sure this time that innocents didn't pay the price for her boyfriend's depravity.

The outside indicator light flashed orange on the Honda Civic, and she overtook a large white truck. The other vehicles in her slipstream appeared content to stay behind it. Coulter gave it a few seconds before following the Honda. On the far side, it had settled down to a cruising speed. Coulter drew his foot back from the pedal – he didn't want to come too close. He touched lightly on the brake and fell in behind. There were no other vehicles between them now. This was too close. He didn't respond when she accelerated a little. Stay cool, he told himself. For a second, he had an image of the car ahead pulling into a lay-by, himself following, walking up to the stationary vehicle, just as Burns had done with Seamus, and delivering Biblical retribution. Chance would be a fine thing.

Still, all of that was fanciful. The main thing was that it would get done, and done fast, so he could go home to being a father, a husband, again.

The most likely scenario was that they were going away for a night in some hotel. That might present problems, but if there was even the most brittle romantic bone in his body, there would have to be some occasion when they were alone somewhere, far from eyes that might stray into an incident.

He felt reassured. This time, whatever developed, they would be on neutral ground.

* * *

Wyman was at the window in the front room, the history of the house weighing on his mind. Outside the day had opened up just about on the right side of middling. A few banks of cloud lurked in the distance, but the sun was in lazy form, refusing to get worked up about an Irish summer.

Brenda had rung twice, wondering where he was, who was going to run the house when she went out to work. He texted that Rosanna was back in action and he'd organised for her to pick up the kids. He was up the walls. What more could he tell her?

He wondered when the place had last been alive with the sound of children. Maybe it had gone through decades in the lonesome possession of a bachelor farmer. And now, just as then, it was part of the prevailing economy. Where once farming had been the dominant way to turn a buck, now everybody was reduced to scrambling for a slice of the drugs market. When you got down to it, what was going on was basic crop rotation. Spuds and vegetables were out, weed was in.

The room was dark, despite the hour, its large square sash window under the shadow of a sycamore bordering the space outside. When this house was built, it was designed to defend against the more inclement elements rather than letting in the light.

There was a Van Gogh print of wheat in a field on the wall over the fireplace, and a framed sepia-toned photograph of a young girl that could have dated from a century ago. A grand piano stood forlorn, yet perfectly at home, in the corner; a pastel two-piece suite took up the centre.

He heard a clanging sound from the rear of the house. He couldn't fucking believe it. Abigail was back there in the kitchen, banging pots and pans, as if she was his wife, summoning him to address what ailed her. He could take that shit from Brenda. That was part of the contract. But, Jesus, this woman was getting carried away with herself.

Once they'd got into the house it soon became apparent that any need she had for passion had abated in the course of the flight from Pure Mule. For his part, the piling on of more stress had rendered him severely horny. Once they were through the front door, he had backed her up against a wall, next to an ancient mirror bordered with dark oak, but she had ducked out from under his arms. Now he just felt irritated.

Abigail's head came around the door. 'Is there anything to eat in this house?' she said. Her eyes were wide, looking for trouble. She walked into the room, hands down by her sides, ready to leap to her hips in a strop flourish. She liked her grub, he knew that, but, to be fair, they hadn't eaten today.

'I could eat the Lamb of God myself at this stage,' he said. 'But the last thing we need is to draw attention to ourselves by going into some local shops. If they have any shops out here in the sticks.'

Now the hands did rise to her hips. 'So what are we going to do? Sit here and starve?'

'Maybe you could give a shout to your angels to pop in with a takeaway,' he said.

She looked at him as if everything that was pissing her off had just crystallised. 'Fuck you,' she said, and walked out of the room.

Wyman closed his eyes. OK, he could have held back. He knew the angels were a touchy subject, not to be trifled with. But he wasn't here to be anybody's punchbag.

He pulled out his phone, tapped in a text to Karen: Middle Kingdom calling. We need food.

Abigail walked back into the room just as the text was entering cyberspace. 'I think we have to talk,' she said.

Oh, Christ, not now. 'Listen, Abi, everything is up in a heap at the moment. You want to talk, that's fine. We'll do it once we get over this stuff that's happening today. Karen is on her way down with this … man who is a serious criminal. Let's just get past his visit and then we can talk. Right now, I'd like to get to work on the plants. I've texted Karen. She'll bring food for us. Could we just get to work? I promise, later we'll talk.'

Abigail was twisting a strand of her hair with her right index finger, fashioning a rope from it. She took her finger away, patted down the hair. 'I'm just a handy lay for you, amn't I?'

Wyman looked to the ceiling. The cornices were done in white plaster, circular patterns that were in fashion fifty years ago. They didn't make them like that any more. 'Abi,' he said. 'You've got the wrong end of the stick.'

'Have I?' She walked over, stood directly in front of him, waiting for his eyes to come down and meet her accusation.

He let out an exaggerated breath. 'Yes, you have. You know my situation.' His hands went up to present the case for the defence. 'Everything is a bit complicated right now. But I told you, we can talk about it. Come on.' He reached out to her, but she recoiled from his touch.

'What exactly do we have, Kevin?'

Did she really want him to answer that? They had a good time once or twice a week, fucking each other's brains out. They had a laugh now and then. They had the here and now. They had, as Bob Seger might have told her, tonight. Who needs tomorrow?

'I don't know what we have, Abi, all I know is that we have … something, and right now that's as much as either of us can handle. Look what we're at. How can things get serious in the middle of all this?' He spread his hands wide in the room. 'We're growing dope. It's not exactly where love stories begin.'

He could see her face was crumbling now that she'd manipulated a crisis from a drama. He told himself she would cool down by the time Karen and the other guy arrived.

'You're something else,' she said, her voice breaking free of composure. 'You really are.'

He moved towards her but she was through the door before he got anywhere, slamming it behind her. He stood there and willed Karen to arrive now so that this little outburst could be parked. He could hear her going towards the kitchen, then footsteps approaching again. He braced himself for screams and tears, but the door handle didn't move. Instead, he heard the front door being pulled shut with abandon. He moved to the window, saw her march across the gravel to the Seat Ibiza. Should he go after her? He was torn between his dignity and having to explain her absence to Karen. Fuck it, he said to himself.

The car gunned off up the driveway in a trail of spite.

* * *

Karen's eyes stayed on his wallet. Burns looked at her, rising panic on his face. The car swerved slightly, but they were all alone out on the motorway, the next vehicle a good fifty yards ahead of them.

'Listen, I'm a bad passenger. Will you keep your eyes on the road?'

'Sorry,' she said, turning to focus on driving. 'Where did you get that?'

'This?' He held up the wallet. He had just pulled it from the pocket of his tracksuit bottoms to locate a card for a little record shop in town, where he could still get his hands on some vinyl, as if he was a preacherman, spreading the gospel. 'You saying I stole it?'

'No, no, but it's salmon skin, right? I know by looking at it. Here, show me.' Her hand went out. He pulled the wallet back, as if she was a mugger. Then he copped on to himself and handed it over. She ran her left hand around it, feeling the coarse texture, the threaded fins, the fish's skin. 'I'm interested in this stuff,' she said. 'Me and my husband, we were going to get into it, making fashion accessories from salmon skin. He got the idea from somebody back here who was already doing it.'

They were coming up fast on a truck. Karen put her left hand back on the steering wheel, the wallet nestling between her fingers. She looked in the rear-view mirror: nothing behind for at least twenty yards or so. She hit the indicator and accelerated past the truck.

Back in lane, she went on: 'We were going to start up a business putting that stuff together.' She passed back the salmon-skin wallet.

'Yeah?' He looked down at it, as if it held secrets he'd only just copped on to. 'I know a guy who does it here. Maybe he's the same one your husband had heard about. They call him Jimmy the Fish.'

'Jimmy the Fish?'

'Yeah. I've a lock-up down in the North Wall, and his workshop is next to me. Jesus, the smell in there would send skunks out with their hands up. He gets the skins in from Howth and puts them through this chemical process, all these ancient machines chugging and farting all day long. And then he hangs them up on these lines, as if he was drying his jocks or something. Anyway, it works. He gave me this wallet, and a credit-card holder that I've back at my place. But he's done all sorts of shit with it. He's made boots for women. You'd look good in them. He had some models that are on the telly pose in them. They're the business all right.'

Karen looked over at him, but his face was pretty serious. He was intense, she'd give him that. Sometimes you could almost forget that he was a criminal. She wondered whether he had ever done anybody serious harm.

'It struck a chord with Peter,' she said. 'The idea of doing something different that was new. We were going to have a go at it in Sydney. Set up a whole operation. When he first got the idea he thought about importing the skins from Ireland, but that would have been crazy. Bringing them halfway around the world. But Peter said we could market it as an Irish thing. He mentioned Fionn MacCool.'

'Who?'

'Fionn MacCool. The guy who burned his finger on the salmon of knowledge.'

'Right,' Burns said, but Karen could tell he hadn't a clue about Fionn MacCool.

He said, 'One thing, though. You need to know what you're doing with those skins. I mean, they can be a bastard if you don't go about it the right way. It took Jimmy the Fish a while to hit on the right formula. One evening when I was down at the lock-up, we went for a few scoops and he told me about the trouble he'd been having. When he started out, he showed it to this kid in art college, and she thought all her Christmases had come as one. She said she wanted to design and make a dress, skimpy little number, with the skins. Jimmy was all on for it. He saw money coming out of the bushes all over the place. So she did it, and it worked out well too. He'd a photograph, pretty cool. The student wore it well. Sexy, even, that little dress, and you realise that it's all made from the skin of fishes.'

Karen kept her eyes on the road. She wondered whether Burns was trying to visualise her in it. She'd never thought you could do that with the skins but, hey, that's business for you.

'Anyway, that was fine, but a few weeks after she had it in this college exhibition she was at home in her bedroom and she noticed a bit of a smell, but she didn't pay it much heed. She wasn't at home all that much, being in college and that, but a few days later she went into her room and the place was ponging. She opened the closet and the fucking dress was disintegrating, skins falling off it and down onto her shoes and the smell nothing short of wicked.'

'Wow,' Karen said.

'Yeah. So, you see, it just kind of shows you need to know what you're at if you get into any kind of business. It can take a while to get things right.'

Karen switched her eyes from the road to Burns. 'I think I could make a go at the fish-skin thing.'

'I wasn't talking about fish skins,' Burns said.

'OK. But your friend, Jimmy the Fish, he did get it right, didn't he? I mean, it came good in the end.'

'Oh, yeah. He's flying. But fish skins and weed, they're from different worlds.'

Chapter Eighteen

Karen rolled the Honda to the front of the house and killed the engine. There was one other car there, Wyman's Golf. The small talk had run its course.

'OK,' she said. 'Just a quick thing. You and Kevin have a bit of history?'

'His problems are connected to Pascal. Nothing to do with me.'

'Oh,' she said. Wyman had told her there had been some physical stuff, but nothing you'd write home about. That was how he had described it.

'Anyway, none of that has anything to do with me or this operation. I'm just assuming that everybody can get along when we go in here.'

Burns looked her in the eye. 'If anybody's holding grudges, it ain't me.'

Karen nodded, and got out. Burns followed, setting one foot on the pebbles, as he surveyed the house across the roof of the car.

Wyman opened on the second rap. He had a wooden mallet in his hand. Karen took in the tool, her eyes asking whether it was a weapon.

Wyman looked at it. 'Just sorting out the bathroom. Pump acting up in there.'

Karen handed him a brown paper bag. 'Sandwiches,' she said.

'Abigail's not here,' he said.

'I was wondering where her car was.'

'You've just missed her.'

'Is she coming back?'

'I doubt it.' Wyman's face was neutral, innocent, but he had to know that she knew Abigail's leaving had nothing to do with the work.

Now wasn't the time to address the issue. She turned to Burns, who was standing behind her, and waved her hand to effect an introduction that she knew was not needed. 'You know each other,' she said.

The two men exchanged what would pass for nods, and all three entered the house, leaving the door ajar.

Wyman led them into the front room. He opened the bag and dipped his hand in, pulling out a wrapped sandwich. He began to unfurl the wrapping with his right hand, manoeuvring things without letting go of the mallet. Burns looked around the room, surveying it as if he had some professional knowledge of the interior of farmhouses of a particular vintage.

'Welcome to the Middle Kingdom,' Karen said.

Burns was looking up at the cornices running around the ceiling's edge. 'Where's the weed?'

Wyman spoke through a mouthful of ham, cheese and white bread. 'Jesus, we're in a right hurry.'

Burns said nothing.

Karen said, 'I was just going to give you a rundown on how we manage things here before showing you around.'

'The grand tour,' Wyman said.

'Kevin ...'

Burns turned to face him. 'Nice to see that you found something useful to do with yourself.'

Wyman said, 'And you're gainfully employed.'

'What did you say?'

Wyman took another bite of the sandwich, his eyes staying on Burns. 'Doing Nix's bidding. I suppose somebody has to.'

'Eat your fucking sandwich.'

Karen moved towards them. 'Kevin, maybe it would be best if you went back to doing whatever we interrupted and I can show Mr Burns around.'

'No problem – but be careful. This guy can turn nasty at the drop of a hat.'

Burns took two steps forward, entering Wyman's immediate orbit, and said, 'How's the porn business these days?'

Karen reached over, placed her hand on Wyman's arm, just above the elbow. 'Kevin, please, I really don't have time for this.'

The two men held each other's eyes for all of three seconds until Wyman broke into a smile. 'I'll be upstairs,' he said.

When this was over she'd give him an earful. Bad enough that he and Abigail were loving up, but now his other problems were surfacing in the business.

Wyman turned and walked through the door. The sound of stairs creaking beneath his weight drifted back into the room.

Karen said, 'Could you cut him some slack?'

'No problem,' Burns said. 'He didn't tell you about the tape?'

'What tape? He said you called to his house one day collecting debts for your boss.'

'But he didn't tell you about the tape.'

'I don't care about ... What tape?'

'He got himself in a tangle with this woman who wanted money for a little roll in the hay they had in a hotel. She taped the whole thing, and when he didn't want to play husbands and wives with her, she went looking for money. He asked Pascal to sort out the woman, so me and Charlie Small went to talk to her and got the tape. Except Pascal is holding on to it as collateral until Wyman fixes up with him. Nobody told you anything about this?'

Karen could feel a little pressure at the front of her head. There was too much going on. She thought of Abigail, and what she might make of the whole thing. It would be better for everybody if it remained beyond the reach of her emotions. How had she missed it? She knew Kevin Wyman wasn't an angel, but this. She looked at Burns and beat back an impulse to ask him what he'd done to get his hands on the tape.

'I don't want to know anything more about it,' she said. 'If I knew … Look, can we just do what we have to here and I'll bring you on to the other houses? Please, I have a business to run.'

Burns shrugged. 'Fine by me. I'm not looking for any trouble. But I'll tell you one thing. He's changed since I met him a few months ago. He's a lot cockier. Maybe he thinks he's a big-time operator now, but a man can get too cocky.'

* * *

Coulter was doing his rag. He couldn't believe he'd lost them out here in the back of beyond. It was as if the bog had opened up and swallowed their car, all the way into the heart of a Bond movie.

He was on a side road now; man, they were all side roads out here. He passed a house set back from the road by a sloping concrete yard. He saw a black and white dog materialise in the rear-view mirror and take after him.

Up ahead on the right there was what looked like a quarry of sorts, huge, gaping potholes filled with water, a large sign in blues and greys shadowed by trees caked with the dust kicked up by a thousand heaving trucks.

He kept going, but his right foot was now more delicate on

the accelerator, slowing down to a pace of uncertainty. After a few miles – more houses, a cottage shop with a roof of thatched straw – he pulled in and did a three-point turn. There was no way they had come this far.

He retraced the car's tracks at a leisurely forty, his gaze arcing left and right in search of a clue. He kept note of the miles clocking up.

Then he spotted the blue Honda Civic, way in behind a bank of poplars that rose up over a stone wall at the side of the road. The vehicle was parked next to another in front of a large house that had to host a farm, Coulter reckoned. He reversed the car until he arrived at an opening on the left, parking on a grass track that led to a corrugated-iron gate.

He killed the engine and listened to his own breathing. A faint chorus of birds called from beyond the confines of the vehicle, but nothing else. This was it. Perfect. He didn't possess a silencer, but out here his deed would go unheard. The luck was with him now, just as it had been absent on his last shot at this.

He felt around under the seat until his fingers touched the cold steel barrel. He pulled it out and let it fall into the long pocket of his fleece. He bent down to fish deeper into the recess beneath the seat until he touched the woolly texture of the balaclava. This he deposited in the other pocket. He had been ready for a long time. Now he was prepared.

It took all of thirty seconds to walk back to the point where he'd spotted the Honda Civic through the trees. A quick sconce up and down the road revealed he was alone. He climbed the wall, one foot after the other, and then with his left hand flat on a stone at the top, he leaped to the other side, landing in a soaked patch of grass. Cold water seeped into his bones. Shit. He had to remember that he was out in the country now.

He made his way through the trees in long agricultural strides.

As they ended, he paused behind a slim trunk, and surveyed the house.

The two cars in the yard were empty. Curtains were drawn on the upstairs windows. On the ground floor, four windows, two each side of the front door. He saw something move behind the window to the left of the door. He ducked back behind the tree trunk on instinct, but it would never have hidden his bulk.

He set out across the fields to give the house a wide berth. The best way of entry was through the rear of the place. He felt exposed as he walked, the grass long and bent from the elements, reaching halfway up to his knees. He could hear a dog somewhere, the squelch of his shoes and his legs pushing against the grass. Then a noise exploded in his ears. He threw himself into the long grass, his right hand reaching inside his pocket. He raised his eyes to see in the distance the source, a fucking cow, big stupid eyes staring at him, as if trying to figure out why this grown man was on the deck.

He was at the back of an outhouse within a minute. He moved against the whitewash, turning a corner, where a yard opened up. The back door was there, set between two windows, larger than those at the front. He pulled the balaclava from his fleece pocket and slipped it over his head.

He stepped onto the yard, the gun now in his hand. He was exposed again as he walked. Then he was at the door. He reached down and tried the handle. It fell down at his touch. Open.

* * *

'OK, let's look at the product.' Karen came out of the kitchen after Burns, waved towards the stairs. He began ascending in slow, deliberate steps, each met with a creak underfoot. Karen was about to follow when somebody came through the back door, wearing something that covered all of his face but the eyes and mouth. He was carrying a gun.

She froze. The man raised the gun level with his eye, arm outstretched, pointing it directly at her head. His left hand went to the mask, the index finger crossing his lips, as if they were both part of some conspiracy.

He moved towards her, gun in hand, finger on his mouth, and then he looked up and over the stairs' banister to meet the eyes of Dara Burns. Burns betrayed no shock. He took off, two steps at a time, and disappeared around to the right on the landing, hopping over the lines of tubes and cables.

The man grabbed Karen by the collar of her jacket, pulled her towards him until her ear was at his mouth, the gun barrel touching her right temple. He spoke in a whisper. 'You won't be hurt if you do what I say. This is between Burns and me.'

Through the waves of fear, Karen could feel something warm between her legs. She'd pissed herself, here at death's door, her life flashing before her.

'Who else is in the house?' he said, that low growl again, pulling at her collar as he spoke.

Words wouldn't come to her. She shook her head. He grabbed her hair, yanked, and she reacted with a yelp for survival.

'The car outside. Somebody else is here. Where?'

She still couldn't speak. She pointed up the stairs with all the enthusiasm of Judas. The man turned her until he was at her back, and wrapped his left arm around her neck. 'Let's go,' he said. She couldn't move until his knee met the back of hers, prompting her along. She began mounting the steps. She could smell a faint hint of sweet deodorant from him. His breathing was heavy on her ear, the barrel of the gun taken from her temple and pointing ahead up the stairs. An oily waft drifted from the weapon.

She looked up to the landing, the spaghetti junction of cables, Kevin's fuse board nailed to the wall, the ancient wallpaper peeling off. She had never noticed the faded yellow wallpaper before, never noticed a lot of things she had taken for granted. In the turbulent dreams that sometimes haunted her sleep, she had never seen the business taking this turn. A lunatic pushing her up the stairs to a violent death. She didn't deserve this. She wasn't a bad person.

Now she was sobbing.

She stepped onto the landing. The grip on her neck tightened against her breathing. The gun was at her temple once again.

He looked to the left. There was nothing in there but the bathroom and a box room. To the right the landing opened up wider, leading to three bedrooms, where all the growing was done.

'What's in there?' the man said. The gun was pointing to the left. She thought she could see it tremble, and it occurred to her that he might be as scared shitless as she was.

'Bathroom,' she said. Her voice sounded far away, as if from the recess of a dream, dark and disembodied.

'Burns,' the man shouted. She heard a tremor in his voice. 'It's either you or the woman. You want another woman to die for you? Get out here.'

A tumbling sound came from the master bedroom, as if somebody had fallen. The man wheeled her around to face the door. It was ajar, like an invitation. He pushed her ahead of him.

'Burns,' he said again. 'Come out. Come out and face me like a man. How many people have to die for you?'

Karen closed her eyes. She was being pushed towards the door, opening into her death. She didn't need to see where this was leading. Why her? Why now? She had been burdened with the same luck as Peter, involved in something a bit dodgy, doing no harm to anybody, and then finding Fate had it in for her, throwing her into this world of guns, just as a storm had driven Peter to his death. She felt her feet kicked against the door from behind, as if she was a rag doll. And then everything started to go crazy.

* * *

When he first heard the commotion downstairs, Wyman was in the bathroom, tightening a connection between the cold tap and a pipe leading to the pump. He stopped, listened, heard the stairs creaking with urgency. He pulled back the door and saw Burns hopping over the cables, pushing open the door to the main bedroom and disappearing inside.

Wyman closed the bathroom door. He laid down the wrench and picked up the mallet. Confusion was all over him now. Where was Karen? Had Burns done her some harm and was now up here looking for him, looking to finish off the job? He waited until the creaking stairs served notice of more action.

He heard Karen saying something. Then the shouting voice. It wasn't Burns: somebody else was in the house, somebody who must be looking for the weed.

Kevin Wyman tightened his grip on the mallet, waiting for the stranger to come through the door. He had to keep it together.

More shouts. They were moving away from outside the bathroom door. To stay here was to invite trouble in rather than meeting it head on, where he might have some chance of a fair shake. He leaned over, and gently pulled the door to open it more than a crack. Somebody was pushing Karen towards the bedroom, a gun in his hand, a balaclava over his head, shouting to Burns as if he knew the man he was looking for was on the other side of the bedroom door.

Wyman stepped out onto the landing. The man was a few yards in front of him. Wyman held his breath and gripped the mallet for all it was worth. He'd get one chance, surprise his only advantage.

The man stumbled on one of the cables, fell forward. Karen cried out as the two of them went tumbling, pushing open the door to the bedroom and falling across the threshold. The man got back onto his knees, the gun now sweeping an arc around the room. Wyman moved fast, swung the mallet hard from behind and connected with the side of the man's head.

He went down on top of Karen, who was motionless on the floor.

The gun spun from his hand, coming down between two of the pots. Wyman moved towards it but Burns beat him to it. His hand reached down and scooped up the gun. He pulled the man across Karen, knocking pots, weed tumbling, but the body was limp.

Burns pulled it clear of Karen. And then he looked at the weapon in his hand, as if examining how best to use it. He pointed it at the balaclava on the floor and pulled the trigger.

Wyman watched as the material exploded, bits of matter flying off across the plants, blood running from the wound.

His ears were buzzing. He looked at Burns, who was standing there with the gun in his hand, his lips moving, but Wyman couldn't hear anything.

Karen's head came up, hands splayed on the floor in front of her, looking to the dead man a few feet away. She raised herself up into a kneeling and then standing position and turned to Wyman. Her lips were moving too, but he still couldn't hear. Had it really happened? Had a man just been shot to death in front of his eyes? Karen moved towards him. He gathered her into his arms, a pair of innocents abroad caught up in a nightmare.

He looked to Burns again, and saw now that the man's brow was beaded with sweat. He felt the heat for the first time, the intense glare from the mounted lamps shining down as if onto a movie set.

The gun was still in Burns's hand, hanging loosely by his side. Burns switched his gaze to the body. He reached down with his left hand, delicately taking the hem of the balaclava in his fingers, trying to avoid the blood that was now spreading out and washing up against the pots.

Burns pulled it free of the head. The man's eyes were closed. His face was pale in death. The first thing that occurred to Wyman was that he didn't look like a killer.

* * *

'Why did you kill him?'

The three of them were in the living room. Karen was sitting on the couch, her arm on the rest. Burns had his back to her, looking out on the parked cars through one of the long windows. The day had turned out dull, but it didn't look like rain. Kevin Wyman stood by the fireplace, talking to Burns's back.

'Why?'

Burns turned to face him. 'Are you a fuckin' psychologist?'

'What?'

'Who said I killed him? Man was lying there, after you assaulted him with a deadly weapon. Who says he wasn't dead before the bullet hit him?'

Wyman's mouth fell open. 'What are you trying to say?'

'I'm not knocking what you did. You saved her life, you probably saved mine, but I doubt that that's what you were out to do. He looked to be gone when he went down that time. You know how to use a hammer.'

Wyman looked at Karen. Her head began to shake gently. 'I didn't see anything. I was too busy being afraid.' She closed her eyes. 'Did you know him?'

Burns turned back to the window, as if he didn't want to deal with the question. 'Never saw him before,' he said.

'But did you know him?'

'I've an idea who he is. Was.'

Karen opened her eyes, looked over at Burns, but he still wouldn't turn around. 'He said something about a woman dying. Is he the same man who shot your girlfriend? Is that why you killed him?'

Burns shook his head without turning to face her, but there was no conviction in it. Wyman kept his eyes on the man's back, knowing now what had gone down. At first, upstairs, as the buzzing in his ears began to subside, Wyman really thought that he and Karen were next, that this guy had lost it and was going to leave them all dead, laid out among the plants.

But nothing happened. Burns placed the gun on one of the pots, sat it there in the shadow of the flowering buds, as the three of them turned to leave the room. The smoke had begun to clear in Wyman's head. This was something between the dead man and Burns. It had nothing to do with him and Karen. They weren't going to be killed. Not now, anyway.

He moved from the fireplace to the couch, stood directly behind where Karen was seated and addressed the man at the window. 'He was coming after you, wasn't he?'

Burns wasn't for turning. He let the question sit between them.

Karen said, 'What does it matter, Kevin? There's a man dead upstairs.'

Now Burns said, 'She's right. The big problem is the body. At least there's plenty of room around here to get rid of it.'

Wyman said, 'What are you talking about?'

'It isn't going to bury itself.'

'You want us to take that man's body and dump it somewhere?'

Burns walked into the centre of the room, stopped before he

got close enough to be in the other man's face. 'Have you a better idea?'

Karen said, 'Oh, Christ.' Her head was forward now, almost on her lap, hands massaging her temples. 'What are we going to do?'

Wyman placed a hand on her shoulder. That was twice he'd made physical contact in the twenty minutes since it had all happened. In the time they'd worked together, they had never touched, beyond the handshake when they'd first met. He felt as if he was invading her space, going beyond the point where she was comfortable, but she looked so vulnerable right now, he didn't know what else to do.

He couldn't handle the thought of going back into that room. The body was one thing . . . but the blood, up there, caked on cannabis like a Crimestoppers advertisement.

Burns was talking bullshit. Kevin hadn't killed the guy. He'd just reacted as any homeowner would if he happened upon an intruder. He was entitled to defend his home, his family, and Karen qualified as family. The guy had a gun to her head.

'Say we were to leave now, head back to the city?' He saw that that made both of them sit up and listen.

'Say we were to just leave things as they are, lock up and head. Would you know anybody who might come down and do a job on the place, you know, with the body and the mess and all that?'

Burns said, 'You want me to get a hold of somebody who might clean this place up?'

'Yeah.'

'Anybody in mind?'

'How the fuck would I know? You're ... in that world. Aren't there people in your line who do this sort of thing?'

Burns's face lightened to a smile. 'Sure, they're in the *Golden Pages*. Under "Disposal".'

'Fuck you.'

Burns turned to Karen on the couch. 'This isn't *Pulp Fiction*. This is the real world. There are no body-disposal companies. That body upstairs is real, real and dead. We're stuck with it.'

Wyman moved towards Burns with a speed that could have been trouble. Burns tensed himself, but the other man walked out past him, going through the door at pace.

'I think this is a bit too much for him,' Burns said.

'Him and me,' Karen said. 'Are we really going to have to bury that man?'

'No other way around it.'

She shook her head, as if trying to shake away what was happening. 'How did he know? How did he know that you'd be here? I mean, don't get me wrong, but if he was just looking for you, how come he ended up coming down here and ... involving all of us? I never ... Jesus.'

Burns took his eyes from her. He stood there in the middle of the room, looking at the back wall, where the piano was. 'Luck,' he said. 'That guy had no interest in what you're doing here. He must have followed us down. Just shitty luck. For you anyway. For me? Maybe things might have worked out different if he'd got me in his sights somewhere else.'

'He followed us? You mean he followed me. In my car? How did he ...' She let the question trail, but Burns had no notion of going after it.

When he spoke, his voice had fallen a notch. 'I think we'd better see how your friend is doing out the back.'

When they walked from the kitchen into the yard, Wyman was out beyond the far shed, in the fields, bent over as liquid spilled from his mouth. A buzzing sound came from him, and he reached down to pull his telephone from a pocket. He looked at the screen, his frame still bent over as if he was carrying an unbearable load.

Burns called to him from across the yard: 'Aren't you going to get that?'

Wyman turned towards them, his face all pain and disgust. The phone in his hand rang out.

Chapter Nineteen

They moved to opposite ends of the body. Burns placed his hands under the guy's armpits, Wyman had him just below the knees. The legs felt stiff, cold, dead. He looked at Burns, the fella's grip, his face, all business, like this was no big deal.

'On three,' Burns said, as if they were lifting a couch. 'One, two, three.'

Wyman reversed out the door, stumbling once as he hit a pot, knocking it over. Karen was standing on the landing, her face on the edge of horror. She had said she wasn't going into the room, where the white lights would show every line on the man's face, every crease in his clothes, every sign that death had claimed him. She had a burlap bag in one hand and a plastic bag in the other. The latter contained the effects that Wyman had handed her after he had removed them from the body. There was a wallet with a band of fifty euros, a credit card, the rental form from the car agency and a couple of cardboard business cards, advertising places in Málaga, Spain. Two sets of keys were there too, one of which was quite obviously for a car. Burns lifted it from the rest, and pocketed it.

The man's wallet also held a picture. When Burns pulled it out,

Karen asked to see it. She held it out and three smiling faces of young boys looked back at her. She replaced it in the wallet.

Out on the landing, she moved forward to the body, like a priest, and wrapped the burlap bag around the head. She had found it in a stack Wyman had stored in the back kitchen. She said she'd go along with this but there was no way she could look into the dead man's face.

To Wyman's eyes, she appeared completely wrecked. He wanted to reassure her that it was all right, that it wasn't her fault they had stumbled upon this nightmare. He could feel something else too. *He* wanted to reassure *her*, not the other way around. The balance of power between them was shifting. He was the one in control now. He was the one who would have to keep the show on the road.

Having applied the funeral touch, Karen reversed into the bathroom to give them room. Behind her, the pump coughed. The lighting on the stairs was dim, a dark yellow from a naked bulb.

Wyman raised the legs up higher as he descended, keeping a balance on everything. Above him, Burns looked down, his face a stone. Once they landed on the ground floor, Wyman reversed towards the front door, making room for Burns. Then Burns led the way, bringing the man head first out through the corridor to the kitchen and out the rear door into the yard.

Darkness had fallen across the midlands. The wheelbarrow was parked by the door, like a hearse from the cheap side of town. Burns got around between the handles and eased the body into it. Wyman let the legs hang out over the barrow, rigor mortis ensuring that they stuck out at a comical angle.

There was a light above the door, but nobody turned it on. There was no fear of it attracting any attention, but this wasn't work you wanted to do in a glare.

Karen materialised beside Wyman, a torch in her hand. She reached over and he felt her touch the sleeve of his shirt, reaching out for affirmation in the presence of death. She switched on the torch, careful to keep its beam away from the body. A shovel and pick were resting against the wall, where Wyman had placed them once they had agreed on the plan. Now he picked them up, shortened his grip to the midway point on the shaft of the shovel, held the pick loosely at the height of its grip and waited. Burns looked at the pair of them. He picked up the barrow's handles and began pushing it across the cracked concrete, the body bouncing in time with the front wheel. Once or twice, Wyman thought the fella was going to tumble out, trying to escape the fate that awaited him, to be hidden in the middle of nowhere, rather than afforded a proper resting place.

Wyman kept pace with the barrow, his hands full of the gravedigger's tools. Karen walked on the other side, torch in hand, the beam's shaft breaking out into the night. The pace was just north of funereal.

Out beyond the yard, the night opened up wide and black. Wyman thought he could see the Slieve Bloom mountains blotting out the horizon to his left. Upstairs, a half-moon, yellow like a section of melon skin, sat high in the night. There were stars too, sprinkled like shards of glass, and no sign of clouds. Wyman could feel the night like he never had before, breathing on him, warning and welcoming at the same time.

Underfoot, the ground was soft and tricky with the print of cattle hoofs. Burns appeared to be having some difficulty keeping the body balanced in the barrow, but there was nothing more Wyman could do. If the fella fell, he fell. And they'd just have to pick him up.

Wyman's left foot stepped on something slippery. A saucer of cowshit. They kept going. He wanted to talk to Karen. They had said barely a word since she and Burns had arrived in the house, trailing death. He wanted to see where things were at. They had to get away from this, from Burns and his world that was not theirs.

Nobody had spoken since they left the house, when Karen eventually said, 'How far are we going?'

'Another bit,' Burns said. A sound came droning from the distance. They all stopped, Burns resting the barrow on the ground. They turned to the source, beyond the shadow of the farmhouse compound. A light was jumping between the hedges, sound of the engine suggesting something more than a car, maybe a tractor. Wyman thought of the young guy they'd met when he and Abigail had arrived earlier. What had he been doing with himself for the rest of the day till now, his life unaffected by the seismic shift that had occurred here?

They pushed on, until a grove of trees at the field's boundary loomed closer.

Burns set down the wheelbarrow. He walked around in a little arc, his feet kicking at the topsoil.

'OK,' he said. Karen shone the light on his face. There was still nothing that said he was out of his comfort zone. Either the guy was made of ice or he didn't find any of this insane.

* * *

Karen watched the pair of them at work and concluded that Kevin looked more suited to this business. Burns had the pick, swinging it without rhythm, grunting like a tennis player each time it hit the earth. He looked to be tiring from early on. He might know about killing, but he wasn't somebody who'd ever spent much time in the company of a shovel.

Kevin worked at a steady pace and seemed unruffled. His thrust of the shovel was firm, the arc through which he swung it perfect, and a neat pile was forming to the side of the hole. Of course, she remembered. Construction had been his game, back before they'd met, before all this.

For the most part, she kept the beam on the point of digging, where Burns's pick softened the earth and Kevin's shovel dispatched it. After a while, once a hole had begun to form, progress slowed, Burns moving in, then retreating to let Kevin get rid of the disturbed soil.

All around them was darkness. Now and again, she switched her gaze to the corpse in the barrow, back there in the shadows, as if it might at any stage leap from its hearse and declare that the joke was over, everybody could go home.

The man was dead. He had died just a few feet from where she had lain, awaiting the end of her own life, scared stiff, losing control of bodily functions, the pungent aroma of weed the last thing she was going to smell before leaving.

That had passed. She was still here, even if this other guy was gone. She wondered about his family, the three boys. What tides of bereavement had he left in his wake? Where would bereavement lead any spouse, like herself? All the way to the desperate plains out here where she was now overseeing the last rites of another life.

What had Burns done to this man? She looked down at him, his face on the fringes of the shaft of light. On the journey down here, she'd thought she had located a piece of him that was human. His passion for music, the way he spoke of those blues guys from long ago, his thoughts on the fish skins. He had been in danger of coming across as a regular guy, not like that other thug, Charlie Small. And now this: the mask had slipped, the brute inside released.

And what now? When they had taken the body from the room,

and she had allowed them to pass from the landing onto the stairs, she had slipped briefly back into the bedroom. The gun was no longer on the potted plant where he had left it after the shooting. Where was it? What did these people do with witnesses? Surely he didn't intend to do away with the two of them out here, making a grave for three instead of one.

Anything was possible, but she wouldn't die again as she had upstairs.

The sound of another vehicle came from the road across the fields. She looked over and followed the broken shafts of light, normal people going about normal business.

'This has to be deep enough.' Kevin's voice came from the hole. The two men were now up to their thighs in it. Karen moved the beam to Kevin's face. His brow was damp. She switched to Burns. The sweat was washing down over his eyes. He was taking a breath or two to work up to a response.

'I think so,' he said. He laid the pick down with a sense of finality. He looked to his hands, and in the light of the beam Karen could see that they were raw with the threat of blisters.

Burns grabbed the side of the hole and levered himself out. Karen's eyes followed him. If anything was to happen it would happen now, with Kevin in the hole, handy for burying if he was shot on the spot. She brought her hands together and noticed a tremor.

Buns leaned over the edge of the hole, his hand extended. Wyman took the offer and pulled himself up. The two men turned and walked to the wheelbarrow, each going for one end of the body without consultation. Burns took the shoulders, the burlap-wrapped head touching his midriff. They moved across until both of them were at the lip of the grave. Karen held the torchlight on the body. She could see in the periphery of the shaft of light the two men nod silently at each other. 'One, two three,' Burns said, and the body went down.

It took them all of ten minutes to backfill. Nobody said a word on the return to the house.

* * *

Burns said that he and Wyman would go looking for the car. Karen could stay back at the house, making sure everything was in order and cleaned up. He said it like an order, not a suggestion.

They drove out in Wyman's Golf and swung left onto the road, retracing the journey out here, everything now black, the half-moon faded behind a bunch of deep purple clouds. They passed a few houses, where no light burned. It was now well after midnight. There was no car to be seen. 'What do you think?' Wyman said.

'We need to find it. It looks like it was hired so wherever it's got there's going to be trouble.'

'How far do we go? At this rate we'll be heading back towards the city pretty soon.' He thought of Karen at the house. She was tough, but since the shooting, he'd seen something that had never been there before.

Eventually, Burns said to turn around. Once back at the entrance to the Middle Kingdom, he suggested they keep going along the road. Within thirty seconds, they came upon it, pulled into the side, in front of the corrugated-iron gate.

Burns got out and tried the central locking on the car. He turned to Wyman and nodded.

Back at the house, he parked the car to the side, where it couldn't be seen from the road. Then they were standing, the three of them, at the front door.

Wyman said he'd lock up. Karen looked at him, her eyes saying they would talk when she'd dropped Burns off.

* * *

The car felt cold when she sat herself in. Burns got in the other side, shut the door and just looked straight ahead. The sound of the engine kicking into life assaulted her ears. She took a deep breath, released the handbrake and set off.

Nothing passed between them for more than ten minutes as they drove through the night, the world around them asleep, Karen trying to rid herself of the image of a man's body in the ground.

At the first sign for the motorway up ahead, she broke the silence in a voice that was impaired and hoarse. 'Are you going to tell Pascal Nix?'

Burns stared ahead when he spoke. 'I have to.'

'Why?'

'I'm working for him. He's got a stake in that operation back there. I could be putting him in danger if I didn't tell him what was going on.'

'Well, I'm not going to tell anyone. You can rest assured of that. And Kevin won't either. Just in case you get the impression that we might. I want you to know that.'

Burns said, 'Who would you tell?'

'Nobody. I mean nobody.'

'You saw a killing back there. You saw somebody being shot.'

She looked at him, but he was still focused on the road ahead, like, she felt, one of those lawyers in a courtroom drama who refuses to look at the witness when asking questions.

'It has nothing to do with me. Or Kevin. I know you and him

didn't get off to a great start, but he's solid. I can vouch for him.' Even after she said it, she knew how stupid it sounded.

'You were part of it,' he said. 'You and him were as much a part of it as anybody.'

Is that what he wanted to hear? No problem.

'Yes, I suppose we were. Everything is just … fucked.' When they had gone out looking for the dead man's car, she had gone upstairs to the master bedroom, where the blood had dried on the leaves and buds. The light from the lamps ensured that it was broken into little crumbles, like muck brought into the house on the sole of a shoe. She couldn't face doing anything about it, just shut the door and left the place undisturbed.

There were only two vehicles ahead of them on the motorway, two pairs of red lights coming closer as Karen accelerated, wanting to leave all that as far behind as humanly possible.

'Could you slow down?' Burns said. She saw anxiety on the man's face. With all she knew of him, all he must have been involved in, he was scared of the possibility of a crash on an empty motorway in the dead of night.

She let things sit for a few minutes before saying, 'I really would like to know who he was. Are you really serious that you didn't know the guy?'

'I think I know who he might have been, what his problem was.'

'There was a photo in his wallet, three boys. Were they his kids?'

'Like I said, I never saw him before in my life. If he was who I think he was, then he thought I had it coming to me on account of something that happened.'

'But you're not going to tell me.'

He just looked ahead, letting her know she had better turn back from that enquiry.

'So what's going to happen?' she said.

'What's going to happen is nothing. There's a body back there and if the law gets involved everybody could be in the frame for murder.'

'But he was the one who was attacking. I mean, if Kevin or you hadn't done anything, I could be dead now.'

'Just remember that. But it doesn't mean the law would see it that way. I'm not taking any chances. This goes no further than you and him. I'm not going to prison. You get that? There's no way I'm spending my days locked up like an animal. This goes no further.'

Karen kept her eyes on the road. Her stomach was acting up now. They passed a sign for the turn-off to Maynooth.

'You weren't expecting any of this, were you?' He was looking across at her now, for the first time since they had set out.

'Of course I wasn't.'

'You just thought you were getting involved in a little business.'

'I knew it wasn't knitting jumpers.'

'No, but you thought there wasn't much to it. That you just get all your skittles in a row and go to work.'

'I'm not stupid.'

'I don't think you are. But you thought the only big problem in this game was the law. That once you could keep your business beyond the reach of the law, everything should work out all right.'

'Sure,' she said.

'But out here, where there is no law, all sorts of shit can happen. You never thought about that.'

'Well, thanks for filling me in. I know all about it now.'

* * *

Wyman heard the news a mile short of his home. It was on the hour on Nova, a rock station he had programmed in because much of the stuff on it went back a decade or two.

'Gardaí have found drugs to the value of two hundred thousand euro in a cannabis-growing operation in the midlands. Early yesterday morning, officers from the National Drugs Unit raided a house in an estate in the village of Coomray. A major operation was uncovered but no arrests were made.'

The gardeners had slipped free. They might well have been gone since that day last week when Wyman happened upon them. The news gave him a lift. There was still hope for Pure Mule; the money was still waiting there to be harvested.

By the time he reached home, the house was in total darkness. He sat for a few minutes in the car, listening to the engine cool and the silence of the night beyond. The clock said it was three thirteen a.m. Brenda would be getting up in a few hours, and out the door before the kids began to stir. She'd want a chat before going to work. She could want all she liked.

He shut the door of the car gently to kill any noise. The front-door key scratched in smoothly, and when he opened the door, the alarm's warning hymn sang out from the control panel on the wall just inside. He punched in the code, and remained stock still for a few seconds to see if anybody had been disturbed. Nothing.

Light poured out at him from the fridge when he opened it. He took the two-litre plastic bottle of milk from the door and drank deeply from it. Of all the sins he committed in this house, the one that really got up Brenda's nose was drinking from the milk bottle.

He thought he heard something from down the hall, but concluded it was one of the kids wrestling with a dream. Then his phone blasted twice to tell him that a text had landed. Karen, asking was he up. He dialled her number and she answered on the first ring.

'Hi.'

'Where are you?' Wyman spoke in a voice that was finely calibrated just above a whisper.

'Sitting in my car here in Phibsboro. I thought I'd ring before landing home.' He didn't need any elaboration on that score. She didn't want to go back to the house and find Abigail waiting. The last thing either of them needed now was that.

'You dropped him off?'

'Yeah. I'm still alive.'

'Do you know where the … gun is?'

'I had a gander around when you were gone with him looking for that car, but I couldn't find it.'

'So he must have it.'

'I thought of that. Kevin, if we'd been stopped by the guards on the way home, and they found a gun on him, where would that leave me?'

'It didn't happen, so forget about it. What do we do now?'

'I don't know. The whole thing is … I can't get that man's face out of my head.'

'Welcome to the cabaret. But there's more to it than that, Karen. The fella, we don't even know his name. He came down there, broke into the house all set to kill somebody. I mean, we were acting in self-defence, right?'

'Even Burns?'

'Yeah, well, fuck him. I wasn't the one who shot the man in cold blood. I just stopped him killing you. Seeing somebody get shot and die there and the blood and the whole thing, it's horrible. But my conscience is clear. It was self-defence. If you're going to break into a house, and he wasn't just a burglar, then that can happen.'

Karen said, 'He had a family. In his wallet there was a picture of three little boys.'

'Karen, I'm sorry, I really am, and if I could turn back the clock I would, but that guy wasn't an upstanding citizen. He wasn't even from the same side of the street as you and me.'

'Burns said he has to tell Pascal Nix about the whole thing.'

'Fuck.' Wyman saw Nix standing there, taking this in, handling a rope, forming it into a knotted lasso, and throwing it over him, tightening the knot, another debt, another recorded incident to hold over him.

'I don't know where this is going to go, Kevin.'

'I'll tell you what I think. I think we need to get cracking on harvesting what we can. We've put too much into this business to watch it go up in smoke now over something that has nothing to do with us. We have to meet tomorrow and sort out the house in Westwood. And the raid in Golden Eagle Valley was on the news on the way home. Guess what? No arrests. The Chinks must have scampered. So we can go down there, take a scoot around and see if we can get some work done. We can leave the Middle Kingdom to last – I'm in no rush to go back there. We can salvage something from this, Karen, and then take stock.'

He heard something behind him, prompting him to leap from the chair and whirl around. Brenda was standing in the doorway, framed by a shaft of light from the hall. She had Ciara in her arms.

Wyman said, into the phone, 'I got to go. We'll talk tomorrow.'

He couldn't see Brenda's face properly, but he could feel her contempt.

'How long were you standing there?' he said.

* * *

Burns received three texts from his boss over the course of the day and into the night.

Now he was at home, the clock pushing for three thirty a.m., Brownie McGhee wailing that he was born with the blues.

He texted Nix: You still up? The reply was immediate. Burns turned down the music and dialled the number. 'Pascal?'

'How're you?'

'You're not in bed.'

'Not technically.' Burns thought he heard something in the background. He'd never taken Nix to be much for whoring, but that didn't mean he was entirely abstemious either.

Nix said, 'Where the fuck have you been?'

'Busy.'

'Are you going to tell me about it?'

'Things didn't go too well.'

There was a silence on the line now, challenged only by the sound of a distant giggle, maybe from across the room, the whore having been told to get out.

'I'm listening.'

'You remember my little problem – Jacinta's little problem?'

'Who?'

Now Burns was pissed off. The guy couldn't even remember his girlfriend's name. 'The problem at my house. What happened.'

'Oh, yeah, yeah, sure. What's that got to do with our friend in the horticulture business?'

'The problem showed up again. Today.'

'Fuck.'

'Followed us to the … garden.'

A heavy breath came down the line. Burns could see Nix's head at work, silently conveying to him, That's your problem, fella, don't drag my business into it.

Burns said, 'Problem's over, disappeared. But now we've got another problem. Well, two, to be exact.'

'These problems have names?'

'You know them.'

'I'm with you. Well, what are we going to do?'

'I'd like to talk to you before we do anything. By the way, you still got that tape?'

'Tape?'

'Our friend doing the *Kama Sutra* for retards.'

'Yeah. What about it?'

'Might come in handy yet.'

* * *

Abigail's car was outside the house when Karen turned into the road in Stoneybatter. When she stepped inside, she saw that Abigail's bedroom door was closed. So she was home, safe and secure. For that small mercy Karen was grateful.

She threw her shoulder bag onto the couch, went into the kitchen and closed the door behind her. She filled a glass of water from the tap, pulled out a chair and sat down. Abigail had placed a bucket on the table. She must have been expecting rain to come dripping through the makeshift Velux window, but all was still dry.

Karen tried to remember the last time she felt so alone. Back in Coogee, on those nights when she couldn't sleep, and the balcony beckoned with the sound of the waves; she loved this time, the hours before the dawn, nestling between one day and the next. There was just her and the night, a private congress of peace. Yet it was also a luxury because she knew that, just a few feet away, a warm bed awaited her. And when she returned there, she'd lay and listen to Peter's breath, as steady as the sea, and she knew that, no matter what, everything in the world was fine, as long as they were together.

Now it was a few weeks short of a year since he'd been gone. She wondered whether her bereavement was entering a new phase. She had made it through the early straits, kept herself busy, had had a fling that must go down as the biggest mistake of her life, and thrown herself into business. Now, maybe, it was all catching up on her. Maybe she was getting the first pangs of a dull pain that would stay with her for the long haul.

She couldn't get that man's burlap-wrapped head out of her imagination. Lying there on the wheelbarrow, awaiting burial, and she hoping against hope that he might leap up out of it at any moment. None of this would have happened if Peter was still alive.

She let her head drop into arms folded on the table. Within seconds, she was asleep.

Chapter Twenty

Spits of rain on the window woke Wyman from a sleep that had never got further than shallow. He was in the spare bedroom, having cleared the bed of the various large toys, empty suitcases and handbags that had been occupying it. The floor was entirely covered with junk, bar a small path he had beaten from the door.

He leaned out of the strange bed and checked his wristwatch on the floor. Six fifty-five a.m. They'd be up and about in the next fifteen minutes, his wife, his children, launching into another ordinary day.

He wondered about the guy – the man with no name – out there behind the house, the earth in which he was entombed now softening, turning moist from the rain. If he was in a coffin, none of that would matter, not that it mattered anyway.

His thoughts distracted him from the sounds that led to Brenda sticking her head around the door, before presenting herself in her maroon cotton dressing-gown. He had bought that for her one birthday, a lifetime ago when only the mundane interfered with their happiness.

She shut the door gently behind her to keep disharmony from the children's ears. 'We have to talk,' she said. Last night, while she'd stood there with Ciara in her arms, only their eyes had spoken.

'Now?'

'I don't have time. I have to go to work to keep this family afloat. Can you make a point of being here this evening?'

His head was still on the pillow. He looked at the ceiling. This evening? Jesus, woman, you've no idea. I could be locked up or dead by then. 'I'll try,' he said.

That did it. Her voice went up a notch, shouting through a whisper. 'You'd better do more than try. I can't put up with this any more. I won't put up with it. Where were you for the last two days? You sneaked out of here like a thief before I could even talk to you on Tuesday evening.'

Now Wyman looked at her. She had a face that was drooped in tiredness, wrecked even, and he knew that he didn't look too hot himself. Here they were, kicking the shit out of each other over small things, while he was trying to get the big things right.

'I had organised for Rosanna to be here before you went to work. I had told you I would have to work overnight on Tuesday. But when you came in with that puss on you I knew there would be no peace. So I just left. You want me to apologise? I'm sorry, OK? Right now, Brenda, work has me in a bind. I need to sort out a few things and then we can get back to normal.'

Brenda's hand went to the door, not, Wyman felt, en route to exit, but more to ensure that nobody entered at this point.

'Well, let's talk about your work, shall we? What kind of employer needs you to work on private houses through the night?'

His hands went to his head, massaged his face, up onto his hair, pulling at it between his fingers and down again to rest over the jaws. The construction he had built for her about this work he'd come into over the last three months always had dodgy foundations. He had mentioned Pascal Nix, a businessman with a lot of property interests, and just in case Brenda ever encountered Karen, he had told her that she was Nix's project manager.

'Not now, Brenda. I told you, once this is over, everything will become clear. But right now …'

'Well, I'm sorry, Kevin, but that's just not acceptable any more.'

This was the recurring point in their arguments at which he went spare, and she knew it. When she threw out words like 'acceptable' and 'inappropriate', she began to sound as if she was dealing with some underling in that fucking insurance company where she worked. Whenever, at the height of a row, she abandoned plain English, he kissed goodbye to basic civility.

He threw back the duvet and rose from the bed, reality banished momentarily, to answer the clarion call of marital combat. 'You think you're the only one with problems … You have no idea, not a notion in your head …'

A sound came from outside the room: Daniel calling for his mother. She opened the door and told him she was coming, then turned back to her husband. 'You be here this evening. I'm not waiting for another day to find out what exactly is going on.'

He gave it a few minutes, listening to the house coming alive, and when he reckoned all were lapping around the breakfast table, he got up and showered.

By the time he arrived in the kitchen, the two children were togged out for school and Brenda scrubbed up, her face of fury lost behind a layer of mascara.

'Say goodbye to your father,' she said, and Wyman heard it as if it was intended to be a final farewell, rather than just bidding them adieu for the day. He told himself to cop on. The two kids came over and he hugged them. He didn't want to ask about the pick-up.

As she headed through the door, Brenda gave him another look coated in contempt. 'In case you're interested, Rosanna is picking them up from school. Her mother has given her the loan of a car to help us out.'

After they were gone, the silence pressed in on him. The radio could only bring bad news; music would not lift him from his current station. He toasted two slices of bread, stood by the kettle as it whistled to a boil, and afterwards he drank slowly from a cup of coffee. For the best part of a year, before he'd got involved in the business, he had found himself here of a morning, alone with the rest of the family gone to their days. He could reach back now and review that pit where he had thrashed around, his usefulness as an earner made redundant, the rhythm of a working day displaced, picking up the pieces of his career by hanging washing on a line.

Now that, too, was a memory. Things had moved on and 20:20 vision was haunting him with the lost possibilities that that period might have presented. He could have looked into retraining, or just getting involved in something to make himself feel useful, instead of moping around and obsessing on getting his rocks off.

If he could sort this out, if they could just reap the dividends of one harvest, he wouldn't act the fool next time around. All he wanted was one more chance.

The day was dry when he went outside, but yesterday's heat had been withheld. He stepped into the Golf and pointed it for the city.

He had gone just over a mile when the car materialised behind him. Headlights flashed. His first instinct was panic. Burns had considered the situation overnight and was now coming after him. The headlights flashed a second time.

He wasn't stopping out here in the middle of nowhere to be dragged from his car and taken away to the same fate as the man he had buried last night.

He turned onto a long straight stretch of road, winged on each side by bungalows sitting behind split-rail fences. The rear-view mirror told him the car was overtaking. He looked out his window to see Detective Garda Nora Cummins waving madly at him to pull over. He could see beyond her to Detective Sergeant Paul Gohery behind the wheel of their vehicle. Relief flooded through him, but only for a moment. Apart from Burns or his associates, the last people on this earth he wanted to encounter right now was this pair of cops.

He slowed at the end of the straight stretch, indicated and came to a stop. The car ahead of him pulled in also. The woman got out of the car and walked back to him. He lowered the window.

'You're not going to play silly buggers, are you?' she said.

He didn't reply.

'Follow us,' she said. 'You know the Livery Arms about a mile down the road here? Pull into the car park.'

He nodded. She walked back to her car. He looked in the rear-view mirror. There was nothing on his face that betrayed the events of yesterday. Or so he told himself.

* * *

When he'd heard the knock on the door that day, nearly three months ago, he had feared the worst, but it turned out to be much worse than that. It was about a fortnight after his meeting with Nix in Philly John's to sort out the blackmailer. Since then, things had opened up with Karen's operation.

Nix still had the tape, which Wyman hadn't bargained for. The bastard had said he was keeping it safe and it would be returned when the last instalment of the debt was paid down. Wyman didn't like any of it. When too many things are put on the long finger, the digit is liable to break, but what could he do? The guy had him by the short and curlies. Anyway, with the new work possibilities, there were some signs that life might improve this side of Judgment Day.

So when the sound of somebody at the door reached through into the kitchen that afternoon, he froze for a second. Was there some problem? Had Nix sent his goons again? Daniel and Ciara were looking up into his eyes to see his reaction. He told them to go on into the sitting room and play in there.

Wyman stuck his head into the broom cupboard, and came out with a child's hurley he'd bought for Daniel. He went to the door, hurley in a long grip behind his back.

Once he opened it, he knew immediately they were the law. One man, one woman, and no two ways about it. He was overweight, tight haircut, his shirt, tie and jacket too casually applied for anybody who was selling anything. She had on a black trouser suit from last year's mail-order catalogue, hair tied back in a bun. Nice face, but again, if she had been selling merchandise or religion, she would have added some class of a smile.

'Kevin Wyman?' the man said.

Wyman moved sideways, placed the hurley against the little oak table. The eyes on the pair of them followed his every move.

'Were you expecting somebody else?' the woman said.

'What do you want?' Wyman said, realising afterwards that he should have been more polite.

'I'm Detective Sergeant Paul Gohery, this is Detective Garda Nora Cummins. Could we come in for a minute?'

'Is there a problem?' he said.

The female garda came in. 'That's what we're trying to find out,' she said.

They accepted the offer of tea, made comments about how nice it must be to live out in the country. Wyman noticed how their cops' eyes were hard at work, taking in everything, including the laptop on the table where they sat.

By the time he'd organised the tea, it began to dawn on him why they were there. When he sat down, confirmation came with the first question.

'Do you know Sabrina McFarnham?' Sergeant Gohery said, the question light with innocence.

Wyman gave the impression of rolling the name around in his head, hoping that his face wasn't already providing an answer. 'Can't say I do,' he said.

The woman had extracted a notebook from somewhere about her person. She flicked it open, removing the top of a pen with her teeth.

'Are you familiar with the website smooch.com?' she said.

Nix had assured him there had been no rough stuff. A low rumble of panic began to rise within him. Surely they hadn't killed her. 'What's this about?'

It was back to the sergeant. 'We're investigating a complaint, a serious complaint. Ms McFarnham was assaulted in her home. She alleges that she was attacked and suffered what she describes as a sexual assault. She believes that the assault may be connected with her … liaison with you. So, Kevin, let's go through this again. Can we take it that you know Ms McFarnham, that you met her through that website?'

He hadn't reckoned on things going down this route. The brief surge of relief that she was actually alive was quickly smothered by dread. It was important to hold it together.

Detective Cummins intruded on his thoughts. 'She gave us the name of the hotel where you met, Kevin. The record shows she booked a room. The barman confirmed that he knew her to see. He also gave a rough description of her companion that night, and he's willing to take a look at a line-up if that's necessary.'

'I never laid a finger on that woman,' Wyman said, his voice heading into choppy emotional weather.

'She's not alleging that you did. Well, apart from your … liaison in the hotel.'

Sergeant Gohery let that sit there for all of three seconds before adding: 'But she is alleging you hired the two men who attacked her. In her home. They broke in and assaulted her. According to Ms McFarnham, there was a sexual element to the assault. That's serious stuff, Kevin, sexually assaulting a defenceless woman like that.'

Wyman looked over at the cop. 'That woman isn't defenceless. Whatever happened, she's not that.'

'What did happen, Kevin?' This from the female cop, the question reaching out to him in empathy.

Wyman got up and walked to the back window. He looked out on the expanse of a lawn rolling into a line of planted fir trees at the back of the property. He didn't deserve this. He'd made a mistake. One thing had led to another and now here he was, the focus of a garda investigation into a sexual assault. He was back there again, in that hotel, nursing his first pint, pushing away the apprehension. If only he had responded to his base instinct at the time. If only he had finished his drink, got up and walked out, gone home to his wife and children, prepared to negotiate the trough. Instead he'd been led by his dick.

'Who were they, Kevin, the two men?'

He turned. The pair of cops were looking up intently at him.

* * *

Twenty minutes after they had arrived, things began to crystallise. He spilled it all out, the debts, Pascal Nix, that woman – he looked at Cummins as he found himself reeling in the word that nearly jumped from his mouth – how she intended to destroy him. What was he to do?

'So you hired two thugs to get the tape back,' Gohery said.

'I didn't hire anybody.'

'That's what it sounds like.'

'I asked Pascal Nix could he help me out.'

'Help you pay your debts to him,' Gohery said. 'That was your pitch, wasn't it? How could you sort him out if this woman had a call on any cash you had? It was like a payment in kind. Help me get rid of her and I'll be able to pay you back. You knew Nix was a serious crim. Not much difference from actually hiring them.'

Detective Cummins asked the obvious: 'Why didn't you go to the gardaí?'

He shook his head. No point in revisiting terrain that had been ploughed to death. He had striven to keep things under wraps. Open court was the last place that he wanted this business aired. At one point, his daughter pushed meekly at the door. The two cops suddenly melted into smiles, parking their interrogation until the child's wants were seen to. Wyman got up and sourced a smoothie in the fridge, turning away from his daughter so she wouldn't see the anguish on his face.

When she was gone, the cops got back on track, but their questions began to stray from the details of his liaison with the woman.

They kept coming back to Nix. How well did he know him? Who else had he encountered?

When he described the visit to the house he had received from Charlie Small and his new partner wanting money, the pair looked at each other.

'They,' Sergeant Gohery said, 'fit the description Ms McFarnham gave of the two men who assaulted her.'

Wyman was too shook to feign surprise. He had guessed that they were the muscle Nix had dispatched. 'What did they do to her?' he asked.

'The one she describes as being as fat as a fool, he got into the rough stuff. Tied her up, slapped her.'

Cummins said, 'And then he presented her with his member. She says that scared the life out of her. The other one intervened before things went further. But it was a joint enterprise. Both of them will be facing a serious stretch. And this tape, did you get it?'

For a second, Wyman saw this pair and some colleagues sitting around a draughty room in a city station, viewing the tape of him trying to fuck away all his frustrations.

'Nix has it. He – he says he'll return it when I clear the slate with him.'

'Do you believe that?'

'What choice do I have? At least it feels safer than when it was with that bitch.'

Neither of the cops reacted to his description of the victim.

'OK, Kevin,' Gohery said. 'This is where things stand. You'll be asked to give a formal statement. Along the lines of what you've told us here. After that, we can see. If what you're saying can be proved, then maybe you're not on the hook for this, but if you slither off, then Nix will be on it good and proper.'

'What if I don't co-operate?'

'We'd have no choice but to interview Nix, and tell him the guts of the case we have against him. I don't know how he might take that.'

Wyman sat down at the table opposite the two cops. His head fell into his hands.

Cummins said, 'There is one other possibility.'

'Pascal Nix,' Gohery said. 'He's a bad piece of work. I mean really bad. If what you're saying is true, then you might be in a position to help us.'

Wyman looked up from his despair. 'What are you talking about?'

'You said you're going to have to work for him in order to pay him off,' Gohery said. 'You're not a crim, Kevin, you're a tradesman, a businessman. But I'd guess that he might use you to work on some of his properties, maybe even his home. You might get to see a lot of things that could help us build a case. Like I told you, this guy is a real scumbag, and we'd like to get him off the streets. If you can contribute to that, I don't know.' The sergeant turned to Detective Cummins, and something passed between them.

Cummins said, 'This crime we're investigating, Kevin. It's possible that it could run into the sand, if nothing turns up. I mean, you weren't in that room when Ms McFarnham was assaulted. If you were willing to help us out, I don't know. These cases can be difficult to prove unless officers are willing to work their asses off and concentrate on them to the detriment of other work.'

Wyman said, 'I thought there was a serious sexual assault involved.' He was seeing a lifebuoy in the distance now, bobbing on the waves.

Gohery said, 'It wasn't as serious as some of the assaults we come across.'

Cummins said, 'I've seen some victims of sexual assault that are really traumatised, but Ms McFarnham, well, she appeared more intent on going after you rather than the individual who attacked her. And Paul has come across her before.'

Gohery said, 'Yeah, last year I investigated a complaint that she was trying to extract money with menace out of a guy from Cavan. Big farmer, big family. He was looking for a little excitement.'

Cummins said, 'Not much excitement on a farm in Cavan.'

'Same deal as she tried on with me,' Wyman said.

'We couldn't prove it. The point is, Kevin, everybody is entitled to protection from the law. It's just that some are more deserving of that protection than others. You're entitled to it too. And if you were willing to do your bit in the fight against crime, well, as I say, there's plenty more pressing issues calling on the energy of a strapped force than sorting out revenge for somebody who thought she could blackmail a poor sucker.'

'What do you want me to do?'

That was how they left it. Low-grade intelligence, they called it. Keep his eyes and ears open whenever he did any work for Nix. There would be no question of him giving evidence in court, of this they assured him. They agreed to touch base each month.

He'd met them just twice since then, each of them once. Their third meeting was now overdue.

He had given them a few titbits. There was the time that Nix had asked him to wire up a little shed at the back of his home, which he'd set up for his teenage son. Wyman took in the security system that was in place at the house; he noticed how there was always a guy hanging around, most likely there to provide protection in case anybody got it into their head to do a number on Nix.

Another day, he was sent to an apartment down in the docks to sort out a blown fuse board. Three flights up, one of those jobs that had little more than paper for walls.

Once inside, the first thing that struck him was the soundproofing along some of the walls. He was met by a woman with a hard face and dilated eyes. And then another hooker from

Central Casting emerged from one of the bedrooms. Over the course of the hour he was there, two other women called to the house and you'd want to believe in the fairies to think that they were gathering for a coffee morning.

He saw no harm in throwing that morsel to Detective Cummins when he met her next. She wasn't impressed. 'Running a brothel isn't exactly the Valentine's Day Massacre,' was how she'd put it. 'We need some class of a smoking gun, Kevin, not this Mickey Mouse stuff.'

At least it was something to show them that he was doing what he could. And all the time, he played it cool. They couldn't have a clue about the business or they would have said something. But this was the last thing he needed today.

They couldn't know. There was no way they could have any idea about what had gone down last night.

* * *

The Livery Arms had a mock Tudor frontage and a disappearing clientele. It had had a thorough refurb about a decade previously to cater for the thickening belt of commuters in rural County Meath. Estates had risen up in the middle of nowhere during the property madness. Between that and the proliferation of one-off bungalows, the gap for a local hostelry began to widen. The Livery did the job, and served the place well, complementing the evening trade with some choice food during the day.

Now, under a pincer attack from the recession, drink-driving laws and the availability of cheap booze, its core clientele had drifted away. Physically, the place was getting shabby around the edges.

The car park was empty as Wyman followed the cops to the

far reaches of the tarmac, partially hidden by the gable end of the premises.

He watched as Cummins got out, opened the rear door on her side and held it for Wyman. He walked over and sat in. She shut it and walked around to the other side, sliding in beside him.

Detective Sergeant Paul Gohery turned to greet him, but did so without a smile. 'How've you been, Kevin?' he said.

'Grand.'

'And how's work?'

'Bits and bobs. You know yourself. Not much happening.'

Cummins reached forward from her position to the front passenger seat, her hand returning with a brown A4 envelope with a hard back.

'You haven't been answering the oul dog-and-bone,' Gohery said.

'Yeah, last few days I've been up the walls. Just didn't get a chance.'

Gohery's left arm went across the back of the front passenger seat, and he turned once more to regard Wyman. 'You're not holding out on us, Kevin, are you?'

Wyman effected what he hoped was a look of pure innocence. This was where the tough got going. He'd been drawn in once by this pair but it wasn't going to happen again. It couldn't happen again.

'What do you mean?' he said.

Cummins pulled at the envelope and drew out a number of photos. She began handing them across to Wyman. He took the first one and immediately recognised the house in Westwood, sitting there on its terrace, looking innocent to the world.

The second photo was from much the same angle, apart from the presence of a powder blue Honda Civic parked on the street outside, and a woman walking up the path to the front door.

The officer passed a third photo. A close-up of the woman on her way back out of the house. Wyman knew the face, knew it very well.

'Do you know this woman?' Cummins said.

'She looks familiar.'

'She looks familiar?'

'Yeah, that's what I said.'

Cummins passed another photo. Same location, same angle, same woman in different clothes. This time she was walking down the path followed by a man. Cummins placed her index finger on the image of the man.

'Does he look familiar, Kevin?'

It could have been taken on any one of maybe a half-dozen times when he and Karen had gone to the place together in her car. 'Oh, yeah,' he said. 'Nix told me once or twice to go there and check on the electrics.'

'Cut out the oh-yeah shit, will you?' Gohery said. He was looking in the rear-view mirror. He turned again to Wyman. 'Once upon a time you had a problem about consorting with some unsavoury types. Now you're involved in the grow-house business. Things aren't exactly looking up for you, Kevin. The woman, who is she?'

Keeping the head, that was what it was all about now. Yesterday was still out of their reach. The way they were playing this, they thought Nix was behind the operation, or at least they wanted him to be.

'She does a little work for Nix,' he said. 'Looks after that house for him.'

'Name,' Cummins said.

'Karen.'

'If she isn't a pop singer I presume she has a second name.'

'I've never heard it,' Wyman said. 'Where did you get these photos?'

'Operation Nitrogen is a splendid affair being run by our colleagues in the drugs unit. Somebody in there thought we might be interested in this stuff. They gave us a little present.'

Gohery looked in the mirror again. 'How many grow-houses have you done work on for him?'

This was it: shit or bust.

'Just that one.'

'Are you sure?'

Out of the corner of his eye, he spotted Cummins's fingers playing with the flap of the envelope, as if waiting for words that would prompt her to pull her latest trick from the bag. 'Of course I'm sure. I think I'd remember something like that.'

No photo was placed before him.

Gohery said, 'This isn't good, Kevin. We try to cut you some slack and you spit in our faces like that.'

'Ah, come on. I just didn't mention going to that place. I didn't think it was important.'

'Don't insult our intelligence. You didn't think it was important that Nix was growing drugs? The way things are looking, Kevin, that oul case of yours might have to get some closer attention.'

'What are you saying?'

'Either you co-operate properly with us or you might as well tell your missus you've a big trial coming up that will involve the screening of you and Ms McFarnham going at it like rabbits.'

'What more can I do?'

Gohery said, 'It's time to piss or get off the pot, Kevin.'

Cummins said, 'You can let us know the next time Nix is in the grow-house. We could do with a little advance warning. Operation Nitrogen is keeping an eye on that house. We've got them to hold off until we can bag Nix. You can get him there for us.'

'No way. There's no way I'd be able to manage that.'

Gohery turned again. 'You'd better find a way.'

Wyman didn't respond. He couldn't make up his mind whether he was relieved or scared shitless. They didn't have a handle on what was going on, but they wanted him to set up Nix? His life wouldn't be worth living.

Cummins spoke in a voice that had dropped to a notch of concern. 'This stuff isn't happening in a vacuum,' she said.

'What do you mean?'

She looked to the rear-view mirror, where Gohery gave a nod. 'Two men have been killed in the last few months because Nix thought they were talking to the gardaí.'

'Oh, for fuck's sakes.'

'The second was just last week. Traveller guy who'd been brought in for questioning. He wasn't even close to Nix.'

'And was he?'

'Was he what?'

'Talking to you.'

Gohery said, 'He didn't get a chance. From what we gather, Nix is getting paranoid. The fella he had shot three months ago, Stanners, he used to work for Nix. He was shot in front of his wife and kid.'

'Great. And now I'm talking to you. What are you trying to do to me?'

A van swung into the car park, described a wide circle on the gravel, and came to a halt a few feet from the front door. Gohery turned in his seat, kept his eyes on the vehicle. It looked to be a Hiace.

Cummins turned her head to look out the back window. 'What do you reckon?'

'I reckon these gentlemen are casing the joint, looking to make a few bob.' He pulled a phone from his inside breast pocket, his eyes on the rear-view mirror all the time. He opened the car door and stepped out, took off towards the van. He'd got about halfway there when the van's engine gunned into life. The driver swung it around and drove off. Gohery tapped digits into his phone, returned to the car and sat back in. 'Where were we?' he said.

'We were explaining Kevin's options to him,' Cummins said.

'Oh, yeah. Well, Kevin, it's make-your-mind-up time.'

'I don't understand.'

'Well, let me make it simple. And this time, I don't want any misunderstandings. Your life could depend on it. We have to decide whether to assign you protection on the basis that your life may be in danger.'

'Is it? My life?'

'We don't know. All we know is that if that psycho as much as sniffs a possibility that you've been telling us what brand of rasher he eats for breakfast, then form suggests he won't want you hanging around in this life for too long.'

Wyman felt the space in the car closing in on him. 'Why should Nix think that I'm talking to anybody?'

Cummins said, 'You've been damn all use to us, but we still don't want to lose you.'

'Thanks.'

Gohery turned around again, looked Wyman in the eye. 'There is one other possibility. If you could place him in that grow-house, give us a tinkle at the right time, and then give evidence, a new life awaits in the witness-protection programme.'

'Abroad,' Cummins said.

'Abroad?'

'Yes. Somewhere you don't have the toll of doom in your ear, morning, noon and night.'

'Your call,' Gohery said. 'You're not in immediate danger so you've a few days to think about it.' He turned the key in the ignition.

'Take care of yourself, Kevin. You might be able to do your country some service yet.'

Chapter Twenty-one

Burns slept soundly without dreaming, and when he woke, he lay in his bed for a long time. He had never shot a man in a mask before. He had worn a balaclava a few times himself, had on the night he and Charlie Small did Stanners, but he'd never actually done somebody who'd been wearing one until yesterday. The reversal of roles was weird.

A particular moment kept coming at him. For a second, as his ears had started ringing, and blood spilled through the balaclava, he feared the identity of the dead man. A moment of panic had gripped when a stray thought told him it could be Pascal Nix. Immediately he reached down and pulled the balaclava away, strange relief coming over him when he saw a face that he just knew belonged to Coulter, an amateur on a safari of revenge.

Why would he have expected Nix? There was no problem between them. As far as he knew, Nix was perfectly happy with him. Neither had Nix any grounds to suspect him of betrayal or skimming, or plotting with Fat Charlie Small to do anything contrary to their main focus, the enrichment and protection of their boss.

After a time, Burns got out of bed, slipped into a T-shirt and went out into the living room. He pulled back the blinds to welcome the day, natural light pouring in brighter than he had imagined it could. Summer had arrived when he'd been otherwise engaged.

He turned on Sonny Terry and Brownie McGhee, looking for some solace in Sonny's harp. He got it, too, on the first track, 'Drinkin' In The Blues'. If he wasn't mistaken, Lightnin' had helped out the two boys on that one.

Once the kettle boiled he spooned a cup of instant coffee into a cup and filled it, using the remainder of the water to boil an egg. He sat down, leafed through the book *Deep Blues*. He'd bought it on Amazon a few months back after coming across it on a website. He never got round to reading it, but he knew he wouldn't. He wasn't a reader. Back in the day, when his grandfather had unreeled the stories of the bluesmen, Burns pulled in the tales, but he was not one to read for himself.

Maybe Nix had come into his head because he'd been around long enough to expect the unexpected. The business was like the sea, constantly moving through peaks and troughs. Nobody stood still. Fellas were always being thrown overboard, often getting the heave-ho from where it was least expected. The only loyalties that endured were tied in family, and even those could be sundered if pressure was high, or the stakes of self-preservation raised. Why couldn't it have been Pascal Nix behind the mask? It didn't matter that there was no problem between them. If Nix had a bad night he might just turn.

He ate the egg, then washed the saucepan, plate and cup, wiped down the worktop and swept the floor. He gave the kitchenette the once-over, satisfied that everything was where it should be. There were a few stains on the tiled floor from last night when he'd arrived home with muck on his shoes.

He took a Brillo pad from the packet under the sink and scrubbed the stains clean. Then he washed the pad under warm water, placed it on the draining board and pulled a sheet of kitchen towel from its rack to dry his hands.

He went over, took the guitar from the stand and sat down next to the table. He killed Sonny and Brownie with the remote, opening up a silent platform on which to perform for himself.

He tried it one more time, 'Got the Blues, Can't Be Satisfied', the song he'd been learning from the sheet music. Still no good: his fingers resisted all instructions from his brain, withholding rhythm, playing half dead.

After two minutes, he gave up. Things just weren't happening. He raised the instrument from his lap and balanced it against the table.

He had always known that one day there would be witnesses. No matter what degree of planning went into it, the day would come when a witness would be there, watching him shoot somebody in the head, shoot his way to twenty years in a cage, and there was no way he could ever contemplate that.

The way he had always envisaged it, instinct would take over. A wife or girlfriend in the wrong place would just have to be dealt with. Nothing personal, you weren't part of the deal, but it's you or me.

He had never thought a situation like yesterday could arise. The moment to act had been after he'd unmasked the dead man. He should have turned to Wyman and let him have it in the face. Then there was the woman. She had been lying on the plants at that stage, her head buried in the weed that had brought her to this point. She wouldn't have known where it was coming from. All it would have taken was one behind the ear.

What bothered him now was that doing either of them never occurred to him at the time. He wasn't thinking of them as witnesses. Everything about how the situation had unfolded pointed to them being accomplices. Without Wyman going at the guy with the mallet, Burns would have been a dead man.

He could locate it now, the dread that coursed through him from head to toe as the guy had made his way towards the bedroom where he, Burns, cowered. There was nowhere to hide. He had picked up a pot, intending to throw it once the guy came through the door. He knew it would have been nothing more than a defiant gesture on the precipice of death, but that was the only way he knew how to go. And then, when the guy fell, and Wyman came at him from behind, he saw a sliver of a gap and pushed right through it. Luck had been smiling at him once more.

That was all very well, him and his new buddies seeing off that fella. But no matter which way he played it, he couldn't see Pascal Nix looking at these things through the same lens.

* * *

'If I tell you this, you have to promise never to breathe a word of it.'

Abigail nodded, keeping calm, bursting to hear all. 'You know you can trust me,' she said.

'I know.' Karen leaned across the table, a little circular affair that ought to have been barred by law from accommodating more than a single diner. Abigail had got the call last night that Heaven's Gate was down an angel and would she be willing to fly into the breach? Now she was on an early lunch break, but the café had filled up ahead of schedule.

'So, could you just tell me? I mean, all you've told me since you arrived in at all hours is that Kevin is all right, which I'm happy about. I think. But apart from that, you could have taken off for the clouds yesterday, gone on the razz at an angel party and arrived back just in time before you turned into a pumpkin. So I'm ready, Karen. I'm ready to hear everything.'

The café hugged the perimeter of Smithfield Square, famous for its horse fairs and fruit markets, but the bubble years had put paid to that. Old cobblestones had been replaced, the fruit people thrown out, and a mini city of apartments thrown up. Now the place had the infrastructure of some corner of New York, but the through traffic wasn't much better than you'd find on a winter's day in Pyongyang.

Karen began to unspool the story. She went back over the trip down with Burns, and then she remembered Abigail's walk-on role in the day. 'Jesus, I completely forgot. I'm sorry.'

'Nothing to be sorry about.'

'You and Kevin.'

'I came to my senses. That business over in the other place, Pure Mule, the raid and all that, it was a blessing in disguise. It brought a few things out into the open.'

'So what happened that you took off? I'd brought food for you.'

'Thanks. I'd like to have met your friend, the criminal. Just out of curiosity. But I'd had enough of Kevin. Every fling has its day, and ours had passed.'

'I'm sorry.'

'You warned me and I'm just glad I got out before it went any further. It was fine while it lasted. We'll always have Pure Mule.'

Karen looked at her, the crooked grin she put on when she switched into self-deprecation.

'Anyway, that's my sorry tale. So, what happened?'

It took ten minutes to share the whole thing, amid the casual diners and lawyers who had drifted up from the Four Courts. At least twice Abigail's mouth fell open in response to the latest detail. At the conclusion, her hand crept across the table and took Karen's. She said, 'What are we going to do?'

Two tears rolled down Karen's cheeks. 'You're great, you know that?'

'What are you talking about?'

'"We". You said "we".'

'Oh, shut up. So what do you think?'

Karen drank from her cup again, but the coffee had lost its warmth. She looked her friend in the eye. 'Kevin thinks we should get this crop out, pull in the money, then wait and see.'

'So you're not going to the guards?'

'To tell them what? I saw a man being killed in the house where I'm running an illegal drugs business?'

Abigail's eyes looked up towards the ceiling in search of some answers in her head. 'I see your point. I see Kevin's point, even if he is a bastard. What do you feel like doing?'

'Running. Going back to Australia, starting out again. I knew that there might be complications, but I never thought things could get as terrible as this. A man has been killed.'

'But it's really nothing to do with you. I mean, men are shot in pubs in this city all the time. The publicans aren't to blame. You were going about your business, showing somebody around, and then a maniac turns up with a gun. It's not your fault.'

'He had a photograph in his wallet,' Karen said. 'Three little boys.'

'Oh, God.'

'So you agree with Kevin?'

Abigail leaned back in her chair, looked around as if a good answer might be floating on the currents of food smells. 'Why not wait and see? Do what has to be done today, see how much of this harvest you can get. You have somebody to sell it, don't you? You're entitled to make some money, Karen. You've worked your ass off for the last three months – you've really put your heart and soul into this. See if you can't get something out of it.'

Karen's phone began trembling on the table. The name on the screen was Kevin. She looked at her friend. 'I'm going to take this outside, OK?'

'It's the bastard, isn't it?' Abigail said.

Karen got up and walked outside. A knot of suited men were standing close to the café's door. She moved a few feet in the opposite direction.

'Where are you?' Wyman said.

'Having lunch.'

'With anybody I know?'

'What do you want, Kevin?'

'We've work to do.'

Karen held back for a second. Yes, they had work to do.

'OK, we might as well go to Westwood, chop down the rest of the trees.'

'No. Not Westwood.'

'Why not?'

'I think we should go down to Pure Mule.'

'What's wrong with Westwood?'

'Not today.'

'Today is the perfect day for it. The other night you said we do Westwood first. Why head off down the midlands when we've work to do here?'

'Karen, I'm not going to Westwood.'

'Why?'

'I'm just … I'm nervous about the place. Who knows where's next to be rumbled? Thing about Pure Mule is that the Vietcong weren't nabbed so there's no reason for the cops to think anybody else is in the estate. In one way, it's beautiful. Where better to go than back to the scene of the crime?'

Karen said, 'Let's not talk about crime scenes for now.'

'OK, but we're going down there, not Westwood.'

'This is strange, Kevin, but I'll trust you. And the other place, when do we face into that?'

'Tomorrow. We'll just go down, in and out in no time, and that's it. I think the expansion plans we had for that place have just gone south.'

* * *

Albert College Park was buzzing, the smell of fresh-cut grass in the air. Burns cycled through the gate on Ballymun Road and dismounted. The park opened out below him to his right in a carpet of grass, interrupted here and there by groves of trees or patches of growth. It felt good, stepping from the busy thoroughfare into an oasis. One path ran down, parallel to the road outside, the other moving away from the bustle at right angles. He took the latter, walking with his left hand balanced on the Trek's handlebars.

Two mothers wheeling buggies passed by, lost in their conversation. A blue-uniformed park attendant was moving along the path with caution, spearing bits of rubbish. Burns noticed the trees were full and heavy with leaves. It was a good time for growing anything, even in the natural world.

He spotted Nix up ahead on a park bench, togged out in a grey suit that was crumpled yet somehow he was overdressed for a park at this hour of the day.

Nix turned as Burns arrived, then looked back out on the expanse of grass. A man and a boy were pucking a sliotar to each other, the man rising dramatically with one hand to snatch the sliotar from the air.

'Tried that game once when I was a kid,' Nix said. 'An uncle brought me down to the local club. It went grand for a while until we were playing this other crowd, from somewhere out in the north of the county. Lad on me was handy and there was only one way to deal with him. They didn't want me back. I wasn't too pushed either.'

Burns said, 'From what I hear, Dublin are doing good at it now. The culchies had better watch out.'

'I'm surprised at you, Dara.'

'It wasn't straightforward, Pascal.'

'It never is, but a witness is the worst form of species known to man. Two of them is a fucking disaster.'

Burns held his tongue. Out on the grass, the man and boy packed in. They came together and made off towards one of the park's gates, the man's free arm wrapped around the boy's shoulders.

'This was your personal business, Dara, but you can understand that, on account of our relationship and it happening on my premises, I'm involved. And that's something I can really do without. We're going to have to fix it.'

'Both of them?'

'What do you think?'

'The woman's less likely to talk.'

'What the fuck is this? The three-twenty at Leopardstown? I can't take any chances, Dara. You know that. I don't feel too hot about any of this. I liked that woman. She had a bit of get-up-and-go in her. But she knew what she was getting into and she's become a problem. There's no way around this.'

'When?'

Nix released an exaggerated sigh, as if the weight of his decision had been staining the whole morning for him. 'I've got an appointment this afternoon so it will have to wait until tomorrow. Don't ring them till the morning – give them less time to think too much about it. Tell them you have to go back down to that place. Go down with Karen. Get me the directions. This job needs more than one man. Charlie will go in the van, arrange to meet him there. I'll come to give a hand after it.'

A woman togged out in a grey sweat suit approached the bench, her arms going like pistons, feet pounding out the path. Burns waited till she was past.

'What about the weed? There's three full rooms of it down there, must be seventy or eighty grand's worth of the stuff.'

'That's why I'm coming down. What you need to do is find out from Karen where the other houses are. Before you deal with her. We can get the stuff together down there tomorrow when they're dealt with and then do the other places. This thing is a mess, but we could get out of it with a few euro in our pockets.'

* * *

Wyman hit Coomray an hour after leaving home, the signature tune for the three o'clock news booming out from the car radio. The journey had been uneventful, sparse traffic on the motorway, and even less once he'd hit the trunk roads. There wasn't a soul to be seen in downtown Coomray. He got a good gander in the door of the convenience store, saw a shape he reckoned was one of the staff in a housecoat of rainbow colours, bent over in one of the aisles. Otherwise there was nothing happening.

His imagination conjured up a movie scene in which everybody has been evacuated from the village to set up a confrontation with the bad guys. These days, with everything that had gone on, his imagination was really all over the shop.

He swept the whole vista with his eyes, looking for some sign of life, a hint that strangers might be in town, waiting for somebody to show up. Nothing.

He cruised past the entrance to Golden Eagle Valley. An

old Ford Escort came towards him, the driver low in his seat, crowned with a flat cap. He raised an index finger from the top of the steering wheel to salute Wyman, as if they knew each other.

Wyman nodded, and immediately turned to look down into the estate, between the mounted stone eagles. From what he could see there was a whole lot of nothing happening in there. He drove on a couple of hundred yards, pulled into the entrance to a field, did a Huey, and retraced his route. He had intended cruising by once more, but everything so far suggested that he was on safe ground. In any event, just driving into the estate didn't confer guilt on him.

He turned in slowly and downed gears to second. Number five was dead to the world. He kept going, passing the houses on left and right, a car parked outside one, a van crowned with a taxi plate outside another, no sign of life on the road. Even the ghosts had left town.

He kept it a steady twenty, right down to the end, to the T-junction. He could see the Chinks' house now, the only sign of life there a yellow-jacketed garda outside.

Back up at number five, he pulled in, got out and walked straight up to the front door. The waft inside was worse than he had remembered it. He knew this was to be expected while the drying was going on.

Upstairs, everybody was behaving themselves. In the master bedroom, all was in full bloom, awaiting the end, to be cut down and harvested. The stink in the drying room nearly pushed him back out onto the landing. He held his nose, and walked among the hanging plants, his fingers feeling the parched buds. According to the book, these lads should get maybe another twenty-four hours, twelve at least before they were fully dried out.

Wyman picked one bud from a stalk, rolled it in his fingers and watched how easily it broke. No need for any more. They would do just fine.

He got to work within ten, picking the buds from their stalks, going between the rows. At times he thought the smell might overpower him, knock him for six, until he fell into a deep dreamy coma, where he could float on narcotic waves, his body added to the missing list, only to be found days or weeks later here among the plants, unconscious, but not in pain, alive and happy as a pig in shit.

These thoughts comforted him as he went about his business, the plastic bag in his left hand filling with green gold.

It was at least half an hour before he heard the front door. He went down and, guided by caution, slipped out through the rear entrance and walked around the house to meet the visitor. As he'd expected, it was Karen. She was looking a bit better today, the weight around her eyes having lifted. She wore a red summer dress, with a navy cardigan and sandals, shades pushed onto her fringe. She was looking good all right. After their initial encounter, once she'd set out her stall, he'd never looked at her in the way he was now. But the other day, when she'd been on the verge of falling apart, when she'd leaned on him, he'd felt something for her that was bothering him. Maybe now that Abigail had given him the bum's rush. Maybe was a fine word.

'Get out your green fingers,' he said. 'We've work to do.'

They worked well together, neither slacking as they patrolled the lines, picking and bagging, picking and bagging. Small talk occupied them for a while, tossing over and back about the power of the humidifier, how the nutrients performed, how long it would take to get the second crop under way, as if this was all that occupied them.

Then Karen said, 'We're due some money from Creole.'

'Fuckin' right we are. He must owe us – what? Fifteen grand?'

'Ten at least,' she said. 'He hasn't been in touch. I'm going to call to him in the morning, see what the story is.'

Wyman stopped for a moment, rubbed his right hand on his jeans. 'See, the money's rolling in. You sort that out, and what we harvest here today must be worth another thirty. By this time next week, we'll be in some serious dosh.'

'Is he hanging around your head?'

Wyman looked up. Karen's face was framed between two stalks and the line from which they hung. Her eyes had that look again, that of a little girl lost – he had first seen it after the shooting. 'I'm trying not to let him,' Wyman said.

'It's not easy.'

'We were accidental tourists, Karen. There's no more to it. What we've got to do is concentrate on getting this crop away and rebooting. We've come too far for things to blow up in our faces.'

'What about Burns? Is he going to leave us alone?'

'Why wouldn't he? It's not as if we can go to the cops. It was self-defence, as far as I was concerned. He didn't get rid of the body on his own. Look, let's just try and … not forget it but put it aside and get on with this. We have to keep focused.'

Karen bent down to pick up some buds that had fallen through her fingers. 'I thought focus was my thing,' she said.

'Yeah, well, everything's been turned upside-down. Look, we'll get this done, and cut up a few of the plants inside, hang them and we'll get out of here. We can leave the harvest downstairs. You see how Creole is fixed tomorrow and I can come and collect this stuff. How does that sound?'

'Sounds really focused.'

* * *

'It's not working.'

'Shit. That's bad news.'

Charlie Small didn't know what else to say. Nix just came out the door of the place across the street, where they had the little brass nameplate that he couldn't read from this distance, up there on the red brick at the top of the stone steps, next to the front door.

He walked across to where Small was sitting in the LiteAce as if he had the weight of the world on his shoulders.

And then he sat in and just said it wasn't working.

What can you say to that? Under no circumstances can you make a joke about it. Men had had their balls burst on a bench vice for less. No question of telling him it's possible to have a happy and fulfilling life without a full head of hair. Don't even think of suggesting that, according to myth, losing all your hair can make you horny as hell. You just have to feel the guy's pain.

Even now, when all sorts of shit was going down, nobody would dream of telling Pascal Nix that it was high time he got a bit of perspective. And certainly not Charlie Small. He knew where his bread was buttered. So, all he could say was 'Shit. That's bad news.'

He had got the call from Nix an hour ago, telling him to pick him up at the hair restoration clinic, over on the southside. Small found the street, just on the far side of the canal, where the houses began to grow in size, and were a throwback to an earlier vintage. He'd been sitting in the car for ten minutes when Nix finally came through the door and stood for a moment at the top of the steps, looking up at a blue sky, where the sun was putting in a rare, if powerful, appearance. His face immediately turned grey, as if he expected the rays to do damage to his unprotected crown. Then he finally came down and walked across, folding himself into the passenger seat. Baldy cunt just didn't know how good he had it.

'Drugs, man. You want to get fucked up, they always do the job.

But you need them to fix you up and more often than not they turn out to be useless.'

'You got a drug for your hair, Pascal?'

'Finasteride. They use it for prostate cancer, but a side effect is supposed to be what they call hair retention.'

'Fuck.'

'Yeah, well, it's not working. The one time you're looking for a side effect, it's nowhere to be seen. The guy inside, Thatcher, he told me I'm going to have to get the full monty.'

Charlie Small looked at him, wary not to tread on anything sensitive, yet obliged to show concern. 'The full monty?'

'A fuckin' transplant. Thirty grand.'

'Thirty grand? Fuck me.'

'Thatcher, he says it like he's used to people walking in there and just doling him out thirty grand. Maybe he is, but he shoulda known that somebody like me doesn't have that kind of cash in his back pocket.'

'You ever think of ... ?'

Nix gave him a look that was a road sign, warning him to turn back fast. 'What are you going to do? Walk in there and tell him what? A transplant or your life? That's not too bright, Charlie. Apart from anything else, a fella like him knows people. All sorts are getting new hair these days. He told me that one of his clients was a leading member of An Garda Síochána.'

'You think he was trying to tell you something, not to get any notions?'

Nix reached around for the seatbelt and pulled it across his midriff. 'Maybe, but none of that's on anyway. I want a transplant, I got to fork out for it, and that brings us to our current dilemma. OK, let's go. I got to get back to Philly John's to do some work. I'll fill you in as we go.'

Small pointed the van towards the canal.

Nix said, 'I made a mistake.'

Small let it ripple there between them, an aftershock of his boss displaying some human frailty. Eventually, he said, 'We're all human, Pascal.'

'I should have let you travel with the woman down the country. You would have handled it better. Now look where we are. Dara's brought his dirty laundry with him and we're all getting covered in shit.'

Small felt a surge within him, a fleeting version of the recurring abdominal pain that plagued him occasionally, but it was transmitting something more than just the knowledge that he'd pigged out beyond his limit. It felt like power flowing towards him. 'I know where you're coming from.'

'You sorted out the other issue?'

'Creole? Yeah. By the time I left he was singing like it was his wedding.'

'You didn't go too far?'

'Naw. He had to go and get fixed up, but nothing that would come back on me.'

'Good. I'm sorry, Charlie. I should have sent you down the country. You wouldn't have left me with this mess.'

Small let that hang there: those kind of comments didn't merit any reply that would make things even better. It had taken a long time, but a crisis had finally forced Pascal Nix to appreciate him.

Nix said, 'What do you think of him?'

'Who?'

'Dara.'

Small looked for a word. 'Weird.'

'What do you mean, weird?'

'He's not like other people I worked with, Pascal. I mean, he's not into booze, he's not into whoring. He plays the guitar.'

'What?'

'He's a fucking musician. The blues. He told me about it one day – he was talking about all these black fuckers I'd never heard of. Johnny Johnson or something. Crazy shit, but he takes it serious too. You can't get a rise out of him about it.'

'But he's straight, yeah?'

'Pascal, I didn't know where to go with this. But Mickey Rickshaw, just before we did him, he said the cops told him somebody else was feeding them stuff about you.'

'And you tell me this now?'

'I thought he was just looking for a way out. Now I don't know. Dara's weird. You just don't know where you are with him.'

The van was stopped behind a line of traffic. Small could see across into the still waters of the canal. A Luas train was coming down the tracks, heading for the city.

'How would you feel about doing him?'

Small had suspected that that was what they'd been leading to. He knew Nix couldn't handle any kind of grief. And this business, the dead guy down at the grow-house, the witnesses, the money on the line, that was enough grief for any man.

'You know me, Pascal. I'll do what has to be done.'

'But could you manage it?'

'What are you saying?'

'He's good. He's never been fingered for anything, never left a mess behind him. He knows the score.'

'And I don't? What the fuck, Pascal?'

Nix leaned over, extended a hand, placed it on Small's arm, just below the elbow, as if he was laying healing hands on a bone that had leaped to offence. 'I told you. I shoulda sent you down there. You know how I value you, Charlie. If you think you can handle it, that's fine by me. This has just become too messy. I like Dara, even if he is a bit weird, but he's carrying a lot of baggage and I don't have room for that any more.

'I've told him to go there tomorrow with the woman. He knows you'll be along in the van to give him a hand. Wyman will be there too. I'd suggest doing Dara first, just to get it out of the way. The other two won't present any problems.'

'Are you coming down?'

'Sure, I'll be down after, to help you clean up.'

'I'll need you. Sorting out three bodies will be no joke.'

* * *

There were four vests on the bed. Two were grey, one white and the last, which looked a bit bulkier than the others, was black.

Burns turned to the homeowner. He was a squat man with bulging eyes that provided the name by which he was widely known – Frog Eyes. The bed was in a room upstairs in a semi-detached house, out in the western suburbs. It had taken Burns the guts of forty-five minutes to cycle out there, a rucksack on his back, dodging between the traffic as he went from one cycle lane to another.

He'd got Frog Eyes' number from another man when he'd enquired where he might get what he was looking for. The other man had said Frog Eyes was your only man. Burns had heard of him – with a name like that how could he not have? – but they'd never met. So far, Burns had been impressed with the guy's sales pitch.

Frog Eyes pointed to the vests, sitting there on a pink bedspread. 'You got to keep it out of the sun,' he said. 'And don't get it wet. When you're wearing it, make sure you've something more than just a light top over it. I wouldn't put it on under what you're wearing now,' he said, pointing at Burns's sports top.

Burns looked at each of the vests, picked them up one by one, and held them in his right hand, as if to weigh them. He unzipped his top and slipped one of the grey numbers over him. It felt bulky, as if he'd just acquired a hide rather than another layer of skin. He walked over and back across the room, Frog Eyes viewing his gait with approval. 'You're a natural,' Frog Eyes said.

'A natural for what?'

'Some fellas, they put them on and they can't even walk properly. But you're built for it. You're like a tank, man. If you're stopped by the law they wouldn't have a clue that you're tooled up.'

Burns rolled his shoulders. It felt all right. He could live with it. When he had shown up at the house, it was obvious that his reputation had arrived before him. Frog Eyes had presumed he was just looking to upgrade a vest. His face had twisted in surprise when Burns had told him he'd never had use for one before.

'No shit, man,' Frog Eyes said. 'Fair play to you. It's a jungle out there.'

Now Burns tried on the black model. There was less bulk in it, but he could feel it heavier on his body. 'You do any sort of a warranty?' Burns said.

'A what?'

'Like a warranty. You know, you buy something and it's a guarantee that you'll get your money back if it doesn't do the job for a year or so.'

'Oh, yeah. I've a warranty on everything. Fellas who found out too late that the vest didn't work, they haunt my dreams. You're some fucker all right.'

Burns allowed himself a smile. He could see that Frog Eyes

was a survivor, the kind who owed his longevity to caution and charm rather than muscle and inspiring fear.

'This one,' Burns said, tapping the black vest on his chest. 'How much?'

'For you I can do it for a ton.'

'With lines like that you should be selling cars, man.'

'Yeah, well, I used to but things happen. These vests, you wouldn't fucking believe it. They're flying out the door. Lot of people out there are nervous, lot of fellas walking around expecting to meet their end. What about you? Is it somebody in particular or just being careful of everything?'

Burns let that sit for a few seconds, more for his own benefit than the other man's. 'I think somebody's got the idea that their world would be a better place without me right now.'

Frog Eyes issued the nod of a sage. 'I hate that,' he said.

Chapter Twenty-two

After calling for the third time, Karen decided he wasn't picking up. She had also dispatched two texts without reply. Creole was acting the maggot. He owed her, by her reckoning, the guts of ten grand, and now he was giving her the runaround.

She arrived on Leeson Street just after eleven, and spotted a parking bay nearly directly across the road from Creole's place. She pulled in and sat there for fifteen minutes, keeping her eyes peeled, girding herself for what she expected to be a confrontation.

In that time, one woman came through the front door, young, casually dressed, with what looked like a green shopping bag in her hand. Karen remembered her, the woman she had met on the threshold the day she'd come with the case of weed. She skipped down the path like somebody without a care in the world. A few minutes later, a man sauntered up. Karen recognised him as Jamie, the guy who had come on board to sell.

He was carrying two white plastic shopping bags. He buzzed, turned to face the street while he waited, and leaned down to the buzzer to confirm his identity. Then he was gone through the door.

Karen's phone trembled on the seat beside her. Caller ID blocked.

'Karen?'

The voice was hesitant on her name, as if unsure whether he had licence to address her in such an intimate manner.

'Hi.'

'This is Dara.'

'I know.'

'We have to meet. There's unfinished business down at that place we were in the other day.'

'Really?'

'Yeah. We need to sort out a few things about the vegetables.'

'The vegetables?' She wasn't sure whether he was talking about the weed or the body.

'So, I can meet you and we can go down there.'

She saw the pair of them pulling in on a layby, somewhere beyond the motorway, out in the midlands sticks. She saw a scene she always remembered from *The Sopranos*, Steven Van Zandt's character Silvio, pulling off a main road, driving Adriana, the fiancée of Tony's nephew, Christopher. She had just revealed that she had been talking to the cops. Silvio stopped the car in a wooded area, got out, went around and dragged Adriana from the vehicle before shooting her.

It was crazy that that sort of thing would enter her head at this time. There was nothing to fear from this guy. Besides, if she didn't show up, what became of all their work?

'I – we – me and Kevin, we'll meet you down there.'

'How will I travel?'

'Listen, I just can't make it. We have business to do in the morning up here and it would be too awkward. Surely you have some means of going down.'

'I just thought, you know, you seemed interested in the blues, I could fill you in some more.'

She pulled the phone from her ear, looked at it as if it had just spewed out something from outer space. This guy wants to talk about music? 'Sorry, but I can't manage it. Why don't we fix a time? Me and Kevin will be down by two o'clock. We can give you a lift back up to the city if you need it.'

There was a pause on the line.

'Hello,' she said.

'Yeah, OK, if we have to do it that way. I might take that lift back from you. See you then.'

She threw the phone across onto the passenger seat. She felt cold after the conversation, wishing that somebody was there to warm her up.

Her focus switched across the road again.

In all her dealings with Creole, she had never felt that he could pose a threat. Even this other guy, Jamie, he didn't come across as somebody lifted from a world where violence was the currency. Yet who knows?

She reached over for the phone again, punched in her security code and tapped her fingers absently on the screen. She could ring Kevin. She could get him to come as back-up. She let the thought ping around for a while, as the phone screen reverted to its saver.

She got out and walked across the road. She moved slowly up along the footpath on the other side, turning once she was two houses away from Creole's, waiting for opportunity to happen along. She saw the woman in the distance, the same one who had come out a few minutes previously.

She turned and walked in the opposite direction, and once the woman entered she ran down and followed her up the path. The woman turned the key in the door, and sensed somebody behind her. 'Can I help you?' she said.

'I'm just calling to Creole,' Karen said.

'Oh, hi,' the woman said, now recognising Karen from their previous encounter. 'How is he?'

'Sorry?'

'How is he today?'

Karen wasn't sure what was expected of her reply. 'Oh, he's fine,' she said.

The woman mounted the stairs, stopped at the landing on the third floor. Karen smiled at her and continued on up the steps.

She knocked on the door. Sounds fed through from inside, a voice, maybe two, something being moved. Then the door creaked open, Jamie's head appearing. The look he gave her would never have passed muster on a sales course. He opened the door wide, and walked back into the room, letting her follow. She shut the door, turned and saw the back of Creole's head over the chair he was seated on, beside the dodgy couch. It was wrapped in a bandage, like the ones you'd sometimes see on rugby players.

She noticed dark patches on the floor, which didn't look like anything that might have been spilled from a bottle or cup.

Jamie walked around in front of Creole, looked down at him and said, 'Guess who's just arrived?'

* * *

She walked over to where Jamie stood, turned and saw a face she barely recognised. Beneath the bandage that ringed his head, there were large patches in shades of purple, black and yellow. His jaw appeared to be out of place, mouth held at a crooked angle. His right arm was in a sling.

When she spoke, it was just above a whisper. 'What happened?'

Creole's eyes conveyed what she could only interpret as contempt.

She turned to Jamie.

'Your friend Charlie Small paid him a visit. He got out of the hospital this morning. He gave them my number in there, so I suppose I'm taking care of him. He has to eat through a straw.'

Karen waved her hand towards Creole, as if enquiring after the provenance of a piece of art. 'Charlie Small did this?'

Creole's eyes stayed on her, saying, Yeah, he did this, and who's to blame for it?

'When?' she said, addressing Jamie.

'Day before yesterday. The girl downstairs, Maggie, she found him on the landing outside, thought she'd heard something moving. Rang for an ambulance.'

Karen didn't want to ask, but Jamie kept going. 'Two detectives visited him in hospital. He didn't say anything. Fuckin' right he was too. At least he's alive now.'

'Oh, my God.' Karen moved around, sat into the couch without a care for what might emerge from it. She extended a hand towards Creole, as one might to the bereaved. All the time, his eyes never left her and she told herself that he wasn't blaming her.

She looked up again at Jamie, the interpreter. 'Did it have anything to do with our business?'

'What do you think?' he said.

Creole was still looking at her. She could see it now clearly. It was contempt. She rose again from the couch. 'Is he going to be all right?'

Jamie shrugged. 'He's not going to die. But he won't be climbing up ladders to paint anything this side of next Christmas. Can't see him doing much dealing either.'

Creole's lips moved in a sound of desperation, words melting into each other, sounding like somebody with a genetic condition, spittle appearing on his mouth and falling onto his chin.

'I suppose you came for your money,' Jamie said.

'Money?'

'The money we owe you. The weed went like hot cakes.'

She didn't know what to say. How could anybody think about money at a time like this? Yet that was what she had come for, what she had sat outside mulling over in the car, a sense of betrayal rising in her, that Creole was trying to pull a fast one on her. And now this. Who had betrayed whom?

Creole made to move again, this time reaching forward, his face twisting in pain at the effort. He picked up a pen with his left hand and began scribbling on a pad that lay on the table. Karen could see that it already had a number of words scribbled unevenly.

He moved the pen slowly; it jerked in a hand that was unaccustomed to writing. Then he sat back, his eyes still on fire, but his task done. He looked up at Karen and nodded towards the pad.

She leaned down to get a proper sconce. The words were uneven, drawn as if by a child, but there was no mistaking the message conveyed: 'Fuck off.'

Jamie was looking at her now, his face saying that he was interested in how she would broach the matter of money under these circumstances.

Karen said, 'I'm sorry.'

Jamie nodded towards the patient. 'So he is. Sorry as fuck that he ever met you, I'd say. I'm not sorry yet, but I don't want to get to a point where I might be.'

Was he threatening her, or just condemning her for coming into their lives, waving opportunity in one hand, hiding dangers behind her back with the other?

'Whatever money is there, you can put it towards Creole's medical bills,' she said.

She felt low, addressing Creole through a third party because he had been silenced, all because of her. She swept the room with her eyes one last time. It was here, in this excuse for a home, that her dreams had begun to foment all those months ago. It had been a plan conceived in creativity, fused in logic, and blind as a bat. Creole, sitting there now with his jaw wired, face purple, black and yellow, and eyes boring into her, had warned her the first time she'd come here. He'd told her to give Pascal Nix a wide berth.

But she had been focused on the possibilities, the challenge, the buzz. She had picked the wrong line of business, the wrong associates. And this was where it was ending, back in the scene of the dream. She saw the blood on the floor again, little patches, soaked into the timber boards.

'Goodbye,' she said. Creole's eyes held their hate.

She closed the door after her on the way out.

* * *

When he saw Brenda walking into the pub, Wyman tried for a second to view her as another man might. She was well preserved, negotiating the foothills of middle age with grace and aplomb. Her looks, the high cheekbones, eyes of green mystery and full lips, were all still intact. She moved with confidence in that business suit of hers. How come he hadn't noticed all that in the last year or so? All he'd ever seen was her harried over the kids on the way out to work, or looking wrecked on her return.

He was sitting in a new-fangled pub. It was a pub only in the sense that it sold booze. In any other society it would have been a straightforward eatery. Brenda's office was across the road. Last night had been another disaster: he hadn't arrived home till after midnight. She'd told him this morning it couldn't wait. She'd meet him for lunch.

And here she was, looking mighty fine. She still had something, no question about it. A momentary stab hit him. What if she had frequented this place regularly after work? She'd had the opportunity.

He saw her now as he never had before, sauntering in here after work in the company of a colleague, some jumped-up little fuck who knew how to wear a suit, while he himself was at home playing the role of primary care-giver. He saw her as a cougar, prowling this bar in search of some action, a queue forming to make her feel all woman.

He saw her now as a part of his life that had floated away as their world was turned upside down, caught in the whirlwind of debt and role reversal, where nobody knew who they were any more. He was here to get her back. The arsing around was over. It was time to reclaim his stake.

They hadn't made time for themselves, that was the problem. A few months after the company had gone bust, Brenda had sat him down and talked about the 'challenges' they would face. That was another of her words, 'challenges', as if they were about to set off and trek the Himalayas. He recalled now that she had referred to making time for themselves, but time was one thing he never had.

He hadn't much time to make his pitch here today. Just before he'd arrived, Dara Burns had phoned him. A meeting was set up for this afternoon down in the Middle Kingdom. The fella wanted to 'sort things out', he said, which Wyman took to mean they might have to move the body. In any event, there was weed to harvest, and the way Wyman saw it, this Burns guy would be happy if they threw him a bag, ten grand or so maybe, and get things back on an even keel.

He reached forward and sipped again from his sparkling water.

Brenda presented herself in front of him, wearing a face that hadn't left her desk, all business and concentration. He went to get up, to offer her a greeting, but she reared back slightly, like a wary foal. You'd never have thought they'd been married for the last ten years. Or, he reckoned, maybe you might. He knew his wasn't the only marriage that had been thrust onto the high seas of debt.

'What would you like?' he said.

'They do a good half and half combo,' she said. 'Liam behind the bar is getting it for me.'

Liam? First-name terms with a barman? How well did she know him? How much time did she spend here, in this world he knew nothing about?

She sat down on a stool opposite him.

'The kids were all right this morning?' he said.

'Yes. Rosanna is collecting them.' She spoke with a firmness befitting an insurance-claims executive, rather than a wife or mother.

'I'm glad we got this chance to talk,' he said.

She kept her eyes on the table in front of her, homing in on a beermat that illustrated a cartoon image of a footballer in an Ireland jersey.

He ploughed on: 'I think I need to let you know what's going on.'

Now she looked up. 'You think that, do you?'

'Brenda, let's try to do this in a civil manner. I know things haven't been the easiest, but let's just try to get through this. For the sake of the children, if nothing else.'

'I want you to move out, Kevin. I think we need a break.'

'You're not serious.'

'I've never been as serious.'

Wyman felt a pang he located to his childhood. It used to hit him whenever a toy, the prospect of a trip somewhere, was withheld as a punishment for his behaviour. This, though, was insane.

'Brenda, you're not thinking straight. We've been through a tough time. Nobody died. We're coming through the other side. That's why I'm here today.'

'Where were you the night before last?'

'Do you really want to know?'

'Actually, no, I don't. For a long time, I wanted you to tell me what was going on. Coming and going at all hours, involved in this work, as you call it, and yet there didn't seem to be much money coming from your end. For a long time I was hoping you'd tell me what was going on and maybe we could deal with it. But now, I don't care any more.'

She stopped as the guy behind the bar, Liam, bent down in his starched white shirt and dickey bow with a bowl of soup and a sandwich. He placed them in front of Brenda.

'Can I get you anything?' he said to Wyman, who replied with a dismissive hand, as if the idea of food right now was preposterous. Liam retreated towards the bar. Brenda unfolded a napkin, placed it in her lap and tasted the soup.

'Brenda, can you just back things up a bit? I know things haven't been on an even keel. I was desperate so I had to take what work was going. But that's all coming to an end now. The whole thing will be done and dusted in the new few days.'

She raised her head from the soup. 'The days have melted into each other, Kevin. I've had it. When you've been at home, your head has been somewhere else. I know you've been good with the kids, but I can't take it any more. I've enough going on right now not to have to deal with this.'

Wyman opened out his arms, inviting her on. 'Look, what do you want to know? I'll tell you everything.'

'I'm gone beyond caring, Kevin.'

'Come on, if you're going to tear me apart from my children, the least you could do is give me a reason. I have nothing to hide.'

'OK. Well, for starters, who exactly are you fucking? I presume it's that Karen woman you're working with.'

Wyman's mouth dropped open, to express disbelief at such a notion. 'I am not fucking that Karen woman, as you call her, or anybody else. Give me a break.'

'I don't believe you. I always knew you were no angel, but cheating on me . . .'

Wyman registered the mention of angels and tried to ignore it. 'What do you want me to do? Swear on my children's lives?'

'No, please, don't do that. Don't lower things to that level. I told you. All I know is that you are no longer in this marriage and only in the house as a babysitter. I can't handle this any more. I've spoken to Rosanna, and she's been really good. She says she can delay going to Germany for a month until I get an au pair.'

Wyman's head was shaking again. He was trying to break free from all the madness. Brenda spooned some more soup, as if she was actually enjoying it, which did nothing for Wyman's composure. He leaned forward, his voice lowered.

'I'm going to tell you this. I may be putting my life in danger by doing it, but the family means too much to me. I've got involved with some people who I didn't know were mixed up in serious crime. I thought I was employed to do maintenance on these houses, but it turns out there's something more serious going on. The gardaí want me to help them out. And if things work as planned, then we could go into the witness-protection programme, the whole family. It could be a new start for all of us, somewhere abroad.'

Brenda's face didn't betray any surprise, shock, concern, nothing he had been hoping for. He drove on: 'It could be a clean slate, far from all the shit we've had to put up with for the last few years. Somewhere that the kids will have a brighter future. What about it?'

She finished the soup, pushed the bowl into the middle of the table. She lifted the napkin and touched it to the sides of her mouth, her expression remaining stone constant. She hadn't touched the sandwich. 'You're something else,' she said. 'You ask me to listen to you, to understand you and you lay that … utter bollocks on me. I hope she's worth it, whoever she is.'

Brenda stood up, looked down at him, as if he was deserving of some pity. 'You can collect your clothes this afternoon but, if not, wait until I'm gone to work tomorrow. We can sort out something about access to the kids for the time being. Goodbye, Kevin.'

He thought he detected a tremor in her voice at the end, the first sign of humanity since she had walked in. It provided him with a smidgen of comfort. She'd see. When the whole thing went down, when the cops came calling, she'd see he'd spoken the truth, that he had been right all along.

He was so lost in indignation that his phone had rung three times before he heard it.

* * *

'Hi, how're you?'

'Not great.'

There was a pause on the line, as if that answer wasn't what had been expected, or wanted.

'What's wrong?' Karen said.

'Brenda has just told me to get out of the house.'

'Sorry to hear that.' Another pause followed, long enough, Karen considered, for a suitable mourning period. 'Our friend was on to you.'

'Yeah. We're meeting him down there this afternoon.'

'Kevin, I'm not going.'

'Why not?'

'I'm out. I went to Creole's place this morning. He was badly beaten up. They left him in a bad way. That's it for me. I'm not chasing my losses any more. And I'm not just talking about the investment.'

'Are you taking the piss?'

'Sorry. No. I just can't do it any more. I need a new start.'

'You are serious.'

'Yes.'

'This is a great time to land that on me. My wife has just thrown me out and now you're jumping ship. Karen, we spoke about this. Something can be salvaged.'

'Kevin, that's the kind of attitude that got you into trouble in the first place. Not knowing when to stop.'

Wyman said, 'Nix isn't going to be happy about this. You don't file for bankruptcy in his world.'

'He'll have to chase me all the way to Australia.'

'You're leaving the country?'

'Today. I know it's short notice. I know we've worked well together. But after what I saw in Creole's, none of this is worth it any more.'

'Wait a minute. You're fucking off? Clearing out of here, and letting everybody else carry the can for you back home?'

'That's not how I see it, Kevin. You came into this with your eyes open. I'm not a quitter, but this stuff is way out of my league. Count me out. Let Nix take what's there. That'll more than cover what you owe him. Go home, Kevin. Start out afresh. Just walk away. I hope things work out with your family, I really do.'

The phone went dead, hung up in a rage. Karen replaced hers in the shoulder bag sitting on the handbrake. She sat there for a while. Then she pulled the wedding band from her finger, opened the bag and another zipped compartment within it, where she placed the ring. She looked at her bare finger. Bare and new, ready to move on. Thirty seconds later the driver's door opened and Abigail sat in. She handed an envelope to Karen.

'Sorry for the delay,' she said. 'They're something else in that bank. They want the queues to stretch just to force people to do it all online. Anyway, there's six hundred in there. Are you sure it's enough?'

Karen leaned over, squeezed her friend's arm. 'You're an angel.'

'Not quite, but I'm working on it.'

Karen raised the envelope, held it between them. 'I feel bad about this.'

'What's there to feel bad about? It's my running-away money. At least somebody's getting to run away on it.'

'I'll have it back to you within two months.'

'Don't rush. Wait to get back on your feet. Although, knowing you, that won't take much time.'

The car turned onto Dorset Street. It was straight all the way from there to the airport. Karen looked out at the streetscape, people going about their business, a pair of shell-suited junkies, a young couple who had 'student' written all over them, a man for whom the streets looked home.

She was seeing it now as if from a news item on TV, as if she was back in Sydney already, her eye caught by some story that had travelled around the world from Ireland, a snapshot of the natives back there. For a moment, it felt as if she hadn't really been back here for the last year, as if it had all been just a voyage around her bereavement, time away from herself. She didn't belong here any more.

Even now, before her final exit, she wondered how in the name of God she had ever got carried along on her journey of the last few months. How had she managed to hook up with so many losers since she'd got back here? She'd never thought of herself as a loser. Maybe she was just lost, wandering around in Loser-land. Now, being driven to her escape hatch, she felt like she was going to find herself again.

'Penny for them,' Abigail said. She released the handbrake and crawled off from a traffic-lights queue. The road ahead was rising out of Drumcondra and towards the airport.

'I wish things had worked out differently,' she said.

'Hey, that's deathbed stuff. You've got years and years, a long way into the future. Don't get ahead of yourself.'

'No, just the business. Did it have to end like this, a complete cock-up?'

Abigail gave herself a few moments to consider that one. 'Fate, baby. That's all it is. Nothing you can do about it. It comes along and pees on the best-laid plans.'

'Lovely. For a while there, I thought this thing would work out. There was one day, oh, about six weeks ago. I was out in Westwood in the afternoon. I went upstairs and sat in the growing room, my back to the wall. I took it all in, the smells, the sound of the water at work, even the heat. I looked at the plants and – I know this sounds crazy – I felt something for them, as if they had, I don't know, feelings, do you know what I mean?'

'No, but I'm trying.'

'Anyway, I just felt so much in control of everything, including my life. It was the first time since Peter's been gone that I felt everything was going to work out.'

'And it is, Karen. But it won't be here.'

Chapter Twenty-three

There was a roadside sculpture up ahead on the M6 depicting the stages of the moon, when Charlie Small brought up the business of the bodies. 'Will we get Wyman to dig his own grave?' he said.

Burns nodded slowly.

Small said, 'What about the woman? I couldn't stand there, listening to her keening, while Wyman is shovelling. Maybe we could get her to do some of the work, but you know the way women are in situations like this. What about we do her inside the house, bring him down the fields to dig a hole big enough for the pair of them, deal with him and then go back for her body?'

'Sure,' Burns said. 'All that's left then is backfill the hole.' He turned to Small. 'I reckon we can handle that.'

Burns looked out on the sculpture, six stages of the moon, mounted on bog oak, standing tall against the flat brown and green plains of Westmeath. The first three phases, from a sliver of a crest up to a half-moon, were spaced apart, the last three all the way to the full moon bunched together. Just like life, Burns reckoned. The closer things got to the end, the faster they went.

Charlie Small, he noted, was dressed in much the same clothes as he had been on the day they'd visited Wyman over the man's debt. The black leather jacket, the brown slacks that left plenty of leg room for excess flesh, and crowned with that ridiculous pork-pie hat. He was togged out in his sports gear, Adidas, from the navy hoodie down to the runners, looking like a man about to take on a marathon, although he didn't know of anybody who'd ever done a marathon carrying a bulletproof vest.

Small extended his left arm out in front of himself, checking his wristwatch.

'They'll be here at two, right?'

'That's what she told me.'

'OK, and you reckon we're, what, twenty minutes away now?'

'As far as I remember.'

'So we'll have the guts of an hour to set things up. If Pascal gets down soon, we could be back in Dublin for dinner.'

'Eddie Rocket will have the red carpet out for you.'

Small's face was full of dreamy pleasure. 'Hey, I might even risk the carvery in Philly John's just to celebrate.' He laughed his same old laugh, all the way down to a fit of coughing. Burns smiled, didn't say anything.

The radio was tuned to some station pumping out wallpaper pop and disco tunes from a bygone age. Burns thought he recognised Diana Ross, a lady who, if she'd been born at a different time, could have been another Bessie Smith, the Empress of the Blues. She might have had to put on a little weight, get rid of those sequined dresses she was poured into, but she'd had the voice. And then she'd gone and spoiled it all by doing that disco gunk.

He thought for a moment about the guns on the bed of the van behind where they sat. There was a Glock 17 pistol and a pump-action shotgun, wrapped in a chenille bedspread the colour of the sun in a black canvas hold-all. He hadn't had the chance to get a good gander at Small, see if the fella was carrying himself somewhere among the folds of fat.

'Hey, we're turning into some team,' Small said. 'This will be our third clip together. Well, third and fourth if you count the two of them. Maybe we should go into business for ourselves.'

'Yeah,' Burns said. Not once on the journey had Small cracked any joke about the guitar, not even in the lightest way. Something had changed all right. Maybe the fella was getting sense, or maybe he was on his best behaviour.

'What would we call ourselves?' Small said.

'I don't know . . . Little and Large maybe.'

Small gave it some thought, his face staying serious. 'You're a funny fella, Dara. Little and Large.' He reached over and turned up the volume on the radio. It was some noise from years ago that rang a bell, but Burns was too busy thinking about other stuff.

Fifteen minutes later, the LiteAce arrived at the entrance to the Middle Kingdom. The gate was chained and locked.

'You don't have a key,' Small said.

'With all that went down here the last day I wasn't too sure I'd be coming back. Drive on up the road. There's a little opening where the dead guy parked.'

Small downed gears, allowed an impatient Lexus to overtake them.

'Don't give him the finger,' Burns said, sensing that Small wouldn't be able to resist drawing attention to himself.

'What the fuck do you take me for, Dara?'

They pulled in tight with the corrugated-iron fence. Small got out and Burns slipped across to the driver's side, then followed him. Small went around the back, opened the door, leaned in and dragged out the hold-all. He locked the door, went around and locked the driver's door.

The day hadn't yet made up its mind whether it was going to stay dull or let the sun come out to play. Burns could hear birds calling in the high-pitched screech that made him think of somebody being tortured. The drone of a car engine carried from somewhere in the distance, but it didn't rise, or give any hint it was heading this way. Everything was as quiet as could be. Perfect setting to do some killing.

Burns led the way across to the stone wall, set back from the road by a grass verge. He found a gap where he could stick in a toe, and gripped the top, hauling himself up onto it. He stood on it, looking down at Charlie Small.

'No way,' Small said.

'What?'

'I can't get up on that.'

Burns jumped back down onto the grass verge. 'Do you want a leg up?' Even as he said it, he knew there was no hope. If anything went wrong, Small could crush him to death.

'Just wait there,' Small said. He walked back to the van, the hold-all swinging from his left hand. He unlocked and opened the back door, leaned in and came back with a white contraption, which Burns recognised as a two-step ladder. Jesus Christ.

Small stepped up on the wall first, then sat down and lowered himself to the other side. He landed in the dyke, the water pouring into his shoes.

Burns followed, pulled the ladder up after him and threw it down on the other side.

Then the two of them set off between the trees towards the house. Nobody spoke. The birds sounded more relaxed now, the tone of conversation approaching civil. They walked across the gravelled driveway. Small spotted the rented car parked off to the side. 'The shovels are still here, aren't they?' he said.

'Sure. There's one shovel and a pick. That's all you need.'

* * *

The airport was all go, black with bodies, alive with the sound of feet and hurried voices. 'One thing about the state of the country,' Abigail said. 'It keeps the airport busy. People can't wait to get the hell out of here.'

Karen nodded. They had walked into Departures from the multi-storey car park, Karen trailing her bag behind her. It was, she had noted, one of three she had bought in Dunnes Stores in preparation for harvest. The other two were in Westwood and Pure Mule. This one was being used for a different operation, but one no less clandestine. 'I don't know,' she said. 'If things had been different, I'd have been happy to stay here.'

Abigail stopped in her tracks. 'Come off the stage,' she said.

'No, I mean it. It's home, Abigail. It's hard to beat home.'

'Oh, yeah, sure. If you can ignore the way it's been hammered into the ground. The muppets who run the show, the mé-féiners, the shysters and conmen. Yeah, apart from that, it's Hell on wheels.'

'You get that everywhere. Even in Australia.'

Karen couldn't shake that feeling that was hanging around her. The one that sat there like a monkey on her shoulder, prodding her to burst into tears for a reason she couldn't quite put her finger on. She didn't really want to leave, but there was no other way to get past what had gone down here. She could stay, and lie on the bed she'd made, but to what end?

She had only been in business for three months, but she could feel the burden of an employer. She had responsibilities, but she had discharged them to the best of her ability. Abigail didn't really have a stake in the business. Kevin had changed, begun to push the boat out further since the thing down in the Middle Kingdom. OK, he had nowhere to run, but he was a big boy. He'd been mixed up with Nix before she'd ever come along.

The sight of Creole, battered and bruised, kept niggling at her. She shouldn't have to carry that. He had been dipping into that world for years. It had only been a matter of time before he'd fall foul of somebody. She shouldn't have to carry that.

She picked up her ticket at the self-service machine. Abigail pointed to the departures gate, and they made their way over. At the end of the queue, they hugged, Karen holding on tight, trying to keep it together.

'You're going to be OK,' Abigail said.

'Yeah. And so are you. You'll come over in the autumn, for a holiday at least. The flight is on me.'

'How could I turn that down?'

'We'll stay in touch through Skype.'

The queue had begun to move. They said goodbye again, as Karen went along the lines between dividing ropes. As she arrived at Passport Control, Abigail blew a kiss, turned and walked for the exit. A wave of emotion flooded over her as the man dipped into her passport.

* * *

The way Burns saw it, if it was going to happen, it would be quick. Small mightn't be the sharpest tool in the shed, but he knew he was dealing with a pro. He wouldn't take any chances once they were inside the house. Neither would he fuck around with hands up or any of that malarkey. It would be swift and with surprise, out of the blue.

They were standing at the front of the house, looking in on the dark living room, the two of them peering past the flaking paint.

'I'll go around the back,' Burns said. 'There's a window that's handy enough. I'll come through and open the front door for you. How about that?'

'Sounds good to me,' Small said. He had the look of a man who was out beyond his depth. Not in terms of the job at hand, but just the environment. Already his feet were soaking. Now there was a premises that wasn't easily accessible. And, no doubt, his mind must have been full of the thought of traipsing off through a bog at the back of the house to dispose of the bodies once the job was done. Burns thought he detected more than discomfort in that pudgy face. There was fear too. He could nearly smell it.

Burns went around the side, past the parked Avensis. He stepped onto the concrete yard at the back. The barrow was where they had left it the other night, waiting like a hearse for the next body. The pick and shovel were leaning against the whitewashed wall of the shed to the rear of the yard.

He took the Sig Sauer from his pocket, reversed the grip on it and swung the weapon at a pane of glass on the upper part of the back door. He reached in carefully, and unlatched the lock, then turned it. The smell of weed hit him as he walked through the kitchen. A buzzing resonated through the house from the fuse board upstairs. He thought he could hear water at work, nourishing the plants. If things went to plan, he would be in some serious money by this afternoon.

He moved lightly through the kitchen, out into the hall. He pulled back the double Yale lock, and swung the door open. Charlie Small was standing there, awaiting entry. He looked shocked because Burns was pointing a gun at his head.

'Leave down the bag, and move back,' Burns said.

'What the fuck?' Small said.

'Do it.'

'Dara, what's going on?'

'The game is up, Charlie. I'm one body that's not going to be buried today.'

* * *

The angles played out in Wyman's head all the way down there. With Karen out of the loop, Nix and his cronies might look differently at things. They might want more control, and Wyman didn't know that he could work at close quarters with those people. If they were willing to carry on as things were, himself stepping in as Karen had stepped out, then new prairies of hope could open up.

For a second, he saw a future in which he was running the show, maybe with a few underlings, maybe even some of those Vietnamese lads on board to do the heavy lifting. He would make a packet, get out and go legit with plenty of seed capital. Construction would be in the doghouse for a while yet, so he might look at other possibilities.

Then again, they might tell him his services were no longer required. Nix and his goons might be moving in, getting their hands on the whole operation in order to rightly fuck it up. In that scenario, he might get the tape, be told his slate was wiped clean, and a farewell drink. He'd be pissed off, seriously pissed off. Until today, that would have meant he'd be heading back to Brenda with his tail between his legs, resuming his role as house-husband, bad and all as that was. Now, with his home gone, his family sundered, he'd have nothing.

There was another possibility, one that loomed larger the closer he got to the Middle Kingdom. They were going to tie up loose ends. That would mean selecting a few more bodies to join the one that was buried out in the field. His, to be specific.

Whatever qualms they might have had about killing Karen, those were no longer an issue. But how could he know?

Once he'd walked into the house, it would be too late. His fate would be surrendered on the threshold, up for grabs among these scumbags.

There was one other possibility that began to take shape the closer he got to his destination. It was a good plan, with small downside risks. If it came off, he would walk away with something to show for his time in this game, and he'd be in a position to woo Brenda back to his side.

Kevin Wyman downed gears, and came to a halt. He was on the road outside the Middle Kingdom. He was early by at least half an hour, but with good cause. He wanted to see the lie of the land before deciding on his options.

The gate was still locked. He had the key, but wanted to do a quick recce. He dropped to second gear and crawled along the road. There was a vehicle up ahead, on the left. He saw the LiteAce, and the sight of it sent a chill down his back. They were there. Waiting for him. Waiting to sort things out.

The van was empty. He pulled into the side of the road, left the engine running. He got out and crossed to the stone wall. Now he could see the front of the house, and two men were walking across it towards the side. One, whose bulk said it had to be that thug Small, was in front. Behind him, Wyman recognised Dara Burns, training a gun at the back of Small's head. Fuck that for a game of soldiers.

Wyman skipped back across the road, got into the car and took off. Twenty yards up the road he looked in the rear-view mirror but nobody was there. Only then did he begin to relax.

* * *

They walked around by the side of the house to the back yard. All the way, Burns kept his weapon trained on Small's head. There would be no cock-ups. He'd never done anything like this before, kept somebody alive for a while until it was time.

'Stop there,' he said, as Small arrived roughly in the centre of the yard.

The fat man turned, and said, 'Dara, we have to talk.'

Burns could see that he was trying to play it cool. He'd been rumbled, but his life was still all to play for. 'Your phone,' Burns said. 'Take it out and place it on the ground.'

'Dara—'

'This has nothing to do with you. It's between me and Nix. Do as I say and you walk.'

Small shrugged, but he didn't look convinced. He took a phone from the pocket of his leather jacket and placed it on the ground.

'OK, over there, near the wall,' Burns said.

'You're going to put me up against the wall?'

'Move.'

Small took short steps. He didn't hear Burns creep up behind him and swing the butt of the gun into the side of his temple. He let out a yelp, and bent over, hands going to his head.

'That's just in case you get any notions. Now, on the ground, face first.'

Small began to weep. 'Dara, please ...'

'I'm not going to shoot you. If I wanted to I'd just blow your head off now. Get down.' Small lowered himself to the ground, trying to avoid falling over on account of his bulk and his fear. Burns retreated to where the phone lay. He picked it up and punched keys, scrolling down through the contacts section until he arrived at PNIX.

He pressed the 'message' icon and began typing: Burns done. What time you come. He sent the message.

He looked at Small. The safest thing would be to shoot him now, there on the ground, no fuss, not having to listen to any of his bullshit. But then he'd have to get rid of him. A lot of graves were going to be required today. By his reckoning, Wyman and the woman wouldn't show up for another half-hour at least. If he could get Nix done by then, it would make everything a little easier, cut down on the space where fuck-ups thrive.

The phone in his hand pinged with a text: Great. There in 15 mins.

Small lifted his head from the ground, turned and looked up at him. 'Dara, I got an idea.'

'Yeah?'

'Why don't you let me give you a hand?'

'OK, you can do that. Get up. There's a shovel and pick over there and a barrow. You've got some digging to do and we haven't got all day.'

* * *

Wyman pulled into the square in Kilcormac. By now, the place had taken on a sheen of reassurance for him. It was here that he'd stopped the night he'd encountered the Chinks in Pure Mule. That was – what? – less than a week ago, and now everything had changed. There was little in the way of action in the early afternoon. The Café Royale was closed, the butcher's open, but few bodies on the square.

He knew he should be grateful. He could have walked in on those scumbags waving their guns around, and he wouldn't give great odds on him walking out of there again.

He punched a number into his phone.

'Hello,' the voice said.

'You know who this is.'

'Yep.'

'Our little talk the other day?'

'I'm listening.'

'I have something that I reckon might get me away from here, new name, new life.'

'That would have to be something big.'

'It is. The individual who has been a sore on your arse for the last while is, I understand, heading down to a farmhouse in the midlands. I'll text you the exact directions after, OK?'

'Hooray, the man's going to buy some cattle, retire to the country.'

'Listen, will you? The other two gents we spoke of before. They're down there already, armed and, if you ask me, about as dangerous as they come. The place is also one of Nix's grow-houses, OK?'

Wyman let that sink in, so that the guy might realise how serious he was.

'There's something else too. In a field out the back there's a body that was recently buried. You'll find he's been shot and I'd lay short odds that the bullet will match one of the guns the psychos in the house have on them. Are you with me?'

A silence of digestion followed. Then: 'Where are you, Kevin?'

'I'm safe. Safe and all ready to experience the joys of the witness-protection programme, a new start for me and my family.'

'If all of this is kosher, there'll be no question about that. Where are you?'

'Don't worry. I'll be in contact. Have to clear up one little matter and then we can play ball. But I'm beyond the reach of that crew, so nobody can touch me.'

'I'd be happier if you came in.'

'I will, but I need a little time. Don't worry, I'm as safe as houses.'

* * *

Charlie Small's pork-pie hat was still on the ground, sitting there on the cracked concrete. He put down the barrow and bent to retrieve it. His composure was back on an even keel now after the little hiccup earlier on. He picked up the handles of the barrow again, the hat now on his head, and he kept going, out beyond the yard, onto the bumpy terrain of the field.

'How far?' he said.

Walking five yards behind him, the gun trained on his back, Burns said, 'Over there by the trees.' Small saw three oaks at the bottom of the field.

When they arrived in the trees' shadow, Small put down the barrow again and turned around. 'It was nothing to do with me,' he said. 'Pascal said it had to be that way. If I hadn't gone along with it, he would have done me too. Dara, please, there's no sense to this. I can help you.'

Burns said, 'You're helping me now. Get the shovel and dig.'

Small looked at the ground around him. 'How many are you going to bury here?'

Burns had been thinking about that. Four of them in one hole. He could do with one of those mini diggers they used when fixing up the roads. 'Just dig,' he said.

Small pulled the shovel from the barrow. One look at the guy and Burns knew that he'd be getting little in the way of a hole out of him. Bad and all as he would have been with the shovel the other night, Charlie Small would be a disaster.

His phone began ringing. No, it was Small's phone in his pocket, like a call to drag him back from the lip of his grave. The caller ID said PNIX. He looked at Small, and both of them knew who it was. Help or hassle just beyond the punch of a button on the phone. It kept ringing. Small made a step towards Burns, as if he might somehow reach for the button. Burns straightened the gun in his hand, levelling it with Small's head.

'Dig,' he said, through the ringing. And then the sound stopped.

'He's going to know,' Small said.

'Know what?'

'That you did me. That you're going to do him.'

'Dig.'

'And what? You'll shoot me when I'm standing in it?'

'I'll shoot you now if you don't get going. I haven't made my mind up yet what I'm doing, but the way you're going on you're making it up for me.'

Small's face was changing, as if it had passed through the depths of fear and come out the other side. All that was there now in the pudgy folds of flesh was contempt. He knew there was no way back. All that mattered to him now was that he experience some breath of freedom before his leaving.

The ping of an SMS landing sounded from one of Burns's phones. He looked to his pocket and Charlie Small made his move.

He raised the shovel and began charging towards Burns. 'Fuck you, weirdo,' he said, the shovel in front of him. as if he was an extra in *Braveheart*, the pork-pie hat sailing from his head.

Burns looked up, and cracked off a round, but the gun wasn't fully level and he caught Small somewhere in the abdomen. Small grunted but kept coming. Burns shot again, and this time the bullet ricocheted off the blade of the shovel. Small was upon him now, the two men tumbling over onto the grass. Burns looked up and Small was on top of him, twenty-two stone of hatred pushing down, trying to crush the life out of him. Small's eyes were wide with the possibility of survival. His hands came up and linked on Burns's throat. Burns still had the gun in his hand, but he couldn't pull it free. Some part of the fat man's anatomy was crushing down on the hand. He pulled once more, finally getting it out, just as his breath began to contract under pressure from Small's hands around his throat. He brought the gun up to the side of Small's temple, and suddenly Small's face changed again, victory fleeing, to be replaced by the inevitability that he wasn't getting out of this one.

Burns closed his eyes when he shot, but he still felt Small's brain matter raining down on his face. The pressure on his neck eased, and he heaved the dead man off him.

* * *

The Aer Lingus flight to London was delayed by twenty minutes. Karen got up from the plastic seat, raised the handle on her wheelie bag and took off at a leisurely pace around the departures area. She knew that a stretch of her legs would be at a premium for the next twenty hours or so.

When she arrived in Heathrow, it would be a rush to get the transfer bus to Gatwick, where she was on standby for a flight. Her composure had returned. It had been inevitable that there would be tears on departure but they had been cathartic, and now, on the horizon, she could see the first streaks of a new day in her life.

Her phone began ringing. Caller ID blocked. She hesitated. Nobody could get her now, not physically, but if somebody reached out for her emotions, trying to pull her back on some pretext or threat . . . Curiosity got the better of her.

'Karen?'

Oh, no.

'Hello, Jake.'

'Karen, where are you?'

'I'm … in Dublin.'

'OK. Could you meet me? I'm after getting bail. That was the longest three months of my life, thought I'd never survive it.'

'You're out?'

'Yeah. For how long I don't know, but we'll take it one day at a time. Any chance you could meet me at the train?'

'Don't think so, Jake.'

'Come on. Even if everything is over between us, we could be friends.'

'Really?'

'Well, more than friends. I was thinking while I was inside. Remember those questions you were asking me about the plants, and I thought you might be getting involved in the game? OK, I should have known you wouldn't go walking into something like that cack-handed, but you got me thinking. What if we went into business together? My trial won't be up for at least one harvest, maybe even two. We could make a serious amount of dosh in that time. With my knowledge of this line and your head for business, we could go a long way . . . Karen? Karen? Karen, are you still there? Oh, for fuck's sake. Running out on me again.'

* * *

Pascal Nix threw his phone onto the passenger seat. Something was not right. He was cruising now, the speedometer on his Lexus rarely tipping above fifty. He had left the motorway just a few minutes ago, heading cross-country now, not completely sure of where he was going.

Why hadn't Small picked up when he'd rung? If Burns had been sorted, as the text had said, then what was the problem? In his mind's eye he saw Charlie Small digging a hole in the middle of nowhere, his phone in his jacket a few feet away, too far to waddle to before it rang out. But why hadn't he called back?

Right now, the itch was bothering Pascal Nix. It wasn't a physical thing – or, at least, it didn't manifest itself as such. It was in his head, tearing at his every thought. He knew the itch, knew how it had kept him alive before. From his life's vantage, here in his early forties, he could look back on occasions when the itch had kept him out of harm's way.

There had been the time, nearly a decade ago, when the itch had told him not to walk into a house in the north inner city where he'd arranged to meet some people. He had parked his motor, got out, one foot on the ground, and got back in, propelled to turn the key and get the fuck out of there. The following day, he'd learned that a hit had been set up on the other side of the front door, waiting to dispatch him to kingdom come.

There had been other times when the itch had repelled him from danger. Once, when he was in a house that was a veritable armoury, he'd gone out the back to take a leak in the wee hours. He had stood there for a minute, admiring a full moon, bothered by something he just couldn't put his finger on. Whatever it was had prompted him to drift down the back garden, from where he'd heard a commotion inside the house. He was over the fence and away in two seconds flat as the ERU bundled through the front door. The lads inside had ended up cooling their heels for the guts of ten years in the Joy after that little affair.

Those were the two occasions that came to mind as he drove through the roundabouts necklacing Tullamore. And he had it now, bugging the shit out of him. But what could he do?

Charlie Small wasn't capable of organising a piss-up in a brewery, and there was too much at stake to leave him to his own devices down there, sorting out bodies and the weed. He had no choice but to keep going.

He ran a hand across his head and looked over at the phone, dead on the passenger seat, willing it to come to life. Ring, Charlie, ring, and let me know that you haven't fucked up already.

He'd make the appointment when they got back to Dublin this evening. Once that was sorted, the first thing he'd do with the cash was put it away for the operation. You had to look on the bright side. This whole affair had turned out bad, but at least he'd be walking away with some cash. You had to take the positives.

A clean break from this cock-up, a fresh start, and what better way to get into it than with a new head of hair?

He didn't see the two Mondeos coming up fast behind him. As the second overtook, he looked across and what he saw took his concentration from the road. The two guys in the back seat had heads on them that couldn't but belong to some of An Garda Síochána's finest, and they were in a mad hurry somewhere. Once the second car had passed he could see the flashing blue light in its rear window.

When Nix's eyes reverted to the road, he was driving towards the hard shoulder. He swerved again, slammed on the brakes. The motor skidded across the road, coming to a halt, the front wheels resting atop the dividing white line on the carriageway. He could hear his heart pounding. He looked up. A car was approaching the way he had come. He turned the key, crawled over to the hard shoulder. Now he was facing back the way he had come.

'Fuckin' hell,' he said. He looked in the rear-view mirror, knocked down the indicator and got back on the road, heading for Dublin. His mind was a jumble but, through it all, he couldn't help noticing that the itch was no longer bugging him.

* * *

After Burns rolled the dead weight of Charlie Small from him, he got up and began digging. But it just wasn't the same when he didn't have somebody on the pick.

After a few minutes he gave up. Maybe he'd go along with the plan Small had proposed on the way down here. When Wyman and the woman showed up, he'd get Wyman to do the digging.

He left the tools under the oak tree, next to Charlie Small's body. As he set off back across the field, pushing the barrow, he could hear birds somewhere, chirping excitedly, as if spreading gossip.

Back at the house, he washed his hands at the sink in the kitchen, splashed a little water on his face. Blood was carried down the plughole. He took the hold-all, with the pump-action and the Glock in it, and swung it up onto the kitchen table. When he unzipped the bag, he could see that both weapons were ready for use. There was a couple of clips in there as well, as if Small had expected he might need serious firepower. He zipped it up again, and dropped it on the floor.

Upstairs, he found the weed in an industrial black bag in the corner of the drying room. He dragged it out onto the landing, thoughts going through his head about how much it must be worth. If he made fifty grand out of the whole thing, that would be enough to keep him honest for the next year.

Downstairs, he looked out of the front-room window, but decided that was too restrictive. He went out through the back door, and around the side of the house. He stood against the gable end, listening. His one hope was that Nix would show up first. If Wyman and Karen came, it could cause all sorts of problems. The drone of a car's engine rose and fell from the road. Then a louder drone, had to be a tractor.

He could hear a dog somewhere in the distance, but little else. This was going to work out, but where was he? Come on, Nix, come to me and let's end all this.

Maybe he should bang off another text, get some idea of where the fella was. He tapped his pocket. Nothing. He checked the other pockets. Neither of the two phones was there. They must have fallen out during his struggle with Small.

For a second, he felt exposed. Once Nix was done, he'd have to have a line of communication with the other pair. Shit, there was nothing for it but to leg it back down and get them.

He broke into a jog when he got behind the house, picking up speed, as he kept his eyes on the terrain underfoot, dodging between hoof marks.

Down at the trees, it took him a few seconds to locate his own phone. He scoured the grass until he spotted Small's model. Another missed call from PNix.

He turned and made his way back up towards the house, noticing for the first time the heat in the day. He still hadn't figured out what he was going to do with all the bodies. Just as he rounded the whitewashed outhouse and stepped onto the concrete of the yard, he spotted a man walking around the side of the house. He was wearing a navy windcheater with the Garda insignia on it. He had a handgun raised, facing skywards, ready for action. Burns drew his weapon, just as the man spotted him.

'Halt, Gardaí,' the man said.

Burns brought his gun up, but he wasn't fast enough. The shot hit him in the chest, throwing him back, the vest keeping the bullet out. He looked up, cracked off a round, but as he did so the cop had ducked back around the side of the house.

Burns felt dizzy as he got to his feet, but adrenalin propelled him across the yard, his eyes on the corner behind which the cop had disappeared. He thought he saw something move and shot again.

And then he was through the door, like a man who had just found shelter from a storm. He grabbed one of the kitchen chairs, and jammed it against the door handle. Then he crouched below the window, out of their range. He had a feeling of just having lost something. It wasn't dissimilar to how he had felt when he had walked into Beaumont Hospital to hear that his gran had died. Except this time it wasn't any person who had checked out on him. No, this time he'd been left by the one thing that had accompanied him everywhere he went to do his thing. This time, luck had run out on him. Well, almost. At least he was still here. At least he still had choices.

Chapter Twenty-four

He moved with greater speed than he'd thought he possessed. Crouching below the height of the window, like a Neanderthal man, he grabbed the hold-all from the table and ran through into the front room. Once there, he threw himself to the side of the tall window. He unzipped the bag, and pulled out the pump-action. He checked the Glock.

He sat there for a moment, his back ramrod straight against the wall, eyes closed, until a smile creased across his face. How else could it be? In the end, order was what it was about, and his plan had lacked that final element.

Even if things had worked out, and he'd done the four of them down here, what end would it have served? Small was a player, who had reached too far. Nix? Well, he was a regret. The whole thing would have had a neater ending if only that fucker had shown up and received his just deserts.

No, the plan was all right as far as it went, but that wasn't far enough. Everything could be traced back to the day he had made the mistake with that hit on Coulter's brother. The code by which he lived had been polluted that day. There was no going back. From then on, it had been inevitable that his own time would come, but his wildest dreams had never washed him onto the shore where he now found himself.

'Hello in there,' a voice boomed, through a loud-hailer, as if it was talking to a boy in a bubble.

'Nobody has been hurt yet. I'm asking you to come out through the front door with your arms raised. Leave your weapons behind in the house and come out. There is no chance of escape from here.'

Burns leaned over and knocked out the corner pane of the window. He shot out through it with the Sig Sauer, just to let them know they could go fuck themselves.

Nobody'd been hurt yet? Oh, man, if only you knew.

Yesterday, when he had figured out what was going on, how Nix was going to get rid of him, as if he was something the cat had dragged in, he considered for a second taking to the road. But where would he have gone? London? He might as well have bought a one-way ticket to Mars. There was nowhere to run to. The contours of his life were traced over a small part of this city, with the odd excursion out of there, across to the southside, down to this shithole here, but he couldn't start a new life beyond the world he knew.

When he'd first taken up the guitar as a hobby, he had been a few years into this life. Every so often, he saw himself one day walking away, becoming a musician, a bluesman of his own day. He'd all the material needed to write the songs. Mississippi John Hurt had nothing on him when it came to tales of death and injustice.

And as long as he kept going, that image could foment in his mind, providing hope that one day he might get out and follow his dream. Of course it was all horseshit. Even if Robert Johnson himself was providing the lessons, Burns knew his enthusiasm could never be matched by talent. He just didn't have it. And now he wouldn't need it anyway.

The sound boomed in again.

'Come through the front door with your hands raised. Leave your weapons behind you in the house.'

Maybe Robert Johnson had the right idea. What point was there in living life by somebody else's strictures? Prison would be no life. More than anything, he would have no room in there for his head. From what he knew of it, that was the worst thing. You never got to be alone with yourself, and solitude was what he lived for most of the time.

So, yeah, apologies, Mr Johnson. You lived it your way, the talent was yours to do what you wanted with, and if that meant whoring around and pissing it down the drain, then fair play to you. I didn't give you a fair break, man. You were entitled to more from me.

He unzipped his hoodie, unstrapped the vest, pulled it up over his head, and threw it on the floor. He put the hoodie on again, zipping it up. He stuck the Sig Sauer in the pocket of his sweat-pants, and took the pump-action in his right, the Glock in his left. For a moment, he thought of emptying all the weapons before he went out, but the way his luck was going, that might mean he wouldn't get out of here dead.

He stood up, his back still to the wall. They'd write a song about him some day. Whenever the next blues revival came about, and tales of outlaws were again plundered for tunes, they'd write about him. He could hear it in his head now, Mississippi John Hurt's melodious guitar, the opening chords of his favourite song, 'Stack O'Lee'.

He walked out of the room, stood in the hall behind the front door, and he heard the last verse of the song.

Standin' on the gallows, head held way up high
At twelve o'clock they killed him, they was glad to see him die
He was a bad man, cruel ol' Stack O'Lee.

Burns turned the lock in the door, his hand still on the Glock. He stepped out, the day fine now. He began shooting from the hip, cracking off three rounds before feeling the bullets slam into his body, lifting him off his feet. The last thing he saw was a pair of boots running across the gravel towards him.

* * *

By Wyman's reckoning, the amount of weed already cut and dried in Pure Mule could come to sixty grand. At least that was something he could walk away with for his time, his efforts, and the stress levered onto his marriage as a result of all this. Nobody could deny him that. With a bit of luck, the opportunity would arise to unload it, even if he would be under Garda protection. There were ways and means around these things and he was still on for one last throw of the dice in this business.

He drove straight into the estate and parked outside number five. He wouldn't be there long, and once he was on his way he didn't care who blew the roof off the gaff. Immediately he closed the front door behind him, he knew that something was not as it should be. The hold-all with the weed was in the hall, as if somebody had left it there in readiness to leave. He walked into the sitting room and found himself staring down the barrel of a handgun held by one of his Vietnamese friends. This was the man he'd encountered when he was out for his midnight walk. Suddenly, the priority of walking out of here with something tangible began to recede. Right now, if he was given a choice, he would just be happy to leave with his life.

The guy waved the gun, indicating that he enter the room. The guy reversed now, urging him further in. He circled Wyman, and moved to the front window, where he pulled across the curtains, the room now falling into darkness.

'Is there a problem?' Wyman said, failing to sound as casual as he was trying to sound.

The guy didn't react at all. Just stood there, staring at him, looking to be nearly as shitless as Wyman was himself.

He didn't see the other guy come up behind him, but he felt the arm across his throat, and the knife being plunged into his chest. His body went on fire, the guy with the gun fading behind clouded eyes. His legs lost their strength, but he couldn't fall: he was still being held up. The second wound felt worse. Now he was fading, and falling, down to the carpet, curling into a heap, hands to his chest, sticky with blood.

He heard something, not talking as he knew it, but people conversing as if in a dream, but that must have been the Chinks hatching a plan. He didn't want them to leave. He didn't want to be alone right now, even if the only company was the pair of fuckers who had just done him.

He heard a door pull, and he knew now the house was his. From where he lay, he could see the peach-coloured couch where he and Abigail had romped a few short days ago. Where was an angel now when he needed one?

He had nearly made it. If only he had listened to Karen and quit while he was ahead. He could have saved his marriage, he could have raised his kids at home, but now it was all slipping away.

He saw himself running home to his mother after school when he was seven, having received the only beating he'd ever had in his childhood. Then he was a sixteen-year-old, messing with his friend at the back of the class, a copybook in front of him blotted with doodlings. He was walking down Second Avenue in New York, the streets like tall canyons, blowing him along on a gust of freedom. He saw Brenda as he'd seen her that first night, his future in her eyes, and he saw her in the labour ward, pushing Ciara into the world. And then the images came no more and it was all gone.

* * *

Twenty-six hours later, the Qantas flight touched down at Kingsford Smith Airport. Karen Riney looked out on a day that was as dull as it gets in a Sydney winter, which was something approaching a fair to middling spring day back in the old country.

Her body ached and her mind was lost between the days.

She breezed through Immigration with her residency permit, and Baggage Reclaim was prompt. Once through into Arrivals, she was taken by the shrieks. All around her there were the cries of families. Some of the hugging scenes lapsed into a production.

She walked out into the day, a slight drizzle falling. Friends in Bondi Junction were expecting her – she'd made contact with them in Gatwick. She stepped into a taxi and told the driver where to go.

'How's things back home?' he said.

She looked at him again. He had the head of a farmer and the accent was somewhere from the south, maybe Cork. It was as if her native country was still trying to hold onto her, here at the far side of the world.

'All right, but it's good to be back,' she said.

The driver pointed to a case on the front passenger seat. 'You missed all the commotion over there,' he said. 'I see on the Twitter that there were shootings and stabbings down in the midlands. Sounds like the place is going gaga.'

Karen wasn't listening. The case he'd pointed to was familiar, brown with those woven diamond patterns that weren't quite leather. 'Your iPad cover,' she said. 'Don't tell me it's made out of fish skins.'

He reached across and picked it up, handed it back to her. 'Well spotted. Got it as a present from my mam. She sent it out for my birthday. Fella back there is making this stuff from salmon skins. Can you believe that?'

'Oh, I can,' she said. She ran her hand across the tanned surface. It felt just like Burns's wallet that day, just like the wallet Peter had brought home to Coogee in her other life. 'I certainly can, and if I've anything to do with it, they'll be made out here pretty soon.' She paused as if something had just occurred to her. 'The midlands, you said. Where in the midlands?'

'Some farmhouse down there on the Offaly-Westmeath border. Guy was apparently a big-time crim, a hitman for hire. He was surrounded, walked out shooting as if he was Jimmy Cagney in one of those black-and-white movies. All those guys are head cases, you know that.'

Karen didn't need to hear the name. She felt cold. She didn't want to hear the name for her next question. 'You said stabbings?'

'Yeah – they're saying it might have been linked. About twenty miles away, in one of those ghost estates. They reckon it was Vietnamese fellas growing pot that did it. Apparently that fella was straight enough, just got involved in the drugs business to pay off debts. Things are pretty fucked back there, aren't they? By the way, where are we going?'

'Where are we going?' Karen said.

The driver looked in the rear-view mirror. 'That's my line.'

She shook herself back to the here and now. 'Coogee, please. The boardwalk.'

He switched on the wipers, let them describe a few beats, then switched off again.

She would sit on the boardwalk and watch the waves coming in through the drizzle. She needed a link to the past once more, to that time before Peter had left, before she'd gone back in search of something that was no longer there. She needed closure.

It didn't matter what had happened. There was nothing on her that might bring the law in her wake, nothing that had left a trail to her door, on the far side of the world. It was all wrapped up now and posted to the past. She looked out on the Sydney morning, willing a new start, but the sadness wouldn't leave her alone.

Acknowledgements

Many thanks are due to a number of people who assisted me in one form or another in completing this book. In particular, for their input in terms of ideas, research, review and reading, I'd like to thank Ronnie Bellew, Gearoid Collins, Liam Ormond, Dave Flynn, John O'Driscoll, Shane Coleman and Eoin Sweeney. Many thanks are due to Michael McNamara for the Blues, and Johnny 'the Fish' Fitzgerald for the skins.

I'd like to thank all at Hachette, particularly Ciara Considine for being, as usual, an inspiring editor, and Hazel Orme for her excellent work.

Finally, much appreciation for my family for the time, space and love that helped me to get the thing done. Special mention goes to the hardy men, Luke and Tom, and, as always, Pauline, to whom this book is dedicated.